BUZZARD LOVE

BUZZARD LOVE

A DETOUR ON THE ROAD TO PSYCHIC STARDOM

A NOVEL

GEHLA S. KNIGHT

iUniverse, Inc.
New York Lincoln Shanghai

BUZZARD LOVE
A DETOUR ON THE ROAD TO PSYCHIC STARDOM

Copyright © 2006 by Gehla S. Knight

iUniverse books may be ordered through booksellers or by contacting:

iUniverse
2021 Pine Lake Road, Suite 100
Lincoln, NE 68512
www.iuniverse.com
1-800-Authors (1-800-288-4677)

This is a work of fiction. All of the characters, names, incidents, organizations and dialogue in this novel are either the products of the author's imagination or are used fictitiously.

ISBN-13: 978-0-595-39940-6 (pbk)
ISBN-13: 978-0-595-67761-0 (cloth)
ISBN-13: 978-0-595-84329-9 (ebk)
ISBN-10: 0-595-39940-1 (pbk)
ISBN-10: 0-595-67761-4 (cloth)
ISBN-10: 0-595-84329-8 (ebk)

Printed in the United States of America

FOR JOSEPH WHO BELIEVED IN ME AND FOR RICHARD WHO TAUGHT ME TO
BELIEVE IN MYSELF.

PORTLAND, OREGON
JUNE, 2005

"THOUGH LEAVES ARE MANY, THE ROOT IS ONE."

YEATS
THE COMING OF WISDOM WITH TIME

MARION COUNTY, OREGON
SPRING, 1977

1

Josie munched on a slice of pepperoni, patrolling the porch with a pensive frown. She looked upward at the cotton wool clouds squatting over the strawberry fields. Raindrops were strung along the clothesline, popping like corn as they hit the hood of her stranded Ford Pinto. This was the fifth straight day of rain in a gloomy, sodden spring that so far had not lived up to the promise of the budding lilacs. soaked or soggy

Rain made mud; mud made ruts, and ruts made rivulets in the county road meandering through the pudding-soft patch where her Nashua hunched in the mire. The aluminum trailer shimmered in the drizzle, moldering beneath a giant oak in the Jewel Grove Trailer Park.

Water dripped from the tarpaper roof to the ramshackle porch and splattered against the door she had swung wide open. A steady stream gushed from the downspout and splashed like Multnomah Falls at her feet. This was a sky flood. Every March the lush Willamette Valley soaked up the deluge and percolated the excess in a mushy soup, leaving an islet in the muck where her trailer roosted. manure, dirt, mud

Josie's battered Nashua crouched on four squidgy Goodyear tires sunk like dunked Oreos in the glop. In 1956 the Nashua rolled across the Cascade Mountains, its striped awning rolled like an umbrella beneath the slender curve of the roof. Every bump and pothole inspired the musical door chime (forty dollars extra, plus tax) to sing out a tinny rendition of "Ramblin Rose." The Jewel Grove Trailer Park in Silverton where it settled was merely a clearing beside the county road winding through meadows full of milkweed, nettles, grasshoppers and second-growth Douglas firs. The park soon filled. Metal mailboxes linked like orthodontic braces bordered the washboard road, and in the middle of a permanent puddle sea, a cinderblock laundry and tennis court completed the amenities.

Too soon to suit some, the Jewel Grove slipped into seedy seclusion. New rigs with peaked roofs and fake cedar siding displaced the old trailers, and by the mid seventies, most had abandoned the Nashua and moved their newer doublewides to mobil-home enclaves bulldozed out of the woodsy patches dotting the rolling hills of the Willamette Valley bursting with blossoms, berry vines and manicured fields. Swimming pools, brick patios and fancier names seemed to suit the ritzier clientele even if their windows looked out on lube shops, fast-food eateries and car lots instead of the nut orchards and wheat fields left behind in Silverton.

Josie took a look at it all—dripping and hissing like a busted steam boiler. The whole scene was as depressing as her funky mood. Oh, well, she sighed listlessly, arching her back while both hands cinched her waist. It was home, and it suited her just fine. Didn't matter much what the rainy weather brought. More mud on her boots, her doorstep and in the trailer didn't bother her. Wading through puddles the size of eastern seaboard states to wash her clothes was a drag, but she was used to it. The laundry could wait anyway. Till hell froze over if necessary. Josie never was much for housekeeping. Waste of time really. She had better things to occupy her talents—important things. Like predicting destiny and toying with fate. Dirty clothes could pile up to the ceiling. The grimy floors could buckle, warp and fucking fall apart for all she cared. It didn't really matter much in the grand scheme of things, did it?

Her ruminations were disturbed by the rattle of a loose tailpipe and the clatter of an old Dodge coughing up the county road. Josie squinted to get a better view of the liverish blob splashing through the puddles. She knew that car. It was Roger's. This was going to be a lucrative day. Roger always had a gullible ear and an empty head for business. Just what the situation called for given that the Pinto sinking in the muck outside her door had no battery and needed a muffler. Roger was just who Josie wanted to see sloshing toward her homestead: a sucker with cash in his pocket.

He waved through the slap of windshield wipers when the car stopped under a drippy tree. "Hi, Josie!" he hollered as he got out and planted both feet in water which soaked his socks. "Awful wet today, ain't it?"

"This is Oregon, remember? Makes the fir trees grow."

"Damn!" A splat of rainwater trickled down his collar. "I hate this weather."

"Ditto. Come on in."

He hop-scotched to the porch, stepped over a crusty cat dish stuck fast to the welcome mat, dodged a mortally wounded dishwasher and followed her across the threshold.

Inside, Josie's Nashua put average messy and musty to shame. The plush settee wedged beneath the louvered window offered the only uncluttered seat. The piece was threadbare and lumpy but pretentious nevertheless—Josie's sole claim to traditional decor. Scarred by decades of indifference since it had graced a Victorian parlor, it was home these days to Josie's cats who shredded its upholstery, coughed up hair balls on the cushions and occasionally urinated behind its faded walnut wings.

In front of the settee was a drop-leaf table draped with a crimson curtain. Josie's crystal ball was centered on a plastic doily. She sat thigh to thigh with Roger whose baseball cap dripped rain on the ratty carpet as they gazed into the clouded glass.

Josie cleared her throat, closed her eyes and let her head fall back in a practiced swoon. She had to prepare herself for communion with the spirits from the afterlife who guided her to the future. Besides, she felt a headache coming on, and neck stretches always seemed to help ease the tension.

Roger took a deep breath and siphoned out the air carefully so as not to disturb her psychic vibes. "Whatcha see, Josie? I need to know by Friday, remember?" He aimed a finger at the ball as if he were going to punch the ON button.

"Stop! Watch what you're doing. Interference can be very dangerous."

"Jeez. Sorry, Josie."

She took deep breaths and exhaled slowly, steaming her mojo. Then she began to stroke the globe with the licentious fervor of a harem master. Josie's eyelashes fluttered, and a pink blush sprouted on her cheeks. This was always her favorite part. It was the mystical thing –the magical transformation from ordinary Josie Wallgood to Madame Josephina. Turned her on every time.

"You see anything yet?" he whispered.

Josie caressed the crystal ball. Her milky eyes, the color of faded denim, gleamed. "It's coming, Roger. I'm beginning to see a shape through the mist."

"Jeez, Louise." All he could see was his own reflection in the glass—distorted so he looked like Jimmy Durante.

"I can see very plainly now. It's as clear as daylight."

"Can you see Marilyn in there or what?"

"It's not that simple. But this isn't looking good. This is some bad shit."

"How bad?"

"Bad."

"You sure about that? Maybe there's flyspecks on it or somethin'. You got any Windex?"

"It's bad, Roger. I'm positive. I can see clear as day."

"Maybe you could switch channels—tune in somethin' else that looks better."

She drew back and squared her shoulders. Her clients were so ignorant of the professional process. But then Josie knew that single digit IQers were always the best marks—because they believed. *Really* believed. "Roger, there is nothing wrong with my psychic reception. I have a message for you. I can see it right here, and it's a bummer. A real heavy downer. Oh, crap." Suddenly she lurched forward, flopped across the table and let her arms fall to her sides.

"Holy Christ, what is it?"

"Awww... I can't see anymore...These are megadose vibrations coming through. I hate it when this shit happens."

"Christ almighty, Josie. What the hell is it? John Deere goin' bankrupt?"

"Worse than that. It's a good thing you came to see me today, Roger. This is way too heavy for you to handle alone."

"I knew it. I could feel it when I got up this mornin'."

"It's big and bad—heavy-duty psychic shit."

"Is it a curse? Is that what you see in there? Can you get rid of it?"

Silly question—she was a pro. Once she had labeled their psychic problem and cast a spell to torture the demons afflicting her clients, the only element left to complete was the pricing. There was more to fortune telling than honing in on a sucker's ego. Josie prided herself on her showmanship. She knew how to stick her hand out at just the right moment. Strip away all the phony astral bullshit, and this was just show biz, a one-woman stand-up routine. And timing was everything in a headliner act, wasn't it?

Josie turned both palms up under Roger's quivering chin. "That'll be fifty bucks."

"Fifty? But you ain't even told me anything yet."

"First the fifty."

"Can't we make it twenty now and twenty-five next payday?"

"Jesus, Roger, can't you add past ten with your shoes on?"

"How's about if I mail a check then?"

"Do you finish talking long distance and then put your money in the slot, or do you pay first and then get your call put through?"

"Say what?"

"It's fifty bucks in advance, and then I can reveal the spirits' message."

"It was only twenty-five last time, Josie. I'm runnin' short till Friday."

"Look, do you want me to help you with this or not?"

"Sure, Josie. But fifty bucks?"

"This is not a cheap curse, Roger. This is a serious, badass zap this bitch's put on your head. Now what do you want me to do? I can tell the spirits here to just forget it and let her fry your brains for you." She folded her arms across her chest and stared at the ceiling. Cobwebs were woven like Belgian lace around the defunct overhead light fixture. And she noticed a square of gypsum ceiling tile about to surrender to gravity. Might have to fix that before it came down and bonked one of her customers.

"I'm a little short. Can't I owe you till payday?"

Her glare sizzled like firecrackers. "The spiritual world does not accept IOU's."

"Okay, okay," he groaned, pulling out his wallet. "But this'll clean me out."

"What's it worth to save your soul, huh? I can see a very dark shadow hovering over you, Roger, but if you're willing to gamble with your future until Friday, I can't be responsible for the consequences."

He jerked out two twenties and a rumpled ten. "I'm in. No way am I lettin' those zombie freaks mess with me. Here. Just do your thing, okay?"

She scoffed up the cash and tucked it in her pocket. In a second, Josie was back in tune with the celestial sphere and rapt in powerful, meditative tremors that impressed the hell out of him. "I see this dark, foreboding shadow hovering over you." She rubbed the globe so hard he half expected a genie to pop out. "She's mad as hell. This is a wig-raising rage, Roger. I see fire in her eyes."

"It's Marilyn! I know it's her. What's she gonna do, Josie? Tell me for crissakes. You got my fifty bucks so tell me."

"Patience."

"I know it's her. I know it. Woman wants me dead, too. She used to tell me she'd shoot my balls off if she ever caught me foolin' around, but I thought the coast was clear once she was six-feet under. Ain't that reasonable, Josie?"

"We're talking celestial omniscience, spiritual sanctions here, Roger. Forget reasonable."

"Can't you just put some kinda zap on her or somethin'?"

"Will you let me concentrate? Just be quiet and don't interrupt." Without his seeing, she peeked a look at her wristwatch. It was almost two. Her favorite soap started in ten minutes—she'd have to move this along. "I see the faces of your spiritual guides."

"It's Marilyn, ain't it? I know it's her. Why's she torturin' me like this?"

"Yes, it's your dear departed wife. And Marilyn's angry. Pissed to the max."

"Hell, she was in a bad mood for the last twenty years."

"She's suffering in the spiritual domain. I see blood coloring her astral aura."

"I thought passin' over cured all them female troubles."

"Never mind that. She wants to get a message through to you—a warning. She's wandering in the mists that separate the living from the spirit world. Her soul is in pain. She's reaching out to you, Roger. She's keening—"

"—What's that? Is it like skatin' or sleddin'?"

"—calling out to you from beyond the veil—"

"—Weddin' veil? What the hell is that all about?"

Plebeian ignorance was such a bore. No one ever appreciated the tolerance required of a true artist forced to endure the tedium of the *hoi polloi*. "She's pissed, Roger. Very angry with you."

"Right. I figured that."

"She says you haven't visited her grave since last Christmas."

"I drove by—don't that count? It was right after New Year's—the seventh, I think. Her birthday." His eyebrows folded in a puzzling frown. "Or was it the ninth? Hell, I forgit. How many points is that gonna cost me—forgittin her birthday?"

"You've neglected her memory, Roger. The date doesn't matter."

"Don't suppose they celebrate birthdays where she's at, do they? She never told her right age anyhow—shaved off five years before she even turned forty."

Josie silenced him with a stare strong enough to strip the paint off his car. "Will you shut up and listen for a minute? You're disrupting my spiritual connection."

"Sorry."

"No matter what day you were there, it's been too long. She feels you let your love die since the funeral. You've forgotten all the good years she gave you, all the good times you shared as man and wife. And what's even worse, you've neglected her grave."

"Hell's bells—I went and put a load of weed killer on it last month."

"No, no. She feels you've tarnished her memory thinking about another woman."

"She knows about Ginger? Damn! What's she say about Ginger? She knows I'm gittin married again. I feel it, Josie—her curse. It's like a bad case of chili-pepper runs."

Josie flashed a wicked wink. "Oh, that's not all she knows."

"Oh, damn! I knew it."

"She warns you to beware of earthly devil-doers."

"Jesus! What's that? You mean like Jehovah's Witnesses or somethin' worse?"

"Like witches."

"Witches? You sure about that?"

"I don't make mistakes in interpreting messages from the spiritual realm."

He scratched his head. "They still got witches flyin' around? I thought the Pilgrims wearin' those funny hats burnt em all up."

She bit her lip to keep from leaping across the incredible chasm separating their intellectual territories and short-circuiting his brain with a metaphysical thump. Much more of this convoluted conversation, and she'd definitely have an industrial dose headache.

Roger was still trying to dam his stream of conscious dribble. "Who woulda thought—witches? You mean like the gal on TV who wiggles her nose and makes Tallulah Bankhead show up?"

If Roger were a turkey, he'd be known as the dumb one.

"Not Tallulah Bankhead, for crissakes."

"Yeah."

"*Moore*head," she corrected him peevishly. "Agnes Moorehead." All these irritating sidetracks were wearing her out—like fighting off a herd of carnivorous gnats.

"Really? You sure about that?"

"Positive."

"Well, they're both Heads anyway, right? Probly related."

"Will you please shut up and listen for crissakes? No wonder you've got this bad-assed hex laid on you—you're not paying any attention."

"Sorry. So she's sicced a witch on me, huh? Is that it?"

"A witch with orange hair and a blue Cadillac."

"Goddam. She knows about the Caddy?"

"Of course, Roger. She sees and knows all in the spirit world." Along with the rest of Marion County's gossip mongers. Roger's poor taste in girlfriends was no secret to anybody who could read the top line on an eye chart and hear their alarm clock go off.

"Jeez, Josie, does she know about everything?"

"Of course."

"I mean *everything*."

"You have no secrets from the spirit world, Roger. None." Josie was intrigued. Roger was runner up as the most boring man on the planet, even if he had taken up with a blonde floozy in a K-Mart wig who sat on his lap while they tooled down Market Road in a bright blue *sedan de ville*. Maybe there was something more entertaining Josie could get for her trouble. Most of the time, Roger's recollection talents were neck and neck with a frozen fryer from Safeway.

He fidgeted and peered over his shoulder. "Jesus, Josie, I never even told Ginger. Oh, Christ on a crutch. I'm a goner then. If she seen me from the other side doin' that stuff with Badger, then there's nothin' you can do to get the curse off me."

"Badger?" His black Labrador retriever. She could imagine this bony Romeo sprawled with his drawers down and the dog lapping at his floppy appendage, and it made her want to laugh. Only Roger's extreme agitation stopped her. That and the fact that she knew for a certainty he had another twenty-dollar bill in his pocket.

"I never meant nothin' by it, I swear! I was lonely before I met Ginger. Jeez, Josie, I ain't like the first guy ever done it."

"You messed with your dog?" Josie feigned disgust, suppressing a giggle.

"I didn't mean nothin' by it, Josie. Oh, god! Is she gonna strike me dead now or burn my house down? Am I like damned or somethin'?"

"This is bad shit, Roger, but try and relax. I can fix this."

"You can?"

"I know how to do this. I can fix it—make it so Marilyn can't see a thing."

"Well, damn, Josie. Do it. For god's sake, do it. I can't live like this. Ever since she passed away, all I do is think about her blamin' me for everything, especially with Ginger and all." Roger stared out the window. It was dirtied with fly tracks, dust, fingerprints and cat nose smudges. "Goddam, Josie. They know it all up there, don't they?"

"There are no secrets in the other world."

"What'm I gonna do then?"

"She'll forgive you, Roger. If you make amends."

"How? Like promises or what?"

"She wants you to visit her grave and prove how much you loved her."

"How do I do that?"

"She wants you to kneel down beside her headstone." She gazed deeper into the crystal ball for a signal. This was beginning to amuse her. "The message is very strong. She wants you to do it right there, Roger."

"Huh?" His jaw flopped open.

"Do it. You know."

"What?"

"It."

"You mean… do *it* right there?"

"Yeah. Do it."

"Right out in public?"

"You owe her, Roger. The living must atone to the dead for their past transgressions if they are to find true peace in this world."

"Oh, shit!"

"You have to seal your eternal bond with a public consummation of your love."

"You mean like doin' it right out where God'n everbody can see?"

"That's what she wants, Roger. That's what it takes to appease her spirit. If you could do it for Badger, you can do as much for her."

"Christ! I can't do that. I'm a workin' man, not some fairy from California exposin' himself in broad daylight. And besides that I'm a Christian, once a week anyhow. I'd like as not get my ass thrown in jail. Her grave's right across from the post office annex for crissakes. I'll get locked up for sure."

"That's the deal, Roger. The spirits have spoken. If you want forgiveness, these are the terms."

"What about the curse she put on me and Ginger? Would that fix it?"

"Yes—you'd be free."

He pulled at the back of his neck. "Hell, I don't know. I can't do it, Josie. Not the consumin' part and shit. How about if I just do it in my bedroom with the lights off, huh? I could get her pitchure out. That sounds fair, don't it?"

"It has to be at her grave in front of God and everybody. She feels you owe her."

"What'll happen if I don't do it? What'll the curse do? Kill me?"

"Worse."

"Worse?"

"Ginger's hair will fall out."

"Christ!"

"And your pecker will shrink up until it's no bigger than a pea pod."

"Shit, she can do that?"

"Roger, all things are possible in the spirit world. Your departed wife is no longer bound by the rules governing our universe." Josie could already smell the lone twenty in Roger's wallet. It was as good as hers.

"So what can I do?"

She smiled and patted his arm. "Don't worry. I have a plan."

"Thank god, Josie. You're a gem, you know that?"

"I could go out to the cemetery and visit Marilyn's grave for you."

"Jeez Louise, Josie! Would you do that for me?"

"I could make amends. I have special powers to appease the spirits."

"You'd be doin' me a huge, big favor. Pullin' some crazy stunt like that—sounds like some shit Marilyn would dream up just to have my ass behind bars."

Josie's palm turned up. "Twenty bucks, Roger."

"Twenty? You'll clean me out."

"You're complaining about twenty bucks for all I'm doing for you? You want to explain to Ginger why she'll have to turtle wax her head?"

He already had the money on the table. "Take it. Here. I ain't got no problem with that. Hey, Marilyn never could rest anyhow till she'd emptied my jeans. Take it."

"Thank you." The bill disappeared into her cache. "Now all your astral vibrations should be in harmony. The wedding can go forward now with the spirits' blessing, Roger."

"Thank god for that."

"Don't worry. I can take care of everything. We'll call this a down payment. After I've gone to the cemetery and expiated your bad karma, you can give me another fifty, and you'll be freed forever from Marilyn's spell. Her spirit will forever remain behind the celestial veil."

"What?"

"Your future happiness should be the most important thing in your life right now."

"Yeah, sure, but—"

"—so you don't have to worry about a thing. It's only money, Roger. I can fix it so you won't ever have to worry about Marilyn interfering with your life again. You and Ginger can tie the nuptial knot in peace. Now how much is that worth?"

"Am I gonna get some kinda guaranty?"

"Trust me. I've done this before. Don't worry about a thing. Leave everything to your psychic advisor. Come back on Friday, and we can wipe your spiritual slate clean."

"But we're gettin' married on Friday, Josie. Ginger has everything all planned—we're even havin' a weddin' cake. Piggly Wiggly has a chocolate marshmallow with raspberry fillin', half off if you buy fifty buck's worth of groceries."

Josie managed a condescending smile. "How romantic."

"You guaranty this'll take care of that hex she laid on me and Ginger?"

"Absolutely."

"I couldn't even get it up if I hadda worry about Marilyn spookin' me ever time I got the urge, if you get my drift."

"Exactly."

"We're drivin' down to Winnemucca to play the slots. We reserved the honeymoon suite at the Truck-Star motel. Hell, we even gotta waterbed." He smirked unabashedly. "Great, huh?" *Wink, wink.* "More traction with wave action, right?"

"Stupendous," she fibbed with a straight face. Josie got up, steered him past a pile of old magazines and caught his arm as he slipped on a stray sock.

His cerebral light bulb winked on as he slalomed to the door. "You mean to say, I gotta come up with another fifty before it's like a done deal?"

"Cash."

He gave in with a shrug. "I guess as how it's worth it then. Guaranteed, right?"

"One-hundred percent."

A gold-capped incisor illuminated his grin. "That takes a load off, I can tell you."

"Good. See you on Friday then."

He punched open the door and jumped off the porch into the mushy yard. "Thanks, Josie. You're a goddam jewel. You sure as hell got me out of a tight spot." He yanked open the door of the Dodge and waved as the car splashed through the potholes.

If Roger Bumledder had the brainpower of a stuffed parrot, he could visit Marilyn's grave, leave a bunch of flowers and feel just as good. But then Roger wasn't likely to question a celestial source of authority. He was too well trained by twenty-four years of mind control from a stern, bovine wife who allowed him little room for independent thought.

Josie shut the door and pulled out her cash. Not bad for today. Now it was time for her soap opera and then maybe a bubble bath in the miniature pink tub filled with old newspapers and hair curlers. She stuffed Roger's money in her piggy bank atop the old Norge and hurried to turn on the TV.

2

Josie flipped off the tube, slid her feet into fuzzy slippers and snow-shoed to the bantam bedroom. She switched on the radio. The dial swung past a country and western steel guitar, a voice as dry as month-old cornflakes extolling the virtues of Five Day Deodorant Pads and stopped on a familiar Tom Jones number. Josie hummed her way to the bathroom, emptied the tub clutter, turned on the tap and dribbled jasmine oil in the faucet stream.

An orange cat as big as an NFL football twisted its ears toward the open louvers. Then it jumped off the toilet seat and whipped a bushy tail around its haunches. Gold eyes bored into Josie's face until a spark of recognition flared.

"You hear somebody, Goldie?"

A plaintive mew was her answer. Actually the cat had already recognized the whine of the groaning engine and squeaky frame coming up the lane. It was a familiar sound announcing a slow-walking human who smelled of dogs. Not a welcome visitor. Goldie leaped onto the sticky floor and made her exit as gracefully as possible, just in case Josie imagined the cat might be scared off by this smelly interloper.

Josie refastened her skirt and peered outside. It was Hobart Ames her neighbor. He'd moved out last winter actually—taken his trailer south to Arizona. But he came back with a shaggy-haired woman named Farrah who convinced him to camp on the soggy slope of Cully Marsh three miles east of the Jewel Grove Trailer Park. So there they were, the two mangy misfits Hobart and Farrah, living like gypsies in their old trailer with no electricity, no running water, no john. Josie could usually smell Hobart before he got to her door. Smelled like wood smoke, sweat, dirty socks and garlic.

"Hi," she waved from the porch as he climbed out of his truck. There was only one door, on the passenger side. The old GMC had only one headlight, too. Had two fenders though—one blue and one primer red. Two tan hound dogs were in the back, yapping and barking at her.

"Hey, Jo," he called with a good-natured grin. "How's it goin', Girl?"

"So so. You?"

"Fine." He ran a hand through his hair. A bristly beard covered his jaw. Hobart was a good-looking man before Farrah got ahold of him. Now he could pass for a laid-off logger, a skid-road slider, a Depression drifter one step ahead of all his earthly goods. Shame. Josie had seen definite possibilities in Hobart.

"You doin' okay with all this rain?" She knew damn well he was gearing up to borrow something. He never stopped by unless he was bent on taking something of Josie's back with him.

"Well, it gets a little messy. Say, I was wondering, Jo," he hemmed, pulling on the back of his neck. He shushed the dogs and stared at his muddy boots.

"Yeah? Whatcha need?" No sense standing out in the rain for a half hour making small talk until he got up the balls to ask for it. Whatever it was. Probably wanting to throw some laundry in with hers and use the washing machines. Damn drizzle made it hard to hang clothes out to dry. Even Gypsies resorted to Speed Queen technology in weather like this.

"Could you come on down to the house and see Farrah, Jo?"

'House' seemed like a gross overstatement. Even for Hobart. His midget trailer was no more than a tin dugout with a shanty privy and a wrecked VW bug hunkered down like a banana slug in the reeds and blackberry vines at Cully Marsh.

"What's wrong?"

"Well, that's just it, Jo. Farrah sorta needs to tell you herself."

"Tell me what?"

He scratched his head as rainwater trickled down both cheeks. "Can you come out—just for a little bit? I'll give you a lift."

"You mean like now?"

"Farrah says it's important or I wouldn't have come over."

"You don't have any grubby duds to toss in the washing machine?"

"Nope."

"So you don't wanna borrow anything?"

"Nope."

She shrugged. Didn't make any sense to her at all. She hadn't spoken a dozen words to Farrah since Hobart brought her back with him. Didn't matter.

Hobart was a friend, and she had nowhere else to go especially. What the hell? She could always use the opportunity to work on Hobart and try to talk him into moving back to the Jewel Grove where he could take up semi-civilized habits again.

"Sure. Come on in outta the rain, Hobart. I'll get my coat and lock up."

"Thanks, Jo. Thanks a lot." He clomped up to the porch and shook the water off his jacket.

His clothes were shabby even by Salvation Army standards. A safety pin closed his wool shirt, and his jeans had both knees ripped out. But when he smiled, Josie could lose herself in his marble-blue eyes gleaming like the Caspian Sea. Yeah, she mused as she went inside, Hobart had definite possibilities. All he needed was a good scrub, maybe a spritz of Old Spice, a shave and a pair of dry socks.

Josie turned off her myrtlewood lamp, grabbed her parka, latched the door and pocketed the key. She followed Hobart across the muddy yard to the truck and climbed in. Didn't help much to keep her out of the weather—the rain flew in through the open cab and soaked her to the skin.

Hobart started up the engine, ground the gears into reverse and backed to the road. When he headed east and switched on the lone headlight, Josie felt a blast of cold slap her in the face. The windshield was mostly busted out on her side.

"Jesus, Hobart. You need a new truck."

"Yeah. I need a little work done on this thing. Need a new carburetor."

"That's not all you need. *Ow!*" Her head banged on the metal roof as they plowed through a pothole the size of Lake Tahoe.

"I sure appreciate your coming over, Jo, on such short notice. I hope I didn't spoil your evening or anything."

She hated to admit that her plans so far had consisted of cutting her toenails, reading the last chapter of *Love Adorns Adelia* and maybe masturbating with a giant pepperoni sausage if the mood struck her. And it usually did after finishing off a romance novel. Adelia was about to get drilled by the horny hero. Took him almost four-hundred damn pages to get around to it.

"It's okay, Hobart. You're a neighbor."

"Well, not technically anymore, I guess. But thanks."

"How long are you gonna hang out down in that swamp? You oughtta hook your rig back up at the trailer park. How can you live without indoor toilets and TV?"

He downshifted to negotiate a corner as the truck choked and spewed a trail of blue smoke. "Oh, it's not so bad, Jo. I don't watch TV anyhow."

"Weird."

"Farrah and I like it. Did I tell you there's a pair of blue herons down at the pond this year? They nested in that old cedar log."

She wrinkled her nose. Birds were not her thing. "Gee," she mumbled with the same enthusiasm the discovery of a new zit stirred in her bosom. "No kidding."

"There's a family of muskrats that moved in, too—bet we're gonna have babies."

"Cute." She wrinkled her nose. Rodents were rodents.

"And you oughtta see Farrah's stuff—it's beautiful."

"Oh, yeah. I forgot she paints." *Yawn.*

"How she does it, I don't know, Jo. But those watercolors of hers look so real, you expect to see the birds take off and fly right out of the picture."

"You don't say." She had painted once herself, bought a kit for fourteen ninety-five at Payless, connected the dots and came up with a watercolor of a Chinese coolie feeding a giant panda. The bear had the number nine showing through right between his eyes. Looked like a target at a carnival shoot. Dumbest picture she had ever seen.

He leaned against her as his hand worked the floor-mounted gear shifter. Josie felt a shiver of warmth slide down her thigh where he had touched her. Hobart had wonderfully masculine features beneath all those baggy duds: a belly so lean she couldn't pinch any fat at all between her fingers when she hugged him. His shoulders were as wide as an aircraft carrier, and his waist was shamefully smaller than hers. Hobart was six-feet tall, naturally hunky and barely broken in at thirty. His thick, curly hair was the color of cinnamon, and he had the bluest eyes she had ever seen outside of a Revlon ad.

What he saw in this Farrah person was beyond her comprehension. Farrah Whateverhernamewas didn't even have any boobs. She was all knees and elbows and hair. That was her good feature. Her mane was so thick and wavy she had enough for two heads. It was the color of oiled rosewood, naturally spiraled down her back like a doll's wig. There was no such thing for Farrah as a bad hair day. Bitch. But she wore glasses as thick as Coke bottles, had long, skinny arms and insect legs like Olive Oyl. And Farrah's feet were big enough to go water skiing without the skis. Now what could a man like Hobart see in a geek like that?

The truck lurched over a hump in the road, slid through a puddle and groaned its way down a winding trail toward a winking light. Must be the Hobart homestead. Josie would probably ruin her good boots slogging through the muck in his yard. If she could call this muddy swamp a yard. Even if Hobart was a friend, this was going the extra mile.

They stopped, and Hobart turned off the engine. He wiped a stream of rainwater from his face and took hold of Josie's wrist before she could crawl out. "Jo, I gotta tell you something before we go in."

Maybe Farrah had a killer case of herpes or something. Or maybe she'd tripped out on some acid and was ready for the rubber room. Whatever. Josie was here because of Hobart anyway—Farrah's problems didn't interest Josie much.

"She wanted you to come really bad, but I don't want you to think we're like taking advantage of you or anything. You know what I mean?"

"No."

"Well, I mean, I'd like to pay you whatever you usually charge. I know you're a friend and all, but this is important to me, Jo."

"Charge for what?"

One hand groped behind his back for the grimy, rumpled bill he pulled free of his pocket. "Would ten be okay?"

"For what?"

"For helping Farrah out."

Before she could answer or glom on to the ten, there was a loud bang as the trailer door flew open, and Farrah aimed a flashlight at the truck.

"Josie? Hi. Come on in. I have some peppermint tea and fresh scones."

Scones? This was one strange lady. Living in the middle of a fucking swamp in a tin-can trailer, and she makes scones? Weird times ten.

Hobart came around to the passenger side and hoisted Josie in his arms before she could sink into the muck. He carried her inside and closed the door behind them.

"Thanks for coming, Josie. I really appreciate it. Here. Let me take your coat. Sit down. I'll pour some tea." Farrah scurried off to the back of the trailer and clattered china cups in the glow of a spitting kerosene lamp.

"No trouble," Josie said, shivering. She was drenched. Hobart might as well have carted her down here in a wheelbarrow for crissakes.

Josie took a look around. She had been in Hobart's trailer before he pulled out and left for Yuma. It was smaller than her Nashua, rounded at the back like a stinkbug. But now it was unreal. There was a hooked rug on the floor, green plants sitting under the tiny windows, china plates and watercolor pictures on the sloping walls, knotty pine cupboards shining with lemon oil and a wood stove purring in the corner. It was…well, homey. Farrah was a sick cookie. There wasn't any trash anywhere. No litter. No mess. Place even smelled clean. As a matter of fact, Hobart didn't smell so bad himself now that she thought about it.

Farrah scrunched up on the mini divan beside Hobart and set down a tray with tea mugs and a plate of scones. A pot of homemade jam and real butter made Josie's mouth water. She could smell the peppermint.

"Thanks." She slurped the hot tea and felt her insides warm up. She was cold and wetter than a sea slug. This was cozy. Maybe it wasn't so bad being here.

Farrah smiled warmly. Her eyes were the size of buckshot behind her thick glasses. She laid a bony hand over Hobart's knee, and Josie could count each red knuckle. She glanced down at Farrah's deerskin slippers—they looked big enough to hold the entire US Olympic bobsled team. Hobart must be half blind. Or maybe he had some sort of a foot fetish.

"Josie, did Hobart tell you about my trouble?"

She put her tea down and munched on a scone. "Nope. Didn't." She slathered butter and jam on the second half and wolfed it down. Delicious.

Farrah looked up at Hobart for a moment. He nodded sympathetically.

"Josie, I'd like you to talk to someone for me."

Gulp. Smack. "Uh, sure. Who? Somebody at the trailer park?"

"Not exactly. It's someone I used to know a long time ago."

Crunch, munch. "Oh. You mean somebody from Arizona?" She licked jam off her thumb and reached for her tea. *Slurp.* "Who?"

"It's someone who was very close to me."

"Oh, I get it. Your ex old man, huh? He's coming up to Oregon, and you don't want him to bug you and Hobart, right?"

"No, Josie. It's not like that at all. Didn't Hobart explain?"

"Explain what?"

"About Max."

"Max?" Josie put the mug down. "Who's Max?"

"My father."

"No shit."

"I want you to talk to him, Josie. I want you to ask him to leave me alone."

Josie's eyes narrowed. Her tongue dug out wads of dough between her teeth. She swallowed and folded her hands in her lap. This was turning out to be a business call and not a social visit. Interesting. "Where is your dad?"

Hobart interrupted for the first time. "He's long gone, Jo. He was sent to Korea when Farrah was just a baby."

"So he's dead?"

"Yes," Farrah sighed. "I'm afraid so."

"He died in the Korean War?"

"That's right. In 1953. I was just a baby. My mother married again when I started school, and Dennis is my stepdad. I never thought much about Max until…" She checked Hobart's expression before continuing. "Before this happened, Josie."

"What happened?"

"He came back."

"Came back where?"

"Here!" Hobart pointed at the floor beneath Josie's wet boots. "The bastard is scaring the shit out of her, Jo. Tramps through the place at night, leaves the door wide open and leaves footprints down at the marsh."

Josie cast a cynical eye in his direction. "You're kidding, right? Putting me on?"

"No!" Farrah twisted her skirt between her thumb and forefinger. "It's the gods' truth, Josie. I swear it. You have to help me. I don't know what else to do."

"You're kidding."

Hobart wrapped an arm around Farrah. "For god's sake, Jo, if you won't help us, just say so."

"Look, if any of this shit is true—and I doubt it—then this is some pretty heavy duty paranormal voodoo you're messing with."

"That's why you're here."

"Hey, I'm just a fortune teller." She laughed. Nobody smiled back. "You know. It's a con. You know that, Hobart," she pleaded with her eyes locked on to his. "You know I just con these suckers for a buck. Jeez, you oughtta know that."

"I was counting on you to help," he mumbled dolefully.

Farrah reached over to grab Josie's hand. "Please, help us. This is important."

Josie stuffed another scone in her mouth and chewed. This was totally fucking weird. When Hobart lived next to her at the trailer park, he would come over in the evenings, share some plum wine and laugh with her about the goofy stories she made up for the suckers. He knew it was all bullshit. And he still had the balls to drag her ass out here in the middle of the swamp and ask her to talk to a dead man? Who was conning who here anyway?

"Josie, say you'll do it. *Please*." Farrah squeezed out a singleton tear.

"I know you can do it, Jo," Hobart seconded. His fingers kneaded Josie's clammy flesh and made her toes tingle. And it wasn't the peppermint tea this time. "Sure, I know you spin some tales for the suckers once in awhile. You just tell em what they want to hear, right?"

"Yeah. It's business, that's all."

"Sure. I know that. But I also know, Jo, that you have something. Something very special."

Farrah nodded and put her head on Hobart's broad shoulder. She stifled a wispy sigh. "It's a gift, Josie."

"Oh, yeah? What sort of a gift?"

"You can reach people, Jo. Lost people. Lost souls. Everybody says so. If there is a way to connect with the spirit world, you have the formula."

"I do?"

"I know you do, Girl. I've never doubted you at all."

"No shit?"

"So when can we start?"

"Uh, I guess anytime really." Josie started to pick up her mug just as a gust of wind blew the door open, slapped against the trailer's skin and let in a backlash of rain that watered them all down like hothouse plants.

"It's *him*!" Farrah shrieked.

"Sonuvabitch!" Hobart flung himself at the door and slammed it shut.

"Jesus," Josie gasped, awash in slopped tea, scone crumbs and rainwater. "I think I better get my power tools."

"Power tools?"

"My crystal ball, my opal ring and the Bhutu necklace with the cock feathers and snake bones. This is heavy duty shit here."

Farrah sighed and clasped her hands. "Thank god. I knew you'd do it."

Josie reached for another scone. "This is not gonna be easy." And it definitely ain't gonna be cheap either, she thought to herself as she sank her teeth into the warm crust. This was opportunity with a capital O. "Don't worry," Josie reassured her newest marks with her mouth full. "I can handle it. Definitely."

They nodded and smiled back gratefully.

3

The storm quit kidding around by ten o'clock. The gusts were rocking Hobart's trailer like a hammock on a tramp steamer. Water slid off the hump-backed roof and puddled on the tapioca turf. By ten-thirty, when Hobart put on his rain poncho and headed outside to shore up the frame, the little aluminum ark with Arizona plates was listing to starboard.

Josie sat with her legs tucked underneath her, munched a ginger-snap—homemade probably—and sipped red wine. Rain pelted the trailer's flanks behind the built-in sofa and beat a steady taps. She would have gone back home, fed her cat—Goldie was bound to be overdue for her tinned tuna pâté—finished off her romance novel and crawled into bed, but the old GMC truck wouldn't start. Hobart nearly drowned sitting in the open cab pumping the accelerator, fiddling with the choke and slapping the dashboard after each engine spasm.

So here she was—stuck out in the tules in this camper-sized crackerbox with Big Foot Farrah and Hobart who was tromping in and out trying to staunch leaks, sliding boards under the sinking axles or coaxing the truck into turning over. He was so wet by now that he made a puddle when he stood still for a minute, and his hair dripped like a string mop.

Farrah didn't seem at all perturbed by the weather or the enforced company. "You know, Josie, I'm really glad to have a chance to get to know you."

"Oh, yeah?" She made a grab for the last cookie.

"Hobart talks so much about you."

"Yeah?" The conversation was finally starting to get interesting.

Farrah's mole-like eyes fastened on hers as she manufactured a look of genuine admiration. Josie was confused. Maybe there was more to this Farrah than weak eyes and big bones. After all, Hobart saw something, didn't he? And Josie had always thought Hobart had more sense than most of the men she had met since coming here.

Josie liked Hobart—a lot. She would have liked him even more if he hadn't packed up and taken off for Arizona without even giving her a chance to see if they couldn't have come to some sort of understanding between the two of them. Whatever it was that Hobart seemed to be lacking in life, he had obviously found with this skinny painter. Maybe Josie could have accommodated him just as well. Maybe not. At least, he should have given her the chance to find out.

"So what's he say about me?" Josie felt thumps beneath the floor as Hobart wedged another support against the frame.

Farrah twined a ringlet of glossy hair around a bony finger. "He likes you, Josie. I know that. As a matter of fact, when we first met in Yuma, he mentioned you right away."

"No kidding." Josie didn't like to dwell on the night Hobart Ames called her long distance from Arizona, told her all about the crazy scene there with artists and big brains living off some university grant to study the sex lives of cactus or some far out shit. Farrah had hitched out to Arizona from the Bay Area, was selling her artwork at the Yuma mall, communing with the Aztec gods, eating maize pudding and crashing in a commune hung up in the mountains. Sounded about as appealing as camping out in Death Valley with no toilet paper and a busted fly swatter.

"You were the only person Hobart said he missed up here, Josie."

"Oh, yeah? For real?"

"And he said he thought you were really smart. He told me how you had come here all by yourself after your old man got busted and everything." She leaned forward and pressed a hand on Josie's thigh. "That must have been a real downer, Josie—losing someone close to you. I can't imagine what I would do if anything happened to Hobart."

She brushed cookie crumbs off her lap. "Yeah, well, it happens, you know. It's not like he croaked or anything."

"No, but it's a downer all the same to be deprived of the companionship of someone you love a lot."

"Well, it wasn't exactly the world's greatest love affair or anything. More convenience than anything else—plus the grass was free."

"All the same…" She looked down, not sure how to end this tortuous conversational track.

"But I had an uncle who dropped dead. Had stomach cancer—first they took that out, then they hacked out his intestines." Josie bit off a hunk of cookie and chewed with her mouth open. "Had to eat nothing but baby food at the end. Disgusting. He'd get halfway through a jar of smashed carrots and then upchuck in his plate. Gross. Died when all he could keep down was pureed parsnips—no wonder, huh?" *Gulp.*

"So did I tell you that's how my mother went?"

"She get down to the mashed parsnips?"

"She had cervical cancer, and they just kept cutting more and more of her out, you know." She shuddered and rubbed her belly. "Finally—well, she went real slow at the end. It was awful to watch someone you love go through that."

"Yeah. I know what you mean."

"My stepdad has a drinking problem, so it was pretty much just me and Mom the last few years. Except for my godmother, my Aunt Philippa. That's my mom's sister—there was just the two of them growing up. They were orphans. Anyway, I dropped out of school a year before Mom passed away and went to California to get my art thing going."

"Yeah. Fascinating."

"I didn't know my mother was dying. It must have been a terrible ordeal for her when I left. Hobart was my lifeboat, Josie. You know what I mean? But I always wondered what it was like for Max." Her glance drifted off to the wall and lingered on a watercolor of plowed fields surrounding a drab Dutch barn. "He had such a violent death. I bet my mom had nightmares about it. People do, you know. My painting helps fill the empty spot his death left."

Josie's gaze followed. One of Farrah's own works no doubt. Kind of depressing, Josie thought, looking at it. Nothing much to see really. Bleak. Boring. Oh, well. It wasn't any worse than the coolie and the panda picture with the dots showing through the paint—made the Chinaman look like he'd been shot with a rivet gun.

"I mean," Farrah went on, "what was it like for him at the end do you think?"

"He got killed in Korea, huh?"

"My mother got this telegram—she saved it, and I read it when I was in high school. It just said he had been lost while in combat action with his platoon. I think they were like trying to take this hill, and the North Koreans were falling back, and then all of a sudden, there was this big rush of new troops they brought in, and the American soldiers were all just like slaughtered." She spread her hands and fanned the skinny fingers. "Like maybe a hundred or so

just got mowed down in their foxholes or something. My D
in front of the whole Korean army and kept firing until he ra
tion while the rest of the guys took off. He got a medal for th
Bronze Star. My mom kept it in her bureau drawer. It was alw
reason my dad didn't come back home to us, you know—like he sacrificed himself to save some of those other guys. Only they didn't make it either, but at least he tried, you know?"

"Yeah. Sad. Like Audie Murphy, huh?"

"Was she a Korean war widow, too?"

"Him. Hey, don't you ever watch war movies? John Wayne and Audie Murphy are the best. *Pork Chop Hill* is my favorite."

"I don't know much about film stars."

Such ignorance was hard for Josie to fathom. "Too bad. So old Max was a genuine hero, huh? What happened to him after the medal thing?"

"I think my dad was shot in the head—like it was blown off or something. My mom never did look in the casket or anything."

"So they brought him home?"

"Oh, yeah. He's buried somewhere in the States, I think."

"You mean you don't even know where he's at? Didn't you go see his grave?"

A blast of wind rocked the trailer, and Farrah pulled her sweater around her bony shoulders. "You see, this is the really crazy thing, Josie. When they brought the coffins home, I think parts of my dad were missing. His casket was sealed. They just told my mom which one was his. I guess they identified the bodies by the dog tags."

Josie knew that much from watching World War II movies about Iwo Jima with Hollywood heroes like Jeff Chandler who never seemed to grow a beard even after weeks on some remote island with no Burma Shave or anything. Gross. The television news pictures on Viet Nam were even grosser. They showed raggedy palm trees and GI's blown to bits in the muck. Sometimes there wasn't anything left but dog tags. Josie had lost at least three good friends to the war in Southeast Asia. Nam was worse than anything Audie Murphy or Van Johnson had come up against. Vicious blood-sucking bugs, leeches, mud like hot paste, booby-traps, burned bodies stacked up like shishkabobs in the smelly paddies. The TV news showed Marines piled up at the medevac stations like slaughterhouse carcasses—they hadn't even salvaged their dog tags. Some of the nastier bits weren't even big enough to bother about bringing back. They were officially listed as MIA's which probably meant their bones were rotting away in the jungle somewhere. Maybe that's what had happened to Max.

"But then after Mom had buried him, they wrote and said there was a mistake, and they were going to dig up Dad's grave and send it to Iowa. They said it wasn't Dad but somebody else in the casket. Mom didn't remember who they said it was."

"Jeez," Josie exhaled in disbelief. This was getting even weirder.

"So they dug up Dad's casket and sent it off to Iowa, and Mom never did get Dad's remains."

"She had his dog tags, huh?"

"Yeah. But no body. I mean, like everybody in Dad's platoon was blown to bits. So Mom figured that maybe his dog tags just got blown off the body, especially if he got hit in the head. I mean, it makes sense, don't you think so?"

"I guess."

"So we never had a body. Maybe he is buried somewhere or parts of him are with somebody else. Mom used to tell me she thought that could have happened. But I don't know for sure." She lowered her voice and clutched at Josie's hem. "Don't you see, Josie? That's what makes this so damned creepy. If my Mom were alive, this would just about kill her."

Josie blinked at the illogic of this observation. "Okay, so let me get this straight. You think you saw your dad hanging around here?"

Farrah didn't shrink from Josie's sarcastic smirk. "Yes. I did."

"So why do you think it's Max's ghost anyway?"

"What do you mean?"

"It could be lots of things, right?"

"Like what?"

"Well, like this storm. You know, wind makes a lot of funny noises and stuff. Hell, the wind blew my door open once before I got the latch screws tightened."

"I thought you were supposed to be tuned into psychic phenomena, Josie. Is this like a test or something? Do you need to find out if I'm serious about this? Is that it?"

This woman was nuttier than Josie had suspected. There was not a hint of doubt in her belief that a Casper creation was skulking around this swampy hovel. What a bunch of bullshit. This was a stunt even too silly to pull on her gullible clients. Nobody would fall for something this stupid.

"Look, Farrah—by the way, what's your last name anyway?"

"It's just Farrah. That's my artistic signature."

"Uh huh." She took another slug of warm wine and licked her lips clean. "So your real name is like Buttblaster or Snotlicker, huh?"

Farrah's face flushed. And it wasn't warm in the trailer anymore. As a matter of fact, Josie could feel a definite draft seeping through the knotty pine paneling chilling her backbone.

"Nothing like that. Why do I need more than one name?"

"Cuz everybody has one, that's all. So what was Max's name?"

Farrah was easily derailed. "Swidnik."

No wonder, Josie grinned. Farrah Swidnik sounded more like a Hereford lung disease than the world's greatest living watercolor *artiste*.

"So what makes you think Max Swidnik has turned up as some kind of ghost?"

"Well, what makes you so certain he hasn't?"

Josie had to think a minute. She hadn't expected to be put on the defensive. "Cuz I know better. This is bullshit, Farrah. Nothing but a buncha bullshit. Ghosts, spirits, afterlife crap. It's all bullshit. I thought Hobart would have known that."

"It is not bullshit, Josie. You're just telling me that to try and make me feel better. Don't bother. I've already been through all this. I know what I see and hear. And I know this is Max. So if you're wondering whether I'm really serious, I am."

"Okay." She crossed her arms over her chest. "Tell me how you know this Max Swidnik is sneaking around in the swamp down there."

"I have a picture of him. Of course, it's old. He was only twenty-four."

Farrah got up, opened a drawer and took out a snapshot album. She handed it over to Josie who flipped through the pages—pictures of a bushy-haired little girl beside a very pretty, angelic woman with light hair. Farrah stopped her at one picture. It showed a man with a squarish head, a crewcut that exposed his thick ears and a trace of an uncertain smile which belied the starched GI fatigues and stiff posture. He didn't look a thing like farinaceous Farrah.

"This is my mom, and this is Dad—Max."

"Uh huh." Average, average. Ho hum.

Farrah flipped a few pages forward, past a skinny baby with squinty eyes and crocheted booties two sizes bigger than her mittens. This kid was built like a praying mantis with curls, Josie observed. A photo of Farrah in a frilly party dress showed a knock-kneed youngster with a fuzzy fright wig, fire-starter spectacles and red galoshes the size of Coast Guard dinghies. Another shot—Farrah in pigtails and striped shorts wearing sandals with silver buckles. Josie smirked. Looked like snowshoes. With those enormous ambulators Sergeant Preston could have mushed barefoot through the Yukon. Sasquatch didn't have paws that big.

"This is my third birthday." A gangly toddler with a bright hair ribbon and red mary janes was framed by party balloons. If her folks had her footgear bronzed as keepsakes, they could have chartered the hulks out as river barges. "And here is Mom and Dad on their wedding day." A happy, smiling couple. Mom was a dainty doll. Max was a tough-looking marine.

"So?" Josie handed the photo album back.

"Well, so I know what he looks like. And I saw him face-to-face, Josie. It scared the hell out of me. I heard someone in the living room, and I got up to see what it was."

Living room was an exaggeration. Josie had seen bigger coat closets.

"I came out here, and there he was."

"Where?"

"There." She indicated the chair wedged against the wall and the triangular, three-legged maple end table attached to the doll-sized sofa. "He was sitting right in that chair, Josie. And he just looked up and stared at me."

"So what'd he look like?"

Farrah's cheeks reddened. "What do you mean? I just showed you his picture, didn't I? It was *him*."

"I mean, did he have a head? He hadn't aged or anything?"

"That's not it at all, Josie. You're missing the point."

"Which is?" About time they got around to it.

"Are you going to take this seriously or not? I need help, and if you don't want to help me, just say so."

"You want me to help get rid of this ghost even though you know I think this is bullshit, right?"

Their eyes met. Farrah looked away first. "Josie, you're not going to believe this, but he was sitting right here. In that chair. I could have touched him. It was real. And you know what else?"

"Surprise me."

"I could smell him. There was this odor about him, something like I had never smelled before. Like old oil at gas stations—like that. That's what he smelled like."

"Uh huh."

"And cigarette smoke. My Dad smoked Camels. Almost every picture my Mom had of him, he was smoking a cigarette."

"Uh huh."

"And he smelled like that. After he had gone, I could still smell that odor."

Josie restrained a cynical smile. "So did he just get up and walk out the door?"

"No," she said dreamily, staring at the chair. "He just sort of vanished. One minute he was there, and then he wasn't."

"No way."

"But he might have gone out the door. The door was open. I had to close it before I went back to bed. You know, at first I thought it was just a dream."

"Or a burglar."

"No. Nothing was disturbed. No valuables missing."

Yeah, right, Josie was thinking cynically. Like there's some real valuable shit here to steal—scones and musk oil.

"I didn't want to believe it was him at first either. I kept telling myself it was a dream. Maybe I was just sleepwalking. That's what I thought. But then he came back, and Hobart saw him, too. So I knew it couldn't have been a dream."

"So what'd Hobart see?"

"He saw a man down at the marsh. He was looking off into the distance and smoking. Hobart wondered what he was doing—if he was a trespasser. He thought he might be bothering the herons so he went down to say something. And when he got close behind the man, the guy turned around and smiled at him."

"Fascinating," she yawned.

"And then he said 'Hi.'"

"Sounds pretty spooky to me alright—saying hi. Pretty scary stuff."

"Josie, you just don't get it, do you?"

"Get what? Ghosts talking to people?" She rolled her eyes. "The ultimate bullshit, Farrah."

"No, no. Max is *here*. He's come back, and I know what he's looking for. I know what he wants."

Suddenly Hobart swung open the door and tramped inside.

"Oh!" Farrah yelped, startled by the intrusion. "Jesus, Hobart. You scared me."

Duck farts must have spooked this lady. Josie was unimpressed. Totally. This was all pure, unadulterated bullwhackey.

Hobart stood there leaking and dripping like a sieve. "If this fucking rain doesn't quit, we're gonna float right down to the pond, Farrah. Better get your boots and come on outside. Josie, if you don't mind, we could use your help, too."

"Me?" After all, she was still technically a guest, and she had serious reservations about being pressed into labor. Ten bucks didn't buy a long night of slogging around up to her ass in mud, wet and cold.

"I'll need you two to help carry some lumber down from the shed so I can shore up the trailer and keep the water out. I'm gonna dig a trench on the south side to see if I can get the water to run off some." He gave his head a final shake and slammed the door behind him.

Farrah got up. "Come on, Josie. We better get out there."

Josie didn't budge. There was one more swallow of wine in the bottle, and she drained it. "Why don't you just move back to the trailer park? If God had wanted people to live in swamps, he woulda put pontoons on Nashua's."

"Please, Josie," Farrah urged as she punched both arms into a rain slicker. "Hobart needs some help." When the door opened, a splash of rainwater cascaded off the roof and drenched her before she could broad jump into the ooze.

Josie pulled an old hat over her ears. Hobart was right—she could feel the trailer listing to one side. She had to step up to get over the doorsill. This was like abandoning ship. One way or the other, she was gonna get wet.

Shutting her eyes against the onslaught, Josie plopped into the soggy goo and sank to her boot tops. This was really the shits. What self-respecting ghost would hang around a dump like this?

4

When Hobart dropped Josie back at the Jewel Grove Trailer Park, she clomped like a Frankenstein monster up to her porch, her boots caked with muck, her hair tangled in slimy knots down her back, and her best skirt grungier than a flophouse mop. She was beat and wounded besides—her right hand sported a gash where a splinter had nailed her as she toted boards from the woodshed.

After the old truck clattered off, Josie staggered into the bathroom and peeled off her clothes. When she checked herself in the vanity mirror, she saw red circles under her eyes, mud smeared across her cheeks like camouflage makeup, a bruise purpling her chin and berry seeds stuck between her teeth.

"Crapola," she muttered, turning on the tub's hot water spigot. "This is the pits. I am never—repeat *never*—going out to that rattrap again." She shook off a boot and scattered dirt clods across the linoleum. "Hobart is nuts living out there in that Pogo swamp with that four-eyed freak." She stood up naked and stepped into the rushing water. "Ghosts. What a bunch of freaking bullshit."

She sat down and reached for the soap. Before long, the bathwater turned the color of old khaki. She dunked her head in the sudsy broth and washed her hair.

If these homespun hippies wanted her to exorcise a ghost, she'd do it. At least it would be more entertaining than reading for some mooning adolescent who wanted to know when Mr. Right would come along. Maybe Hobart and Big Foot would present a challenge, something to test her special talents. That could be interesting, she mused, sinking in the bubbles.

So far this week, Josie had stashed almost two-hundred dollars in her cookie jar bank. Not bad for honest work. Sure beat slinging hash up at Denny's in town or grubbing for that parsimonious jerk at the Pack-A-Sack who had the gall to offer her a job last winter. Horny, old bastard. Josie was doing okay. Better than okay since she could almost afford to get the Pinto running again, and then she just might look into buying a color television. At Hall's Appliance Mart, she could put twenty-five dollars down and sign a contract for the balance.

This psychic-gig wasn't so bad for the money. She never could abide being chained to a desk all day and taking orders from some brain-dead clone. This was self-enterprise. Just what her sociology professor had pounded into their heads with all his lectures about the proletariat's struggle in a capitalist society. Well, Josie had taken his advice to heart. She had refused establishment traps and instead located herself comfortably in her own business enterprise. And so far she had done pretty well. There was this trailer, paid for free and clear. Not much to some maybe, but it was cozy, cheap and accommodating to her cats, clutter and chaos.

Her face crinkled as the soap bubbles popped under her nose. With a satisfied sigh, she squeezed her eyes shut and let the warm water slide over her breasts. Her knees were drawn up under her chin in the midget-sized tub. She wrung out a dingy washcloth and draped it over her exposed thighs to trap the heat as she soaked.

Maybe the trailer park wasn't much to look at, but it was decent. Besides, there was a colony of creative artists in permanent residence here. It might seem like a boondock staging area for rednecks to the indifferent trespasser, but Josie knew better. There was a sculptor she knew who used to crash in the old Winnebago Brave by the laundry—he had a piece in a gallery at the coast that went for over a thousand dollars. It was a conglomeration of windshield splinters, old radio knobs, plastic soda straws, gold glitter and jellybeans Super-Glued to a 1955 Plymouth hubcap. He called it Chrysler Karma in the Cosmos. Not bad.

Josie had plans about renovating the old Nashua, too—really fixing it up. Someday when she had the time and energy to get into it. Right now it was enough to make the fifty-dollar monthly rent payment to the old queen who owned the trailer park and keep the Nashua's pipes from freezing in the winter and the roof from leaking Willamette Valley rain on her head.

She poked a toe out of the water and studied the wrinkled skin. Where had all the easy times gone anyhow? Somewhere in the last few years—maybe 1971 or 73—she seemed to have misplaced her youth and optimism. Suddenly the future looked a whole lot closer, and she didn't recognize her own past when she bothered to look for it. 1977 was here already, and she had barely reconciled the decade piling up years like firewood outside her door.

Josie had dropped out of the University of Idaho at Caldwell in her second semester to move in with Taylor Thump when she thought she was pregnant, had a humongous case of genital herpes and a killer head cold to boot. It turned out that Taylor was already planning to crash with three other coeds, and after a month, he decided to hitch a ride to Haight Ashbury and launch a career as a psychedelic herbal estheticist. Just as well, Josie consoled herself, rummaging through the cupboards after he left. Taylor had about the worst case of bad breath she had ever come across. He exhaled an exhaust that reminded her of rotten eggs, diesel fuel and dead fish. He could use some high-powered herbal absolution.

By the time Taylor's minivan hit the Frisco city limits, Josie knew she wasn't pregnant, and the herpes turned out to be a common yeast infection. After she had finished off the last Saltine and scraped the peanut butter jar clean, she decided it was time to find another partner. Fortunately the building was full of accommodating fellows in or out of class, stoned or straight who were happy to exchange a meal and a little conversation for Josie's cuddly company. That free-spirited journey lasted a couple years, and then it dawned on Josie that her life was standing still in this time-warped world. She had to strike out on her own.

She couldn't go back to school. Besides flunking all her second term subjects, she had been busted for smoking weed on campus. She had absolutely no money, nothing of value really, and the very last thing on the face of the planet she wanted to do was to slink back home to her parents. Those establishment-loving, uptight, Anglicized, porcine prudes would have slapped her ass in a Catholic school and branded her forehead or something. So she had picked up a Timex watch and a Kodak camera from K-Mart (it was amazing how lax their clerks were) and hocked them for a bus ticket to Las Vegas where she planned to parlay her pennies into a fortune. That didn't work out.

The Greyhound bus broke down outside of Nampa, Idaho, and while they were waiting on the shoulder of the highway for a tow, Josie stuck out her thumb and accepted a ride from a farmer with no front teeth.

When she climbed down from the truck, all she could see for miles was the tops of green onions shooting up like soda straws through the crinkly soil. A mile up the highway she staggered, breathless and disgusted, into a service station and doused herself with the water hose. She was so hot steam rose off her body as she cooled. She licked her salty lips and rested on the cool grass in the shade of a sycamore tree. That's when she saw the sign. It was a magic marker on the road to her deliverance: *Fortunes Told*. Just what Josie needed. She had no idea if she should head one way or the other, and maybe she could use a little professional guidance.

She got to her feet and shuffled down the dusty trail to the doorstep of the clapboard cottage with purple hands painted on the front windows.

A woman pulled the door open and surveyed her with a sneer. "What the hell do you want, Girlie?"

"My fortune read."

"You got any money?"

"Some."

"How much?"

"How much is a reading?"

"Five bucks."

"I only got four."

"Sorry." She tried to close the door in Josie's face, but a boot barred the way. "Hey, it's five bucks, Girlie."

"Well, how about just reading four-fifths of my fortune then? Four bucks is better'n nothing, right? Besides, I don't see any customers lined up behind me here."

The woman made a mental tally of her financial fortunes and held out her hand. "Okay. Four bucks."

Josie dug deep for the crumpled bills and handed them over. She was shown into a crummy living room full of snotty-nosed kids, mangy dogs and old newspapers.

The fortuneteller sat her down at the kitchen table. Josie wasn't impressed so far. The seer's ass was broad enough to block a New York subway. She had badly dyed cordovan-colored hair and a big, black mole on her forehead. As she flexed her shoulders, Josie could see hairs sprouting like sagebrush under her arms. She wore a cheap, silver spoon-ring on her right thumb and a huge turquoise stone with the gold-tone finish just about worn away. Everything about this woman screamed fake, cut-rate, make-do, half-assed cheap.

She pushed aside some dirty plates and grabbed Josie's hands. "Now relax and concentrate on your wishes," she burped with a bored expression.

Josie jerked away. "Where's your crystal ball?"

"I don't need a ball."

"Oh, yeah? Well, for five bucks, I expect more than just my imagination, Lady."

"You only paid four. And for four, you get what I say you get."

Josie took another look around and wrinkled her face. "This place hasn't even got a beaded curtain or anything."

"So?" She wiped her mouth with a beefy arm. "What's so muckin fuch about a beaded curtain, huh?"

"Look, I been around, Lady. You gotta promote yourself. Nobody's gonna believe in this shit." She pointed at the magazines on the floor. "*Reader's Digest?*"

"So?"

"What's that stink? Sauerkraut and wieners?"

"Look here, Girlie—"

"—nobody's gonna shell out five bucks for this shit. You gotta have a little atmosphere. You have absolutely no sense of the theatrical."

"Fuck that. You want your four lousy bucks' worth or not?"

Josie peered at the woman's blotchy face. "Say, you're not even a Gypsy."

"No shit. I'm from Annapolis. My folks are Dutch-Irish. What a dumb ass."

"What's your name?"

"Ethel. Now shut up and give me your paw before I throw your ass out."

"Nobody's gonna believe anything an Ethel says about the future. Don't you even have a professional name? Like Madame Urania or Sister Selena?"

She got up and stuffed Josie's bills down her front. "Look, Girlie, why don't you buzz off before I call my old man, okay? You're a pain in the ass."

"Hey! Wait. So what am I gonna get for my money?"

"Nothin' but a boot in the ass, Girlie." She opened the front door and stood with her hand on a mammoth hip.

"You're kicking me out?"

"You got it, Girlie. Get lost."

"You can't do that."

Suddenly the bathroom door swung open, and a burly guy with tattoos up both arms strode out. In one sweep, he hoisted Josie and deposited her on the stoop.

"Hey!" she yelped as he let go.

"Take your wise-ass mouth and get the hell off my property before I call the cops, you hippie bitch."

What seemed to be just another rude rip-off turned out to be prophetic. Josie stomped back to the gas station and bummed another ride. She was thinking about how that crone had gypped her out of four bucks. Josie could do better than that, and she wouldn't have her customers booted out the door feeling like fleeced sheep. Style—that's what Josie would provide. All she needed was a little practice. This racket had definite possibilities.

She was snared by another sweet-smiling huckster who gave her a lift into town and then up to his house in a clump of trees as tall as skyscrapers. He had a scar on his cheek where a cougar had swiped him, he said, although Josie found out a year later his ex-wife had laid him out with a can opener. His name was Bucky. And he always smelled of pine pitch and cherry tobacco. Josie was really happy with Bucky at first. She practiced palm reading on him, and he was so impressed, he gave her a five-pound bag of homegrown hash. Before long all the stringy-haired tokers in the neighborhood were bartering good grass for a little of Josie's hocus pocus. It seemed like more than a fair trade.

Josie hung out at the county library and read all the books on Tarot, Psychic Awareness, ESP and Occult Mysteries she could find on the shelves. Bullshit mostly. But there was one constant she flagged in each edition: for every conceivable scam, there was always a ready sucker. People just had to put their faith in something or somebody who promised easy answers. It was human nature. The trick was to cash in on peoples' inherent weaknesses. Nobody wanted to face the fact that shit just happened—even if they had to pay Josie to tell them they were going to inherit a bunch of money or find their true love. They needed to believe that their futures were predetermined by Fate and thus avoid personal responsibility for their miserable, mangy lives.

Business was booming for Josie—more or less. The barter business anyway. She blew everybody away with her mystical predictions. She was always paid off with quality weed and welcomed everywhere in exchange for a little psychic pizzazz. But then Bucky got busted—he was growing enough marijuana in the woods behind his shack to turn on the entire Russian Army. So before the narc squad showed up to blowtorch the bushes, Josie packed up her gear and hit the road.

Out on the Interstate, she had climbed up into a yellow KW cab-over headed west. The driver was named Jim Bob and looked just like a character from some dime store southern novel. He chewed tobacco, spat out the side vent every few miles and had the eight-track cassette cranked up on high as he barreled down the I-5 freeway with Ferlin Husky and Percy Sledge. He bought her a chicken-fried steak dinner at the T&R Truck Stop near Albany, Oregon, and showed her pictures of his kids: Ginny Mae, Jim Bob Junior, Billy Boy and Pansy Ann.

"This here's my wife," he grinned, flashing another bad snapshot. The woman had hair as high as an African termite mound and sparkles on her bat-winged glasses.

"Curly Sue?"

Her sarcasm eluded him. "Zella. Her daddy named her for her granpaw who was in WW one."

"Interesting," she mumbled, spearing a chunk of meat with her fork.

"He got a dose a that mustard gas, ruint his lungs, used ta cough up yeller blood."

"No kidding—yellow blood. Lucky for him he didn't get any of that ketchup gas, huh?"

"Zella's the onliest one in the fambly got herself named for a French gal. Zella's for mamzella—that's what they call their gals over yonder—in France."

"Fascinating," she lied.

"Her littlest brother was named Buford Bap*teest* Hoopsmutter on account a his mama was a Baptist from Jackson. They's Mississippi Hoopsmutters an a Bama branch, dontcha know."

"A Mississippi Hoopsmutter, huh? Gee."

"But my little Zella is the onliest one named French."

She choked on a mouthful of biscuit. "French, huh?"

"Zella Lulinda. Course she was Zella Lulinda Snapsatch fore we married on account of she married off real young ta this feller she done went ta church with since she was this high." He lifted his left hand about three feet from the tacky floor.

"You're kidding. Snapsatch? You're making this up, right? Putting me on?"

He put the pictures back in his wallet. "Nosirree. Bare-assed truth, Missy. He run off. Heerd he took up with a one-eyed chippy over to Coon County what got nine kids all deef as a post."

"I don't believe this."

"On the Gospel. Now she's all mine. She's my sweet little Zella Lu. Cute as a brand new bug, ain't she?"

"Cuter." If it weren't for the sequined glasses, it would have been a close call.

Josie was experiencing a Faulkner flashback attack by the time they climbed aboard the KW and started eating up the asphalt again. And the truck stop gravy must have been recycled crank case oil—she had heartburn hotter than a fire eater's fart.

In the eerie cab light, Jim Bob's face glowed like a new moon. "You know, Sugar, you ain't half bad lookin' yerself."

"Thanks."

"Bitta fancy fixins, an you'd be a genuine looker."

"Gee, thanks, Jim Bob. I don't know if I could ever be as attractive as Zella Lu though."

Jim Bob didn't even read her put-down. "Hell, Sugar, all you need is a little winnder dressin' ta show off whatch ya got there." He was trying to imagine her thin body without the bulky Army surplus jacket and baggy skirt that hung to her shins. Reminded him of a bag lady from the old folks' home. It wasn't a vision that inspired him half as much as T and R's chicken-fried steak had. Jim Bob liked a little meat on his bones, and this gal sure didn't have much sizzle. Matter of fact, his passenger looked more like a burlap bag full of coat hangers. Not much for a man to get ahold of in Jim Bob's opinion.

He took his foot off the gas, geared down and pointed ahead at the Market Road exit. "This here is where ya want off, Sugar." He was working the gearbox like a juggler catching batons. "Market Road exit ta Salem. Puts ya straight inta town, Missy."

"Thanks, Jim Bob. I appreciate the ride." The KW shivered to a stop on the shoulder, and the diesel purred like a lion as she climbed down.

"Be seein' ya sometime, Sugar."

"Doubt it, Jim Bob. Can't imagine running into you again."

"Cain't never tell," he drawled with a quick spit out the side. "Cain't never tell where our paths might get crosst, but I'm gonna recollect whatch you tolt me, Sugar. Wham! Right?"

"Yeah. Wham. See you." She grabbed her backpack and jumped down.

"Don't take no wooden nickels now." He put his foot down, and the tractor grunted as it rolled back onto the pavement and disappeared in the darkness, a rectangle outlined in orange and crimson lights bleeding into the night traffic.

By the time she had crossed the freeway and headed down Market Road, she knew what her future promised. Her jacket pocket was stuffed with Jim Bob's money. It all seemed so easy, she wondered why she hadn't figured it out sooner.

She had emptied out Jim Bob's thick billfold on the trip across Oregon to the capital city. Josie had spun the long-haul driver a tale of romance and fantastic fortune from the astral advisers she decided she might as well quote to make it seem official. Then at the truck stop, after Jim Bob finished off three cups of black coffee and a slab of lemon creme pie, she had held his hand and peered at the creases and lines on his sweaty palm. She closed her eyes, let her head fall back in a swoon and told him he was going to come into a fortune someday. Purely by chance. Dumb luck.

"How much ya reckon?" he had asked with a silly grin.

"I see a lot, Jim Bob. As much money as you make in a year."

His eyes bulged. "You ain't jokin' me, Sugar? That's a bundle—more'n twenty thousand net."

"You make that much driving a truck?"

"That ain't no ordnary rig sittin' yonder, Missy, an I ain't no ordnary wheel jockey neither." His lips parted in a wider grin that showed more gums than teeth.

"Well, I said as much as you make in a year." No reason. It just sort of came to her. Like remembering the state capital of Nebraska. Didn't even know she knew it until it just tumbled out of her.

"Whew! That's sumpin, Sugar. You yankin' my chain?"

"Of course, not. I said a lot. A fortune, Jim Bob. So if you make twenty thousand, then that's how much money we're talking about. Minimum."

"How's it I git this here money again?"

"You're just minding your own business, Jim Bob, and wham."

"Wham?"

She slapped the table. "Wham! You just fall into the gravy. How's that, huh?"

"Hot damn, Sugar. I like them apples. You're good—damn good." Jim Bob thumped her on the shoulder and handed over a twenty-dollar bill. "Hell, seein' as how I'm goin' ta strike it rich, I figger I'll share the wealth, right, Sugar? Go on an tell me some more."

"You're just driving down the road minding your own business—"

"—and *wham!*"

"Exactly. That's what I see." If she closed her eyes, she could almost visualize the shiny KW screeching to a stop, all eighteen tires smoking as its chrome hood ornament zeroed in like a B29 bomb sight on a pile of new, green bills scattered across the center line.

He squirmed in the slippery vinyl booth. "Damn! I like them apples, Sugar. Wham, huh?"

"Wham," she echoed with a bored sigh.

"Wham! Twenty goddam thousand, you say?"

"At least."

Jim Bob liked the money prediction even better than the one she made about the redhead. Truth to tell, Josie liked the romantic forecast better, but he balked at slipping more money in her direction when she pushed it. He liked hearing about the cash rendezvous—"whamming" it, he repeated as he laughed. So she told him the whole story again—how he was just cruising down the highway in his KW and running right over a pile of brand new bank bills. Jim Bob would wait till she finished, then his big, bullfrog eyes would shine, and he'd slap another twenty from his thick wad in her palm. Easy as pie. Hard to believe he was willing to pay her so much for such claptrap.

But he handed over the cash nevertheless, and at the Market Street exit she jumped down from the purring KW with a hundred and thirty dollars in her pocket, a full belly and a new unbridled optimism for the future. This was easy. She was born to it. It was bullshit with an attitude, wishful thinking at professional prices. Telling the suckers what they wanted to hear.

After parting ways with Jim Bob and his KW, Josie bit the bullet of first-floor capitalism and slaved in a Salem diner. She had a hard time saving money—there was always a better place to put it than in her cookie jar. There were a few local yokels and drifters who captured her attention for a few months at a time, but finally she scraped together her meager resources and decided to strike a blow for independence and seek her fortune. It was time to link up with the supernatural forces directing her future.

Josie had a stake big enough to buy the Nashua trailer at the Jewel Grove, get a secondhand brocade curtain she outfitted with a beaded hem, a slightly sick, potted palm and a real crystal ball from a discount store in Portland. She made the sign out front by herself, decorated the fence around her space with purple and gold stars and nailed up three giant red arrows leading spiritually starved suckers straight to her trailer.

Customers came. Living was easy. Well, almost. She still didn't have a cassette tape player, and the Ford Pinto she had bought for four-hundred bucks broke down on her the very first week. But she had a Zenith console TV that worked good enough to watch *As The World Turns* and enough money to go to a show when she felt like it. And she could tell—definitely—that she was on the upswing. Success was only a matter of time. What Josie really wanted was her own television show. That was her dream. The pot at the end of her rainbow. One of these days, she'd be on national television, make so much money she couldn't count it all, come back and live in real style. It all seemed plausible. Josie was good. Everybody told her so.

Most of the time, it didn't seem possible that the time had flown by so quickly since she bounced off Jim Bob's semi. Things that had seemed so promising when she first arrived looked like white-trash flotsam now. Even the old Pinto was on borrowed time. But she was making progress. Absolutely. What she needed was a break. A super score. Once a real opportunity knocked on her door, she'd be ready. It was just a matter of timing.

Josie slathered soapsuds over her breast and surveyed her meager cleavage beneath the waves. Once she was a slim, speckled mermaid with tawny braids and an upturned nose, front teeth like a chipmunk and rosy cheeks. Now there were lines crisscrossing her face like Union Pacific tracks, silvery streaks running through her hair and slack skin hanging on her thin frame. Even her boobs seemed to be surrendering, sliding toward her navel without so much as a pardon. Oh, well. The tide was about to turn. She could feel it.

She stuck a toe under the faucet and stretched. Her plan was to strike it rich, get a client with a bankroll the size of Texas and a brain no bigger than a dust mite's ass. Then she'd buy herself a Lincoln Continental with a Landau top and wire wheels and head for Boise to see her folks. Maybe by now the decade had mellowed the pair. Actually, in their last Christmas card, they had seemed a little reluctant to nag. That was progress. If it weren't for the fact that her wimpy brother had made it through law school and now was some big-ass jerk in Seattle making super big bucks, or that her kid sister had married a professor at Cal Tech and went to Europe every summer—well, those were just unfortunate circumstances, that's all. One of these days, Josie would outshine them both. Her folks wouldn't be able to believe how enterprising her middle age could be.

She sighed and dunked her head under the water. It was depressing to think of it in such maudlin terms. Middle-aged sounded like one step from senility and death. And Josie was only thirty-five. Just. She was still in her prime. Too much sun and outdoors had tanned away the bloom of youth in her fair English skin, but it wasn't as if she was really old yet. There was still plenty of time to blossom into the full-grown future she had imagined riding west in that Kenworth semi with Jim Bob. Plenty of time.

She turned to spy a spider tip-toeing behind the sink. A dust ball as big as an orange rolled across the floor and collided with a wad of used tissue. Josie sank back and closed her eyes. Oh, well. She was meant for better things than sacrificing herself to this old tin can. One of these days, she was going to hire a maid. And a cook, too. Besides, she didn't even have a vacuum cleaner that worked. First things first. As soon as she finished her soak, she was going to get dressed and hitch a ride into town. She had definite employment plans—a bona fide exorcism in the works. That meant a real payday down the road. She might as well start considering how to allot her prospective earnings. Maybe even look for a real deal on a new TV—no more vertical hold going berserk in the middle of *General Hospital*.

But first she'd buy some white wine, a T-bone steak and frozen French fries. And then Josie Wallgood was going to feast.

5

The kindergarten teacher who lived in the Airstream with the plastic daisies in the window gave Josie a ride into town. The day was warming up; the clouds were bubbling across the dishwater sky like beer foam. Fruit trees were budding; hyacinth and crocus were blooming in Willson Park surrounding the state capitol, a marble icon of art deco chic with a gold-leaf logger standing atop the dome in what many Oregonians compared to a glitzy bowling trophy. At least it was unique, and today it was postcard picturesque with the fountain sizzling, and the flower beds aflame.

Josie wrapped her sweater around her shoulders and walked down Commercial Street to Hall's Appliance. The store was cool and quiet. She was the sole customer.

A salesman approached. "Hi. Can I help you with something?"

"Yeah. I'm thinking of getting a new TV."

He was a medium tall guy with wavy, ash blond hair combed over his ears. He wore a striped tie that clashed with the brown sports shirt and maroon slacks wanting a professional crease. He had eyes the color of melted chocolate and a tanned face anchored by a Marlboro-man mustache and dimpled chin. Josie noticed a tiny mole below his right eye.

He smiled and steered her toward the front display window. Two sets were tuned to a *Flying Nun* rerun. "What size did you have in mind, Miss? Portable or one of the new entertainment centers?"

She flipped her hair back. He wasn't bad looking, a little corny in the leisure suit duds but earnest and not half bad at all. At least, he was friendly rather than pushy. "I was thinking of a portable color set. Something sorta compact—I have a real small space."

"Great. Okay, let's see now." He rubbed his palms and took a good look up and down the aisles. "Too bad you missed our Presidents' Day sale, but we're having a spring clearance actually. I can give you a real deal on this floor model here. It's a Motorola full color with high fidelity sound speakers, VHF, simulated walnut grain case, nineteen-inch screen."

She cocked her head to one side and looked it over. It seemed just right for her little trailer. Josie was especially taken with the fake walnut case. It looked pretty good to her. "How much?" she asked, already deciding she would take it even if she had to work out a payment plan for the balance.

He bent toward her in a conspiratorial pose and winked. She could smell his shaving lotion and shampoo. He had a nutty flavor to his breath. "How's two ninety-five ninety-nine sound?"

She crinkled her nose. "Too much."

He moved even closer. Their shoulders and hips touched.

"I can make you a real deal if you'd like to take this home today with you, Miss."

"Okay. How much?" She could count little flakes of gold in his irises.

"How much can you put down?"

"Depends." She wasn't exactly a fool.

"Hey, I'm Bob Johnson. Nice to meet you." He offered his hand.

She took it and gave him one firm shake. "Josie Wallgood."

"My pleasure. For sure."

She eyed him suspiciously while studying the deep tan at his throat, the untrimmed mustache, the mismatched clothes and scruffy shoes with knots in the laces and the scars on his hands. This was no slick salesman of the month. He was no Bob Johnson. "What's your real name?"

He looked over his shoulder toward the office, leaned into her and brushed his hair back from his forehead. "I'm not Bob Johnson?"

"Don't look like a Bob Johnson to me. How long you been doing this?"

"A month. As a matter of fact, you'll be my first floor sale. I think I'm gonna get the ax at the end of the week anyway. So hey, you want the Motorola, I can make you one helluva deal."

"Thanks. I got two-hundred bucks."

"Well, how about twenty-five cash down, and we put the rest on contract?"

"Far out. I gotta hold back enough to buy a battery for my car."

"Okay. It's a deal." He whipped out a pad from his coat pocket and licked the tip of his pencil. "You want it delivered, Miss Wallgood?"

"Sure—if it's free."

He started writing up the order. She watched him peruse the serial numbers, fiddle with the adding machine trying to figure the carrying charges and interest and then pause to stroke his bushy mustache.

"So what's your real name anyway?"

He tore off a strip of adding machine tape. "Cain Reeves." He had a bashful grin that made her smile back. "Cain was my mother's maiden name. My Dad's name was actually Revescu, but it got changed when he emigrated. Bob Johnson is better for a salesman, don't you think? Everybody remembers a Bob Johnson."

She shrugged. "Guess so."

"I sorta got stranded out here in Oregon when I lost my job. Not much happenin' in these parts, is there?"

"Guess not. Depends."

He handed her a sales slip. "Just sign at the bottom there. The payments are only fourteen-fifty a month. Think you can handle that?"

"Sure. No problem." She took the pen and printed her name and address on the contract.

"So what do you do?"

"I'm a fortuneteller—psychic reader."

"Hey, far out. For real?"

"Yeah." Her face softened in a self-conscious grin. "Fraid so."

"Well, I wouldn't put that in the employment space there."

"You wouldn't?"

"Why don't you put somethin' like, uh…" He pinched his chin and lowered his eyes thoughtfully. "How about putting down human relations consultant, self-employed?"

"You think that'll help the credit app go through?"

"Trust me."

"Okay." She crossed out her preliminary scrawl and wrote what he suggested. Then she took out her purse and laid down the cash.

"I never met a fortuneteller before. You seem pretty normal."

"Come around and have your fortune read sometime."

He looked at the contract. "Uh, you live out on Silverton Road, huh?"

"Yeah. The Jewel Grove Trailer Park. I gotta sign out front. Can't miss me."

"You want this delivered tomorrow?"

"Great."

He tore off a pink copy of the paper and handed it over. "So, thanks."

"Sure. You gonna get canned, huh?"

"I'm not much of a salesman."

"Oh, yeah? You did great."

"It was a cinch to hustle you—you're a fox, Josie."

"Oh, yeah?"

"Yeah. You got an old man or anything out at the trailer park?"

"Nope. Just me and my cat."

"Well, maybe I'll stop by sometime."

"Yeah. That'd be cool."

They stood awkwardly toe-to-toe, staring at the washing machines and refrigerators lined up all around them.

Josie folded up the sales contract and shouldered her bag. "Well, I gotta take off. See you. And thanks for the deal."

"No problem. Thanks for comin' in, Josie."

"Yeah. See you later maybe." She sauntered out, stuffed the contract in her purse and waited until she had crossed the street before she let herself think seriously about this unexpected encounter.

He seemed nice—a fish out of water in that crummy appliance store. He looked more like a carpenter than a salesman. There was no doubt that he was coming on to her. She had some open ends right now. Maybe the timing was right. Even if he was almost out of a job. He looked like the type who could handle a shovel well enough. Farmers and sawmills always needed strong-backs. He'd find something.

Josie had a strong hunch that beneath the tacky suit and bodacious necktie, there was a sinewy chest with butterscotch hair she could graze, arms as strong as crowbars and necessary drilling equipment slung like Matt Dillon's long-barreled forty-four inside those trousers. She could see herself cuddled up with this munchable candy-man, and just thinking about it made goose bumps break out all over.

Maybe this was all a matter of astrological timing. Josie was ready for a new romance. Time was slipping away.

Josie walked another block, stopped in at a drugstore to buy a Coke and strolled out into the splotchy sunlight. She had to figure out a ride home—might have to stick out her thumb. She didn't need to.

A horn honked. A rattle and clunk followed, and Hobart's GMC shook itself to a stop at the curb. He leaned out and motioned for her to climb aboard. "Hi, Jo. Goin' home?"

"Yeah. Thanks." She climbed up into the cab and hung on to the dashboard as the truck lurched off and rattled through the intersection.

Hobart's hair was flying in the wind from the open cab. He had on fresh overalls and smelled like Ivory and wood smoke. Goddam, she thought as he shifted gears. There was no way to avoid the issue: Hobart was a gorgeous hunk. Maybe now there would never be a chance for her to taste this delicious specimen—not as long as spooky Farrah was around.

"Thanks for helping us out last night, Jo."

"No problem."

"Good thing the rain stopped, huh?"

"Yeah." She looked out the cracked side window. The park blocks were mint green. The faint scent of fruit blossoms in the air reminded her it was almost April.

"You get much flooding out at your place?"

"Nope." Didn't matter to her. So long as her little Nashua stuck like a bull-frog in a mud hole, she wasn't worried. If the water rose over the trailer's wheels, she'd just hang out on her porch and watch the ducks paddle by.

"I really appreciate your helping us with the other thing, too, Jo. Farrah has a lot of confidence in you, you know."

"That Max business—it's bullshit, Hobart. You know that, dontcha? Bullshit."

"It's real, Jo. I know. I've seen him. It sounds crazy as hell, but what're we supposed to do? This is freaking us both out."

"You saw this Max? You saw a *ghost*, Hobart? Gimme a break."

"I don't know what it was, Jo. But it was scary as hell. I saw this dude down by the marsh, smoking a cigarette and staring off into space. He turned around and looked right at me."

Josie was disgusted at such gullibility. "Hobart, so you saw a man. So what? What the hell does that have to do with ghosts? This is all bullshit."

"Look, Jo, I saw what I saw."

"You saw a guy smoking a cigarette."

"How'd he get down to the marsh? He didn't leave any tracks. There was no car. Nothing. One minute I'm down there stacking wood, and nobody's there. The next minute, there he is, Jo."

"So what's that prove? He coulda come from anywhere. Maybe he was just out taking a walk. Ever think of that? Or is that too simple for Farrah to figure out?"

Hobart kept silent for an entire city block. "Josie, you don't really like Far-rah much, do you?"

"Not much." She felt better being able to say it straight out to his face. He asked her so she answered. Simple as that.

"She's the sweetest girl I've ever known."

"She's crazy, Hobart. She's got you living out in the tules, mucking around in the swamp all the fucking time while she paints pussy willows or some shit."

"It's beautiful stuff, Jo. She has a feel for nature that comes right off the canvas."

"Yeah, yeah."

"And she's starting to sell quite a bit."

"Big effing deal."

"So what is it with you and her?"

"I just don't think she's right for you, Hobart."

"Oh, yeah?" He shifted the GMC into third and bounced it over a bump that made Josie's jaw ache. "Don't you think I'm the best judge of that, Jo?"

"No. You got a piss poor way of judging women. I know." She firmed her mouth and avoided looking at him.

"What do you mean by that?" His voice had an edge that she did not miss. In fact she was happy to hear him somewhat remorseful over their missed opportunity. "Who'd I ever misjudge?"

"Me, you bastard. Why'd you go to Arizona anyway? I was only two trailers away for crissakes."

His tone softened as he reached out and stroked her arm. "Oh, Jo. You're my best friend. You know that."

"Sure."

"I had to take off for awhile, that's all. New horizons—you know. Nothing was happening for me here. Farrah fit everything together for me. I didn't know you felt like I abandoned you or anything."

He had aimed, fired and missed the mark by a mile. She was damned if she was going to bare her soul anymore by making stupid admissions to Hobart Ames. To hell with him. She would focus her energies on the appliance salesman instead.

"Forget it," she mumbled. "I just don't much like Farrah, okay? Leave it at that."

"Okay. But Farrah thinks a lot of you, Jo."

"That's fine with me."

"And she's trusting you to help her get rid of Max." He slowed the truck down, cranked his head to one side and tried to catch her eyes. "Josie?"

"Huh."

"You are going to help her, aren't you?"

"Maybe. But it's all bullshit. Why doesn't she call in a priest? You see the *Exorcist*?"

He didn't talk all the rest of the way out Silverton Road. At the fence, he stopped the truck and let it idle. The pickup belched and hiccuped like a cranky tractor.

Before she climbed out, he touched her arm. "Jo, is there anything I can do? Farrah really needs your help."

She jumped down, slung her bag over her shoulder and slammed the door that didn't quite close. "Okay. If she wants me to get rid of Max's ghost, then it's gonna be a straight business deal, okay? Just like any of my other clients—straight business. Nothing else, okay?"

"Sure."

"And I charge for exorcising evil spirits. A lot." She hoped she had discouraged him, but he only answered with a broad smile. "A lot, Hobart. Probably over a hundred."

"Sure, Jo. Whatever you say. Whatever's fair."

Her brows arched over her milky eyes. "You got any money, Hobart? I can't take IOU's or firewood or shit."

"No sweat. Farrah's mom just passed away. Farrah's the only child—she's got a check coming. Don't worry about it."

"Oh, yeah?"

"Whatever you need, Jo, we'll take care of it."

"You mean like an inheritance or something?"

"Yeah. We'll have plenty. Money's no problem. Don't worry about it."

Dubious, she squinted into the sunlight and shifted the bag on her back. "Well, I'll let you know. You get the money together, and I'll start doing my thing."

"Super, Jo! I'll tell Farrah. You need anything?"

"No. Just the money. At least a hundred to start. Then we'll go from there."

"No sweat. Thanks, Jo." He revved up the engine, and the chassis shook like a Mixmaster.

She waved as he drove off, trailing a stream of blue exhaust. She headed toward her trailer, avoiding as many puddles as she could. Some people ought to know better. Hobart was an educated person, and here he was offering to pay Josie to whack a ghost for him. Go figure.

At least she had a new TV coming tomorrow, money to fix up the Pinto and the prospect of milking Farrah for a whole lot more than the hundred bucks she needed to prime the pump. Josie was beginning to get lucky. If Farrah had money, real bucks, then there was no way Josie couldn't figure out a way to cash in on their ignorance. If she pulled this one off, she was going to make it worth her while.

She scraped her boots on the porch step, opened her door and reached down to pet Goldie who was stretching her backbone before she ventured out.

"Max Swidnik," Josie hummed as she put down her bag, "your ass is grass."

Goldie flipped her tail and mewed. A definite second.

6

Josie looked around the trailer when she got home and could see plenty to occupy her time: the stainless-steel sink was overflowing with dirty crockery; silverware and empty wine bottles littered the kitchen counter. A rotten onion lay abandoned on the cutting board; breadcrumbs and crackers were scattered like snowflakes on the table. Dust balls rolled like tumbleweeds under the settee and the dinette set. Even the crystal ball was dusty.

Josie grabbed a dishtowel and flew at the globe, rubbing and buffing until it gleamed like a new windowpane. Then she sat down, tossed the rag aside and took another look. If she had the inclination, she could waste the entire afternoon cleaning the place. The rug needed sweeping. The kitchen definitely needed swamping out. There were URO's (unidentified rotting objects) in the Norge she didn't even want to think about. Something dark green and blood red was stuck to the bottom rack and oozed fetid juice onto the linoleum floor when she opened the refrigerator door. What Josie needed was a maid not a mop.

She got up and took a bottle of Coke from the cupboard, rinsed out a glass, wiped some cat hair from the rim and poured herself a drink. She cracked open an ice tray, cooled her soda and flopped down on a chair. She drank, smacked her lips and burped. There was so much to do she got tired just thinking about it.

She emptied the glass and got up to switch on her TV. Before she made herself comfortable in the settee, she toggled on her Westinghouse fan, aimed it at her face and made room for Goldie to curl on her lap. Not much on the tube, but it was better than tackling the laundry or cleaning the sink. She dozed through daytime re-runs of *Mr. Ed*, *Adam 12*, *The Price Is Right* and *I Love Lucy*. When she woke up, it was dark outside.

There were no customers. That was okay, too. Sometimes she went a week without anyone knocking on the door. Then they would all come in a bunch, regulars and transients passing by who saw the sign.

At eight o'clock, Josie heard a car outside. Headlights bounced a high-beam strobe off Josie's front window. The car stopped beside her porch, and a door slammed shut—a customer. Too late really. They'd just have to come back tomorrow. Maybe she wouldn't even bother to answer.

There was just one timid knock. She turned the volume down on the TV and stood there trying to decide if it was worth the interruption to make a quick twenty bucks.

"Josie? You home?"

"Who is it?" She dropped the cat and pressed her nose against the metal door.

"Cain Reeves. Remember? I sold you the Motorola."

She pulled open the door and looked at him. He was wearing cowboy boots, a tee shirt, an unbuttoned, wool vest in gray plaid and blue jeans. Groovy. He was the Marlboro man after all.

He turned sideways and shuffled his feet on the porch. "I…uh, had a hard time findin' you."

"Most people forget to stay on the main road when it makes the Y. You end up at the trout farm?"

He grinned while appraising her with lazy eyes. "The fish farm. Yeah."

"Well, you found me. Is it about the TV?"

"Uhm…well, yeah. The manager wouldn't send your credit app to the loan company. He's kinda uptight, you know what I mean?"

"Yeah. So does this mean I don't get the Motorola?"

"I guess."

Her face sagged. She pinched her hip through the robe. "Well, I could pay cash, I guess. If I have to."

"Sorry. But he's something else, I can tell you."

She felt like flirting. He was up to something anyway. Coming all the way out here at eight o'clock at night just to tell her she had been turned down by some crummy finance company for a lousy two-hundred dollar loan. Maybe he just wanted to see about getting his fortune read. Or maybe that nervous shuffle and shy smile meant something else entirely. She let her eyes fall and didn't see any slack in his worn Levi's.

Josie's ears began to burn. "Did he fire you?"

"Yep. Gave me my walkin' papers this afternoon."

"You're better off."

"If busted is better, I guess. I'm flat broke. You don't know of any jobs around here, do you?"

"Doing what?"

"I dunno. Anything."

"Well, what did you do before you tried selling TV's?"

He scratched his head and tugged at an earlobe. "Play ball. I played ten seasons in the Pacific Coast League. The bigs were takin' a good look at me, but then I tore my knee up."

"Are you a pitcher or something?"

"Nope. Catcher."

"Well, same thing—just different side of home plate, right?"

"The catcher controls the ball, Josie. The pitcher, hell, he just throws the damn thing. The catcher is where it's at—the center of the action. He keeps the game goin'."

"I don't know much about baseball really. Sorry." She crossed her arms.

"Don't you ever go to any games or anything?"

"Nope. Don't watch it on TV either."

"You don't know what you're missin', Josie."

She leaned against the door. "So did you make any money playing catch?"

He leaked pride like a pricked party balloon. "I did okay. Made ten thousand my best year. That's real good money in Triple A ball. I hit .327 my best season with Tacoma, led the league. But see, the bigs got plenty of catchers—it's hard to make a space for a guy in the minors to move up. Trouble was I just never got the call when I was in good enough shape to go."

"Uh huh. So what're you gonna do now you can't play?"

His eyes lingered on the widening décolletage the sloppy robe revealed. "Guess I'm not gonna sell TV's." He tilted his head and put his weight on one foot as he scratched. "Gotta figure somethin' out."

"Guess so," she agreed, letting her voice fall to a sexy purr as their eyes locked together. "So is your knee messed up pretty bad?"

"Some." He grinned bashfully and tapped one boot toe against his leg. "Kinda gimps up on me in wet weather. I can't handle the hard day-labor jobs anymore."

"Shame, huh?"

"Damned pitiful. You got a soft heart for cripples, Josie Girl?"

"Might. But I sure as hell don't know of any jobs around here for a guy with a busted knee."

"Well, sellin' appliances is out, I guess."

"Yeah. Guess so. Long as you're out here, you want your fortune read?"

"Sure. How much is it?"

She took hold of his arm, and with one step he was inside, maneuvering around her laundry and avoiding the cat darting between his legs. "It's on the house," she decided, closing the door. "Have a seat."

He cleared a space on the settee and sat facing the crystal ball. Josie tightened her sash, switched off the television and fluffed her hair. She must look like hell, but he didn't seem to mind a bit.

He still had that gratuitous smirk pasted on his face as he watched her warm up the globe. "Does that thing really work?"

"No. It's all bullshit." She loved the sound of his laugh. His voice was as smooth as cheesecake.

"So what can you see in my future, Josie? Nothin' bad, I hope."

She sank her chin in her palm and stared at the strong arms, the muscular definition under the denim and the shock of mussable hair. The harder she looked, the more she began to see just what she was looking for. "I think you believe in this crap." She watched his eyes for clues.

"You got me there," he laughed. "Yeah. I guess I do some. Don't you?"

"Nope. It's all a matter of observation, memory, common sense and deductive reasoning. That's all it is. Only the suckers think there's something more to it."

"So's baseball."

"Oh, yeah?"

"You gotta figure all the time, take everything in—the batter, his strengths and weaknesses, figure who's on deck, if the pitcher's lost his stuff, if the guy runnin' the bases is a jumper. All the odds figure in. You gotta have a head for details. You gotta lot to remember. I used to study the hitters real hard, you know. I could tell when they were gonna chase a sucker ball, when they were chokin' and when they were hittin'."

"Huh."

"I worked on their heads—psyched em out. It's your brain that fucks up your batting average, see. It's a mental thing. Hell, baseball's more mental than anything."

"It's the same thing with me. Wanna see?"

"Yeah. Lemme see your best stuff."

"Okay. For starters, I knew right away you weren't a real salesman, right?"

"You did?"

"I knew Bob Johnson sure as hell wasn't your real name, didn't I?" Her face broke open in a smug grin. "Took me a couple minutes was all."

"You pegged me, Josie. You did. I gotta give you that."

"That was just from observation. And I also figure you didn't drive all the way out here tonight just to tell me my loan didn't go through. Am I right?"

A rosy blush crept up his neck and darkened his tanned cheeks. "Yeah? What do you figure I'm up to?"

"Probably hoping to get laid."

He froze for an instant, startled by her sudden candor. "Hey, you hit me with a change-up there. So far, you're three for three, Girl. I'm impressed as hell about now. You're somethin', Josie."

"That didn't take any effort at all. You were trying to pull a con on me, but I think you're a decent guy basically."

"Thanks."

"And you're at loose ends right now."

"Sort of, you might say so. When I got outta baseball, I stepped off the bus in Portland with nothin' but my suitcase and a fifty-dollar bill, got a gig cleanin' big shots' offices at night then met a girl who had a thing goin' in Corvallis—she raised poodles, how about that?"

"Amazing." Not half as much as popping zits.

"When she split, I hitched a ride up north to Seattle but got dumped out in Salem when my ride broke down. Hall's Appliance was lookin' for a salesman so I started sellin' GE washers, Motorola TV's, Amana freezers and shit. So now it's back to the startin' gate, Josie Girl."

"You don't know anybody in town who can help you out?"

"I know some people, but they don't exactly wanna know me right now, I guess. Like my boss at the store. And I owe back rent at my place, gotta get enough together to get some work done on my car before I can set out travelin' again."

"Well, you know what I see in your future?"

"Somethin' good, I hope."

"Money. And a partner."

His fingers started a tap dance on his thigh as he watched her stroke the crystal ball. "Who's the partner? You?"

"Me."

"Hell, Josie. I can't tell fortunes."

"You won't have to. That's where the money comes in."

"You don't want me to knock off somebody for you or anything, do you?"

"Nothing like that." Their fingertips touched for an instant. She could feel the electricity jumping from his skin to hers. He was a flesh and blood Tesla coil.

"If it's some kinda scam milkin' Grandma outta her life savings—"

"—nothing like that. You need a job, right?"

"Right. Dead right about that."

"So I'm offering one. Yes or no."

"Okay. I guess I'm in. How much you paying?"

"How much do you need?"

"Well, I got obligations like anybody else."

She tossed her hair back. "Like what?"

"Say, Josie Girl, you tryin' to offer me some kinda bonus here or what?" His voice was so goddam sexy it made her toes cramp and her ears wiggle.

She sidled up beside him and pressed her thigh against his. He was as warm and supple as a fresh donut. "You can clear a couple hundred dollars for a week's work. You interested, Cain?" Her hungry eyes were wolfing down his handsome face. If she had ghost busting on her agenda, then she just might be able to put this hunky lunk to good use. Once in awhile, it was smart to take on an accomplice, especially one as unsuspecting and available as this guy seemed to be. Whatever she needed done, he could do it. No strings. No problems. He was perfect. "What else you got going?"

Cain's lips curled in a half smile. He didn't have many options at this juncture in his journey so he didn't even weigh the odds when she impulsively brushed his mouth with hers. He couldn't open his eyes to catch the subtle little flicker of satisfaction playing on her lips as he surrendered with a limp shiver when her hand lit on his belt.

"Not a damn thing worth doin', Honey," he whispered as they kissed with swollen lips. In the clutch, he took a deep breath and tried to throw out an anchor before she tipped his boat over. "Josie, this is all above board, right?"

"Sure. What else?" God, he tasted good. Like hot sticky buns.

"Nothin' criminal. Just fortunetellin' shit, right?"

"You interested or not?" His conversation had become a distraction. They could hammer out the working details of their partnership later.

He bumped his nose against hers. "Well, I guess we gotta deal then, Josie Girl. So long as you got the bread to pay me. I'm interested in cash deals only, got it?"

"Sure. No problem. This is a business deal. Strictly cash and carry."

"Strictly business." He planted another quick peck on her nose. "You really turn me on, Josie Babe. You know that?"

Finally, she was thinking as he grabbed her like she was a Big Whopper fresh off the grill. "Kiss me, Cain. You taste so goddam delicious, I can hardly stand it."

He obliged her. "You got some kinda healthy appetite, Baby."

"Mhmmm. And I'm about starved to death." Her mouth smothered his.

Then she wrapped both arms around his neck, curled a leg around his waist and pulled him on top of her. He didn't even have to flex a muscle.

7

Cain was even better looking with his clothes off. He had a tattoo of a dolphin on his left bicep and a shiny, half-moon scar across the web of his right hand. His shins were scarred and dented like an old, battered washtub, and his knuckles were as gnarly as a warty oak, but he was lean, tanned, muscular and hungry for a woman. Josie barely whetted his ravenous appetite once he got started.

They cuddled together in the middle of her lumpy bed with the purple, tie-dyed quilt. Cain graciously lay in the wet spot while Josie marveled at the rippled waves on his belly.

"How old are you?" she asked.

"Thirty." He rubbed out his cigarette and held her so tightly she could barely take a breath.

"I'm older than you."

"Don't matter." His hand strolled down her thigh.

"Where you from?"

"Dayton."

Her ear had caught a flat, heartland drawl which threw her off track. She'd never have guessed that this hunky specimen was reared in the Willamette Valley in a sleepy, backwater berg not far from Salem. Dayton, Oregon wasn't much more than a smudge on the county roadmap. The only time Josie had been there was when she drove out to pick berries once and glanced up to see a "Leaving the City of Dayton" sign in her rearview mirror. Whizzed through the whole damn town faster than passing a billboard.

"I didn't figure you were an Oregonian, Cain. Don't sound like one."

"No way. Dayton's in Ohio."

"Since when?"

He swatted her backside. "Since before this pothole was even on the map probly."

"You sure? Ohio?"

"Where else would it be? You ever been to the Midwest, Josie?"

"Nope."

"Dayton's famous for a lotta stuff. Like batteries—you know who Delco is?"

"Sure. My Pinto needs a new battery. I had a Delco, and it died on me."

"Dayton Electric Company—Delco. Started up right there in Dayton. And all the cash register machines are there, too."

"They make those in Dayton, huh?" she feigned a remarkable curiosity. Big deal. Who cared? So far as Josie was concerned, the entire Midwest was one big cornfield interrupted by mountains of manure, grain silos posing as skyscrapers and sluggish mudflows sodbusters mistakenly called rivers.

"Patterson started his factory up right there in Dayton. You've heard of National Cash Register Company, right?"

"Right." So what? Everything had to be made somewhere, didn't it?

"Started right in my hometown and went all over the fuckin world."

"Huh."

"You ever hear of Wright Patterson Air Force Base?"

"No." Didn't care to either, she thought.

"That's where the government keeps all the UFO's they've captured."

"No shit?" What crap.

"They got some special hangar there everybody says—Hangar 18 or some shit. You even try to get close to that place, and the FBI or CIA or somebody comes out and rips your fuckin head off."

"Huh."

"We got all sorts of famous shit in Dayton. Did you know the Wright brothers started up in Dayton?"

"Built airplanes there, huh?"

"Not airplanes—bikes. Don't you know about the Wright brothers? Jeez, what kind of school did you go to anyhow?"

"Oh, yeah, those Wrights—Wilbur and his brother Oliver, sure," she hemmed, hoping to avoid a lecture.

"Orville."

"Yeah, right. Orville."

"You don't know a goddam thing about Dayton, do you?"

"Nope."

"That's okay. I can tell you all about it sometime."

Sounded about as interesting as reading a lunchmeat label.

"So how come you're out here?" she detoured, hoping to be spared a rambling monologue on further highlights of Ohio's fair city.

"I got put on irrevocable waivers—that's fired in your lingo—from the Springfield Cougars. Minor league, single A ball. That's about as low as you can go, Josie, and still be in baseball. I got sent down from Tacoma after I blew my knee out and was on the injured roster for twenty-three straight games. Got released halfway through the season. So I was out. It was all over."

"Just like that? No severance pay or anything?"

"This is baseball, Josie, not General Motors. You play—they pay. You quit and get shit. That's the way it is. I never expected anything but a chance to make it up to the bigs someday, and I came close. That's something. Not everybody can say that." He propped himself up on one elbow. "I got signed to the Reds' farm club after my senior year of high school. The Pacific Coast League picked up my contract nine months later, and I started catching my second season for Tacoma. I was sort of a phenom." He thumped the mattress and closed his eyes again to shut out the glare of reality. "I just ran into some bad luck or I woulda made it."

"What happened to your hands?" She took both his hands in hers and kissed the fingers one by one. None of his fingers was straight.

"I got catcher's hands, that's all. You know, you take some knocks once in awhile. That ball is flyin' into your glove at eighty, ninety plus miles an hour, hard as a fuckin rock. You ever try to stop somethin' goin' that fast?"

"Nope."

"And you got dudes as big as fir trees crashin' into you, feet first, tryin' to knock your ass halfway to Sunday. I got spiked enough, Josie Girl, if I fell in the crick, I'd leak like a sieve."

"Why didn't you play another position—like fielder? They don't have to do much, do they? Just stand around out there waiting for everybody to strike out so they can go back to the dugout."

He rolled over and pinned her beneath him. "You're a strange lady, Josie."

"Why?"

"Because that's just about the dumbest thing I've ever heard."

"What's so strange just because I don't know anything about baseball?"

"Everybody knows about baseball."

"Not me."

"It's the American pastime."

"Not mine."

He bounced his body on hers a few times and rubbed the tip of her nose. "What do you do for fun, Josie? Besides reading that crystal ball of yours?"

"Watch TV." There wasn't really much more to say, was there? Was that what her life was all about? Soap operas, game shows and *Hawaii Five O*? Was that it for crissakes? Didn't sound like much for a lifetime's résumé. Her face crinkled in a petulant frown. "Dammit, Cain. I had plans of my own, you know. Just like you did about playing for the big leagues. Big plans."

He stroked the hair away from her face. "What sorta plans?"

"My own television show. I would read fortunes, give advice to people calling in. I wanted to be the first psychic reader with a big network show."

"You're nuts."

"What's so nuts about that?"

His head nuzzled her affectionately until he sensed the anger had fizzled. "Nothin'. Nothin' at all, Josie. Everybody's got a dream, I guess. Yours probly makes more sense than mine. Mine's all shot to hell anyway. Now I got nothin' to look forward to except hard work and old age."

"Maybe you just haven't found the right partner yet. Maybe," Josie whispered in his ear as he slid inside her, "you and me can figure out something."

"Oh, damn Baby. I got somethin' figured out right now."

"Is it more crap about baseball?"

He thrust into her hard enough to make her eyes water. "Yeah. I'm runnin' down the Tacoma roster right now, see." He squeezed his eyes shut, and tiny droplets of sweat glistened on his brow as he labored. "Garvey, Stan...*unnhhh*...second base, .254, Helena...*unnhhh*...Montana," he moaned. "Ortiz...Renni...*unnhhh*...*unnhhh!* Relief pitcher...*unnnnnhhh!* Langley, B.C."

Josie reached up and anchored herself to the headboard. Cain was lost in the rhythm of their lovemaking, and hit all the bases before reaching home with a climactic lurch.

The sex was good enough. Actually, Josie thought to herself as he finished on top of her, it was better than she had had since she left Bucky. Only this time, the man trapped in her arms wasn't stoned halfway to Nirvana. Cain Reeves made love like he played baseball—letting out all the stops, going for broke. And she had a very good idea how she could put this fortuitous liaison to good use. He was perfect.

Cain had no clear agenda of his own. He had driven out to the Jewel Grove Trailer Park in his ruby red jalopy with his suitcase in the trunk, a six-pack of

Budweiser beer and no plans to move on any time soon. He was making circles, he told himself on the drive out of town. Cut all his ties, left all the bill collectors, hounders, naggers and creditors far behind. No more hustling appliances, lubing cars, pumping gas or tending bar. He was going to sit tight until things took a turn for the better.

The way he saw it on his last day of employment, Josie Wallgood had waltzed right in and invited him to stay awhile. It was in her eyes and the way she swished her hips when she went out the door. Cain Reeves had been wrong about a lot of things in his life so far, but one thing he never misjudged was women. He could read em like a book, he boasted often enough in the dugout. He could pick up women easier than tying his laces. Didn't even have to try hard.

The way he saw it as he sprawled on the bed with cat hairs floating over his face and dirty clothes piled on the floor around him, he had two choices at the moment. He could get back into his jeans, fire up the old Pontiac and head on down the line, or he could keep circling, invest a little time with this weird woman and see what happened. Maybe she had some scheme to turn a few bucks, and he sure could use the money. The trailer wasn't much—hell, it was a rat's nest—but he could help her clean it up. It was better than the pea-green cell at the Senator Hotel with a rattling radiator. This place might even be cozy if he worked at it. What Josie Wallgood needed was a man to shape her up, kick her in the ass a time or two to get off her lazy butt and straighten things up.

When he had recovered his breath, he fumbled for a smoke with his eyes closed. "So how long you been doin' this?"

"What?" She thought he meant fucking.

"Reading fortunes."

She shook the hair out of her eyes and flopped back on the pillow. "Oh. Well, since I came here after I left Bucky. A few years, I guess."

He glanced around the cubbyhole with a critical stare that offended her. "So is there any money in it?"

"Sure. It takes time to build up a regular clientele."

"Uh huh." He exhaled a stream of smoke toward the ceiling and folded an arm behind his head. "So how much do you charge?"

"Twenty bucks for a straight reading. More for specialty stuff."

"Sounds like hookin'."

"Hey, listen—"

"—What's specialty stuff?"

"You know, like making contact with somebody specific in the spirit world. Sending messages across the astral divide. That's extra."

"Like a seance?"

"Something like that, yeah."

"You pay any taxes or anything?"

She batted away a stream of smoke. "Are you crazy?"

"Guess so." He laughed with her. "So are these people—your customers, right?"

"Clients."

"Clients. Right. So are they guys?"

"Both. Women seem to be more into it than men though. Usually men come out and wanna know about getting laid. Women come to find out who their husband or boyfriend is making it with."

He rubbed his belly. "Sounds like a real trip. So you take their money, look into that ball and tell em what they wanna hear."

"Hey, you catch on really quick. That's it. That's exactly it."

"I guess everybody just wants a little reassurance. I can understand that. Hell, I'd like to have you look into that damn ball and see me playin' in the bigs, see my knees all healthy. Hell, I'd pay you to tell me you see that in my future."

Josie sat up, hugged her legs and gazed into his cocoa-brown eyes. "Cain, I can tell you something."

"Yeah?"

"You came out here probably thinking you could get my two-hundred dollars for that Motorola, write me up a phony receipt and take off with my money."

The blood drained from his face. He almost dropped his cigarette. "Shit, Girl."

"I thought of that as soon as you told me about the loan not going through. I thought you were gonna hustle me for the cash and take off. I think it was on your mind at first, and then for some reason when we started to talk, you had a change of heart and just sort of went with the flow." Her hand caressed his cheek. "That's what I think, Cain."

"I thought you told me this psychic stuff was all bullshit."

"It is. But there's science to it. It's not all hocus-pocus. I can still tell things only it's not from the other world—it's from here." She tapped her temple with a forefinger.

He reached up and pulled her down for a long, sweet kiss that tasted like tobacco and sweat. "Josie Honey, I'd be a goddam liar if I tried to argue with you."

"Bastard," she whispered, pecking his lips.

"But it was only for a minute or two. As soon as you opened the door, and we started to talk—just like you said, Josie—all I was thinkin' about then was gettin' you in the sack if I was lucky." He fondled a handful of breast and tweaked her nipple. "And I raked in the whole damned pot, didn't I?"

"Yep. But maybe I'm the one who got lucky."

They embraced. Arms, legs, nipples, lips and toes all meshed together.

"Josie," he breathed into her ear as they cuddled, "I swear this is a lot more than just an easy lay for me. I'm not gonna do anything to hurt you, Josie Girl. If you want me to stay awhile, I will."

"That's cool. I could use some company. And I have a little job you can do for me."

"Whatever you say, Baby." He nibbled on her neck and tickled her with his mustache. "First thing, let's clean this place up, huh? I like things neat and orderly."

"Whatever turns you on."

"You turn me on, Baby."

He was ready to go again. He had more energy than Pacific Gas and Electric. Nothing seemed to wear him down for long. He could make love four or five times at a crack, each time taking him longer to get off so he spent more time pleasuring her blushing body. Josie wasn't used to this kind of one to one, tenderized coupling. Most of her mates had been stoned, soft-bellied philosophers—laid back, lax lovers compared to the animalistic passion Josie fantasized about when she read her trashy romance novels. Cain was hot, sensuous flesh and bone, and he devoured her like a coyote attacking a chucker. It was exhausting, deliriously wonderful fun. By the time midnight came around, she felt as if she'd ridden bareback over the Rockies, and Cain was getting a second wind.

"Hey, Josie," he suggested, rolling out of bed, "what say we fix some chow? You got any eggs? I make a mean omelet." He stood up, hopped into his jeans and reached for a pack of Camels.

Josie was tired, covered with a coat of stinky sweat and jism as thick as jam on her thighs and butt. She didn't have the energy to move a finger. "I gotta flake out, Cain. You wore me out. I'm not hungry." She turned her alarm clock around to check the face. It had run down. "What time is it?"

"Goin' on two. Almost time for breakfast."

She buried her head under a pillow and groaned. "Ohhhh, you go. I gotta sleep."

"Okay. I'll fix you breakfast in bed, Baby." He bent down, gave her a quick kiss and waded through the debris blocking the doorway.

As soon as he was in the kitchen, he whistled and hitched up his pants. This place was a sty. Dishes stacked everywhere like clunkers in the junkyard, rotten food and empty cartons stuffed into the crannies. This woman was a pig. Been living alone too long. Let the place just go to hell. He'd change all that. It was the least he could do.

He grabbed a dishrag, turned on the hot water and began a search for some soap. In less than a minute, Goldie was rubbing against his legs and purring. Cain poured some milk in her dish and started pulling garbage out of the old Norge refrigerator. There was an orange in the crisper with more hair than Pocahontas, a tar pit of blackberry jelly catching debris from the rack above, foul smelling chicken wings with purple blisters and a bowl of orange mystery goo. He scraped and swabbed mold and mildew, mopped the sticky floor, washed all the pots and pans, scrubbed the stovetop and waxed the counters.

Finished at five a.m., Cain lit a cigarette, took a long drag, opened the louvered windows to let in some fresh air and cracked a handful of eggs into the frying pan.

8

By the time Josie staggered out of the bedroom, her new roommate had transformed her nasty Nashua into a sparkling model of domesticity with gleaming linoleum, scrubbed porcelain and polished cupboards. The smell of detergent and lemon spray hung in the air. Criminy—she hardly recognized the place. Where the hell had all her dishes gone?

Josie rubbed her eyes—the range top shone like an Alaskan glacier. She had forgotten that she had two rear burners. For the last couple years they'd been a parking place for her old pressure cooker and iron fry pan with the bottom burned out. "I'll be damned," she muttered, surveying the kitchen with carp-eyed awe as Cain poured himself a glass of orange juice.

"Thought I'd get a head start on the housework. You really let things go to hell around here, Babe."

She could smell her own redolent perfume—essence of ripe sardines and tidal marsh. What she needed was a shower not a lecture on Good Housekeeping from this testosterone jockey. "You stay up?"

"Yeah. It took me all morning to clean this shit, Josie. Jesus, when was the last time you got hold of a broom?"

She flopped onto a kitchen chair and blinked in amazement. The table was clean, polished until the chrome trim sparkled like Christmas tinsel. There were no grease skids, leftover gunk or empty Coke bottles on the shiny Formica. Incredible. Even the sugar bowl was sanitized. All the brown lumps were gone. This man was a goddam hygienic maniac. A neat freak who'd slipped over the edge.

"I don't have time to do much cleaning," she alibied effortlessly, inspecting the saltshaker to see if the green-thingees were still stuck to the top. Nope—all gone.

Cain sat down at the table and drained the orange juice. "I like things neat. So I'll do the cleaning, okay?"

This was too good to be true. She bent down to retrieve a slipper and found only mopped, waxed floor. So where was all her shit? "Suits me. But where's all my stuff?"

"Put away where it belongs. You know, your cupboards were all empty. All your shit was everywhere but where it oughtta be."

"Huh."

"And you need to go to the store and restock. You know you're all outta flour?"

"Don't need any."

"How you gonna make biscuits with no flour? I like gravy with my supper, too. You need flour and baking soda. And you don't have any more eggs. I ate the last one."

"Great. We'll go shopping one of these days."

He leaned across the table and peered into her glassy eyes. "Look, Josie, how about if we make a deal?"

She nodded. Whatever. She couldn't think straight until she had some caffeine.

"I'll hang around until I take care of whatever it is you want me to do for you. And in exchange for room and board, I'll do the cooking and clean the place up. I like things—"

"—neat and clean. Yeah, I can see that."

"And you supply the bread, okay? Money for groceries, gas for my car. A beer or two when I get thirsty. Fair enough?"

"And you'll help me out with the project we talked about last night, right?"

He skewered her with one lazy eye. "We didn't actually talk about it, Josie."

"We didn't?"

"You didn't really tell me anything except that it's nothin' illegal, right?"

"Right. So what do you wanna know?"

"Well, for starters, what the hell is it? You need a hand around here while you're charmin' the shorts off the suckers? Maybe some work on the trailer, haulin' trash, plumbing, what? Maybe you need some help with that old Pinto out there?"

"Yeah. But that isn't it exactly."

"Well? Spell it out, Josie." He tilted his chair on the back legs and pressed his hands on his thighs. "I'm all yours, Babe. Let's hear it."

She wasn't sure where to begin. This might sound crazy if she just laid it out for him. She didn't want to scare him off. Especially now that he had mentioned working on the Pinto—she definitely didn't want to queer an offer like that. But on the other hand, as she sat there and drank up his cowhand good looks and recalled the ferocity of his lovemaking, she felt compelled to be as honest as she could. Chances were he wasn't going to take off before chow call anyhow.

She pushed her hair away from her face. "I have a chance to make some good money. I'm not exactly sure how much yet, but for starters there's a hundred-dollar deposit."

"You mean a job you've been hired for?"

"Yeah. They want me to do a special job."

"The specialty type work you were tellin' me about?"

"Yeah. Exactly."

"Talkin' to dead people? Some creepy mumbo-jumbo with the crystal ball?"

"Sort of. It's complicated, but the bottom line is, Cain, that this client will pay me pretty much whatever I ask for so long as I can deliver."

His chair legs smacked the floor as he bolted forward. "What are you talking about exactly? Deliver what?"

"A ghost."

"A what?"

"You know—a ghost." She got up and grabbed the refrigerator door. When it swung open without a tug of war, she noticed the blue rubber seal had been sponged clean. Goddam. This guy was thorough. She had never seen the old Norge look so gorgeous. And empty. Hmmm…he must have trashed that can of leftover chili she was saving. It had a far out kind of furry life form that had intrigued her. Oh, well.

"This sounds spooky as hell to me, Josie. I'm not sure I wanna mess around with any of this psychedelic shit."

She poured herself a glass of Coke and took a long drink before answering. Her head cleared somewhat, and she could finally focus her eyes. What perfect white teeth he had. And there was that little black mole beneath his right eye. He was better looking this morning than he had been last night. Goddam, she was lucky.

"Look, Cain, there's nothing to it. This Farrah Bigfoot person is convinced that her place is being haunted by some spooky character named Max."

"This ghost has a name?"

"Sure. Lotsa ghosts and spirits have names."

"Aw, Josie, I don't know about this. Maybe you better count me out after all. Look, I can work on your Pinto, clean the place up, but messin' around with spooks and shit just ain't my bag."

She petted his arm. "Relax. Just listen for a minute. This is no different than selling somebody a washer and dryer on credit."

"I don't know."

"It's the same. Trust me. Just a business transaction, that's all. Business is business. Selling washing machines or exterminating ghosts."

"You gotta exorcise some kind of evil spirit?" He got up and thumped the door of the Norge with both palms. "Dammit, Josie! You mean like the priest in the movie?"

"Well, sort of. After all, that's what I do, Cain. That's my professional specialty. Yours is catching baseballs, and mine is getting rid of ghosts. Same thing."

"You gotta be kidding. I don't want to mess around with any bitches screwin' their heads off and talkin' to the Devil. Count me out."

"This ghost isn't like that. Relax."

He tugged at an earlobe. "I don't know. I don't like this shit."

"Look, you saw the *Exorcist*, right?"

"That's what I'm talkin' about, dammit. Scared the holy shit outta me."

"That was fiction, okay? This is reality. Ghosts are not like that."

"Says who? You're an authority, are you?"

"Yeah. Definitely."

"I thought you said this was all bullshit."

She backtracked slightly. "Well, it is. But the point is the suckers don't think it's bullshit. Don't you see what I'm saying? The scam only works on suckers who believe in this bullshit."

"You can't cheat an honest man, is that it?"

"Yeah, sort of. In a way. Same thing."

He sat back down. "So tell me about ghosts. They real or not?"

"Who knows?" His eyes rolled, and she regretted her flippancy. "What I'm saying is that if somebody wants to believe in a spirit, then what harm does it do?"

"But it's all bullshit?"

"Absolutely."

"So how come everybody believes in this junk if it's all a buncha bullshit?"

She sighed. People were so easily led, weren't they? Pathetic. "Look. It's like this. Lotsa people believe in all sorts of weird fucking shit—like Jesus Christ walking on water, having a virgin mother, crawling out of the grave and flying up to heaven. Now I ask you, how crazy-assed is that for crissakes, huh?"

He grinned. "Pretty crazy, I guess—yeah, I gotcha."

"People swallow a lotta crap. That doesn't mean any of it is real."

"But they wanna believe so they swallow it hook, line and sinker. My whole family was God-fearin Baptists—couldn't take a shit without checkin' in with Jesus first."

"Exactly. There are no real ghosts, Cain."

"I know that," he snapped, put off by her maternal reassurance. "But there are some spooky things goin' on. Definitely. Like in the movie."

"The movie was made so people would shit in their pants, okay? To sell suckers tickets. People will pay a lot of money to get scared out of their skins. The truth is, there aren't ghosts who upchuck all over everybody right and left and twist their heads off. That's all bullshit."

"Okay. So what about this ghost of yours? What's Max like?"

"He's some guy who got killed in Korea back in the fifties. And the guy's daughter Farrah thinks he's come back to haunt her. It's all a buncha bullshit, but she wants to pay me a lot of money to make him go away. So what the hell? A business opportunity is the same no matter where it comes from."

"But if you know it's all bullshit, and you still charge her a bundle to go through some rigmarole to get rid of this Max, then it sounds like just another hustle to me. Maybe even against the law."

"It's just business. You think the police come around to every fortuneteller's door whenever some sucker says the crystal ball was wrong? That's crazy."

"Maybe they will if you're hustling people for money to get rid of ghosts that don't exist."

She had reached the end of her patience. "Jesus Christ, Cain. Get a brain in your head. People want to believe in this shit. Hell, they need to believe in it. Even if I charged em triple, they'd still be pounding on my door, begging me to help em. People are natural born suckers when it comes to this type of thing. I know about this. Trust me a little, okay?"

"You swear it's not against the law or anything?"

"I swear. Look, I won't tell you how to pitch catches or whatever if you don't tell me how to tell fortunes and run my business, okay?"

A slow smile wrinkled his face. "You really don't know the first thing about baseball, you know that, Josie?"

"Sorry."

"How about if I take you to a game? We can watch the high school squad practice. Just to get you up to speed. You don't know a goddamned thing. I can't believe it, Girl."

"You let me do my thing with no hassles, trust me, and I guess I'll let you teach me a little bit about baseball."

"A little—hell. Baseball is bigger than both of us, Babe. It's the best part about America, you know that? It's what this country is all about. It's more American than rock'n roll or apple pie or anything. It's the wet dream of every nine-year old kid playin' in the backyard to pitch for the Yankees or the Reds in the Series someday. It's what we all dream about, Babe. The very best day of your life without baseball is worse than the very worst day playin'. You can't learn just a little about baseball." He slid her off the chair and scooped her up in his arms. "It's like makin' love, Josie Girl—you gotta go all the way or nothin'. There ain't no little bit about it if it's good."

She broke out in giggles as he tickled her. "Okay, okay! I give up."

He dumped her on the settee. "You give up too easy, Girl." He kissed her enough to make her ears buzz. "How about if we start off by learnin' some signs?" His hand slid between her thighs and made her gasp for breath. "The pitcher has to keep one eye on the catcher's crotch to get the sign and the other eye on the runner leadin' off. And then the catcher calls the pitch." His breath warmed her eyelids. "That's a slider," he whispered, making her eyes close as he flexed his fingers.

"Ohhhh…oh."

"And this is a fast ball…low and away…" He plunged deeper.

When she finally opened her eyes, he was smiling sweetly at her with an errant lock of hair falling over his brown eyes. "See?" he cooed, kissing her cheek. "Baseball can be fun."

His body felt so damned good connected to hers, better than Thai stick, a bubbly tub on a cold night, high-priced California wine, fresh laundry or April sunshine on her face. Cain was heavy medicine. "You're terrific," she murmured, recovering her equilibrium as he held her close. "Are you sure you aren't some kind of phantom lover yourself?"

"Phenom, Baby."

"Whatever."

"Never had a lady accuse me of bein' that before."

"Well, it's possible." She pinched his belly until he yelped in pain.

"Ow! Hey, I can't keep this up on fruit juice. I already had the last of your eggs, but I'm gonna need a real breakfast before I get to the bedroom."

"Sexual blackmail, huh?" she tittered, flattered he still craved her favors enough to wrestle her back to bed for seconds.

He stood up. From the open doorway dirty clothes, magazines, boxes and litter spilled from under her bed. "I'm gonna swamp out the bedroom, Josie Girl. And when I'm done with that, you better plan on feedin' me a steak."

She crinkled her nose. "What're you gonna do with all my stuff? How'll I find anything?"

"Same way you do now—look for it."

"You have to start cleaning again right now? Haven't you done enough for today?"

"Nope. Can't stand havin' a mess like that to sleep in."

"What am I supposed to do while you're playing house?"

"Go to the store and get me a steak and some flour, eggs, butter, milk, bacon and potatoes. I left you a list there." He indicated the kitchen table. "And you need some more dish washing soap, too."

"That sounds so mundane." She flopped back and shut her eyes. "I'd rather take a shower, have some coffee and watch a movie on the tube."

"No way, Girl. Not today."

She watched him move back to the kitchen, put her dirty glass in the sink and turn on the tap water. "Cain, you agreed to help me with this other thing then, right?"

"I said I would." He turned the water off and reached for a dishtowel. "Let me make sure I got this straight. You got some client who wants you to get rid of a ghost named Max who's haunting her place even though you know damn well it's all a buncha horse hockey. Is that about it?"

"Yeah. That's it, I guess."

"And she's gonna give you a hundred-dollar deposit, and then you're gonna ask for a whole lot more once you get rid of the ghost. Did I get that right?"

"She's inherited some money. I don't know how much yet, but I'll find out."

"I figured it was somethin' like that."

"We could be talking a thousand dollars. Apiece." She watched his eyes flicker.

"And I suppose you want me to help you make Max disappear?"

"So you'll do it?"

"Sure." He came back and grabbed hold of the settee with both hands. As her eyes widened in eager expectation, he dumped her on the floor.

"Ouch!" Her backside bounced on the rug and made the trailer shimmy.

"I figure since you got an extra hundred comin' in, you can go by the appliance store and pick up your Motorola TV."

"That hurts!" She rubbed her rump. Might even have a bruise.

"I'd like to watch the Giants play on Saturday in living color. First regular season doubleheader." He headed for the bedroom. "And don't forget the beer, Babe."

"Hey, you coulda broken something, dammit!" She was still massaging the sore spot on her backside.

"Bottles. Don't bring home cans. Got it? Long-necked bottles."

Josie watched him wade into the bedroom where he began flinging clothes around like a Texas twister. She caught sight of her pink flannel shirt flying by along with an empty carton of powdered doughnuts before she closed her eyes.

9

The sun was sizzling behind bristled hills dredged in a tangle of vegetation creeping toward the edge of the slough. Sluggish marsh water seeped through the ground making it as spongy as bread pudding. The hillsides were striped with precocious forsythia, bled crimson with quince and swaddled like papooses in plush Oregon grape, salmon berry, swordfern, stunted larches and willows. Cully Marsh was a mere dab of color on the Oregon landscape, a freckled speck amid the checkerboard fields so fertile homesteaders claimed to the folks back home that toothpicks stuck in the dirt would sprout a fir tree by morning.

Oregon's capital in Salem may have been the political center of the Willamette Valley, but the burgeoning farmlands, orchards and berry farms of Marion County were the true jewels in the Pacific Northwest's agricultural crown. Created by the great deluge of the Missoula Floods during the last Ice Age when the Columbia River scoured the land as clean as a new bride's fry pan, Oregon's fecund midsection inherited a mother lode of top soil swept from eastern Washington and Montana. The Willamette Valley straddling Interstate 5 south from Canada to the Mexican border could thus lay claim to some of the richest soil in the world. Before World War II, Nisei farmers tilled the black dirt to grow stupendous vegetables and fruit that people drove all the way from Portland and Seattle to haggle over. After most of the Japanese-Americans were interned in camps and torn from their farms, developers moved in and paved over large portions of Paradise. Before the Korean War was over, supermarkets, shopping malls, car dealerships, tract housing and commercial blight spread like poison oak across the landscape, isolating pockets of small-town havens in an undulating sea of golden wheat, filbert trees and berry bushes.

The village of Silverton, nestled in the petticoat frills of the Capital, could have been snipped from a picture postcard. It's modest neighborhoods, quaint storefronts and homespun hospitality belied the splendor of the surrounding geography which had been particularly generous in planting Silver Falls within hollering distance. This treasured spot boasted over a half-dozen waterfalls spiraling down a rocky course decorated with elegant cedar, fir and lush greenery which awed even jaded tourists. Barely a mile from the city limits, the scars of civilization faded away, letting the whispered hush of the nearby forests fool a visitor into believing they'd slipped through Alice's rabbit-hole into a Grant Wood Utopia.

Oregonians were a distinct breed—needing to feel they were only a handshake away from nature even in the midst of traffic congestion on the freeways, barbed wire and Diesel fumes. Look around any corner in the close-knit communities of the Willamette Valley, and it was a cinch to find residents who refused to turn their back on the physical grandeur that drew their forefathers to plunk down their plows and whack a home out of the woods instead of heading for California gold. Everybody seemed to be a gardener, not happy unless their castle was surrounded by greenery, flowers, edible plots producing fresh salad greens on the hoof and a view of a Cascade mountain or two. Those who staked their fortunes on the rich valley land rather than the boondoggle treasure hidden in the streambeds of Sutter County seemed to have made a better bargain. Marion County farmers were on the whole a prosperous lot, wedded to the generous soil and forgiving climate that could make a native soon forget the scourges he'd known back home: marauding mosquitoes, chiggers, roaches, toll roads and muggy summers that smothered the air like wet socks thrown on a campfire.

From one end of the horizon to another, the Willamette vista was a kaleidoscope of eye-popping color, textures and fragrances of bounty and promise locals too often took for granted until ambitious immigrants threatened to stamp their own brand of civility on the countryside. Paradise discovered meant paradise lost, and to avoid the prospect of foreigners encroaching on their private nest, native web-footers settled far enough from town so the fuss and noise of city life were only echoes over the next hill. The Salem movers and doers in their three-piece armor congregated along the capitol mall, hustled deals over coffee at hole-in-the-wall haunts with ivy growing through the walls and considered themselves on parole once they pointed their Beemers and Volvos for the open vistas beyond the Interstate. The Willamette Valley was a hard place to pass through without searching for an unclaimed corner. Sometimes Easterners were shocked to discover such diversity where they expected only lumber mills, loggers and salmon canneries and found instead idyllic farmland, sturdy villages and folks who weren't yet convinced that progress meant improvement.

At Cully Marsh where Hobart's trailer squatted, blackberry brambles as high as a giraffe's gizzard choked the roadsides. Streams fed from icy mountain springs tumbled over the hills to pool in a cattail sea where herons, blackbirds, jays and beaver carried on as if they still held sway over the land. This was a place where a person could keep a safe distance from civilization and still only be a half-hour's hike from a cheeseburger and fries at Silverton's Dairy Delight Drive-In. For Farrah and Hobart, the setting was ideal, disturbed only by the haunting shriek of a red-tailed hawk in the twilight's chill.

As night closed in on the marsh, Hobart's hound dogs circled beside the woodshed and whipped their hind legs in pursuit of tenacious fleas. Hobart Ames surveyed it all, shaded his eyes from the flash of an orange and scarlet sunset and looked across the brackish water where his dinghy nudged the rotten pilings poking through the marl. He couldn't be exactly sure, but it seemed to him that there was a ripple in the still water—not a natural stirring of the evening breeze that rustled the reeds and sent a shiver through the pond. This was a mysterious, roiling wake that shattered the glassy surface and made the stern of his little boat dip and bob. Could be a frog or red-winged blackbird had flopped on board. It was hard to see, but there was something in the damned boat. He squinted and peered at the ruffles spreading across the pond, making the dinghy dance. For sure there was something going on.

"Hey!" He tramped closer and sank into the soft mud. "Get outta the boat there!"

His mind was cataloging the intruders he could account for this evening. Both dogs were plainly visible up by the shed. Now they stood with their ears cocked and their tails up. Farrah was at the trailer cooking. He could smell her curried rice. He hadn't heard a vehicle on the road for over an hour, hadn't seen a solitary soul since he had closed the woodshed and come down to check on his frog traps. His brow furrowed as he watched the boat rocking gently in a dimpled wave. Hobart was more than a little perplexed.

Night shadows were closing in. The road was deserted, no log trucks rumbling over the potholes. There was barely a whisper of a breeze, only a low murmur in the tall grass as he searched the horizon for a familiar silhouette.

He decided against his better judgment it must be a damn bird or muskrat in the boat. Nothing to get excited about. It wouldn't bother him at all if it weren't for this weird business with Farrah and her dad. Maybe there was nothing to it, but Farrah was a sensitive, intuitive woman, and she was convinced it was Max. She ought to know if anybody did. What could Hobart do but try to get her some help? Even if it was nothing but a bad dream, Josie would put Farrah's fears to rest, and they could get on with their lives in peace. No harm done one way or the other.

Hobart hiked down to the edge of the pond, parting the waist-high saw grass as he looked for whatever it was that had caused the commotion. He waded out until the water lapped at his thighs and peered into the rowboat. Nothing there but a rusted bailing can, a woolen sock and both ash oars snug in the oarlocks. No muskrat, no stray cats, no birds. Not even a wet footprint.

"Dammit," he cursed his foolishness as he waded back to shore. Now he was starting to see ghosts himself. Something had made the boat rock around like Elvis, but whatever it was, it sure as hell wasn't a ghost. It was nothing at all. Might have been a big carp under the water. Funny how many things he could imagine when he let himself get spooked.

He stopped when his right foot sank in a depression filling with muddy water. The boot print was nearly as big as his own, and it lead from the cedar log to the muddy bank and into the pond, tattooing the ground with a trail that disappeared in the shallows.

"Holy shit." He looked again. And again. Fresh footprints had appeared from nowhere, gone into the pond in the direction of the boat and vanished. How about that?

Hobart stared into the murky pool. A blackbird perched on a stalk of pussy willow and scolded him for his intrusion. It beat its wings and flew off as he gawked at the transient's signature melting into the mud. The footprints led straight into the water and didn't come out. What the hell was going on anyhow? Anxiety and uncertainty began to brew in his brain the harder Hobart stared.

He waded farther out until the cold seeped beneath his armpits. His boots stuck in the bottom mud. He shivered and swung his arms under the surface. Nothing. It was no more than seven-feet deep at the center of the pond. Bottom was like quicksand out there. No use making a complete fool of himself by slogging around in the cold muck like a damned idiot. Nobody would just appear and then wade into the pond like that. If some hobo had wandered onto the property, traipsed down to the water without leaving any visible footprints until he got to the muddy bank, gone in for a swim and not left any exit tracks, then that was about the damndest thing Hobart Ames could imagine. But if some down-and-outer did decide to drown himself, then Hobart would just wait to see if a body floated up in a few days. Otherwise, he tried to convince himself as he sloshed back to the shore, there was nothing to worry about. This was crazy.

When he got back to dry ground, he tramped around the trailer twice looking for fresh tracks and didn't find any. The dogs hadn't even barked either. Freaky. He took a final look out across the marsh and then opened the trailer door.

Farrah was setting plates on the table. "Hey, Hobart. Hungry?"

He sat down on the step and tugged at his boots. "Yeah. Starved."

"You're soaked. Did you fall in?"

"Nope." He flung off a smelly boot.

"Anything wrong?"

"Nope. Just checking on the boat, that's all."

"The dinghy? Did it sink?"

He flung off the other boot and rolled up his Levi's. He leaked water on the floor. "Nope."

"Well, why'd you get so wet?"

"Just waded into the pond."

"How come?"

"No reason."

"No reason? What would you get yourself all soaked for, Hobart?"

He came inside and closed the door. "Farrah, listen, I won't lie to you."

"What is it?"

"I thought I saw somebody in the boat. I went to take a look, and there were those footprints again."

She blanched and grasped his wrist with both hands. "Like the ones we saw before? Oh, my god, Hobart."

"I followed the tracks from the boat around the pond and then into the water. I don't know where the hell they came from or where the hell they went."

"Oh, god."

"But I do know I don't give a damn." He pulled off his shirt and wiped his nose with a cold finger. "I can't figure it out. I guess it's just as well you asked me to get Josie to help you out. Maybe she can figure this out—I give up."

She clung to him. "Hobart, it's more than just something we can't figure out."

"Don't get into all this mystical stuff with me again, okay? I'm tired, and I'm soaked through from wading up to my chin in the pond."

She knelt and gathered up his wet clothes. "Why'd you go in the water, Hobart?"

"What do you mean?"

"What were you looking for?"

"I don't know—just trying to find out what was there. Maybe some old bum drowned himself or something. Hell, I don't know." He poured water in the sink and scrubbed his arms and hands with a bar of Ivory soap.

"You don't believe that. The dogs never even barked once, did they?"

"Nope. So?"

"So you know nobody gets within a quarter mile of this place without the dogs making a fuss. If some bum wandered off the road, where are his footprints going down to the pond?"

He scrubbed with renewed ferocity. His skin was turning cherry red.

"You didn't see any trace of fresh tracks, did you, Hobart?"

"Nope. Didn't see a goddam thing."

"So it's him, isn't it?"

Hobart rinsed with a dipper of water and took a towel Farrah handed him. "I'd say we don't know what the hell it is, Farrah. If you want to think it's Max, then fine. It's Max. If you want to think it's some kind of practical joke some redneck asshole is playing on us, fine. Maybe it's something else. Could be some nature lover waded out across the pond and came out clear over at the other side. Hell, I don't know."

They sat down knee-to-knee at the tiny table and shoveled in brown rice, curried chicken and canned apricots. Midway through the meal, Farrah got up and lit their kerosene lantern. She turned up the wick until the light made their faces glow. Hobart cleaned his plate and fed the stove with last year's alder logs.

After dinner, as the dogs curled up beneath the trailer, and the night owls hooted their lonesome calls, Farrah and Hobart lay together in bed and stared out at the starless sky.

"I know why Max has come back," Farrah whispered in the dark.

Hobart had started to drift off when her words jarred him awake and made him open his eyes. "What?"

"It's his dog tags. He wants his dog tags. He can't be at peace without those dog tags being with his remains wherever they are. I have to give them back, Hobart."

He rolled over and buried his face in the pillow. "That's crazy, Farrah."

She continued to stare up at the black night and a sliver of moon peeking out from a charcoal cloud. "I know that's what he wants. I have to figure out how to give those tags back. Maybe Josie knows of a way."

Hobart grunted and wrapped the covers over his ear. "Josie said she needs a hundred dollars to do it."

"Okay. That's fair."

"That's like a deposit, Farrah."

"Okay. I'm getting that money from Mom. The lawyer says I should have a check any day."

Hobart stirred. All of a sudden, he was no longer so sleepy. He turned onto his back. "Farrah, you're dead serious about this?"

"Yes. I am."

"How much money are you getting?"

She snuggled up against him. "The lawyer says after all the fees and everything are taken out, my check will be for about a hundred-thousand dollars."

Hobart sat up so fast he bumped his head. "Christ! How much?"

"A hundred thousand. But don't worry. I've already told him I'm going to send a check right away to my Aunt Philippa for half. She like practically raised Mom after my grandparents died. My mother had polio as a kid, and she and Mom were very close. Aunt Philly always looked out for her, you know—made sure nobody picked on her. Mom was really shy, like me, I suppose."

"I suppose is right."

"Plus she's my godmother—she was always like the most generous person with me as a kid. Sort of like a combination grandmother, favorite aunt and fairy godmother. Now with my mother gone, Aunt Philly has nobody really. She never married—had a boyfriend once, I think, but the rumor was that he was married. That's what I heard Mom and Dennis talking about anyway. I felt sorry for her—I mean, Aunt Philly isn't the kind of person to let somebody take advantage of her like that, but then I guess when you're in love, you just sort of do some really nonsensical stuff. It's hard to imagine somebody getting the best of her like that though. She must have been really hurt when they split. It probably did a real number on her psyche, don't you think?"

"He must have made some promises he couldn't keep."

"I suppose. But I never heard her being involved with anybody after that. So now I have you, and my stepdad is getting hooked up with another lady, and Aunt Philly is still alone. So I think she should have half, don't you?"

"Yeah. That's fair."

"I thought so, too. The lawyer is going to send her the money for me. So I'll get a check for the balance, I guess."

"That still leaves fifty-thousand dollars, Farrah." He whistled. "Jeez. I didn't realize it was that much."

"Is anything wrong?"

He reached for a spent roach in a conch shell by the bed. "Money is poison. We have to be careful with it. I don't want it to screw up things between you and me." He struck a match and sucked. After a long, slow sigh, he passed the cigarette to Farrah who took a short drag and tossed the spent reefer back into the shell. Their exhaust plumes coiled upward, intertwined and drifted out the oval window.

She stroked his back. "I know how you feel, Hobart. Money makes people miserable more than anything else. We don't want that kind of life—we're trying to make something better living out here, making it on our own without ripping anybody off or giving in to the establishment freaks running the world. That's still important to me, Hobart—to be true to ourselves no matter what."

"Me, too."

"But we can afford to get a new truck, and I can get the supplies I need to make my own picture frames. We want to do things around the place here like put in a well and a fence for the garden. You'll need things, Hobart. We both will. But the money won't change us. We won't let it."

He hugged her. "I hope not, Sweetpea. I like things the way they are."

She tweaked his ear playfully. "Even when the trailer sinks in the mud, and the privy fills up?"

"Almost the way they are anyway."

Their limbs entwined like warm pretzel dough. "I promise not to do anything foolish with the money, Hobart. We won't do anything we both don't agree feels right."

"And you still feel you have to do something about Max?"

"Yes, I do. Very strongly. I've always had a freaky feeling about Max ever since Mom told me about the screwed up burial and his dog tags being put in with the wrong remains. I never really felt comfortable having those tags, but it meant a lot to Mom for me to have something of his. Maybe it just bothered her to have them. I don't know." She shivered. "I'll feel better when we pay Josie the money and let her take care of this."

"You think she can do any good?" He had always known Josie to have a plain vanilla attitude toward the occult. Maybe Farrah shouldn't place so much trust in Josie Wallgood for something this serious.

"Oh, yes. I could tell by talking to her. She has a gift, Hobart. If anybody can reach Max, I'm sure Josie can. Aren't you?"

He begged the question by nuzzling her neck. "Aren't you sleepy yet?"

"Nope." She reached down and encouraged his restlessness. "Are you?"

He rolled on top of her in one easy motion. "Not anymore."

She dug her heels into the mattress. "What a coincidence."

Outside in the shadows cooled by the marsh winds, the hound dogs huddled together nose to tail, caught the strange scent in the night air and serenaded the moonless sky.

10

Bradley Hammaker snapped his case closed and pocketed the few pink telephone message slips on his desk. His secretary Penny saluted him as he punched his way through the double doors leading to the reception area.

"See you tomorrow, Mr. Hammaker," she said at the same time she lifted the receiver to take an incoming call.

Bradley pressed the down button on the elevator car. He waited, studying the panoramic view of Lake Michigan polka-dotted with white sails fluttering like confetti on the water and tried to ignore the cursive stare of a waiting client leafing through back issues of *Time*.

A bell chimed; the car arrived; the door slipped aside to admit him and his bulky calfskin briefcase, and he stepped aboard. He looked at his watch on the way down to the building lobby. It was three-twelve. He was playing hooky this afternoon. Didn't matter really. For the last four weeks, he'd been billing twenty hours a day doing trial prep for the Harvey Chalmers case. This would be the longest trial he had ever litigated, utilizing more expert witnesses, associates and resources than the firm had ever garnered before. And if he won, he wouldn't have to worry about a secure retirement. He'd already consulted with Abrams, Schift and Pfeiffer, his personal accounting firm, to determine the best placement of his prospective fees in secured trusts, annuities and shares in Grumman Industries.

The elevator opened, and he stepped out into the marble lobby with alabaster sconces, Italian slate inlay and burnished brass handrails on the stairs leading to the parking garage one level below. He palmed his car keys as he negotiated the steps. His white Mercedes was parked at the end next to the

Madison Street door. He got in, tossed the briefcase on the floor and started the engine.

He had an appointment to meet with his client Philippa Mooney at five o'clock on the South Side. She was going to receive a cash settlement in the estate of her late sister Phoebe Mooney Swidnik Poole. Phoebe Poole had succumbed to complications from metastatic cancer, liver failure and alcoholism. At the age of forty-six she had left an estate in real property and life insurance of half a million dollars to her estranged husband Dennis. There was also a trust fund for her only child, a daughter named Farrah Swidnik living somewhere in Oregon. From what Hammaker had learned since Phoebe's death, the daughter was a counter culture hippie who painted watercolors and hung out in backwoods communes on the West Coast. Phoebe's trust fund had been seeded with the ten-thousand dollars of life insurance left to her when her first husband, Farrah's father Max Swidnik, had been killed in action during the Korean Conflict.

There was now over a hundred-thousand dollars in the account, and Farrah was to be the sole recipient. Recently Bradley had received a call from an Oregon attorney named Alan Farnam who represented Farrah. He insisted his client wanted to split the proceeds of the trust with Farrah's maternal aunt Philippa Mooney. He had asked that Bradley prepare the disposition papers for the division of the trust proceeds in favor of Farrah's Aunt Philippa. Bradley could never argue with any transaction in favor of giving money not legally owed to one of his clients.

Bradley Hammaker had never personally met Philippa Mooney, but he'd had a number of telephone conversations with her over the past ten months of probate. Typical old maid, he thought. A fifty-year old spinster, a language professor at the University of Chicago who lived in a one-bedroom apartment overlooking Jackson Park. A personal visit wasn't something he normally would have included in his schedule, but it just happened that this served him very conveniently when he needed an excuse to be out of touch for a couple of hours in the afternoon. In fact, it was perfect. Philippa's apartment was only four blocks from where Loretta Pultz was waiting for him.

He stopped for a light and checked his watch again. Three-seventeen. Right on schedule. Bradley was watching a busty woman with long, braided hair sprint across the street against the light. He slowed to let her cross and admired her breasts bobbing like dumplings in a stew pot.

The only glitch with this Poole probate case was the husband Dennis. He and Phoebe had been separated for over four years. It took Hammaker's office three weeks to find the sonuvabitch. He finally turned up in Salt Lake City living with a woman named Hedda who had five kids and no brains. Dennis had a drinking problem nearly as severe as Phoebe's. Crazy bastard had tried to make threats against the firm and Bradley Hammaker personally. He was demanding the entire estate, including the trust fund set up for Farrah. When he learned his sister-in-law Philippa Mooney was going to get half of the money from that trust, he flew into a rage, screamed he'd come down to the office and tear Bradley's heart out in person. Crazy asshole. There was no love lost between anybody in the Mooney family and Dennis Poole.

Apparently Phoebe's first husband Max Swidnik was a decent guy. A war hero, in fact. How she could have gone from grade A to a loser like Dennis was a mystery. But feminine detours into the choppy waters of matrimony never ceased to amaze Bradley Hammaker. He had charted a few detours himself in twenty-five years of marriage.

Bradley moved into the left lane and swerved around a taxi. He had time to think by himself for a change. It was a good idea to escape from the office for an afternoon. Sometimes surreptitious sloth served to refresh the mind and stir the memory to uncomfortable proportions.

Today as he drove, he found himself thinking of a hot, steamy afternoon a long time ago in a California trailer park off the Pacific Coast Highway. He was wearing a pair of khaki-colored boxer shorts and a wristwatch, nothing more. She was lying on two pillows in the center of a Hollywood bed. Her hair was almost white it was so blonde, and her pussy hair was as fine as corn silk. Her bold, blue eyes tracked him while little dabs of mascara trickled down her cheeks. A scarlatina, orgasmic blush colored her neck and shoulders. She was slick with sweat.

"*You shouldn't have done it if you felt this bad about it,*" Lieutenant Bradley Hammaker, USMC, chided her as he puffed his last cigarette. "*It's no big deal for crissakes. Quit crying.*"

"*I didn't know it was going to be like this, Brad,*" she whimpered, pulling a sheet over her breasts. "*I'm sorry.*" She sobbed into the pillow. "*I'm just sorry. Sorry it ever happened.*"

"*Too late to be sorry, Bibi,*" he grumbled, using his thumb to grind the cigarette into an ashtray.

"*Just leave me alone. Please, go and leave me alone.*"

The sounds of her remorse twisted his guts into knots and made his morning coffee back up in his throat. Goddam women. Never could make up their minds. They had no guts. No guts at all. Couldn't take a risk. Never could stand to take any casualties.

"*Yeah*," he had muttered, kicking a leg into his khakis. "*I'm on my way.*"

"*I'm sorry. I'm sorry.*" She was crying as he dressed.

"*Great time to decide you're sorry, Bibi.*" He clanked his belt buckle into place and groped for his socks and shoes.

"*I want this to be over, Brad. Finished. For good.*"

"*Don't worry, Honey. I'm through. This is the end of the line for me, too. I've had it with your Princess Snow White routine.*" He had grabbed his tie from the bureau. "*Next time you want a roll in the hay, Honey, call some other sap, okay?*"

"*Brad, please.*"

"*I know. Don't tell me—you're sorry.*"

"*Brad, wait!*"

"*See ya, Honey.*" And he had slammed the door behind him.

Bradley Hammaker, gray now and soft in all the places where his body had been honed to the hardness of sheet metal twenty-five years before, put on the turn signal and slowed down. He steered the Mercedes toward the Jackson Park exit. He drove slowly as he started looking for an inconspicuous parking slot.

By now, after all the years of carefully managed dalliances when he was rising like cream to the top of his father-in-law's firm, he had learned to regulate his passion. He never made mistakes, never allowed sentiment or emotional chaos to derail his organizational precautions at discovery. His marriage was sound. His two children Marcus and Bradley Junior were doing well in life, one as a second-year medical student at Johns Hopkins and the other sailing somewhere in the South Pacific while he dawdled on a Master's thesis in marine biology. Things had turned out well. Bradley Hammaker didn't make mistakes anymore. There was only one miscalculation, one error of judgment to blemish his record. That was twenty-four years ago. And now Phoebe Swidnik Poole, or Bibi as she was called, was gone. Nobody left to blame him, remind him of his secret failure. He only had the voice of his own persistent conscience to goad him these days.

He slipped the Mercedes into a space beneath a dehydrated sapling tethered to the concrete with a twist of scrap iron, got out and locked the door. He had a block and a half walk to the entrance of the co-op. It was doubtful he would see anyone he knew, but if he did run into someone familiar in this neighborhood, he could display his weighty briefcase and mention the Poole probate case he had taken a personal interest in. He always had all the bases covered.

He walked faster. Few pedestrians took much notice of the distinguished, silver-haired barrister hurrying along the sidewalk.

Bradley Hammaker was always in control of his actions, always steered by intellectual reckoning. Except for that one time, he damned himself as he caught sight of the droopy topiary by the building door. Just because of that one sultry afternoon when Bibi's guilt overwhelmed them both into quarreling and parting the sheets, he had been forced to carry this oppressing burden of moral deficit with him all these years. Goddam it. Goddam Bibi. Goddam the niggardly Rexall druggist who had taken so long waiting on a pregnant woman with a screaming toddler that Lieutenant Hammaker had rushed out bound for Bibi's without the package of Trojans. Things grew complicated from simple screw-ups, he liked to remind his subordinates. It wasn't a huge, glaring error that made things impossible—it was a compilation of innocuous slips which most often added up to total disaster.

As a matter of fact, Bradley mused as he started up the steps, he wasn't even surprised all those years ago when Bibi called to say she had been to the doctor, and she was going to have a baby. It hadn't surprised him at all. Carelessness always paid off in spades for Bradley. The story of his life.

He stopped in front of apartment 2-D and pressed the buzzer. When the door opened, he stepped across the threshold with the lingering memory of a weeping young woman clutching his jacket at the Union Pacific train station in Oakland. She had a one way ticket eastbound. Bradley was headed for the provost marshall's office in Honolulu. It would be a long time until he heard her plaintive voice again. A very long time.

"Hello," Loretta greeted him.

His recollections of California and Bibi dissolved as he closed the door behind him and dropped the briefcase.

"You're late." The second the words left her mouth, she knew she had erred in scolding her hasty lover.

"I was held up at the office." He shed his jacket along with the heavy case.

"That's alright. Want a drink?"

"Scotch, please. Extra ice." He sank into a chair and loosened his tie.

While she left him to get the liquor, he looked up and caught sight of himself in the mirror. He saw an expensively groomed, middle-aged man with a lined, tanned countenance straight from the cover of GQ, a hard chin and cold, granite eyes staring out beneath hedgerow brows and a finely-trimmed head of thick, silvered hair. Success had brought him some measure of physical refinement in his fifties which promised a graceful decline into a distinguished senior status. But today, as he perspired beneath his tailored silk shirt, he saw only the reflection of Lieutenant Bradley Hammaker in his cotton boxer shorts puffing on a Lucky Strike cigarette.

She returned and handed him the drink. He threw his head back, took a slug and shivered.

"Cold?" she asked him with a stupid frown.

"Just tired."

She didn't speak as he killed the rest of the Cutty Sark without looking at her.

11

Wrapped snugly in her robe, Josie Wallgood fluffed her hair and nuzzled up against her new lover who still smelled like soap from his bath. He turned on the gas beneath her kettle. When the water was hot, she took down a cup, mixed in her instant cocoa and dropped some sourdough bread in the toaster. Cain had the snug little galley gleaming like a Northern Pacific dining car. In a few minutes, he had eggs and bacon sizzling on the stove, buttered toast on the plate and the radio blasting Fleetwood Mac. This magic kingdom was likely to be addictive. Cain was assembled like Rawhide's Rowdy Yates, and he cooked and mopped floors. A hunk of heaven had landed dead center in the Jewel Grove Trailer Park.

Josie sat down at the table, opened up a magazine and started to shovel in a load of breakfast. Before the fork reached her lips, there was a rumble outside, a stomp on the porch and then a knock on the door.

She got up, stuffing in a last bite of toast.

Cain was peering between the blinds. "Customers or bill collectors?"

She wrinkled her nose disapprovingly. It was an affront to her professional standing to suggest she was behind in the rent. As if he were so plush, he could criticize. "Clients," she corrected him in a snotty tone. "Business."

"Cash cows?"

"Of course, cash. I don't take credit."

"Hit it, Josie Girl. This I gotta see for myself." He tossed his dishtowel aside.

"Just be quiet and pay attention," she shushed him as she put a hand on the latch. "You can watch and weep—I'm good."

He flashed a high sign, ducked into the bedroom and pulled the slider closed.

Josie cinched her robe sash and opened the door.

"Hi there," the woman giggled with an abashed grin Josie had come to recognize as a prelude to easy money. "I saw your sign."

"Great. Come on in." She ushered the woman inside and motioned her to sit on the settee while Josie finished her toast and studied her customer. This gal had a beady-eyed eagerness—probably having an affair with some used car salesman and needed some mumbo-jumbo high sign to pack up her knock-off jewelry, ditch the girdle and dump her old man.

Josie uncovered the crystal ball, sat down and tucked her legs under her butt Hindu fashion. "I'm Madam Josephina." Her stomach growled making her wish she'd had time to dig into the scrambled eggs. "It's twenty dollars for a straight reading."

The woman didn't even budge. Her purse remained closed on her generous lap. "What exactly is a straight reading?"

"You want to see into your future, right?"

"Not exactly."

This one was going to be picky. Meanwhile Josie's eggs were getting cold. Maybe she should think about putting business hours on that sign. What kind of geek would want her fortune read before breakfast anyway?

"What time is it?" Annoyed and not afraid to show it, Josie checked the clock on the kitchen wall—it was permanently stopped at twelve oh-two.

"Almost ten, I think."

"Well, I have other appointments this morning so what is it you want exactly?"

"I'd like to ask you questions about someone else. What can you tell me about another person's future?"

For twenty dollars, it wasn't gonna be much. Bargain hunters were always bad news in the psychic-science biz. "It depends on the aura of the person you're interested in. Is this person among the living?"

"Oh, definitely."

"I have to contact their spiritual guardian then. Some are more difficult to channel than others."

"Channel?"

"Connect with. I have to be able to link spiritual energies."

"Oh." She froze in a naïve stare that encouraged Josie to ham it up even more.

"Connect with the person's spiritual guide who charts their astral pathway."

"I see. Of course."

Belief was so often confused with understanding. "So who is this other person?"

"Well, how much would it cost exactly to do this?" Both plump hands still clutched her purse.

Because there was a serious chance that her eggs and bacon would be ruined by the time she finished with this reading, Josie added a surcharge. "If I can get through to their guardian—and there is no guarantee—and then channel into the fourth-dimension, universal psychic perspective—"

"—Oh my..."

"It'll cost you fifty-five dollars. Cash. In advance."

"What if you fail? I mean, do I get a refund if you can't get through?"

"Sure." No chance of that happening. People were such shmucks sometimes—how could anybody disprove an impossibility? If this chubby hausfrau had to miss her coffee and Dunkin Donut to slosh through the rain at ten in the morning to find out what her husband or boyfriend was up to, then it ought to be worth every cent.

The purse finally snapped open. She counted out the bills.

Josie stuffed the money in her pocket and concentrated on her prospect. For starters, she could tell the woman had lost weight recently—the seams on her blouse were stretched, but the material hung loosely across her boobs. Her makeup was thick, applied with an inexperienced hand—the garish, aqua shadow bled into her eyebrows, and her lipstick spotted her front teeth. She wore ugly discount-store slacks with an elastic waist and a pair of spike-heeled pumps at least three years out of fashion. On her left hand, the naked ring finger was grooved from a well-worn wedding band. Dangly earrings with bowling pin charms and Woolworth perfume completed the tacky tableau. She must be a refugee from the Farmers' Co-op, smitten with the hog feed salesman or the pump jockey at the Shell station.

"I can see you with someone. A new man has come into your life."

The woman sat up straighter and pressed her fingers on her chubby knees. "Yes?"

"You have strong feelings for this man."

"Yes, yes. That's him."

Josie looked up and drilled her with a hard stare. "This is the person you want to channel through their astral guardian."

"Oh, yes...yes. That's the one."

"I am getting a sense of conflicting passions—romance...lust...adventure. I also see confusion...frustration."

The woman covered her face with both hands and heaved a sigh of relief. "Oh, god! I knew it. Thank god. You got through to his guide, didn't you?"

Josie squelched a grin. This was too easy. People were so unaware of their own psyches. They radiated clues like heat waves from a Miami window shade and then seemed amazed when Josie came up with something close to the target.

"I sense a feeling of doubt," Josie went on, sniffing the air. Too bad she had left the last piece of toast on her plate—she hated cold toast. Probably soggy by now. "You want to ask a very important question, am I right?"

"Oh, yes. That's it. Yes."

"I see the initial T." That was safe. Going with the most common letters never failed. Every person on the planet had someone close with the initials E, D or T. Just like poker, this game was all about odds. It wasn't a revelation; it was just common sense. Something most of her customers lacked. "This T is very close to you."

The woman's eyes widened in anticipation. "It's Tom…it's my Tom."

"Has the spiritual guide contacted the right guardian soul?"

"Oh, yes. That's him. What is he telling you about Tom?"

She might as well have described his dick to Josie her infatuation was so obvious. Pitiful. Her husband must be some German-born, red-necked farmer with manure on his boots and tobacco juice on his chin. Probably milking Bossy right now or shoveling cow shit in the barn. Pitiful.

"Tom's head is full of many things," Josie hedged as her stomach growled.

"He's thinking about me?"

"Business, financial matters."

"Not any romantic thoughts at all?" she pouted.

"With this man, money always comes first in his thoughts. He's had many lovers." She felt like bopping this asshole, whoever he was. He was going to hump this silly woman until he got bored and then dump her like sour milk. Men were so goddam rotten sometimes. Cold eggs or not, Josie suddenly felt a trickle of compassion for this overweight, gullible figure flying solo on a doomed dime store fantasy. "Your affair does not occupy a special place in his life. You are not the first nor the last to share his bed."

"But what about his feelings for me?"

"He likes the sex." Josie drew back and folded her hands over the crystal ball. "He doesn't know your true heart—he doesn't touch your soul. It's the physical persona he is attracted to."

"Ohhh…I see."

"There is another man in your life who is very important to you. This other person is also very close to you."

Tears dribbled from the Cleopatra eyes, and mascara ran down both rouged cheeks. "What else does the guide say about Tom?"

"I see a strong love bond with this other person. I feel love and forgiveness in his heart."

"Forgiveness? Who needs it?" She dried her eyes with a handkerchief. "Look, since I paid to learn about Tom's feelings, do you have to talk about this other person?"

Josie ignored the sidetrack. "This person—I am hearing a name." Seeing actually. The woman's purse had initials swirled on the leather: PMT. "There are two T's in your life, pulling against each other. One loves you from the soul, with all his heart and mind, and the other loves only the flesh."

"Oh, yes, yes." She twisted the hanky. "Tom is so different from Eddie."

"Eddie is your husband."

"Uh huh." She dabbed her weepy eyes with a cold, disapproving stare.

"His guardian angel is obscuring the connection with Tom's spiritual guide. It's Eddie's earthly aura that appears stronger in my reading. His guide's astral powers are reaching across the psychic divide to deliver a message to you before it is too late to save your fate from ruin and misery."

"Eddie's guide is sending a message? Are you certain about that?"

Josie decided to step on the gas and pull into the passing lane. "I see a woman of great strength, a hard worker—her hands are aged and red from years of hard labor. It's someone who was very close to you, someone you've recently lost." Another safe bet—no way would this hausfrau prance all over the county with Tom Somebody while her mother was still around to point a shaming finger. "She fears you will lose your husband's love and begs you to sacrifice your lustful sins and reward Eddie's faithful devotion before it's too late." She bent over the crystal ball. This was the finale. It was certainly worth the fifty-five bucks if it kept this lady's panties on and shortstopped another tawdry rendezvous at some ratty Motel 6 off the Interstate. "Oh, no…" Josie moaned, fluttering her eyelashes.

"What? What?" She nearly toppled off the settee. "What do you see in there?"

Josie was hit with a sudden shot of amazing insight. The T on her purse must be for Torkler. Through the window she could see the tan Plymouth Fury wagon parked alongside her porch, and she remembered being at the Safeway checkout behind this broad-rumped woman, and in a brilliant flash the name sprang to her lips. Josie could recall the clerk ringing up the sale and calling her dumpy customer by name: "Mrs. Torkler, can I get someone to help you out with these?"

And right out front was the same dirty, tan station wagon she had seen a half dozen times at the Safeway lot. Josie remembered watching the car loaded up with bags of dog food and canned corn. If this pathetic, star-struck loser had paid more attention to the people around her than to the box of mint crème cookies she ripped open at the cash register, she would have recognized Madam Josephina as just another shopper with holes in her jeans. Wonderful how the gifted brain worked so well in a tight spot. This was genius at work. Pure genius and an exceptional memory for detail that separated Josie Wallgood from the sleazy charlatans reading tarot cards and palms while puffing on a menthol butt and letting the cat shit stink up the house. Josie was a real professional. She worked at it.

"Mrs. Torkler, I can see it all clearly. Trust me. The spirits have seen the future, and they are warning you to change course before it is too late to turn back."

"Oh, my god! How did you know my name?"

"The spirits know all, Mrs. Torkler. Your departed mother is praying for your soul as we speak."

"Can't you keep my mother out of this?"

"I can't control the spiritual guides."

"Then tell me what I'm supposed to do."

"Eddie loves you, Mrs. Torkler. Your guardian angel is trying to keep Eddie from damning his soul to hell by committing the ultimate sin."

"You mean Eddie is thinking about doing something to Tom?"

"I can see bloodlust boiling in his heart. He's going to find out what's been going on behind his back. Your departed ones' spirits beg you to give up this sinful life and save your one true love before it's too late."

"How?" She sniffled into her hanky. "They must know I'd do anything for him."

Finally, a little nuptial loyalty. About time. "Don't worry. You came to see me in time. I can help Eddie save your marriage."

Her head snapped up, and her eyes flared like butane torches. "Eddie? Forget my husband. Forget my marriage to that dumb plodder. I mean Tom. He's the one in danger, right? If Eddie thinks he can hurt Tom and get away with it, I'll find a way to stop him with or without anybody's help."

"Look here, I'm warning you. You can't fool around with the psychic powers of the universe, you know. There are forces at work in the spirit world—departed loved ones charged with protecting and guiding you through this earthly life—who will not allow anything to tarnish Eddie's soul. He's the wronged party here."

She was barely chastened. "But what about Tom? He's the one I care about."

"Tom has no defending guardians in the spirit world. He is an outcast, a patron of the Devil himself." How bad could she make this guy? Old Tommy probably had a dose of clap, too, but she doubted the spiritual equivalent would wield the same damning effect. "You fool around with him in defiance of your astral advisors, and you're in danger of being cut off from your guardian angels' protection. You better think that over, Lady. Nobody survives in the spiritual world without celestial guides, you know."

"Who do these dead people think they are anyway to give me advice?"

"People whose spirits ended up on the right side of the astral plane because they listened to their celestial guides when they were here on Earth. You keep screwing with this Tom character, and you'll be in deep-dish trouble. They want me to pass along this warning, Mrs. Torkler. If you want my advice, I'd listen. Never ignore a spiritual signpost."

"But I love him! I'm absolutely bonkers about Tom. I want a divorce. Is he thinking about asking me to marry him? That's what I really want to know."

Josie snorted irreverently. "Marriage? I am getting so many names from the guides that I can't even repeat them all."

She blinked back her surprise. "Names? What names?"

Of all the bimbos, suckers, hookers and sluts Tom has pinned to the mattress before you came along, she was thinking. She clamped her eyes shut and feigned psychic concentration. "The spiritual guides are unveiling the signs. The mist is clearing. Through the fog I can see a K with dark hair and a P with a mole on her face and a C." She was monitoring her client's reaction. So far she hadn't fidgeted. "But there is one very special lady in his life. The curtain is parting slowly." She peeked and saw Torkler lean forward eagerly. "There's someone with false hair, cut short. A friend of yours. A classmate perhaps. I'm getting a J."

"*Judy?*" Her jaw flapped open in disbelief. "Is it Judy Thrillspeck?"

"Your cosmic aura appears as a triangle with three T's which completes the sign of the astrological omen."

"He slept with *her*? The sonuvabitch! I remind him of *her*? That bitch?" Her eyes bulged, and her cheeks were as red as Roma tomatoes.

"I see a vision of Tom and Judy in a car. They are embracing—"

"—He screwed her in the Oldsmobile?" Her spit showered on Josie. "That bastard! I can't believe it. She's at least forty-pounds overweight."

"The picture is fading." Her belly was gurgling like a stopped-up drain. Cold toast and bacon seemed easier to stomach than trying to steer this stupid woman out of the trouble she didn't even know she was in. Josie sat up and covered the ball with the velvet drape. "That's all I can see for now."

"That cow. I oughtta rip her hair out by its black, bleached roots."

"The spirits have given you a warning, Mrs. Torkler. Ignore it at your peril."

She got up, slipped on her jacket and grabbed her purse. "Well, I guess I'll have to figure the rest out by myself."

"Maybe you should give this some more thought before you take any drastic steps. Why don't you come back for another consultation to see if the guides have found a solution to your problem?"

The woman smiled indulgently and hugged her handbag against her chest. "At these prices, Madam Josephina, I think I better work this out on my own." She stepped off the porch and took out her car keys. The sunshine brought out the henna highlights in her frizzy hair. "Maybe I can keep Tom and Eddie both. It's always smart to have a back up, don't you think?"

Josie shrugged. "Suit yourself. I've told you what your guardians advise."

"See, heaven isn't really important to me. So many bastards I know were faithful churchgoers, and I don't even want to be on the same planet with those jerks. Like my mother-in-law for instance. So if Tom is such a sinner that he doesn't make it, then that's okay. It only means we have a better chance of being together in the afterlife if we're both sinners, right?"

What a trivial, obstinate woman. What did either of these guys see in her?

"And maybe if I run off with Tom, Eddie will still take me back if things don't work out. After all, I do have to worry about my old age, don't I?"

"I'd recommend another consultation, Mrs. Torkler. This is a complicated matter, and you definitely need spiritual guidance."

She opened her car door. "If Judy thinks she can hold onto my Tom, then she's got another think coming, Madam. I have a few tricks up my sleeve I haven't even thought about using. We'll see what that fat, bleached slut thinks about that."

"See ya then."

"Bye. And thanks, Madam Josephina. You've helped me a lot." She got in, started up, and drove off.

Josie closed the door and sat down to her cold breakfast plate. Goldie jumped up on the table and snagged a rasher of bacon. Josie didn't have the heart to scold her. Sometimes people were so mean spirited, she just lost all heart for her work.

"Damn it," she cussed as Goldie leaped off the table dragging a bacon rasher. "Now my whole morning is trashed."

Cain came out and turned on the gas burner. "Babe, you're somethin'. You really had her snowed, you know that?"

"It was penny ante. Dumb bitch. My eggs got cold."

"The way you worked her for the dough. How'd you figure out all that stuff anyhow? You got some kinda talent." He searched for the right word. "Like a gimmick or somethin'. How do you pull all that shit outta your head like that?"

She savored the admiration reflected in his gaze. "Trade secrets."

He slapped the frying pan on the stove. "You're a real pro, Babe."

"Thank you," she acknowledged with not even a hint of modesty. "I told you I knew what the hell I was doing."

"You're a real big-leaguer. I'm impressed." He cracked an egg and watched it sizzle in the pan. "Impressed the shit outta me, Josie Girl."

"She was easy."

"I gotta know how you do it—is it like ESP?"

"Don't be such an idiot. Of course, not. It's brains." She tapped her temple. "Brain power, deductive reasoning, reading people. I can read em like you read a T and A mag. It's my profession."

"Like readin' the hitter, right, Babe?"

She shrugged. Somehow baseball just didn't seem to be on the same psychic level.

"Well, I'm impressed. Whatever it is, you got it, Babe. You got those suckers right where you want em."

"Was there ever a doubt?" She reached for the cookie jar and counted her stash. "Two hundred and fifty-five dollars in house money. Not bad."

"And it's gonna get a whole helluva lot better, Josie Girl."

She had suckered that frump into paying twice the going rate for a load of bullshit she didn't even want to hear. And she'd probably be back for a straight twenty-dollar reading later—after Tom dumped her ass in some lousy motel, and her husband wised up enough to hire a good divorce lawyer. That ought to be a lucrative reading. But this was small fry. The big catch, Hobart and Farrah's gig, was going to propel her into the majors. Cain had blown his chances to make it up to the Bigs, but Josie was just getting warmed up.

12

Josie perched her reading glasses on her nose. "Start from the beginning now and tell me what you know about Max." She flipped her tablet to a fresh page and tapped her pencil on her knee, waiting for Farrah to put down her cup.

"Well…" Farrah began with a little, comfortable sigh. She had already counted out one-hundred dollars in cash and handed it over to Josie. Then she made a pot of mint tea, took her marionberry pie from the oven and cranked open all the trailer's jalousie windows to let the marsh breezes cool them off. Once she got through this interview, told Josie all she needed to know about her father, then she could begin to relax. She had definitely done the right thing asking for professional help. "You already know Max was killed in the Korean War and was awarded medals for bravery."

"Right." Josie nodded, eager to hurry Farrah past the basics.

"Well, he and my Mom met during the summer of 1950 when she was spending her school vacation with her big sister—that's my Aunt Philippa. We call her Philly. She lived in Oakland. She was a school teacher."

"Uh huh." Josie hoped she didn't have to scale the entire Swidnik family tree. All she needed was just enough information on Max to make her exorcism believable.

"Anyway, my mom met Dad at a carnival ride. They shared the same car on the Tilt-A-Whirl, I think it was. Corny, huh? I loved hearing Mom tell me that story. Dad was really a good-looking guy, I guess. Mom really fell for him even though he was older than her. He dropped out of college to join the marines. He was from Chicago. The Korean War was just starting up then, I think. He was stationed in California, and he and Mom started seeing one another.

My mother's foster parents weren't that eager to get her back, so she stayed on with my Aunt Philly in California when classes started. She and Dad were dating, and pretty soon things were really deep between them so they got married right after Mom graduated high school.

They didn't have much money, of course. The marines paid next to nothing. So they rented a little place near the base until Dad got shipped overseas." She played with a strand of springy hair while she patted her belly. "Mom didn't know it, but she got pregnant with me before Dad left. When she wrote and told him she was expecting, I guess he was pretty excited. Anyway, Mom moved back to the Midwest with Aunt Philly who got a job teaching at a university. My Dad was home for awhile on leave—I think it was right after I was born. And then he went overseas again and got killed when I was ten-months old. And you remember I told you the rest?"

"About the mix-up with the remains?"

"Yeah. They notified my mom after she had buried Max that they had made a mistake, and it wasn't my dad in the coffin they sent back. So all she had were his dog tags. And we still don't know where his remains are, Josie."

"Uh huh." Josie scribbled a few notes, mainly for Farrah's benefit. Josie had an excellent memory for details. The notepad was mostly for show. "So then your mom married this Dennis person, right?"

"Dennis Poole. I was about six-years old, I think. We moved to Dayton, Ohio."

"That's where they make the cash registers, right?"

Farrah's eyes brightened. "Far out, Josie. Are you from Dayton, too?"

"Never been out of the Northwest. But I know that's where Orville made bikes not airplanes, and the battery king dude lived next door to the cash register guy."

Farrah blinked, not sure she had an apt sequitur for such Osterized observations.

"So what about this Dennis?" Josie went on without a hitch.

"He's my step-dad, but I haven't seen him for awhile. Him and mom separated a few years ago. I think he's in Utah or Nevada somewhere living with a lady who has a bunch of kids. I'm not sure exactly where really."

"He and your mom didn't get along, huh?"

"He drank a lot."

Josie didn't miss the hesitation in Farrah's reply. She honed right in. "How about your mom?"

"She drank some, too. But, Josie, I think it was just because she had lost the love of her life when my dad was killed. I know she just freaked for Dad. Her and Max were so much in love. I always thought Dennis was a little jealous."

"They used to fight about Max?"

"Sort of."

"So how come you split?"

"I guess I just wanted to find out things for myself. My mom was pretty sick. She was drinking more, and she and Dennis were fighting all the time, and I just sort of felt like I could do better on my own. So I split."

"You dropped out of school?"

"My junior year at Antioch. Mom was going back to Chicago, and Dennis was moving out. I didn't want to go to Chicago with Mom. I swear, Josie, I didn't know how sick she really was. I knew she had cancer, but I thought they stopped it. I wouldn't have taken off if I'd known how bad it was. I went with some friends to California and joined an artists' commune in Marin County then finally got to Phoenix and worked in a gallery for awhile until I heard there was a really groovy thing going down in Yuma. That's where I met Hobart."

"Right." No use going over that sappy story again. It's not like it was Cary and Deborah at the Empire State Building. "So did this Dennis do pretty well—where'd your mom get her money from?"

"I don't know really. Except I always knew about this special trust fund set up in my name. It provided the money to buy me a car, college. Everything. We went to Disneyland when I was eight, stuff like that. I guess Mom could get money from the fund whenever she needed it. Mom always dealt with her lawyer about that. I'm not sure where it came from. I guess I always thought it came from Dad's side of the family or something, maybe his GI insurance or the social security check I got as a dependent."

"That's not much. Was Max's family rich?"

"Not that I ever heard of. We don't keep in touch with them anymore. He had a sister who lived in Cleveland, but she's dead now. And I know his dad was a steelworker, but I think he's in an old folks' home somewhere. Maybe he's dead by now. We hardly ever saw him. The one relative I remember was his mother Magda. She was neat. She taught me to make Polish cookies. Granny was a cool lady, but she had a stroke a long time ago, and she's gone now."

"So how much money are you getting from your mom's estate?"

"About a hundred thousand."

Josie's face scrunched up like a toddler's puss at incoming pureed beets. Her eyes bulged. She dropped her pencil. "Where'd she get that kind of money? She musta had lots of life insurance, huh?"

"I guess, but Dennis got that, I think. He's still her husband legally. This other money is all from my trust fund. It was in her name, and when she died, it goes to me."

"Holy Jesus. That's a fortune—a hundred grand. And that's in cash, right?"

"A check probably. I'm splitting it with my Aunt Philly. She'll get half."

"Half? How come?"

"She's all I have left. And she was always so good to Mom, especially when they were little, and Mom had polio. Then she looked after Mom in California and brought her out to Chicago after Max was killed. She made sure Mom had medical treatment, too when she got sick. She was like my fairy godmother, always there for me. I guess I owe her a lot. And she's never married or anything. Her teaching has always been the most important thing in her life so she's missed out on having kids, real relationships and like that. But she made full professor and got tenure when there weren't many women doing it, and now she's a department head. You should hear her, Josie. She's a classical language expert, and she speaks French like a native. She's a translator, too, for medieval antiquities. Universities from all over the world ask her to work on their historical texts. Aunt Philly's really smart, but I guess she's what my mom used to call a spinster. Doesn't really have anybody left but me now. She deserves half, Josie. I'm happy to give it to her."

"Where's she at now?"

"The University of Chicago. She's been there for ages—since I was a little kid."

"You see her much?"

"I saw her last year at Mom's funeral. She gave me some money to get settled out here. She's just so cool. I love her a lot."

"Does she know you're giving her this money?"

Farrah shrugged and put her mug down. "I don't know for sure, but she'll find out when she gets the check."

Josie cleared her throat—her measly hundred-buck retainer stuck in her craw. "So why do you think Max is haunting you anyhow, Farrah?"

"I've thought a lot about this, Josie. I think it's because of the dog tags. He's come back for the tags. Maybe it has something to do with his spirit not being at rest until he claims those tags. What do you think?"

"Could be. You got the tags?"

"Yeah. Would you like them? I'd really feel more comfortable if you took them with you, Josie. If you don't mind."

"Sure. No sweat."

Farrah got up and disappeared in the back of the trailer. In a moment, she returned with a small, red velvet jewelry box. She passed it to Josie and turned away for a moment. "I feel better getting rid of those things."

Josie opened the box. A pair of beat-up dog tags minus chain nested in the satin lining. She examined one: USMC Pvt. SWIDNIK, MAXWELL G. O Pos. For an instant as she stared at the tags, Josie felt a burning sensation creep up her neck and singe her ears. She broke out in a sweat. Must be the heat from the oven. Not enough air in this sardine can. She stuffed the box in her bag and mopped her forehead.

"You okay?" Farrah seemed alarmed at Josie's sudden flush and sweaty mustache. "Can I get you something to drink?"

"How about something cold?"

"We don't have ice."

Oh, yeah, Josie remembered. They were in the tules, in the middle of a smelly swamp with a one-hole privy, a washtub and a woodstove as hot as a steam boiler, two jumps away from Hog Holler and Ma and Pa Kettle's shack no doubt. Hobart must be nuts. But maybe for a hundred-thousand dollar payday, he wasn't so stupid after all.

"How about some pop? You got any Coke?"

"Afraid not, Josie. I can make you some lemonade."

"Great."

Farrah fussed in the kitchen. She took out a knife, a fresh lemon and started to work. Josie was thinking more along the lines of frozen Bird's Eye concentrate served in a pitcher of ice. She was beginning to feel the jittery harbinger of caffeine deprivation. What she really needed was a tall glass of icy Coca Cola. It was time to go home.

"We saw him again the other night. Did Hobart tell you?" Farrah cut and squeezed lemons.

"He mentioned it on the way over. Said you saw some tracks around the pond."

Farrah put the knife down and wiped her hands. "Josie, it was him. He's here wandering around, looking for something—the dog tags. What else could it be?"

"Don't know yet." When Farrah gave her an inquisitorial frown, she stalled with a dose of her professional flimflammery. "I have to consult my crystal ball and do some readings, Farrah. This is complicated. I can't just snap out an answer, you know. It might take me awhile to figure this out."

"Oh, I understand. I didn't mean to rush you or anything. It's just that this is driving us crazy. We know he's here. I can feel him, Josie. Does that sound freaky?"

"No way," she lied. This would be easier the freakier Farrah got. Suckers who wanted to believe the most were the easiest to deceive. Josie wasn't teaching anybody any new tricks.

"Would you like sugar or honey in your lemonade?"

Neither, she wanted to say. Ice and lots of it. But her refreshment choices were limited. She'd stick with the old standard, C&H pure cane sugar from Hawaii. "Sugar's better." She grimaced as she saw Farrah scoop up raw, brown crystals from a paper bag and swirl it into the mixture with seeds, pith and all. This wasn't real lemonade—it was more like citrus stew, lemon slush. Yuk!

Farrah twisted the top off a twenty-gallon milk can on the porch and poured water to the top of her pitcher. She came back to the front and stirred while Josie regretted even being thirsty in the first place. Now she'd have to drink this slop.

"As soon as we get the money, we're going to have a well dug. That'll be great. The water is always so cold from a well, Josie. Here." She handed over a glass of cloudy liquid with seeds floating on top. "And this fall Hobart wants to put a bathroom in. We're gonna have a big hot tub on the deck in back, too. Far out, huh?" She sat down and poured herself a glass of lemonade.

Josie hadn't touched hers yet. "Yeah. Sounds great."

Just before the lemon concoction touched her parched lips, the door was flung wide open, and Hobart and his dogs came in together.

"Hey," he greeted them with a sun-burned smile. "They got an egg in the nest down there. You ever see a blue heron nest before, Josie?"

She was glad for an opportunity to ditch her glass. "We got lots of em around here."

"This is their first breeding season. That's why we don't want anybody messing around down at the pond." Hobart spied the lemonade. "Hey, you make enough for me?" He took off his battered Fedora hat and wiped a band of sweat from his brow. Josie could smell his redolent manliness from where she sat. He crowded in beside her while the dogs whined at the doorstep.

"Take mine. I've had plenty." Josie offered her lemonade.

He grabbed the glass and emptied it before coming up for air. He smacked his lips and wiped away a shred of lemon on his chin. "Ahhh…That was terrific."

"Well, I'm about ready to head back, I guess." She stood up and tucked her pad back into her bag. The pencil had rolled away beneath the couch and wasn't worth the trouble to retrieve.

Hobart put his hat back on. "Just let me wash up a little bit first. Unless you don't mind my stink."

"No problem."

Hobart Ames sweated more than any man she had ever known. He could have outdone the biggest cotton-picking buck on a Louisiana plantation. He had been outside chopping kindling and cutting brush, and his longjohns were soaked through with *eau de masculine*. He still had wood chips in his hair.

"I'll go start up the truck, Jo." He handed off the empty glass to Farrah and went out with both dogs at his heels.

Josie feigned regret at parting company so soon and headed for the door.

"Thanks for coming out, Josie." Farrah caught her in a hearty hug which Josie endured for only a moment. "You're a special lady." More hugs, and Josie felt like she'd been captured by a giant caterpillar.

She freed herself and jumped off the front step. "I'll get back to you when I've figured out what to do. In the meantime, if you have any other signs that Max is hanging around, let me know, okay?"

"Hobart can come right over and get you, Josie."

"Well, that's probably not necessary, but keep track of anything unusual, okay?"

As she climbed up into the truck, Farrah tugged at her elbow. "Are you going to try and contact Max in the spirit world, Josie? Do you think you can get through to him?"

"I'll do the best I can."

What stupid presumption, Josie was thinking as Hobart got behind the wheel. People were absolutely nuts. Crazy as gophers. Just imagine if there really was a way for psychics or whatever to get in touch with people who had passed over into the spirit world. In the first place, who would waste their time asking if Aunt Mabel really wanted Uncle Charlie to prune the rose bush? Jesus, she snorted when the truck sputtered to life. The first question they'd ask is how the hell does it feel to be dead? Maybe it's groovy—no more ingrown toenails, no BO, no hangovers, no stupid bill collectors, income taxes, zits, menstrual cramps or cold sores. And how can dead people still mess with the living? And if they could, then exactly what powers did they have? Could they predict Keno winners? Could they snoop on their ex old man and watch him making it with the next door neighbor right after the funeral? Was the spirit of your high school English teacher hovering over your ass while you sat on the pot doing the crosswords?

And how about God? Where the hell was He if this spirit world was able to open up long distance lines with psychics all on their own? Was He sitting on his Holy Duff just watching all this shit happen? What was it really like to be dead? Was their sex in the spirit world—especially oral sex and maybe celestial orgies? Think about it, she mused with a sardonic grin. Don Juan, De Sade, Errol Flynn, Caligula—hey, they were all toast, and if they had a thing going up in heaven, it could get totally far out and freaky up there.

Did God have sex? Was the spirit world like it was with the Catholics—the nuns and the priests getting it on? Did Jesus and Buddha make passes at angels or what? What about all the dead spirits who got taken out in their prime—Jimi Hendrix and James Dean for instance? Did they ever sneak back and diddle the living daylights out of somebody? What other sensible reason was there for coming back anyhow? It had to be either money or sex. Josie just couldn't think of another reason worth the trouble of spanning the Universal Void. Maybe wet dreams and orgasmic reveries under the covers weren't just dreams—maybe they were the spiritual masturbations of the departed.

Cripes, Josie thought suddenly as Hobart bottomed the truck bouncing over a rut. She could be thumped by the ghost of Harry Houdini or Bela Lugosi. She closed her eyes dreamily. Yeah, maybe even a real hunk like Gary Cooper, Steve McQueen or Victor Mature in that groovy Roman tutu. That was something to think about the next time she woke up hugging her pillow. Definitely.

Hobart pulled into the trailer park and stopped the lumbering truck at her Nashua. He stopped her from jumping out. "So what do you think about all this, Jo?"

"About the ghost coming back to haunt you guys?"

"I thought you said it was all bullshit. You know—smoke and mirrors."

"Yeah, but sometimes there is real, unexplained psychic phenomena, Hobart. You ever hear of the Loch Ness Monster or the Abominable Snow-man?"

"Those aren't supernatural ghosts, Jo—they're some kind of mutant species scientists just haven't discovered yet."

"Well," she defended herself, "that's what this is maybe. Scientists don't know everything and neither do I. I think this is something real, Hobart. Something or someone from the other side trying to communicate with Farrah."

"Honest? You really believe that, Jo?"

"Sure," she said with a piety even a Hoover vacuum cleaner salesman would envy. "You know I'd never charge you guys if I didn't believe it was a real haunting."

He scratched his cheek. "I guess I just don't know what to think. I can tell you that those tracks going down to the pond, coming from nowhere—that freaked me out completely. You understand where I'm at?"

"Don't worry about it, Hobart. I'm gonna get this all straightened out." She clambered down and shouldered her bag. First thing she had on her mind was raiding the restocked Norge and sucking on an ice cold Coke.

"Hey, Jo!" He had to shout to make himself heard over the gasping and groaning of the engine.

"Yeah?"

"You know Farrah is getting some money from her mom's estate, right?"

"Yeah. Farrah told me." No need to appear greedy.

"Well, it's a whole lot more than I figured it would be. So whatever you need, Farrah has it. How much is this gonna cost exactly?"

Josie looked up and tried to appear pensive. In this business, there were always change orders, extras and additional billing opportunities. "As soon as I make a connection to the other side, I'll need at least a thousand. Then we'll go from there depending on how it goes. This is really asking a lot, Hobart. Establishing a psychic conduit with the spirit world isn't an easy thing. It even has some risk, you know."

"Risk?"

"Yeah. The living and the dead don't co-mingle, do they?"

"Guess not."

"Well, there's a good reason for it. It's dangerous for one thing. Unless I'm very careful—and maybe even if I do everything right, it still might happen."

"What?"

"The wrong spirits might come out and take over the transmission. That's pretty scary. I just don't know what might happen."

"Like what? You mean something might happen to Farrah?"

"That's what you're paying me for—to make sure that doesn't happen. Not all the spirits are benign. In fact, some are real bad-asses."

"Then you do believe in this stuff. Jeez…"

"Only when it's real, Hobart. And this shit is so real it scares me." She was pleased with her melodrama so far.

"Can you guarantee that Farrah won't be in any kind of danger? She's my number one concern."

"Hey, I'm the one taking the risks. I'm the one in danger. It's my ass on the line, Hobart, not Farrah's."

"Sure, Jo. Then I wish you good luck. And whatever you feel is fair, we'll pay. It's worth it to get rid of this thing. It's driving Farrah nuts."

"Trust me. I can do it. But it's not easy. It can't be done overnight, and I have to charge enough to cover the possibility that I might not be able to work again for awhile."

"What do you mean by that?"

"Well, it just takes everything out of me when I channel to the spirits. It sort of drains my brain. I can't see a thing for awhile, that's all."

"Well, whatever's fair, Jo. We trust you." He shifted the truck into reverse.

She waved good-bye and climbed up to her porch.

Hobart backed up and bumped down the road. His old GMC clattered, smoked and backfired like a steam donkey. Maybe when the money came, Hobart could get a new truck—one with two doors, glass in the windows and a heater that worked.

13

Bradley Hammaker popped a breath mint in his mouth as he trotted across the street and unlocked the Mercedes. He tossed his briefcase on the seat and fit his key in the ignition. When the engine hummed to life, he checked his appearance in the vanity mirror, straightened his tie and smoothed his hair. Then Bradley pulled the sleek sedan away from the curb and headed toward Jackson Park to keep his appointment with Professor Philippa Mooney.

The afternoon sun was fading. There was a chilly wind blowing in from Lake Michigan. The staked trees along the avenue shivered in the breeze as bits of trash rose in brief flight to sail over the parked cars. Bradley felt the liquor burning a hole in his guts. He should have had a proper lunch today. No matter. Tonight Angela, his socially adept wife, was taking him out to dinner with Vic and Ramona, longtime bridge partners and pals. He'd put away a decent meal at the club and feel fine in the morning.

He slowed the car to a creep as he came to the intersection and looked for address numbers. Once he found the apartment house, he swung around the block to search for a parking place. If he was lucky, he could be in and out within an hour. Glancing at his watch, he saw it was only five after five. Right on time.

He hadn't had time to shower at Loretta's. Her bathroom had a tub streaked with soap scum and hair dye, a rust collar around the drain, chipped tile and blackened grouting. He didn't like to use Loretta's marginal accommodations, but their hurried, humid couplings made a parting absolution necessary. Not today. He had arrived in a piss poor mood, depleted from the Chalmers case. The stress had taken too much out of him. That was his excuse when he saw the false sympathy reflected in her slate stare. She liked seeing him defeated. To hell with her. To hell with Loretta Pultz and her goddam superior attitude.

Truth was, he didn't need her anymore. Whatever it was that had enticed him to her tacky boudoir had simmered out a long time ago. Conscience and a sense of cavalier decency kept him coming back one afternoon a month. After their first few trysts with moments of sheer exhilaration and pride as he made her moan with pleasure, he'd focused on her baser qualities and wondered how she'd attracted him in the beginning. Didn't matter now—that was all over. He doubted if he'd even bother to call her again.

He spotted a vacant space at the corner and stopped. Shifting into reverse, he backed into the slot perfectly and turned off the motor. And if she called him? They always called. Long after it was clear he wasn't coming back. Ego. That's what it was. Feminine ego. They ought to know by now they were just a pastime, a time filler, a change of pace, a professional prerogative, an eclectic hobby. Nothing serious.

Bradley looked at the file once before getting out of the car to make sure he had the address right. Satisfied he was in the correct spot, he locked the Mercedes behind him and walked around to the entrance of the Varsity Building. Professor Philippa Mooney lived on the third floor of an art deco mausoleum with Chrysler Building slashes chiseled in terra cotta valances over the arched windows. Blue and yellow Turkish tile accented the lobby. The elevator had an out-of-order sign stuck to the door, so he walked up three flights and rang the buzzer. He was barely out of breath. Not bad for a man of fifty-four.

She answered the door, immediately ushered him inside a darkened foyer and followed him through to the living room. A big bay window looked directly out onto Jackson Park. There were potted palms, Chippendale furniture, faded Oriental throw rugs and heavy draperies which gave the place the ambience of a museum with musty carpet and linseed oil furniture polish. Probably as buttoned-up and archaic as the old maid herself, Bradley thought as he turned around and waited for an invitation to seat himself.

"Please, let's sit at the table, if you don't mind, Mr. Hammaker." She directed him to a dining room with an ornate sideboard and chandelier. The Duncan Phyfe mahogany table was bare except for a pair of baroque candlesticks. He took a closer look. The silversmith had sculpted a pair of delightful nudes with all the anatomically correct features.

"Excuse me, but those are absolutely lovely," he pardoned his prurient appraisal.

"They're a souvenir from Bruges."

He pulled out a chair for her, but she sat down across from him and indicated he should take the seat himself.

"Please, sit down, Mr. Hammaker. I have fresh coffee if you'd care for some."

"No, thanks." He snapped the locks on his case and retrieved the probate file. "I hope this won't take up too much of your time, Professor."

"I appreciate your coming to see me, Mr. Hammaker. It saves me a trip, and I'm grateful for your courtesy." She gave him a prim, fleeting smile and folded her hands on the tabletop.

"No problem. I'll just go over the papers you'll need to sign." He searched for the blue-tabbed document in the pregnant file.

"Take your time."

He fumbled with his papers, dropped his pen and misplaced his readers. Then he pulled out the wrong folder. Dammit—Philippa Mooney wasn't what he had expected. Not exactly the old maid type. Not the stereotypical prune-faced shrew with the orthopedic shoes, hair bun and body odor he had anticipated, some prim, scholarly recluse with no makeup, support hose, hair on her lip and a flat ass. Philippa Mooney was a surprise, and it made him distinctly uncomfortable. So much so, he had turned into an idiot with ten thumbs all of a sudden. The file he wanted was spilling onto the floor as he clumsily grabbed for it. "I'm sorry, Professor. I seem to be having a slight problem here."

"That's alright. Take your time. There's no hurry."

While he collected the documents, he glanced up to see her studying him with an aloofness he recognized in his judicial overseers. Her eyebrows had a high, natural arch that seemed to signify imminent disapproval. Prominent cheekbones and a broad, unlined brow spoke of an elegant poise. Every detail about her was perfectly tailored, chic with a subtle undertone of sensual charm he could not begin to define. She had green eyes that shone with the brilliance of liquid gemstones behind long lashes. Her skin was as fine as rare porcelain, radiating a natural blush rather than cosmetic artifice.

Her expression was set in a half-smile, the lips cutting a crimson gash in the pale face which formed no creases when she spoke. There was something about the portrait which struck him. A combination of the plaintive look in the eyes, the ivory complexion, the Patrician profile all brought to mind the same familiar features in a smaller, younger, more diminutive edition—Bibi.

Philippa's features were not as delicate as her sister's, rather she possessed a lithe energy in her willowy figure, long-stemmed legs and elegant neck which was more athletic than aesthetic. Auburn hair framed her face like an origami headdress, perfectly coifed in a style that flattered her aristocratic bearing.

He recognized her scent. *Emeraude.* His wife's perfume. This woman was nothing so much as the exact opposite of the person he had imagined from the voice on the telephone. Perhaps he had been lead by his own ingrained prejudices against spinsters and middle-aged professors and thus deceived himself into believing that she could not possibly resemble his former lover Bibi who had faded to a dim recollection now, frozen in his memory as she looked on the day they said good-bye twenty-four years ago.

While he reassembled the file and spread it on the table, Philippa fixed him with a riveting stare. "Mr. Hammaker, I understand that the only reason I am to receive a benefit from this trust is because my niece wishes to make a personal bequest on my behalf. Is that correct?"

"Uh, yes. Correct. Your niece has elected to make this a voluntary gift, Professor. She instructed her attorney in Oregon to give you half of the total proceeds from the trust. That comes to…" He hesitated as he sucked in a lungful of her perfume and consulted his file notes. "About fifty-thousand dollars in round figures."

"The amount isn't important. I want to know the reason for the gift. Tell me about Farrah. Is she feeling any pressure from her stepfather?"

"What kind of pressure?"

"Financial pressure. Surely you understand my question."

"Not that I know of." He sat back and tried to relax. His palms were sweaty as he surveyed his client. Philippa Mooney was fifty-years old, but she hardly looked it. She could pass for forty, forty-five for sure. She was a study in serene confidence. Hers was a common affliction of the professorial ilk, he thought to himself, trying to assuage his chagrin at being taken aback by her appearance. Professors were used to being in command, being the superior intellect among their charges. So were lawyers. Especially senior partners like Bradley Hammaker, Senior. He had planned on keeping this visit brief, simply dictate the terms of the bequest to a grateful client without a hint of adversarial attitude and leave without a second thought. He had been mistaken.

"Frankly, Professor, you should know that Dennis Poole did contact our firm and make himself a nuisance. He's been very upset about this. I want to be honest with you."

"I appreciate that."

"But this has nothing to do with Dennis and your sister's other assets. As you know, this trust was established solely for Farrah's benefit, and this disbursement is not contested. Dennis Poole has no legal standing as far as this trust is concerned. Your niece has every right to do whatever she wants with it.

I think it is a magnanimous gesture on her part to share the money with you, Professor Mooney." He swallowed a lump growing in his throat. Her eyes were as vivid as the headlands he saw blazing through the mist when he caught his first sight of Diamond Head so long ago. "Your niece must think a great deal of you."

"I love my niece very much. I have always tried to act on Farrah's behalf. You know that her mother Phoebe was an alcoholic."

It wasn't really a question, and he didn't want to appear to know too much. What he knew about Phoebe had more to do with memories of the golden girl with the plaintive eyes crying into her pillow than the hardened, defeated woman who had slid into depression, alcoholism and bad health much too early.

"Yes. I am aware of that. I'm sorry your sister died so young—it's a shame."

"She was an invalid emotionally when she married Dennis, and he gave her the crutch of alcohol to lean on. She should never have married him. But then Phoebe probably shouldn't have married anybody."

He didn't know what to say. He only nodded and tried to look away, pretending to study the room. Her eyes tracked him all the same.

"Tell me what you know about my niece. Have you ever met Farrah, Mr. Hammaker?"

"Uh, no. No, I haven't, but your sister spoke of her daughter a lot. Of course, handling Phoebe's estate, I have seen photographs."

"She doesn't look like Phoebe. She takes after her father, don't you agree?"

His heart was thudding, and his cheek twitched. The professor was holding his hand to the flame until the fire scorched his soul. "I understand he died when Farrah was a baby."

"Ten-months old. He went overseas when she was a baby and was killed in 1953. Max—his name was Maxwell Swidnik as you know, of course—was dark-haired like Farrah. Do you think his daughter bears a resemblance?"

Before he could blink, she leaned sideways in her chair to expose a framed photograph of Bibi and Max—a wedding picture. Phoebe was wearing gloves and a silly hat with a polka-dot veil, and Max was in his dress uniform in front of the courthouse steps. He couldn't take his eyes off the picture. It was as if time had stood still, and there was the Bibi of his youth reborn, as fragile as a Botticelli angel.

"I suppose she does take after him in some regards."

"Mr. Hammaker, I want to speak frankly."

He stiffened in preparation of a frontal assault on his privacy. "Of course, Professor, please do."

"I know that Max Swidnik was not Farrah's biological father."

He choked as saliva rushed into his throat in a flood. His voice cracked when he answered. "I beg your pardon?"

"My sister told me that she had an affair with someone at the marine base when Max was overseas. When she got pregnant, she knew it was her lover's child and not her husband's. Apparently Max found out, too. That was the main reason he volunteered to go back to his old infantry unit. He could have stayed stateside."

Bradley unbuttoned his collar and reached for his handkerchief. "I see. I see."

"I have no idea who this man was. Bibi would never tell me his name."

He shivered despite the heat. How in hell did Bradley Hammaker think he could have come to see this woman on her turf, fake emotional neutrality and breeze through this formality unscathed? How absurdly self-assured and naïve had he become after all these years? When had he ever taken this seriously, taken even a moment to calculate the impact this meeting would have on him? He had set and baited his own trap. What a goddam fool he'd been.

"Was he a marine?" He tried to simulate practiced indifference.

"Yes. I know that much, Mr. Hammaker. He was stationed at the base in Oakland. I think he was an officer. Bibi just wouldn't give me many details. She didn't want to involve him in any way."

"I see."

"I don't know the circumstances of it, but I do know she cared for him very much. I knew Bibi better than anyone. She was like my own child. I helped raise her after we lost our parents. She was taken in by a foster family, but you know how that is. As soon as I finished my education and got a job, I had Phoebe come live with me in California. I feel responsible for what happened." Her lips trembled. "It's all somehow my fault."

Without thinking about it, his hand came out and pressed over hers. "You mustn't think like that, Professor Mooney."

"She was so lonely when Max went overseas. They were newlyweds, and Bibi was so young. She was so insecure after being bounced around in foster homes, being sick. She had polio when she was nine. She limped a little. It took her a long time to walk without the leg brace."

He had first noticed the limp when she stumbled on a curb. He had stopped and looked to see if she had tripped. She only smiled and explained about the polio. To Bradley it only made this fairy child even more desirable, more vulnerable and made him burst with protective pride when she was lying in his arms.

"When Max went overseas, Mr. Hammaker, I was working on my master's degree. I was always in a rush, too busy with work, school. My studies and my teaching career were always number one priorities in my life. Unfortunately, I never let anyone intrude, interrupt my agenda with personal problems or demands. As a consequence, I didn't devote enough time to Bibi when she needed me. I rightly blame myself for what happened. Her tragedy was my failure as well."

"I don't think you can take any blame, Professor Mooney. After all, that was so long ago."

She took back her hand and glared at him. "Time has nothing to do with forgiveness or guilt. I am as remorseful now as I was when Farrah was born."

"What does this have to do with the trust fund Farrah is splitting with you, Professor?" He was eager to change the subject.

"I told you that I don't know who Farrah's father was. But of course Bibi did. She did communicate with him after Farrah was born. I know she did. I saw the letters."

His hands were shaking as he scooped up the probate file. "I don't see—"

"—They were from Chicago. From the Palmolive Building. I believe they were from an attorney this man had represent him in this matter."

"What matter?"

"Farrah. You see, Bibi got a monthly payment from this lawyer after Max died until her death. Surely you know the proceeds of the trust fund are from this money."

"Yes, I believe there was something like that explained to me. I understood she had initiated the trust with the GI insurance policy Max left her."

"Every month she received a check which went into the trust fund for Farrah. And anything she ever needed, she would contact this lawyer, and he would see she got it."

"I see."

"Good lord, Mr. Hammaker, don't you understand what I'm asking?"

"Pardon?" he stammered, pulling at his tie. "You're inquiring about the source of the funds in the trust?"

"Not at all. I'm asking you to find out who this lawyer in the Palmolive Building was who sent the money. I know he was acting on behalf of Farrah's father."

"It's possible, I suppose."

Exasperated with his deductive density, she tapped her forefinger on his sleeve. "Mr. Hammaker, I want you to locate that attorney and then find Farrah's biological father. It's that simple."

"Why would you want to involve yourself in that? Frankly, that's a privacy issue I'm sure your sister would not want you to breach. If she took pains to keep the identity of the child's father secret, then it seems we should respect her wishes."

"Respect her wishes? How well did you know my sister, Mr. Hammaker?"

He knew her so well he thought. Loved her harder than he had ever allowed himself to love before or since. Then after they separated, time slowly swept away the hurt and dulled the memories he had harbored so fervently. Once he got out of the Marine Corps and started practicing law in Chicago, he and Bibi had never exchanged another word, never looked into one another's eyes. All their correspondence had been by and through the attorney in the Palmolive Building: Judge Francis Lohman, an ex Illinois Supreme Court Justice, a fraternity brother of his father's. Fran was a man whom Bradley could trust with the deepest secret of his life. Bradley had not seen or spoken to Phoebe Mooney Swidnik Poole in twenty-four years. Not since the day they'd parted at the Oakland train station with Farrah snug in Bibi's womb.

"I'm afraid to say I didn't actually know your sister, Professor Mooney." He flinched slightly at the lie. "Our correspondence has been purely professional since I became administrator of her estate."

"Phoebe named you specifically in the will, Mr. Hammaker."

"And the Court approved the executorship."

Her eyebrows rose. "My sister named you out of all the lawyers in Chicago. I assume she had a reason. Don't tell me she picked your name out of the phone book."

"Not at all."

"You're not cheap. Most people even say your fees are scandalous."

"Professor Mooney, I can assure you we file a complete accounting of costs and fees with the Probate Court."

"I don't care about that. I only want to know about your connection to my sister."

"I believe your sister was referred to our office by another associate."

"Who?"

"I'd have to check my file, Professor Mooney."

"You don't know?"

"Not at this moment," he stalled, red-faced. He was accustomed to cross-examining witnesses, not being on the receiving end. He felt an urge to grab his briefcase and bolt for the door. He couldn't seem to take hold of the laboring oar with this woman. Liars were seldom in control when faced with competent counsel, and Philippa Mooney was good. He wouldn't want to play poker with her.

"Think." She drilled him with a penetrating stare until he had to look away.

"Uhm, I believe it was a colleague in the Hazeltine, Brown firm."

"Hazeltine, Brown and Polli?"

"Yes. If I recall…"

"They're in the Palmolive Building, aren't they?"

"Yes. I believe so."

"You mean to say you don't know where the Hazeltine firm is officed?" She nailed his wriggling, quibbling heart to the cross with one deft hammer blow.

"Uh, naturally I meant to say yes. I believe they're in the Palmolive Building."

"Then it ought to be a simple matter for you to locate the attorney who was sending these checks to Phoebe. You must know this man."

"There are a number of firms practicing law who have offices at that address."

"Don't use that condescending tone with me. Of course, there are a number of firms in the Palmolive Building. But we're not concerned about a number of law firms, are we? We're talking about a particular firm who referred my sister Phoebe as a client."

"Please, Professor." He held up a hand to stop her advance. "Wait, wait."

"The lawyer who handled the trust fund payments may even be the same attorney who referred my sister to your office. Isn't that likely?"

"I can't say really. Why is this matter so important to you?"

"Because I want to find the sonuvabitch who fathered Farrah and look him in the eye!" She stood up abruptly. "He broke my sister's heart for twenty-five years. He bought her silence with his money, Mr. Hammaker. He couldn't face up to being a father, marrying a little nobody orphan from Steubensville, Ohio. I'm sure he was someone well placed with money who thought Bibi wasn't good enough for him. The sonuvabitch never even cared enough to see his own daughter. Not once. That just killed my sister. I know why she drank herself to death at forty-six, Mr. Hammaker. I know who killed my sister, and I want you to find the sonuvabitch for me."

He sat there numbed to the bone, unable to speak or avoid her withering stare. The air he breathed seared his lungs. He couldn't think where he was—here with Philippa in a South Side apartment looking down on Jackson Park or back in Oakland in the steamy trailer, nothing but his boxer shorts on, sucking on a stubby Lucky as Bibi sobbed into her pillow.

"Well? What do you have to say?" she demanded in an icy tone.

He got to his feet, scooted his chair back from the table and holstered his pen in his jacket pocket. "This is outside my professional arena, Professor Mooney."

"Nonsense! You're my sister's lawyer, aren't you? The executor of her estate?"

"I feel we must respect your sister's wish for privacy."

"I'm hiring you, Mr. Hammaker. You can charge me whatever you want, but I am asking you to do this for me and my sister. If you have any true regard for her feelings, you'll help me."

"I don't know what to say. You place me in an awkward position, Professor."

"You could find this lawyer with very little effort, couldn't you?"

"There is the matter of client confidentiality to be considered. The lawyer client privilege applies to all members of the bar. I could never pry into the relationship between another attorney and his client."

"I'm suggesting that you do not need any sort of formal inquiry. For god's sake, I know you hobnob with those old boys at a club somewhere. Over a friendly drink or round of golf, I'm sure you could find out everything I need to know, Mr. Hammaker."

"Look, Professor Mooney, I would suggest you enlist the aid of a private investigator if you really want to pursue this. I can't help you with this matter. Believe me. I'm sorry."

She sat down. "All right. I will. Give me a recommendation of someone good."

"If you call the office tomorrow, I'll give you the name of someone if you're serious about going through with this."

"Of course, I am."

He took out the trust agreement and held it in both hands. His sweaty fingers smudged the paper. "I advise against it, Professor."

"Fine. I've heard your advice. But I can assure you, Mr. Hammaker, I am going to find this bastard. Farrah need never know anything about it. But this is something I have to settle on my own. I never got into this while Phoebe was alive out of deference to her, but now she's gone I'm going to say what I have to say to this miserable, cowardly sonuvabitch."

"If that's how you feel, then what can I say?"

"I think you've expressed your feelings adequately, Mr. Hammaker." Her eyes glistened with restrained frustration and rage. "I'll thank you for a recommendation of someone who can help me."

"Very well. Call my office at your convenience."

"I will. Thank you."

He directed her attention to the agreement and went over the text with her. All the while he read from the document, his heart was racing; his head ached. He felt she was looking right through him, nailing him naked to the wall with her unforgiving stare. She was like his worst nightmare—the ashen ghost of Bibi coming back to haunt him. He wasn't prepared for this. It wasn't fair. Not after all these years of careful planning and discretion. He was shocked at how easily the veneer was peeled back to expose his quivering heart. Twenty-four years, and today time was no protection from the past.

She finally took a pen, swirled her signature at the bottom of the legal document and accepted the bank draft he put on the table. They shook hands, and he left.

Outside Professor Mooney's apartment door, he switched his briefcase to his left hand, started for the elevator, saw the "out of order" sign and pushed open the fire door at the end of the hallway. When he took the stairs, a very pregnant young woman with all the grace of a penguin waddled down the narrow stairway ahead of him and blocked his path.

She looked up over her shoulder, laid a hand on her protruding tummy and smiled shyly. "Sorry. I move a little slower these days."

He took her elbow with his fingertips. "No problem. Can I help?"

"Thanks. It's stuffy in here, isn't it?"

"Yes, it is." He helped her down to the second floor where she grabbed hold of the railing to catch her breath. "When's your baby due?"

"Next month—the tenth. My doctor thought it might be twins I was so big."

"Your first?"

She beamed with undisguised pride. "Yes. My husband is hoping for a boy, but I'd like a girl first. What do you think? Do you have kids?"

The soles of their shoes made the steel stairway clang as they descended.

"Two boys."

"Oh. Did you ever want a girl?"

Her words stung him. Had he really shut that thought out of his mind for all these years? Had it never occurred to him what it would have been like to have a little girl in his life? His little girl. Maybe a blonde toddler who resembled Bibi or a daughter like this young woman to present him with a grandchild? "Yes, I suppose so."

"If it's a boy, we're going to name him Frankie after my husband, and if it's a girl, I want to call her Mary Janice. Janice is my name, and Mary is my mom's."

They came to the ground floor, and he opened the door for her. "So is this going to be the first grandchild?" he asked just to keep the conversation going until they reached the foyer.

"Yeah."

"Your parents must be pretty excited, huh?"

Her face clouded. "My Dad doesn't know about it."

"Why is that?"

She looked down at her belly mound. "Well, he and I don't talk anymore. He isn't really a part of my life."

Bradley felt a pang of guilt. As she walked with him to the corner, he couldn't explain his urge to intrude. "Are you estranged from your father?"

"Yeah. I guess."

"And you haven't even told him about the baby?"

She shook her head.

"You have to tell him. He has a right to know about his own grandchild. What's your baby going to say when he grows up and wants to know about his grandfather?"

"I don't know exactly."

"Whatever happened between you and your father—"

"—It was something awful. I can't even talk to him about it. It was disgusting."

They stood facing one another in front of the apartment building. Her belly nearly touched his jacket button.

"What did your father do if you don't mind my asking?"

"He was with a prostitute."

Bradley started walking. "Believe me, Janice, there are worse crimes a man can commit in this world."

"But that's so filthy—my own father with that disgusting woman. I can't even think about it." She pinched her eyes closed. "It's just so awful."

"Even a prostitute has a soul." He touched her arm gently. "Are you Catholic?"

"Yes."

"Have you confessed the sin of dishonoring your father?"

She looked up with moist eyes. "He's the one who should beg for my forgiveness for what he did."

"Life is a hard lesson for mere mortals, Janice. Try and be more accepting of failure and weakness. Very few of us manage to get through life with clean slates."

"But what he did—"

"—Forgive him. Get over it. Put it behind you. He's your father."

"I can't."

They were at the corner. "Jesus did. So can you."

She brushed a tear from the corner of her eye. "Do you know my father?"

"No. I'm just an interfering old man."

She returned his smile and looked at his briefcase. "You're not so old. My dad's a lawyer. Are you?"

"Guilty."

"I thought so. You look like a lawyer." They laughed together. "I wouldn't know what to say to him. I mean, I haven't even spoken to him since…you know."

"He's still your father. Call him up and start over."

"You think so?"

"Invite him over for dinner. Forget about what happened. Give him a chance to be a part of your life. You only have one father. That's all you're ever going to get—for better or for worse."

She halted at the curb. "I'd like to see him. I mean, I've thought about it ever since I got pregnant. We used to be real close. He always spoiled me a lot since I'm the only girl. There were just the two of us kids when my parents got divorced, and then after my brother died it's just him and me. My mom married a Navy guy and lives way over in Japan. I won't even let my uncle tell my dad where I'm living. It's been kinda hard, but I just couldn't face him."

"You remember the good times you had with your father?"

"Oh, yeah. He can be really funny even though he's real hard with people sometimes. You know, some of his clients aren't exactly—well, he has to be that way, I guess. But he was always so sweet to me. That's why I just couldn't handle this whole thing." She blew her nose with a Kleenex. "Why would he do something like that? So filthy and degrading."

"Young lady, don't bring your baby into this world without letting your father be a part of his grandchild's life. Every child deserves a chance to know where he came from, learn about his heritage. The rest isn't really so important in the grand scheme of things. Look into your heart and find forgiveness. He loves you—he's your father. If the tables were turned, you know he'd never turn you away no matter what you'd done. Forgive him. Call him."

She held her bulging tummy with both hands. "You think so?"

"Janice, I know so." He crossed the street and didn't look back.

14

Farrah and Hobart sat stiffly in the slick, Naugahyde chairs opposite Alan Farnam's battered desk piled high with neglected marriage dissolution petitions,
DUI citations, civil motions and dog-eared State Bar Journals. He was approx-
imately three weeks' behind in his dictation. For Alan Farnam, BA, JD, attorney at law in general family practice in Silverton, Oregon, pleadings sliding
across the court clerk's counter for filing minutes under the statutorial dead-
line were no big deal.

Farnam operated out of an old hardware storeroom semi-redecorated for
office tenants. There were no street level windows. Steep stairs lead to the third
floor facilities where there was a Standard stool and basin crammed in with his
old file storage boxes. Out front, seated behind a steel desk salvaged from the
military auction at Swan Island in Portland, was Myrtle Mudsunk, his able secretary who had been with him for the past sixteen years. She could type out a
discovery motion or a community property settlement agreement in less time
than it took Farnam to dictate the guts of it. She was a pearl. A real legal eagle
for whom no fewer than a half dozen, established firms in the valley had
offered her a substantial salary increase to relocate. Her unswerving loyalty to
Farnam was partly due to the fact that he never treated her as a subservient
employee. They were partners. And they worked well together. His legal acu-
men along with Myrtle's organizational talents kept the practice on an even
keel.

Alan Farnam sat with his weighty paunch pressing against the desk drawer
and adjusted his horn-rimmed glasses. He was sweating despite being in the
mainstream of the Westinghouse fan buzzing away on a file cabinet behind
him. At least sixty pounds overweight, bald with red, pointy ears and a nose

like a Model T horn, he resembled a dissolute Elmer Fudd. But his heart was pure gold, and all his longtime clients would never think of going to anybody else when they had a problem. Certainly not the suave pinstripes in Salem, the State capital. No slick shysters for these plain people. Alan Farnam was plenty good enough for them.

"Okay, Farrah, I think we have everything ready here." He looked over the documents accompanying the Chicago bank draft he had received in his morning's mail. "You'll need to deposit this check in a bank and wait for the funds to clear before you can actually draw on the money." He peered over the rims of his glasses. "You understand that?"

"That's fine."

"This is a lot of money. Money carries a lot of responsibilities. You have plans?"

"Well, Hobart could use a new truck."

Hobart leaned forward. "Not a new one necessarily. Just one with a little more reliability, that's all."

"That's sounds like a good idea. That old Jimmy of yours looks like it's over-due for Tony's." That was the local junkyard. And there were plenty of rigs behind those barbed wire fences in better shape than Hobart's old wreck. "Well, if you'll just sign here, Farrah, the check is in your hands." He slid the papers around for her to peruse quickly. They had already gone over the fine print. She took the pen and added her name at the signature line.

"Thank you, Mr. Farnam."

"Alan's good enough, Farrah. I hardly know who Mister Farnam is around here." He pulled out a carbon of the document, folded it twice and handed it over. "Now there's one more thing, Farrah. There's something else I received for you. I got a letter postmarked from Chicago with a typewritten note explaining that your mother had instructed it be sent in the event of her death. Your mother apparently had entrusted this to somebody's safekeeping for delivery to you after her estate had been settled. And that's just what's been done." He reached inside the manila folder and took out a sealed envelope. Without another word, he reached across the desk and placed it in Farrah's hesitant hand.

"What is it?"

"Just what I told you, Farrah. You know as much as I do. I imagine it's something from your mother she wanted you to read after her death."

"Gee, Mr. Farnham—I mean Alan—it's dated August 24, 1952."

"I saw that."

"That's just four months after I was born." She looked to Hobart. "What do you think it is?"

"Open it up."

"I don't understand why she wouldn't have told me about this before. Why would she wait for twenty-five years to tell me something important?"

"Oh, this is a pretty common thing. Don't worry about it. Lots of people with the foresight and common sense to prepare their estate for their heirs go to the trouble of leaving some sort of communication or directive to be opened after their death." Farnam failed to abate the anxiety creasing Farrah's face and softened his voice to an avuncular hush. "Don't worry, Farrah. She probably just wanted to say something about how special your birth was to her and what a fine young lady she hoped you'd grow into. Something like that. Don't worry about it."

"You think so?"

"Look at it as sort of a gift from beyond the grave. Nothing to be upset about."

She handed the envelope to Hobart. "I don't think I want to open it myself. Hobart, will you please take a look?"

"I think you should be the one to read it first, Farrah. Your mom meant it for you. Don't you think so, Mr. Farnham?"

"That's up to Farrah."

"I don't want to. What if it's bad news? What if Mom was keeping something from me, something that might hurt me if I found out?"

Alan Farnam removed his glasses. "Come on now, Farrah. This isn't anything bad. Don't worry about it. In fact, there's no need to open it at all until you feel like it." He nodded to Hobart who laid the envelope back on Farnham's desk. "No rush. Whenever you're ready."

Farrah got to her feet. "You're right. I think I'll wait a while, if you don't mind."

"Fine. It's yours. You can do whatever feels right to you, Farrah. After all, it's been sitting in somebody's safe for twenty-five years. I don't think a little more time is going to make much difference, do you?"

"What do you think it is, Mr. Farnam?"

He tugged at an earlobe and fiddled with his knit necktie. "Oh, just a personal letter probably. Nothing earth shattering. I wouldn't look at it as any more than that, Farrah. A little keepsake perhaps."

"Well, I still think I'll wait to open it later. Thanks for all your help. Is there anything else I have to do?"

"Nope. This is it."

As they got to the door, Hobart stuck out his hand. "Thanks, Mr. Farnam. We appreciate your help."

Farrah gave Farnam a warm hug. "I'm glad my Aunt Philly got the money. I feel good about my decision to share it with her. I think Mom would have wanted that, and I owe her so much more than money."

"I think it was a very generous thing for you to do, Farrah. Something I don't think I've ever seen the likes of before in my practice. You're quite a little lady. I wish you and Hobart all the luck in the world."

They shook hands all around and left the airless office for the street. The couple walked to the corner, crossed the street and entered the cool foyer of the First State Bank. Farrah endorsed the draft, opened an account and went out with a savings passbook and a checkbook.

"This may sound silly," she said to Hobart as they climbed into the old truck, "but this is the first time I've ever had a checking account."

"I don't like turning that money over to the bank. They never do anything good with anybody's money. I'll like it better when we can get the cash out ourselves."

"That's a lot of money, Hobart. I'm not sure it's safe to keep it out at the trailer."

The GMC started with a bang and a lurch as the chassis shimmied and bucked when they started off.

"I told you from the first, Farrah, I don't like the idea of all this money anyway. It'd been alright with me if you'd given the whole shitaree away."

She snuggled closer and gripped his thigh. "Hobart, just think of the new truck you can buy. No more busted out windshield in the rain. And we'll each have a door." She laughed as they took a turn, and she had to hang on to the seat frame to steady herself in the roll. "And we can put in a well so we can take showers and hey!" Her eyes lit up. "We can build a sauna behind the woodshed and maybe get a washing machine."

He watched her exuberance grow as her shopping list expanded, and by the time they reached Cully Marsh road, he was grinning along with her. "I'm gonna build you the most beautiful bathroom in Swamp City. You can have a claw-foot tub with a brass faucet and porcelain knobs."

"Oh, alright! And I want an ice box."

He pecked her cheek. "You're gettin' mighty modern here, Woman."

She rested her head on his broad shoulder and sighed contentedly as the truck bounced by hillocks choked with berry vines, Queen Anne's lace and vine maple. The air blowing through the open truck was sweetened with the bursting blooms of budding trees, damp cedar bark and wetland muck as deep as the Cascade creeks. Another fragrant Willamette Valley spring was awakening from a long, weary winter sleep.

"What do you think I oughtta do about this?" She held the envelope up for closer inspection.

"That's up to you, Farrah. I don't see what the big deal is. Your mom probably just wrote a poem or something when you were little and saved it all these years. That's all. Just like the attorney said. I don't think it's anything to worry about."

"I don't know." She sighed wistfully and put the envelope in her coat pocket. "It just makes me so sad to think about it—what she must have felt like when she was writing it. Mom always seemed to regret so much in her life, Hobart. I can't bear to read it if she's being down on herself, having her heart broken by losing Max, being alone with a little baby to raise when she was almost a kid herself. Just holding it makes me feel bad. And like Mr. Farnham said, there's no rush to open it anyway, is there? Maybe when I'm feeling better about this whole thing, losing Mom and all, the cancer, my abandoning her—"

"—Don't get down on yourself, Farrah. We've talked this all out enough, haven't we? Look, you can't go around for the rest of your life feeling all this shitload of guilt over your mom. It'll mess up your life just like hers was screwed up."

"I know. But I do feel guilty about it. My mother didn't have a happy life, and she gave me all these opportunities to be my own person, to live the way I want, and I paid her back for all that by running out when she needed me the most."

"She'd want you to do what makes you happy, Sweetpea. That's all there is to life. She made her choices, and you've made yours. Nobody needs to feel guilty about anything."

"I suppose so. You can always put things in a better light. It makes sense when you say it."

"Well, trust me then."

"But the money and everything—it's from my dad really, and I've never felt comfortable with that. I don't really deserve it. I mean, Mom and Aunt Philippa were the ones who took care of me, loved me when there wasn't anybody else who cared. So I figure the money doesn't belong to me really, and you have no idea how good it made me feel to give half to my aunt."

"It was a really cool thing to do."

"There's time then, isn't there—to open the letter? Just in case it's something about my dad or how unhappy Mom was, something to make me feel even worse than I do already."

"Sure, Sweetpea."

"I think you should keep it. It gets me down just thinking about it, Hobart."

The truck careened around a corner, jolting both riders as it wobbled down the last few squiggles in the county road before turning off on the weedy path to their camp.

When they were stopped, Hobart rested both hands on the wheel. "What are you thinking might be in that envelope anyway?"

"You know."

"Something about Max?"

Her dark eyes grew somber. "I feel it, Hobart. You know what I mean?"

"Yeah." He drummed his fingers nervously. "Lately he's got us all pressed out of shape, Farrah. I don't think we oughtta dick around with this shit."

"What do you mean?"

"I mean that goddam piece of paper in your pocket there. It's already got you all freaked out on some kinda head trip."

"You mean just throw it away then?"

"No. Just maybe have a third party open it. If it's something harmless, your mom's blessings or whatever, okay fine. But if it's some shit about Max, maybe some real super-sized downer your mother was on, then we can decide what to do with it. Okay?"

"You mean have Josie open it and take a look first?"

"Yeah. Why not?"

"Why don't you take it over to her, Hobart? Right now. Here." She whipped out the letter and pressed it into his hand. "Take it. Tell her to find out what it says, and then she can let us know. Then I'll decide if I want to read it or not, okay?"

He slipped it into his shirt pocket. "Okay. On one condition."

"What?"

"Once we find out what this is about, we forget about it. Okay? We already got one pissed ghost bugging us, let's just not stir up anything else. Agreed?"

"Alright, Hobart. I hate this spooky shit. It scares me to death."

"Doesn't exactly make me feel too good either." He started the truck as Farrah slid out and waved good-bye.

He backed up and headed the GMC for the county road. When he geared down to make the climb back onto the pavement, the truck coughed itself to a shuddering halt. Its front wheels skidded on the asphalt, and the rear end slithered sideways.

"Shit!" He slammed on the brakes to keep from rolling into the ditch.

There was one good thing coming out of all this: Farrah's inheritance would mean burying this old war-horse in the junkyard and getting himself a truck with the ability to outrun a lame mule pulling a sled full of shit uphill.

The truck clambered on, rattling and smoking a lavender mistral that settled over the roadside brambles like fog. All the way to the Jewel Grove Trailer Park, there was a burning sensation in Hobart's chest where the letter lay unopened in his pocket.

15

Cain tossed his cigarette between his legs and stamped it out. When he looked up, a belching, farting old pickup truck with one door missing, no bumper and a busted windshield was aiming for their porch. He leaned out from under the Pinto's raised hood and wiped his greasy hands on a rag as Hobart stopped and killed the Jimmy's engine. It hissed and pinged as he jumped down and peered at the headless figure hidden in the bowels of Josie's old junker.

"Hi there. Jo home?"

"Josie?" Cain pushed the brim of his baseball cap up just enough to get a peek at his visitor. The guy had thick, bushy hair and wild eyes the color of blue marbles.

"Yeah. Josie Wallgood. I'm a friend of Jo's."

"She's up at the wash house doin' some laundry." Cain moved his crescent wrench back from its precarious perch on the fender and wiped a smudge of oil from his wrist as he bent down over the distributor. "You wanna beer while you're waitin'?"

"Thanks, but maybe I'll just run on up there. I got something for her to take a look at, that's all. Thanks. I'll see you later, Man."

"No sweat."

Hobart started back for the truck, turned around slowly and gave the Pinto a once over. A green sprout was growing on the parcel shelf. "Say, you trying to get that thing to run for Jo?"

"Yeah. Carburetor has more gunk in it than her old Norge. Battery's dead as a doornail, too. She don't drive it much, I guess."

"I haven't seen that thing running for six months at least. I offered to give her a jump, but she always just hitched a ride into town with me most times."

"You live around here?"

"Down in Cully Marsh. I used to live over there." He pointed to a concrete slab overrun with thistle, volunteer daisies and wild mustard. "I had a space here in the park for a couple years. I used to help Jo out when I could."

"Oh, yeah?" He stretched his body across the block to reach a spark plug wire.

"Well, nice talking to you. See you around, huh? You staying for awhile?"

"Just passin' through. Lookin' for work. You know of any jobs around here?"

"You a laborer?"

"Naw. I got a bum knee. Can't do the heavy shit anymore. What about odd jobs? Carpentry, electrical, like that. I'm pretty handy with a hammer and wrench."

Hobart had noticed the scars and knots on Cain's hands. The man was still halfway under the hood of the Pinto shielding his face from view. With the sun behind him and the baseball cap hugging his head, Hobart couldn't see much. "You a mechanic?"

"Just amateur, shade tree stuff." He held up a hand he realized Hobart had been studying. "Baseballs. I used to catch."

Hobart's eyes grew wide. "Far out. Really far out. What team you play for?"

"Just scrub ball—minor league stuff. Pacific Coast League. Busted up my knee and can't even run the bases. Can't take the squats no more neither since I tore the cartilage all to hell." He slapped his leg. "I got a few bumps and bruises, but I can still give a guy an honest days' work."

"Well, if I hear of anything, I'll look you up. As a matter of fact, I'm gonna be doing some work at my place. I could use an extra hand."

Cain squinted to focus through his cigarette smoke. "What kinda work?"

"Gonna drill a well, put in a pump house, add on to my trailer. You any good at plumbing?"

"In a pinch, I'm some better than nothin', I guess." He torqued on a nut and banged the end of the wrench on the fender.

"I might give you a call then. Five bucks an hour sound fair? Plus all the chow you can put down."

"Beer included?"

"As much as you want, Man, and we got homemade berry wine."

"Just beer—keeps me runnin' like a well oiled machine, Man." He grunted as he took another reef on the stubborn nut.

"Great. Later then, Man."

Cain never even looked up as he left.

Hobart got back in the truck and drove around to the wash house. He jumped out, went inside and located Josie pulling wet clothes out of an old front load Speed Queen washer. She turned around when he hailed her.

"Hi, Hobart."

"Hey, Jo. How's it goin'?"

"Great." She yanked out a pink bath towel, lifted her basket and headed for the dryer. She fed in her change, cranked the dial and set her clothes tumbling. "If you're here to find out about Max, it's too early."

"That's alright. Actually, I just dropped by to give you some news. We went in to see the lawyer today and got the money."

Josie tried to hide her excitement at hearing the cash was at last a material asset rather than just a promised windfall. "Far out."

"Well, the lawyer gave us the check, and then he gave this to Farrah." He handed her the crinkled envelope. He sank both hands in his ripped Levi pockets while Josie studied it front and back.

"It's not opened."

"Yeah. That's why I'm here. See the postmark date?"

"August 24, 1952. So?"

"So that's like four months after Farrah was born."

"And?"

"Well, we don't know what's in it, Jo. The lawyer said that some guy from back East had kept it in his safe, and that he wanted Farrah to get it after her mom died."

"So what's the big deal? It's just a letter, Hobart." She handed it back and leaned up against the humming dryer.

"We don't know what's in it, Jo."

"That's because you haven't opened it, Hobart," she scoffed sarcastically, pushing the sleeves of her cardigan up. "What's the big deal about a letter?"

"Farrah's afraid what it might say. Maybe it's from Max." He offered it again.

"Max speaking from the grave, huh?"

"Maybe. This thing has her so spooked, Jo. She's all torqued over her mom's death, quitting school and taking off for California—you know about all that, right?"

"I guess. Doesn't matter much."

"Well, it matters a helluva lot to Farrah. What she doesn't need right now is another downer trip to bum her out about that shit. We just don't want anything to do with it. So we thought it would be better if you just opened it yourself, saw what it had to say and then let Farrah know if she should read it or not."

Talk about easy money. This was like a fence post being paid for standing around all day. What saps people could be. Afraid of a letter? It might just as well be her mother's favorite flapjack recipe for pity's sake. She felt compelled to penalize people for such stupidity. "Okay. Maybe that's a good idea. It's been sitting around for twenty-five years, right? It's just a little spooky to have it come to light now, huh? Is that what she's thinking, Hobart?"

He heaved a sigh of relief. "Yeah. Like that. So will you just take it?"

"Done." It slid into her pocket.

"Thanks, Jo."

"I'll open it later when I'm in a proper frame of mind. If it *is* something to do with Max, then I need to prepare myself."

"Uh huh." He had absolutely no idea what Josie did other than gaze into that crystal orb of hers and make startling predictions and assessments that more often than not were right on track. How she did it, he hadn't the slightest clue. The fact that she was so damned irreverent about her prescient talents only made her more believable as far as he was concerned.

"We don't want to take any chances of blowing this thing at this stage. So I'm glad you brought it, Hobart. Really. This was the right thing to do."

"Thanks, Jo." He turned to go.

"Don't forget I need two-thousand dollars up front, Hobart. I can't start until I have the money."

He blinked. From a hundred bucks to two grand was quite a leap. And they hadn't even received any guarantees about anything. But at the same time, he knew how important this was to Farrah. And to Hobart money was only a capitalistic tool to be used for basic necessities. If Josie needed the money to help Farrah get rid of Max and restore some peace to his situation, then it was okay with him.

"Two thousand?" he echoed without much attitude one way or the other.

"This letter thing is extra. It could contain some heavy duty shit."

"Farrah can't draw any of the money out of the bank for a couple days, Jo. Then we'll get you the cash."

"I can't start until I have the money, Hobart. Be sure to tell Farrah that."

"I will." He paused at the threshold. "Do you need the money before you can open the letter, Jo?"

"This is all connected. It's all the same astral pathway. The letter is the same as calling out to Max's restless spirit."

"Then the answer is yes, huh? We'll have to wait to see what's in the letter?" There was a tinge of disappointment in his voice at not being able to discern the contents of the mysterious envelope and deliver the news to Farrah waiting at home.

"Until then, I'll keep the letter locked up in my personal strongbox, Hobart. It'll be alright. Besides," she added with a spark of her original inspiration for psychic babble, "if the spiritual guides are seeking entry of the dark souls into the earthly dimension through this letter, then we only gain strength by waiting them out."

"What was that?"

"Trust me." She patted her pocket. "Just trust me, Hobart. I know exactly what I'm doing."

"Okay, Jo. See you later." He scuffed his boot on the concrete sill plate. "Say, I stopped up at your trailer…"

She returned to her laundry while she sensed Hobart's stare boring into her backside. Josie could swear she detected a hint of jealous interest—just a touch, but Josie was good at picking up this sort of thing.

"I met that guy working on your old Pinto. He your old man, Jo?"

"Nope. Lost his job, and I let him work out a few meals for fixing the Pinto."

"Maybe I could use him when we start to fix our place up."

"Ask him."

"You don't mind?"

"Nope."

"Well, I'll get back then, I guess."

"Let me know as soon as you get the money. Then I can open the letter and get started on summoning Max's spirit."

She watched him leave. So Hobart had met Cain. Didn't really matter. She had warned Cain about not being too visible with any of her visitors. They had no idea what she had in mind for both Cain Reeves and Hobart Ames.

She smiled to herself. Power was so sweet. So sweet.

16

With her laundry basket full and the dryer tumbling the towels, Josie chuga-lugged the Coke she purchased from the vending machine. Then she hopped up on a dead washer and took out the envelope. Carefully turning it over, she examined the seal and studied the handwriting, got down, went over to a washing machine filling with hot water, lifted the lid and held the envelope over the rising steam cloud. Patiently she pulled back the gummy flap and carefully took out a sheet of plain paper.

She frowned as her eyes sped ahead of her brain at first. It wasn't a letter at all. It was a carbon copy of an affidavit, signed and sealed in Cook County, Illinois, on August 24, 1952. Josie read with her teeth biting her upper lip. She didn't even hear the sound of the dryer or the children playing outside the laundry room. She was fascinated.

Law Offices of Hazeltine, Sampson, Brown & Polli
Twelfth Floor, Palmolive Building
Chicago, Illinois

Est. 1871

Hon. Chief Justice Ronald Hazeltine	Carlyle S. Sampson, Jr., Esq.
Hampton Neely Brown	Quentin L. Brown III
Marion Marbody	Anthony T. Polli
Benjamin Coffin	Byrum Harvey, Esq.
David Schultz	Hollis Eberhardt II
Michael P. Ryan	Francis W. Lohman, Esq., of Counsel

AFFIDAVIT

I, Phoebe June Swidnik, née Mooney, being duly sworn, do swear and affirm that I am the natural mother of Farrah Lynn Swidnik, born April 20, 1952, in Cook County, Chicago, Illinois, who is my firstborn child. I further swear that Maxwell Grady Swidnik is my lawful husband, and that we were married on December 19th, 1950, in Marin County, California, and that Mr. Swidnik is presently serving in the Armed Forces of the United States as a USMC Private 1st Class. I do further swear that to my best belief and knowledge Farrah Lynn Swidnik is not the natural issue of our marriage and that Maxwell Swidnik although lawfully married to me at the time of the child's conception and birth, is not the biological father of my child.

I make this affidavit with the full knowledge and understanding that I do not wish to recognize the name of the true, natural father and that in the event of the dissolution of my marriage I do not intend to seek any financial reward, settlement, alimony, child maintenance payments or any other form of monetary stipend or allotment for the support, maintenance and care of Farrah Lynn Swidnik for so long as she remains a minor in my care and custody or in the event of her incapacitation, illness or any event resulting in her not being emancipated at the age of 21 years. I relinquish now and forever any and all claims against my husband Maxwell Swidnik for any terms of support whatsoever, of any kind or nature, after the date our marriage is terminated.

I swear that the foregoing is true and correct to the best of my knowledge. I make this affidavit freely, without duress, promise or obligation of any kind whatsoever.

Personally appeared before me Affiant *Phoebe June Swidnik* and swore to the foregoing in my presence this 24th day of *August,* 1952, in the County of Cook, State of Illinois.

Signed: *Phoebe J. Swidnik*   Witness: *R.B. Pester* Notary public
Lic. Expires: Nov. 14, 1954

F. Lohman, Esq.
Attorney for affiant

cc: Charles P. Plack
    Plack and Fetzer

Josie licked her lips and folded the affidavit. Inside the envelope was a glossy photograph. It was a wallet-sized snapshot of a man standing on a beach, squinting into the sun as he faced the camera. In the background was the Oakland Bay Bridge, the silhouette of a lazy gull caught circling over the water and a striped towel lying on the sand.

The man was good looking with very dark, thick hair so dense the part was hidden. His khaki pants were neatly pressed. His thumbs were hooked on his belt; the head tilted slightly, and a faint trace of a smile aimed at the photographer. Josie could see metal bars on the shirt collar. She held the snapshot closer to get a better look. There was also a class ring. His aviator type sunglasses hung from his breast pocket. He was an officer—strong, handsome, supremely self-confident—maybe even cocky. He had large hands, a broad brow, wide shoulders and big feet. Sasquatch size brogans anchored him in the sand.

Cain stuck his head in through the open window and grinned when he spotted her. "Hey. What's up?"

"Something very interesting."

"Oh, yeah? How much interesting?"

"A couple thousand at least. And a whole lot more maybe. I think we may have struck pay dirt, Cain. Let's celebrate."

"Suits me. You wanna spring for some bucket chicken and beer?"

"Sure. Only maybe we ought to eat in, okay? I got some serious thinking to do."

He cocked his head jauntily to one side. "Sure. Brain games, right?"

"Sort of," she teased, waving the envelope in front of her.

"Whatch you got, Girl?"

"A ticket."

"Yeah? Where to?"

"Anywhere I wanna go." She held the photo up to catch the sunlight. "Zowie! Forget the greasy chicken. Let's go for a steak at Stuart Anderson's, okay?"

"Do you hear any arguments from me?"

"Come on in and carry the laundry basket for me, will you?"

"No problem, Josie Girl. Don't wanna strain your psychic powers now, do we?" He smirked irreverently.

While she waited for him to go around to the front entrance, she took a second look at the backside of the photograph. There it was. She just knew this was going to be a bank balance in the making for her. She had always wanted to make a major league score, hit it big enough to get something going—maybe a booth at the State Fair, an appearance on *Bewitched* or even her own show, a write-up in *TV Guide*, signing autographs at international psychic conventions, a movie based on her best-selling book *Secrets of A Psychic Phenom.* Finally things were starting to go her way. And all she'd had to do was just wait for the knock on the door. Opportunity really did come to those who waited.

When Cain came in and hoisted the basket on his shoulder, Josie stashed the envelope in her sweater pocket and followed him back to the trailer. Things were different at the home front these days. Ever since Cain had moved in, there was so much space, it was like living in a double-wide. There was counter room in the kitchen now, even a space on the stovetop to set things down. The old Norge looked brand new with nothing crawling under its own power in the crisper bin. Even the freezer had been defrosted. Josie had never attacked the arctic tundra growing in there. As long as there was a slippery slot free for her lone ice tray, she was content. The beauty of Cain's housekeeping was that now there was room for two ice trays in the old Norge. More ice. More cold Cokes. Pure heaven.

She had the new color Motorola, too. Didn't really make much of a difference to her though. Cain staked out territory for every single baseball game broadcast on the planet. Josie had no idea there was so much sports trash on the tube. It seemed more inane than her soaps. Boring stuff, dragging on and on for hours when she was either badgered to come sit beside him and absorb more meaningless statistical data or pretend enthusiasm for what still seemed to her like a lot of nothing played out in agonizing slow motion. Lots of spitting, arguing, scratching and stalling while men threw balls at one another alongside the fence, and the TV camera panned sunburned spectators probably more bored than she was. It just was never as much fun as the first lesson he'd given her on the horsehair settee. Their national pastime seminars never breached that sensual level again.

In the closet-sized bedroom, she tugged on a built-in bureau and took out a fresh blouse. She unbuttoned her sweater, sat on the bed and kicked off her sandals.

"You getting all dolled up?" he asked from the doorway.

"Yep. I told you I wanted to celebrate." She gave him a critical stare. "Why don't you wear a fresh shirt?"

He sat down beside her and pulled off his tee shirt. "So what you got in your pocket, Josie Girl?" His arm wound around her waist and stuck like an octopus tentacle. "Wanna show me?"

"None of your business." She tried to wriggle free. "Not yet."

"Hey, we partners?"

"Partners when I say so, Cain. This is my business. I have homework to do first. I'm not gonna show you anything until I'm ready. So don't bug me, okay?"

"You're the boss." He flounced back on the bed. "So tell me about Hobart, Jojo."

"Don't call me that," she snapped, whipping the hairbrush over her head like a bullwhip.

"This is the guy you're gonna stiff, right?"

"Don't bug me, Cain. This is business, remember? Hobart Ames is a client." She brushed loose hairs off her sleeve. "A well to do client, by the way."

"They got the money?"

"Yep."

"So how much you hittin' em up for?"

"They owe me another thousand-dollar deposit."

"Two-thousand bucks just for a deposit? You ain't even done anything yet."

"Not yet. But I gotta have a decent retainer before I make any commitments. This is strictly legitimate business tactics, Cain. I know about this."

"Hey, I trust you, Baby. So far you've done about zero, and these dopes have paid you a hundred and are on the hook for a couple thousand more. Suits me. Hey, I admire your style." He sat up suddenly. "You know how many goddam washing machines, TV's and clock radios I had to sell at Hall's Appliance to make a thousand bucks?"

"No."

"About four hundred, I think. Of each."

"Yeah, right. And how many'd you sell?"

He pulled her on top of him. "I sold you, Josie Girl, didn't I?"

"You didn't have to sell me—I came in ready to buy with or without your help."

"Hit me where it hurts, Baby." He smothered her snickers with a wet kiss, forced his tongue between her lips then slapped her ass hard enough to raise a red spot under her panties. "So tell me what you're sellin' old Hobart Ames, huh?"

"Maybe something he doesn't even know he wants yet."

"Like what?"

She struggled to free herself. "When I'm ready, you'll know, okay?"

He locked on to her wrist and pinned her with one jerk. "Hey, Girl, if I'm gonna be a team player, I think I oughtta know the score."

"When I'm ready, Cain. Dammit, leggo!"

He released her with an exaggerated sweep of his arm.

She rubbed her skin. "I have to do this my way, okay? I'm not even sure yet exactly what I have, but I know it's even better than I thought. We've gotten lucky. I want to be sure I make the most of an opportunity, that's all. You just have to trust me."

"I do."

"Then don't keep bugging me. Just let me do this my way, okay?" She stomped out of the bedroom and snatched her purse.

He followed, punched his arms into a fresh shirt and tucked the hem under his belt. "No need to bite my head off. We're in this deal together, right?"

"Hobart says you agreed to go over to their place and help him with some odd jobs."

"Just talkin'."

"You didn't tell him anything, right? I hope you kept your trap shut."

"I thought you'd think of somethin' like that."

"Just let me make the decisions, okay? Don't do anything until I say so. And another thing, remember that you don't know anything about my business if anybody asks. You know I read fortunes, and I'm a helluva good psychic, but that's it."

He moved closer until she could feel the heat radiate through his shirt. "Can I tell em about the incredible, spooky head you give, Baby?"

She swatted his shoulder. "Will you be serious for a minute? You don't discuss Hobart and Farrah with anybody, okay? The less you're seen and heard the better for business."

"Our business."

"Just make sure you don't go blabbing anything to Hobart, that's all. As far as he's concerned, you're just a dumb hunk I got to fix my car, okay? That's it."

"You want me to play stupid, huh?"

"How hard is that for crissakes?" she shot back with a flippant sneer. "You're a natural."

There was a flicker of silence—a frozen moment that chilled the air before Cain Reeves whipped her head around by the hair, trapped her in his arms like a spider with a fly and crushed the breath from her lungs. She was too startled to struggle.

He moved his mouth to her ear and whispered in a voice which despite its silky baritone raised goose bumps. "Don't push too hard, Josie Girl. You wanna be real careful I don't push back." He relaxed his hold so she could take a breath. Then he slowly released his grip, grabbed his jacket and walked out the door.

Josie hugged herself, slumped down on the settee and began to shake. Jeez, maybe he was getting weird on her. He was really pissed being under her control. It was all just a macho thing. Maybe that was it.

She heard him start up his jalopy. He was waiting for her. She was buying dinner. And his beer.

She got up, shouldered her bag and shut the door behind her.

Goddam him, she muttered to herself as she climbed in his beater Pontiac. He would regret ever threatening her. Every single word would cost him one way or the other. He had no idea who he was up against. She'd make certain he found out before she was through with him. Sonuvabitch had crossed the line. Nobody did that and got away Scot free. Nobody.

17

Bradley responded to the flashing light on his four-button phone and picked up the receiver while his eyes stayed on the codicil taking up his attention this morning.

"Bradley Hammaker," he answered curtly.

"This is Philippa Mooney. I'm calling to remind you about the recommendation you promised for someone to assist me in finding out the identity of my niece's father. Do you recall our conversation?"

He swiveled his chair to gaze out at the Lake lying like a rippled slab of gray slate as a light breeze scudded steel wool clouds across the sky. Glass and granite blocked his view of the traffic on Lakeshore Drive. "Yes, of course, I do. I thought you might change your mind upon reflection, Professor."

"I think I made my feelings clear the other evening. I would appreciate your giving me the name of someone I can call."

He pinched the bridge of his nose. "Professor, I'd really like to persuade you to let sleeping dogs lie."

"You can't. Don't bother wasting your time. I know what I want to do."

"Alright. Let's assume you're successful and find out who this person is."

"I intend to."

"Then what do you do with this knowledge? Intrude on someone's life, perhaps ruin a marriage or other relationships established over the last twenty-four years? Have you really given the consequences of your plans much thought?"

"Yes, I have. Have you ever considered the pain and tragedy my sister suffered on account of this man? Phoebe is my main concern."

"But with all due respect, Professor Mooney—"

"—Philippa."

"Philippa. As I was saying, with all due respect for your sister, she's dead. What's past is past."

"Not for me it isn't. She was my sister. My only flesh and blood, and someone treated her very cruelly. I'm not going to let him get away with it."

"Then this is about vengeance? A personal vendetta?"

"Yes. I suppose it is."

"Alright. So suppose after you find this person, he isn't happy to be discovered. Have you thought about the repercussions?"

"I'm not planning on shooting the sonuvabitch, although the more I consider that as an option, the more appealing it becomes."

He allowed himself a half grin. She had guts. She was a survivor, a fighter. Not like her sister. Bibi was vulnerable, unsure of herself, easily lead to believe in her own shortcomings. He liked Philippa Mooney. Not only was she physically attractive, charming and sensual in an intellectual way, she was straightforward, blunt. Traits Bradley Hammaker admired. Especially in an adversary.

"My point is that what you're doing may be considered threatening."

"Tough. I'm not concerned with his feelings at all. He didn't give a good goddam about my sister or his own daughter for twenty-four years. Why should I consider his feelings now?"

"He did make generous financial arrangements to provide for his daughter."

"Yes. He paid for his mistake as if it were some damned traffic fine."

"But it wasn't, was it? Legally enforced, I mean. He made all these payments completely voluntarily I understand." He felt a thump in the pit of his stomach. Butterflies swarmed in his guts and made him break out in a sweat. Hadn't he rebutted this same defense for years, lying in the dark, staring at the night while his mind toyed with the guilt? "Why can't you see that as a caring gesture?"

"Caring? Using an intermediary, sending a check every month to salve his conscience, or what I suspect may be the case, to secure Bibi's silence? I think he was afraid of being exposed. It was hush money, Mr. Hammaker."

"Bradley."

"Those payments had nothing whatsoever to do with his regard for Phoebe or Farrah. It was strictly a business deal. Period."

He turned from the window and rubbed his forehead. When he shut his eyes, he could see Philippa seated at the dining room table, her sea-green eyes burning with restrained revenge. There was nothing he could say to dissuade her. Like it or not, she was going to try to destroy him.

"Maybe you don't know all the details. Maybe your sister and this man had an arrangement, an understanding, if you will, between them. I think you're being exceptionally rash in getting involved in their affairs."

"What you think doesn't matter to me, Mr. Hammaker. Please, understand I'm not trying deliberately to be perverse. This is something I have had eating at my soul ever since Phoebe died. I need to do this."

"What about your niece? Does she know anything about her real father?"

"No. We've never discussed any of this. I'm certain Farrah doesn't know that Maxwell Swidnik is not her biological father."

"Then for god's sake, Philippa, think what this might do to her. She's an innocent young woman who just lost her mother. Why put her through the ordeal of discovering she's lost not one father but two?"

Bradley twisted in his chair, stared hard at the Chinese jardiniere beside him, listened to the sound of his own breathing and waited for a reply. Maybe he was being overly dramatic. Maybe he was merely showing concern for a client's family. But maybe, just maybe, he reminded himself sternly, there was truth in every word. Maybe Bradley Hammaker really did care what Farrah Lynn would do if she uncovered his secret. He had fantasized years ago about meeting this young woman, searching her features for clues to his own longing to know her, to claim her. But now the image of this twenty-five year old artist, an unconventional rebel, struck pure terror into his establishment heart.

"Bradley, do you have children of your own?"

"Two sons." Odd, he thought. The lie was harder this time.

"Then you can understand that a child needs to know who brought them into the world. I think that deep down, maybe only in her dreams, she is troubled by the persistent thought that there is something missing from her life."

"Come on, Professor, that's bunk, and you know it. She's leading a very full life from what I understand. Nobody wants to find out a truth that alters their whole understanding of their place in the world."

"I know my niece. Farrah isn't like that. She's a very serious young woman who's trying to find something missing from her life. She's been looking in all the wrong places. I don't know if she'll accept the truth, but I'm going to give her that choice."

"Isn't there anything I can say to change your mind?"

"No."

"Then can I at least delay your taking any overt action on this until we've had a chance to talk some more?" He heard her sigh, and his heart sank. "We could have dinner."

"Bradley, we've already talked about this. I don't see the need to flog a dead horse, do you?"

"No. I mean, what I'd like is just the chance to talk this out with you—in private. Can we at least do that?"

"This is private, isn't it? We spoke confidentially the other evening." She was reproving with a professorial tone he despised. Each time she caught his ambivalence, she tangled him with her verbal lasso and pulled him off his horse. He was not used to this kind of verbal combat from a novice opponent. It was painfully abasing.

"Just let me buy you dinner. All I'm asking is a chance to spend an hour with you and examine all the ramifications of what you're planning. Is that fair?"

"You can stop by the University this afternoon, if you'd like."

"No. Neutral territory. How about if we meet somewhere?"

"Alright. But we must agree first that after we speak, if I'm still determined to go ahead—which I will be most certainly—then you help me or else keep your hands off completely. Agreed?"

"Agreed. But first you agree to listen with an open mind to what I have to say."

"Done."

"Let's say seven-thirty at the Lake Shore Club."

"I'll be there."

"Well, good-bye then," he ended awkwardly, feeling like a schoolboy given a burdensome homework assignment for misbehavior.

"Good-bye." She hung up.

He dropped the receiver back on the cradle and held his head with both hands. He felt an ache in every bone; his stomach churned. It could be the flu. It could be a spring cold virus. He stood up and paced back and forth behind his desk. It could be the same damp dread he had felt overwhelm him when he got that phone call from Bibi twenty-five years ago. He had managed to control his feelings then, to let intellect and not passion rule. He could do the same now. All he had to do was collect his thoughts, plan a strategy and stick to it. Philippa Mooney was only one woman. One person disconnected from Bradley Hammaker's life for the past quarter century. He was going to keep it that way.

He buzzed his secretary. "Penny, hold my calls, will you?"

"Yessir."

He punched another button and found his fingers flying to the numbers without his having to think about it. The phone rang for a long time. Four rings and no answer. Five. He would wait for one more ring.

"Hello?"

The voice was gruff, hoarse with age and too many stogies smoking over whiskey glasses. But it was reassuring for Bradley to hear the man answer who had driven the teenager to his first day at Northwestern University in his Cadillac LaSalle. The mentor's advice to the gawky freshman was still fresh in Bradley's mind: Make your parents proud, and if you can't do that, at least make yourself happy.

"Fran? It's Brad."

"Hey, Hampster! How the hell are you? You haven't called me in a coon's age, you rascal. Too busy making the big bucks now, huh, to remember an old fart like me?"

He tried to sound jocular, but this was a man he had never tried to patronize. "I've been preparing for trial. You know—too much to do and not enough time to do it."

"That's what they pay you for, Hampster. How much you bilking the public for these days? Hundred-fifty bucks an hour for a twenty-hour work day?"

"Twenty-two hours if I've got my figures right."

"Make it while you're young. Old farts like me envy you guys making senior partner before your fiftieth birthday. Smart-assed bastard, Bradley—you always were a snot."

"Super snot, in fact." Bradley could hear the old retired jurist puffing on another cigar.

"So what the hell's bugging you, Hampster?"

"Oh, just called to see how you were getting along," he stalled. "Just nice to hear a friendly voice."

"Only people who call me these days are twerps wanting some sage insight on a constitutional case I heard way back when Adam and Eve were still dating or old broads with butts like battleships trying to get a fourth for bridge. What's wrong, Bradley? Angie and the boys okay?"

"Fine. Everybody's fine."

"Then spit out what's on your mind. You got a new typist with knockers like fenders on a Great Lakes freighter you want me to break in?" he chortled.

"Fran, I need to see you about something. Can I come over?"

"Hell's bells. Thelma will cut my throat if I invite company over. She's got the place all tore up, giving the carpets a shampoo and set or some goddam thing."

"Can you come downtown?"

The judge's voice suddenly fell to a scholarly bass. "Is this important, Bradley?"

"Yes. It is, Fran. I need to see you this afternoon."

"Come on over. We can go upstairs and use Bobby's room. There's carpet and drapery people and God knows who else mucking around here today. But if you need to come on out, I'll be here."

"Thanks, Fran. I'll see you in about an hour."

"I'm working my way through a bottle of Early Times while I finish the *Trib's* crossword. Jesus, this retirement schedule is killing me, Bradley. Hard to keep up the pace, you know what I mean?" he joked with a bittersweet laugh.

"See you soon."

Fran Lohman hung up without a good-bye.

Bradley took his jacket off the rack by the door and slipped his arms into the sleeves. As he straightened his lapels and pulled down his shirt cuffs, he thought about the granite and tile mausoleum where Judge Lohman lived in Brookfield, a half hour drive from the city. The house, built in 1901 and remodeled by Fran's father in 1928, was surrounded by three acres of woods, a fishpond and neglected crabapple orchard where Judge Lohman had once built his son a double-decker tree house. The property was within sight of the Chicago Zoological Park.

Bradley grabbed his briefcase and switched off his desk lamp. It was apt they would be meeting in Bobby's room. That was Fran's only son killed in Vietnam in 1967. He was a career officer, academy graduate, the pride of Judge Lohman's life. The old man had never recovered from the loss. What remained was a shell of the once fierce, unassailable jurist who had risen to the top of the legal tier and given it all up after Bobby's death to stay home, do puzzles and watch television with his wife Thelma. His only voluntary outside activity these days was to visit Bobby's grave every Sunday. He always took a carton of Pall Mall cigarettes, a box of Stover's mints and one single red rose to the cemetery—Bobby's favorite brand of smokes, candy and a symbolic remembrance of the three-dozen red roses he had delivered to his wife's hospital room when his son was born. Thelma was thirty-six years old at Bobby's birth, and Judge Lohman was forty-six.

He had waited all his married life for Bobby's arrival, and everything in his busy, demanding schedule revolved around his son. Losing him, sacrificing his immortality in what proved to be a futile, stupid war in support of all the establishment evils his three daughters protested, drove the old judge close to the edge of sanity. These days he was completely apolitical, atheistic and totally unrepentant for past sins.

Bradley Hammaker strode through his office, told Penny he would be back in time for his four o'clock conference and left the building. Once outside on his way to the parking garage, a shaft of sunlight poked between the skyscrapers and stabbed at him like a laser beam. He raised a hand to shield his eyes. The word retribution came to mind as he hurried out of the light.

18

"Did you ever meet Max Swidnik?" Bradley asked his old mentor after they were seated on the worn wing chairs upstairs in the third floor study once the favorite haunt of Robert Cramer Lohman.

"Hell, no. Never met the bastard. Mealy mouthed little prick." He blew a cloud of tobacco smoke toward Bradley. "Sure you won't have a drink?"

"No, thanks, Fran. I have to get back to the office."

"Little nip sharpens the senses." He tilted his glass in a brief toast and took another sip of his whiskey and soda. "Can't think worth a damn sober, Hampster."

Francis Lohman was the one person in the world who called Bradley by that silly nickname. Even his parents had refused to acknowledge the depth of intimacy the moniker denoted in their son's relationship with the family mentor. But it stuck. Over fifty years. By now Bradley saw it as a special link between the two of them. A recognition that with this one person, he could be himself without any professional pretense, male ego or assumption of any social airs whatsoever. This was the one confidante who shared his deepest thoughts. And secrets.

"Fran, I don't know where to start really."

"Well, I assume it's got something to do with Phoebe's death. You wanna know what I took out of Phoebe's safe?"

They hadn't spoken about Phoebe, Farrah, Oakland, Swidnik, any of it for so many years, yet here it was on the tip of this man's tongue when Bradley needed most to refresh his memory. He was so relieved he slumped back in the chair and pressed his tired eyes shut. "Dammit, Fran, I think there's going to be some trouble after all these years. I thought once she died, it would finally be over."

"Hell, it's not that bad, is it?"

"It could be. You know the trust fund for Farrah."

"Yeah."

"Farrah gave her aunt Philippa Mooney half."

"The hell she did. Half?"

"Professor Mooney is on the faculty at the University. She's head of the classical language department. A person of some professional reputation, I understand."

"Smart broad, huh?"

"Very quick witted. Very determined lady."

"What's she after, Hampster? She trying to milk you for something?"

"Nothing like that. She thinks she wants to find out who was making those monthly payments to Phoebe all those years."

"The hell she does."

"She's convinced the lawyer who handled those arrangements knows the identity of Farrah's father. And she wants to find out."

"Jesus H. Kee-rist. What the hell for?" He took another slug of whiskey and wiped his lips with the back of a speckled hand.

"I don't know. She has some kind of vengeful heart, I guess. She and Bibi were very close, you know."

"She and Bibi didn't get on that well the last few years since her husband took off. They were estranged of late, you might say."

"Well, she's very much involved, Fran, with Bibi's past. Bibi never told her sister about me."

"So what's your problem? You can handle her."

"She's on a crusade to find out who Farrah's real father is."

"Tell her you'll work on it, and let her cool her panties for awhile. She'll forget all about it."

"I don't think so. She's not like that, Fran."

"What's she want?"

"I don't know. It's not money. Hell, she hardly cared about the money from the trust fund Farrah gave her. She just wants to find Farrah's father and spit in his eye."

"Bradley, you know I opened the safe and took out the letters Phoebe had saved. Letters from Max and whatnot. I burned them all. There was nothing in there to drag you into this. You're clean as a whistle."

"I never thought Phoebe would violate our agreement, but I had to know."

"There was a diary. That's all, Bradley. Phoebe sent it to me when she found out she had cancer. It was something she prepared a long time ago—right after she married Poole when Farrah was just a kid. It didn't do you any harm at all. Never even broached paternity, just tried to make Poole seem like the apple of her eye. I think it was Phoebe's idea to try to help her daughter establish a better relationship with her stepfather—the gist of it was to tell the kid that Max Swidnik was not the love of her mother's life, and she shouldn't spend her life loving a phantom father when Dennis Poole was flesh and blood. That kinda horse shit. I don't think Farrah ever saw it. Anyhow, I burned the damn thing. There's nothing for Farrah to question now that Phoebe's gone. It's all a dead issue."

"Did Bibi ever talk about us—me?" He knew he could trust the judge not to have left anything damaging to be discovered. But he still wanted to know what Phoebe had thought about their affair during all these years.

"Naw, not much. Mostly, you know, her diary was just something Phoebe kept to ensure her daughter knew something about Bibi's relationships with Swidnik and Poole and how much she wanted Farrah, how she enriched her life and so on and how she wanted her to have a good father-daughter relationship with Dennis Poole. You know, emotional laundry. But she thought it was important for her daughter's sake. I burned it all, Hampster."

"I just wanted to ask."

"Phoebe was my client, Bradley, as well as you."

"As far as you know then, Farrah never had a hint from Bibi about Swidnik not being her real father?"

He sipped his whiskey slowly and played with a frayed thread on the chair arm. "Well, it's this way, Hampster. I think Phoebe was trying to make sure her daughter didn't grieve unnecessarily over the death of a man she thought was her father. She wanted to dispel the notion in her daughter's mind that she had spent her life all fucked up with booze because of losing Max Swidnik in the war. That's all that mattered to Phoebe. She wasn't so concerned with having her daughter follow a trail to your doorstep, Bradley. That wasn't her intention at all if that's what you're thinking."

"Were Farrah and her stepfather close?"

"Never. The guy was a bum. Phoebe should never have married him. I even tried my damnedest to talk her out of it, but she wanted to give the kid a father. It was a mistake of the first order. Farrah and Poole never did get really close."

"I'm sorry to hear that."

"Dennis Poole was a drunk, a loser and a whiner. Not even half the man Max Swidnik was. Max knew the kid wasn't his, but at least he kept his mouth shut. He wanted Phoebe to name you, but she never did. Never. She was a decent woman, Hampster."

"What did she tell Max about us?"

"Nothing really. Only that the baby wasn't his. I don't know exactly how Max felt about that, but Phoebe was pretty sure the marriage was over. I think they would have parted company if he'd made it back from Korea."

"I didn't know that. I always assumed he'd come back and raise Farrah. I didn't realize he knew the truth about the baby not being his."

"In a perfect world, Hampster. You know Phoebe—she had to play it straight. Besides, I think Max had something going on the side himself."

"Who?"

"Some gal here in town. Phoebe told me when she and Max first met, he was engaged to somebody else. The girl got married on the rebound to some GI who got killed himself a year later. I got the impression from Bibi that maybe he was going to go back to his old flame when he got back from Korea. That's what she said anyhow, but hell, he was all messed up, and so was she."

"She had a right."

"Well, what the hell. People make mistakes. That's why pencils got erasers, Hampster. She made a mistake and decided to spend the rest of her life paying for it."

"Then she never told anybody about me?"

"Nope. Not even a clue, Hampster. Don't worry about it."

"God, I wished I'd never got involved in this. Why didn't you let somebody else handle it?"

Lohman patted Bradley's arm. "Don't get your knickers all in a bunch over this. I didn't want to touch the probate given the circumstances of our arrangement over the years. And I thought if you handled the estate yourself, you could sort of see to it that everything was kept copasetic. Bibi agreed with that."

"I didn't know about the diary."

"No matter. None of your business at the time. Didn't matter. That was between her and me. I went out to her place a month before she died and emptied her safe. Just to be sure there was nothing there. Didn't even involve you given the way things turned out."

From downstairs they could hear the whine of a floor buffer. The walls vibrated beneath their feet.

"Goddam. Sounds like they're tearing out the second floor," the judge groused.

"Philippa knows the payments were arranged by a lawyer in the Palmolive Building. She figured out it was someone in the Hazeltine firm."

"How'd she come up with that?"

"Well, we were talking. She asked the right questions. I told you she's not stupid, Fran."

"So what? So she knows some lawyer in the firm arranged the trust fund. So who gives a good goddam if she does?"

"Don't you see what I'm driving at? She knows it was somebody in the firm. She'll find out it was you, Fran."

"So who still gives a goddam? She can find out till the cows come home that I set up a trust fund for some client and arranged payments and withdrawals. That's proof that I'm a member of the Illinois State Bar for crissakes, Bradley. That's all it proves."

"She knows the trail leads to the identity of Farrah's father."

"The hell it does!" he blustered, spilling whiskey on the carpet. "It'll be a cold day in hell when she can poke her pesky nose into a client file. What the hell's the matter with you, Bradley? You sound like some stupid schoolgirl afraid of a pimple before the prom. What's wrong with your head?"

"Nothing. Nothing." He looked toward the window. "It's just that I thought this was a closed matter. Now after all these years, I don't seem to know anymore."

"Forget about it. Tell this nosy broad where the bear shit in the buckwheat, Hampster. She's not gonna get anywhere. Tell her to piss off."

There was a resounding crash from the first floor that sent a thundering herd of footsteps accompanied by shouts to the ground floor.

"Probably taking down the plaster and lath," he grumbled, sucking on the cigar as he slowly rolled it in his fingers. "When Thelma gets the spring housecleaning bug up her ass, the place looks like Warsaw after the Krauts marched through. It'd be a helluva lot easier just to burn the sonuvabitch down and build a new house every year."

"Maybe I ought to try to talk this Professor Mooney out of it, Fran."

"You can't talk a woman out of anything, Bradley. No man in recorded human history has ever done that. Once a female has her mind set on a target and locks on, there's no man capable of reining her in. Somebody tells me they caught a cutthroat out in Montana as big as a Studebaker—that's maybe believable. Hell, yes. The Cubs cinching the Series in four straight? Might con-

vince me of that before I'd swallow some bullshit about a wizenheimer claiming he talked his wife out of adding a sun room on the castle or filling the moat
with koi. No way in God's green earth it's ever gonna happen, Bradley. No way.
Forget it."

"I have a feeling—hell, maybe it's just guilt stalking me after all these years."

"Guilt, hell. What the hell you got to be guilty about? You threw a bad pitch,
but when the sucker went outta the park, you stepped up and acted like a man.
You got nothin to apologize for, Bradley. Don't you forget it. Guilt is a disease
that eats your guts out. If I'd done this or that different, maybe, what if—shit.
Guilt is for fuckin losers. Don't fall into that tar pit for crissakes. Forget guilt.
This was all about responsibility, and you paid the tab in full. Nobody's got any
complaints so far as I'm concerned. And that's the way it's gonna stay." He
drained the whiskey and reached for the bottle on the bookcase beside him. He
dribbled in a double shot and sank back in the chair. "What you got to be
guilty for Bradley?"

"I keep thinking I could have done more, maybe if I'd tried to work it out
with Bibi—something, I suppose."

"You never spilled your guts to Angie, did you? You ain't that stupid."

"No. Never." He looked up suddenly irritated. "Of course, not."

"Well, if this little Miss Nosy pokes around and finds me, then she can just
frustrate herself to death for all I care. She isn't gonna learn a damn thing, Bradley. What transpired between Phoebe and me is confidential, and the file is
sealed. Whatever happened between you and Phoebe is your business, and
you're a damned fool if you ever tell a living soul about any of it."

He sat there and listened to the thumps, bangs and shouts from downstairs
as Fran sipped his Early Times. Bradley could see the folded newspaper lying
on the window bench—the *New York Times* crossword done in ink without a
single strike-over. Mediocrity was stressful for the retired judge.

"To be absolutely honest with you, Fran, I think I may have some sort of
perverted idea about seeing Farrah."

"You want my advice, Hampster?"

"Yes."

"Forget it. Keep it a secret fantasy. It won't work out. Believe me, it's like
looking up your first love and finding out she's got grandkids, varicose veins
and stretch marks on her wrinkles."

He forced a grin. "I suppose so."

A stream of cigar smoke billowed from the judge's lips. "Besides, I hear that Farrah is doing okay. Pretty good kid it turns out. She's an artist. You know that? Not bad, if I do say so."

"What do you hear?" He felt a prick of pride.

"Oh, I heard something about her work being in some show in Sausalito. They got quite an active artists' community out there. I guess her stuff ain't half bad."

"What does she paint?"

"Watercolors. Mostly seascapes—Golden Gate Bridge, Monterey Bay. Not half bad from what I saw."

"You saw some of her work?"

"Once."

"When was that?"

"Oh, a few years back when Thelma and I took a trip out to San Francisco on vacation. Farrah had some paintings at a gallery across the Bay so we took a quick look. That's about it."

Bradley stood up. "You mean you saw her recently? When? When was this, Fran? Jesus, you never told me!"

"Sit down. Have a drink for crissakes. You're as nervous as a virgin at a Mormon picnic." He passed his glass over to Bradley who shook his head.

"When was it exactly? I want to know. You never said a damn thing to me about any of this."

"Well, I don't exactly check in with you when I take a dump either, Counselor. Calm the hell down, will you? What's wrong with you?"

Bradley sat down reluctantly. He felt betrayed for the first time by his friend. What else had he known about Farrah and Phoebe that he had kept from Bradley? "I just want to know about her paintings, that's all."

"I told you it was pretty good. We browsed around and took off. Nothin' much to tell. Phoebe was pretty proud of her daughter's talent. She didn't have much of a head for school, you know."

"No, I don't know, dammit."

"Well, I always felt it was just a social thing. Farrah had to go her own way."

"Is that why she left school? You never told me anything about that, Fran." He tried hard to disguise the vague sense of resentment in his voice. He was beginning to face up to how very little he knew about his daughter—by choice.

"It was like I said—personal problems."

"What sort of personal problems?"

"Well, you didn't need to know the finer details. Farrah never gave a plug nickel for school. Only thing she ever got worked up about was her art. She's got Phoebe's instinct for self destruction, Bradley. No self confidence, vulnerable as a fresh carcass being plucked by buzzards. Couldn't be pushed into life—she had to find her own way. From what I hear, she's got it all together as they say nowadays, doing okay by all accounts. She's got some genuine talent, and she's been shacking up with an Oregon woodsman-type who seems to keep her on the right track."

"I didn't know."

"Of course, you didn't. You never knew a goddam thing about that kid. No need to involve yourself, right? Isn't that the way it was supposed to be?"

Bradley shrank back in the chair and hunched his shoulders. He felt like such a miserable bastard. A sonuvabitch worthy of Philippa's scorn. "Does she drink? God, she's not a druggie, is she, Fran?"

"Hell, no! Farrah's anti establishment, goes her own way, sets her own limits. But she's got a streak of moral courage running through her veins, Hampster. She's always been able to separate wrong from right, and her heart's as big as a buffalo—not a mean bone in that kid's body. Strong as a fuckin ox, honest as the day is long, too. I like to think some of that came from you."

"Maybe I didn't handle this whole thing very well," he admitted, more to himself than to his critic. "I wish I'd had a chance to talk with Phoebe more about it."

"Well, you could have just dropped outta sight. Left her flat. After all, she was married. Farrah could have been all Max's financial problem not yours."

"She was his problem it looks like."

"She was caught in his trap, my friend."

Bradley checked his wristwatch and stood up again. "Fran, I have to get back to town. Thanks for taking the time to see me."

He set the whiskey glass down. "You can see it was a real bitch to fit you in between the demolition derby downstairs and the crossword." He got up with more than a little effort. At seventy-nine, he moved like a broken toy these days, arms akimbo, feet barely rising off the floor in a kind of slow shuffle as he moved toward the door. "You gotta promise me you aren't gonna let yourself get all tied up in knots over this, Bradley."

"Don't worry about it." He barely touched the jurist's arm in guiding him through the doorway out to the third floor landing. A vacuum cleaner motor revved downstairs and made him shout so the old judge could hear. "This is over with! Right or wrong, I did what I thought was best, and it's over now!

That's all there is to it!" He cleared his throat when the racket died down. "Thanks for always taking care of everything for me all these years. I guess that's one reason I never bothered to get involved—I trusted you to keep that part of my life separate."

Lohman eyed him with the skeptical stare of an ex prosecutor. "You're right, Hampster. And now it's over and done with, let sleeping dogs lie."

"Well, I gotta shove off. Take care of yourself, Fran."

"Let me walk you down. I gotta check up on Thelma's house moving project." He went down with one hand gripping the banister and the other resting on Bradley's shoulder to steady himself.

In the foyer, electric cords, open tubs of floor wax and rolled carpets hindered his exit.

"Thanks, Fran. Give Thelma a kiss for me."

"Give her one yourself, you handsome devil," a kindly voice teased from behind him. He turned around and received a perfunctory hug and peck from Thelma, a white-haired lady with twinkly eyes set in a rather plain face.

"Hi, Thelma. How are you?"

"Trying my best to put up with the Judge here. How are you and the boys?"

"Fine."

"Angela?"

"Fine. Just fine."

"Give her my love, Bradley. Tell her to come out and join us for lunch. We'd love to see her, wouldn't we, Fran?"

"Sure. Tell her to come on out, Bradley. We could use some cheerful company."

"Thanks." He stepped out onto the porch and took a final look back at the baggy eyes and drooping jowls of his longtime friend. "Take care of yourself, Fran."

"You, too. I see a few white hairs you didn't have the last time you were here."

He waved and stepped back as a man in white coveralls brushed past carrying a bundle of fat rubber hose. Watching him pass, Bradley's eyes fixed on the wall at the foot of the stairs. The judge moved back, and Bradley saw a magnificent watercolor of a scalloped beach and the Oakland Bay Bridge anchored in a leaden sky with the jeweled hump of Treasure Island silhouetted in the distance. The scene was bathed in pale mauve and gray shadows which seemed eerily translucent. He could almost smell the bay for a moment as he stared at the seascape. When he looked away, he saw Fran catch his gaze and smile.

"I told you she was pretty good." He wagged his cigar at the picture. "Not bad eh, Hampster?"

And then as Bradley Hammaker stood there gaping, the judge turned around and labored back up the stairs one tread ahead of the hose man.

19

It was warm for the beginning of April. Outside the thin walls of the trailer, Farrah could hear the raucous symphony playing down at the pond. Frogs, crickets, owls and raccoons were noisily staking out their territory. There was barely a breeze.

Once she and Hobart got the money, they would have an electric line run from the road out to the trailer. That would be nice. Maybe it would be done in time for her to bask in the whisper of an electric fan on warm summer nights.

Farrah opened her eyes, unsure of what had roused her from sleep. Maybe the dogs had barked. She listened and heard only the music of the marsh stirring the night as she gazed up at the stars. Moon glow bathed Cully's Marsh, silver shards gleaming on the aluminum trailer like sardines swimming in a summer stream. If she could only capture those ethereal hues in her watercolors, she sighed. During the day, she never tired of watching the rays dart like fingerlings among the reeds and grasses, painting the pond apple green one moment then as the sun flitted behind a cloud, casting a charcoal pall across the water. Her brushes couldn't work fast enough to trap the kaleidoscopic wonder of the landscape. Her pictures were at best a poor imitation of God's artistic handiwork, she despaired. Try as hard as she might to capture the soul of the marsh, she always felt something lacking, something vital missing from her art. If only she could name it, put it all together and make her pictures come alive.

Farrah sighed. She had been dreaming. A good dream. She was a little girl sitting on a big, pink towel at the beach. But the sand was wet and scratched her bare legs. And the water was so cold. When she waded into the waves, it bit into her tender skin like a swarm of angry hornets. She had cried as her mother carried her back to the towel and dried her reddened limbs. Then the dream changed to a surreal tableau both disturbing and intriguing. Farrah watched as her mother reached down the front of Farrah's frilly swim suit and extracted something shiny. As the little girl watched, Phoebe held up a gleaming piece of silver and pressed it against the child's lips.

Lying with her eyes wide open in the murk, Farrah saw the dream pictures in her mind and recognized the silvery object as Max's dog tags. The ones she had given to Josie. Thank God, because now he was even invading her sleep. There must be something significant about this dream. She would tell Josie all about it. Just in case there was someway for her mother or even Max to communicate with her through the veil of unconsciousness.

She flung the covers back to cool her bare body. Squeezing her eyes shut to try to force sleep didn't work. So much to worry about—her mother's suffering and loneliness at the end, her Aunt Philippa so far away, the whole disturbing thing with Max and the letter. It would be easier to drift off thinking about what she and Hobart would do with the money. She concentrated on imagining a bathhouse with a tub, a sauna, a flush toilet. As she let her mind wander through the luxuries of modern plumbing, she felt a sudden chill and shivered as a cold draft touched her shoulders.

Just as Farrah reached for the blanket to cover herself, she was enfolded by a pair of strong arms in a comforting embrace. Her whole body was infused with a healing warmth and feeling of unfathomable peace.

She clutched the hands holding her close. "Ohhh, you're so warm, Hobart."

She pressed her face into the pillow, safe and secure in protective arms. It wasn't a sensual embrace. It was a loving encirclement which bestowed an incredible rush of well being. Her appreciation for such unexpected tenderness in the middle of the night inspired her to turn over and gaze at her lover's face.

She opened her eyes and froze. Her heart skipped a beat as she reacted in terror to the emptiness beside her. "Hobart! Hobart! My God! Where are you?"

She heard pounding outside the trailer just before the door banged open, and Hobart's heavy footsteps raced to the edge of the bed where he instantly caught her up in his arms and held her tight.

"Goddam, what is it?" he gasped, out of breath and nude except for his longjohn drawers. His fly was still open.

"Oh, Hobart, I was so scared," she sobbed, clinging to him. "Where were you?"

"Taking a leak." Nonplused by her panic, he buttoned his drawers. "What's wrong? You scared the shit out of me."

She swept her hand across the space beside her on the bed. The sheet was cold to the touch. "I…I thought you were here beside me."

"You were just dreaming, Sweetheart. That's all it was. Just a dream." He lay down and pulled the covers up.

"You weren't here. I was in your arms, and it felt so good, and then you were gone."

"Of course, I was. I had to take a pee. I was only gone five minutes." He put his arms around her and snuggled. "It was just a bad dream. Calm down and go back to sleep. You want me to make you some tea? You wanna split a joint?"

"Oh, Hobart, it wasn't a dream. I was awake. This wasn't a dream."

"It's no big deal. I just slipped outside for a minute, that's all."

"No, no, no!" She sat up, found her glasses and put them on. "I felt someone. They reached out and put their arms around me and held me. I said how warm you were. I was so cold, and then he hugged me, and I was warm, too."

He pulled her down beside him. "It was just a dream, Farrah. Go back to sleep."

She took off her glasses and lay back down but couldn't close her eyes. She shivered with fear even with Hobart's arms around her. It hadn't been a dream. And if Hobart wasn't lying beside her when she woke up, who was? Who had cradled her in such strong arms as if she were a baby and made her feel so safe?

"Oh, Hobart," she whimpered as a tear ran down her cheek, "I know it's him. I know it."

"Don't be silly. You were just dreaming. Don't get all freaked over a dream."

"He was here. He was here beside me…He *was*…" she repeated over and over as he drifted back to sleep without her. "I know Max was here. And he held me just like I was a frightened little girl or something. It wasn't anything bad at all. I don't think he wants me to be afraid, Hobart."

"Hummm…" His voice faded as his mind dissolved in dreams of his own making.

Farrah stared at the night sky visible through the louvered window. She could see stars twinkling and a sliver of moon as bright as a silver dollar.

"I know it's you, Max," she whispered with the tip of her nose uplifted to catch the musky perfume of the marsh. "I know you've come back for me."

20

Cain lit a second cigarette and ambled from the tidy sleeping nook in the Nashua. He took a long drag and watched Josie sitting with her legs curled up under her ass, tugging at the long, silky hair falling disobediently around her face.

"Whatch you doin', Girl?" A curious smile wrinkled his face.

Josie was too absorbed to answer. He smoked for a minute more then joined her on the settee.

"I'm thinking. I have a plan." She put aside her writing pad and pencil. "We have to be careful. This has to be believable. I want to create an exorcism extravaganza with lots of drama. But before we can do that, Cain, I need your help."

He draped a leg over the arm of the settee. "You gonna have me screw my head around in a circle or somethin'? Want me to shove a crucifix up my ass or what?" He smirked irreverently.

"Don't be stupid. This is a quality production. They're going to get every cent's worth of their money for this job."

"How much money we talking about here?" He blew smoke at her.

"I'm going to ask for ten thousand."

His head recoiled as if a line drive had drilled him right between the eyes. "Jesus! You're not askin' for much, huh? Ten grand? Christ, Girl. There's no way they're gonna go for that. Hell, I could put out a contract on the President for that kinda money. You're nuts."

"Believe me, they'll think they're getting a bargain at that price."

"You for real? What are you gonna do? Sic zombies on em?"

"Listen, by the time I wrap this act up, they'll be happy to pay whatever I ask. In the first place, I can guarantee success one-hundred percent."

"Nothin' is ever that good." He scratched his chest. "You ain't that good, are you, Josie?"

"Better. This is like making it up to the bigs, Cain. Major league plays. They buy into this gig because they want to believe. So they're gonna swallow the whole schmeer with the same fervor."

"Hey, I like that word, Babe. Sounds sexy. Say it again."

She blushed despite her best intentions not to let this man beguile her so easily when she was trying to be serious. "Never mind. Point is, they're already hooked."

"First you scare the shit outta these people then you offer to save them from the boogie man for the right price. Is that the bottom line here, Babe?"

"It's more complicated than that, but yeah. That's it. I have a job for you to do. That was our deal, remember? You were gonna help me with this in exchange for staying here, eating my grub and drinking my beer."

"And I cleaned this sty up for you at no extra charge."

"That was your bag not mine. I liked it the way it was."

His legs captured her in a scissors grip. "I can split anytime, Josie. You say the word, and I'm outta here. You can have all this voodoo shit to yourself."

She relented quickly. She needed Cain Reeves. And she was getting used to having clean plates to eat off, not having to spend ten minutes shoveling shit off the bed before she could go to sleep at night. He was growing on her. And that didn't even take into account his formidable sexual prowess which she was finding could become addictive. Definitely habit forming. He just had a way of turning on all her lights. It wasn't natural, wasn't even a good thing probably, but there it was. She didn't want Cain Reeves to go. And as she flashed a disconcerting smile, she knew he understood the source of her dependence, and it made her mad. But there was nothing she could do about it.

"I'm sort of getting used to you, I guess," she confessed. "Let's not argue about this shit, okay? I want to talk to you about business."

He loosened his hold on her. "Okay. I'm listening. So long as I don't have to knock anybody off or wear any kind of stupid swamp monster suit or anything, then I'm all yours, Babe."

Josie leaned forward and locked on to his smoldering gaze behind a veil of cigarette smoke. "Farrah and Hobart are convinced they've seen the tracks of this ghost around their place, down at the pond and around the trailer. They both think they've seen his footprints. They sorta just appear from nowhere and go nowhere."

"Old Max is a sneaky bastard, huh?"

"Ghosts are not known for ringing doorbells and showing up in taxis."

"That'd be pretty groovy—to have old Max show up delivering a pizza, huh?"

"Be serious. Farrah told me once she came out and saw the ghost sitting in a chair in the trailer. Scared the shit out of her."

"Yeah, that'd scare me."

"But you aren't listening, Cain. It's bullshit. You understand? This is all something in her mind. She was dreaming or hallucinating."

"They got any good mushrooms out at their place?"

"Pay attention."

"Okay. So she's seen some footprints and some dude sittin' in her livin' room. What else?"

"That's about it. But it's enough to get them extremely freaked out. I don't think it will be difficult to convince them this is more than just a harmless haunting. And, of course, I'm the one who knows how to make it stop."

"Natch."

"I figure one more credible encounter is all we need at this point. I don't need to overdo it because I have an ace in the hole now."

"You got somethin' in that letter from Hobart. What is it?"

"My trump card, Cain. We're going to give this back to Hobart and tell him it has such bad vibes, I can't open it. I'll reseal the envelope. But what's really in there is going to mean a lot of money to us, Cain. I'm talking about permanent security."

"That much?"

"Maybe even more. I need to finish my homework, but I think I can get even more than ten thousand from Farrah and Hobart."

He swung his legs off the settee. "So what's in the letter worth sellin'?"

She grinned at his ability to cut through to the marrow. "Farrah's mom married this guy Max Swidnik who was in the marines, and he went overseas and got killed in Korea. So then her mom remarries some drunk named Dennis Poole who's Farrah's stepdad. And the whole thing about the haunting is that Farrah thinks this Max is coming back for his dog tags because the government screwed up and lost his remains."

"Yeah. So?"

"So…" She let his interest rise to the boiling point before she let each word slip out like honey dripping on a buttered biscuit. "Max…wasn't…Farrah's…father. The letter said that it was somebody else. So Max isn't Farrah's real dad after all."

"Does she know about this?"

"Of course, she doesn't, you dope. But if she finds out from me and not this letter, then she's gonna be convinced I've got a connection straight to the spirit world. And that's where the fun comes in."

"Tell me about the fun part."

"I lead Farrah step by step, inch by inch toward finding out who her real father is. Think how much money that's worth, Cain." Her eyes sparkled; her cheeks gleamed with a rosy rush welling up beneath the freckles scattered like cinnamon sprinkles on her face. "This is a whole new ballgame."

He reflected a moment then crushed the cigarette stub in an ashtray. "So who's her real old man? That's in the letter, right?"

"It didn't say exactly. But I'll find out."

"You mean it didn't give you names, addresses or nothin' like that?"

"Nope."

"How you gonna find out then? Whatch you got to go on?"

"All I need," she promised with a sly wink. "I have an affidavit signed and sealed and everything. And I got the names of the witness, the attorney who made it up and another guy who got a copy. I'm thinking he must have been the lawyer for Max." She wet her lips suggestively. "And I have something else—I got the sucker's picture."

"What's he look like?"

"Looks so much like Farrah, it's scary. The feet especially." She pulled the envelope out and offered it to him.

"Looks like some GI with those shoes and weird haircut there."

"He's got lieutenant's bars on his collar—can't you see anything?"

He squinted. "Oh. Yeah. An officer type, right?"

"I'm gonna find him."

"How you gonna do that?"

"Look on the back of the picture, Cain. Look carefully."

He turned it over. "It looks like it had somethin' written here in pencil that got erased. I can't see nothin' else."

"It's upside down. Turn it over."

He did and made a second effort. "Looks like a date, huh?"

"1951. See? It has a little mark and fifty-one. And then it has his initials. Look for crissakes."

"Could be E."

"It's a B. See the swirl at the top? It's a B. Here. Give it back." She snatched it back. "It's B. BH—'51. It has to be Farrah's father."

"You really think you can find this guy?"

She got up, gathered her papers and headed for the bedroom and her business stash under the bed. "I'm already working on it. The lawyer who wrote this up was in Chicago—probably still there. These leeches never retire."

"Hey, I gotta buddy in Chicago—Frankie. Him and me roomed together when we were playin' for the Beavers. What an arm this dude had, Josie. He went back home when he got released."

She dismissed his trivia with a shrug. "Anyway, I bet I can still find these guys."

"Played shortstop. He was always tellin' me about this place in Chicago that had girls come right out and dance on the tables—a strip joint with rock'n roll music for crissakes. Far, far out, Josie Girl."

"Whatever."

"Him and his dad went to all the Cubbies' games."

"Hurray for him. Look, who cares? I'm only talking about Chicago because that's where this scumbag lives."

"So he went back home when they dropped his contract, and now he's workin' for some newspaper or somethin', workin' on the printing machines."

"Look, Cain, I don't care about Freddie or whoever the hell you're talking about. Will you listen to me?"

"Frankie."

"Who the fuck is Frankie?"

"My buddy from the Pacific Coast League. Frankie Alveras. Short stop. I just told you."

"God, Cain. Will you shut up about baseball and just listen to me?"

"You gotta one track mind, Josie Girl. I gotta give you credit. You really work at this shit."

"It's my profession. And I'm good at what I do."

"You're movin' up to the bigs, huh?"

She put her head back and her chin up. "I have talent I haven't even used yet."

"I believe you, Babe. You're a regular psychic phenom."

She took his jocularity seriously. "Thank you."

"So what do I have to do?" He laid back and closed his eyes. An hour's labor drilling Josie to the lumpy mattress had tired him out. He had spent the whole day working on the Pinto, doing dishes and then wolfing down an eight-ounce New York steak with Ore-Ida tater tots. He was past due for a long sleep. It was getting too late to talk about this shit anyway, but he felt like humoring her. Whatever it was she wanted him to do, he'd just as soon get on with it.

"I have a cassette tape recorder, and I want you to record a message, Cain. I have it all scripted out. I'm going to have you speak to Farrah, then when I'm doing the exorcism, it'll be your voice on the tape who's responding."

"Hey, Hobart's already heard my voice."

"Don't worry about that. They won't recognize your voice at all when I'm through with it. Besides, they're expecting to hear from Max not Cain Reeves."

One eyebrow arched in disbelief. "I don't know about that, Josie."

"Trust me. I know what I'm doing." She came back to the settee, sat down with a small cardboard filer on her lap and handed him a handwritten script. "This is what I want you to say. And you need to go over it first so you can say it just right."

He took it, read for a minute and began to snicker. "This is totally wild. Freakin' weird, Josie. You oughtta write for TV."

"I could. I have lots of creative talent bottled up."

"You sure Hobart won't recognize my voice?"

"In the first place, you'll be talking to Farrah not Hobart. But even so, he won't be thinking it's you—he'll be watching Farrah freak out. And," she added, reaching out to hand him a plum, "you'll be speaking with this in your mouth."

"What?" He rolled the ripe fruit around in his palm. "You're a crazy woman, Josie Girl. I can't talk with this stuck in my mouth."

"Yes, you can. Try it. You'll see. It'll give your voice an older effect, too. Go on. Try it, Cain."

He popped in the plum, sucked on it while he rolled his eyes to amuse her and then opened his mouth to speak a practice line. Josie listened intently.

"Not bad," she critiqued him. "Do it again. This is definitely going to work."

He spat out the plum. "How are you gonna get this tape out to their place and have it play when you want it to? Ain't it a little suspicious if they hear this thing only when you're around?"

"It's so simple. Look, it's an hour tape, half hour on each side. So your voice recording is on the last minutes of tape. That gives the machine almost a full half hour to run before they hear you. And I will have Farrah there to hear the tape when it's ready. All I gotta do is turn it on when we first go down to the pond."

"You're gonna plant it beforehand, right?"

"Bingo. You're brilliant."

"Glad you appreciate me, Babe."

"And I'm also gonna put these dog tags back at Farrah's. That's where you come in, Cain. I want you to drop these in the rowboat down at the pond." She tossed them in his lap. "You sneak out there about one or two in the morning I figure."

"Nobody's gonna see me creepin' around?"

"No. Not if you're careful. Don't worry about leaving any footprints—they think it's Max tromping around out there anyway."

"Sounds easy enough."

"And he's got dogs. So take something to keep them quiet, okay? If they start to make a racket, Hobart'll be on your ass, and don't park too close to their place. Use your head."

He made an 0 with his thumb and forefinger. "Gotcha, Boss."

She snapped the red jewelry box closed and returned it to her file. "That does it for now. Can you do this shit tonight?" She indicated the cassette recorder.

"Suppose so." He stuffed the dog tags into the watch pocket of his jeans.

"Okay. Let me hear you read through it again."

"Yes, Massa."

"And remember spirits don't talk fast. Go slow."

"Anything else, Chief?"

"You drank all the Coke."

He opened his mouth and aimed the plum. "Breaks, Babe."

21

Bradley Hammaker gave his keys to the doorman and walked inside. He was half expecting her to be there ahead of him, waiting at the bar with a drink in her hand and giving him that dismissive appraisal he hated. He wasn't exactly late. He had been tied up with a long distance conference call. Then he had taken the time to phone Angela. She hadn't even expected him to call her this evening, but he did. He wanted to be sure he wasn't forced to invent a story when he came up the stairs late tonight after his dinner date with Philippa Mooney. It was better to explain it all in advance to his wife. It didn't matter really. Angela had learned to expect him only when she saw him during the final weeks of trial preparation.

He took another look at his watch. It was a quarter to eight. Now *she* was late. He was seated at the table and perused the menu presented with a flourish by the waiter. When he glanced up, Philippa was coming toward him. He stood to greet her.

"Hello." He offered to pull out her chair before the waiter beat him to it. "I was thinking you might stand me up."

She looked at him as if he'd just confessed to the dog eating his homework.

He tapped his wristwatch face. "I was afraid you might have changed your mind, that's all."

"I planned to arrive fifteen minutes after the scheduled time in order to spare you the aggravation of being late, Mr. Hammaker. I have never found a man in your profession to operate by the same earthly clock as the rest of us do. Did I misjudge you?"

Chagrined at her artful logic, he hid his face behind a water glass. "I'm sorry to say you did not. I was involved in a three-way call with Philadelphia and actually was just seated when you came in."

She snapped the menu open. "Well, then."

"But I thought we were past the mister and miss formalities."

Her expression softened as she sipped her water. "So we were."

"Would you like a drink?" He was already studying the wine list.

"A martini. Very dry with a twist."

He nodded to the hovering waiter. "A martini for the lady, and I'll have a Cutty Sark over ice."

They sat facing one another across the linen tablecloth and searched for conversational pleasantries to put them more at ease. Bradley could not help being partly tongue-tied by her penetrating stare which seemed to bore through him as easily as x-rays through cookie dough. He could smell the *Emeraude* and suddenly felt as if he'd downed his third Scotch.

"I like your hair," he blurted. It wasn't what he meant to say at all. He had wanted to keep this strictly professional. He did not intend to let her open a seam in his emotional armor plate. "It's a very becoming color." The drinks were delivered, and he eagerly took a healthy sip before daring to look at her again. "You and your sister seem so different in many ways and yet so similar."

"You've seen Phoebe then?"

"In pictures. She looks smaller." He was grateful the words "thinner than you" had skidded to a halt at the tip of his tongue.

"She was petite. I was the athlete—Bibi was the princess."

He could smell the redolent stink of sweat, animal juices, tobacco and Bibi's sweet perfume all over again. He had accused Bibi once of being a princess, a derogatory barb meant to injure her. He had never thought of it other than as a pejorative he used to wound when they quarreled.

"Blondes and redheads run in your family, I suppose?"

She tasted the martini and caressed the stem of the glass with her lacquered nails. "So it would seem. Bibi had hair like an angel. It was so fine and soft—pure, spun gold. When she was little, it was so pale—almost no color to it. She was what you might call a natural platinum blonde."

"Uh huh." He needed another drink and nearly drained the glass. He could recall how pale Bibi's body was, as delicate as bone china. Her silken, pastel pussy reminded him of a poppy with its wispy petals spun as fine as spider threads.

"I was disappointed that Farrah was so dark. I was hoping she would be fair like Phoebe. Maybe even a redhead like me. I suppose her father must have been quite dark. Phoebe always liked opposites."

He shrank behind his Scotch and pushed the empty glass toward the edge of the table for a refill. The waiter obliged by scooping up the empty and disappearing toward the bar.

"Do you drink a lot?"

"Uh, no," he stammered, feeling his cheeks redden. "Not at all. I was just a little warm, I suppose. It does help the appetite, you know."

"I have a lecture series to prep for tonight so I'll just have a salad. I thought this meeting was primarily arranged so we could talk."

She gave him no ground to maneuver. The trouble with Philippa Mooney was that she didn't behave like a woman. She had all the tactical skills and killer instincts of a man. Of a trial lawyer even. It didn't seem fair. If she had been a courtroom adversary across the conference table, Bradley would know how to deal with her. As it was, he was hamstrung because of her gender. Not to mention the disconcerting fact he was always skating precariously close to the edge of the truth with her.

"I am grateful you agreed to come, Philippa."

"So let's begin the discussion, shall we?"

The waiter returned and looked first to Bradley for a clue about the pace of their repast. "Are you ready to order, Sir?"

"I suppose we'd better," he mumbled, picking up the menu again.

Philippa handed hers to the server. "The house salad please with vinaigrette and a baguette."

He turned expectantly to Bradley. "And for you, Sir?"

"Uhhh, bring me a bowl of soup. You still have the French onion?"

Philippa interrupted before the waiter could whet his pencil. "They only serve the French onion on the weekend, Bradley. The *soup du jour* is creme of cauliflower. But if you want to sleep well tonight, I'd order the beef barley with a whole wheat roll." She nodded to the waiter, and he retreated without another look at Bradley.

By now his ears were burning from her merciless bashing. Bradley felt ten years old, like a poor miscreant under the eagle eye of a stern governess. Maybe there was a reason Bibi was so passive, so compliant and convinced of her own fallibility. How could she ever have stood up to this super woman, this paragon of intellect and intuitive reasoning? For the very first time in his life, Bradley

Hammaker felt compassion for Bibi's cowardice. Who could ever have lived up to the expectations of an older sister like Philippa Mooney?

"Look, Professor, why don't we just put our cards on the table?"

"Fine. What sort of agenda do you have?"

"Pardon?"

"Why is this important to you one way or the other? My sister is just another client to you, isn't she?"

"Yes. If you want to put it that way."

"What other way is there to put it? You didn't know my sister, did you?"

"No." He was certain his tongue stuttered with the lie. She must suspect. It was in those eyes. "I regret that I didn't have a chance to know your sister."

"Then why should it matter to you if I want to pursue this?"

"Because it's a violation of my client's privacy. I think this is an ultimate betrayal on your part."

Her mouth hardened into a hyphen. "That's ironic. For you to call me the heavy in this little drama." She took another sip of her martini and blotted her lips with the napkin. "If I'm the villain, how would you describe Farrah's father?"

He resisted the urge to reach for the whiskey and give himself a dose of courage. "A victim maybe."

"I don't think I understand your reasoning, Counselor. Explain that to me, if you will. I'm confused. I thought my sister was the victim. I thought Farrah was the one deprived of her father's love."

Her supercilious attitude would have elicited a withering assault if she were an opponent standing on level ground. He wasn't exactly outwitted by Philippa Mooney, but he was intimidated. He could allow himself to admit that much.

The waiter returned and put the salad plate and soup bowl down. "Would you like ground pepper or Parmesan?"

"No," she answered for both of them.

He fussed for a few more seconds and then with a slight bow made a hasty exit.

"Tell me how Farrah's absent father is a victim, Bradley. I find this viewpoint fascinating." She poked her fork into the greens and speared a cherry tomato.

The symbolic skewering made him shiver. She had put him on the defensive, and he couldn't figure out how to gain the initiative. "He was shut out of Phoebe's life. He was never allowed to express his feelings about the matter."

"The matter?" She raised her eyes flirtatiously.

He fumbled for the right words, but he was beginning to wobble. "The pregnancy, the baby…Farrah."

"Well, just what do you think my sister did to deprive him of any relationship he could have had with his daughter?"

"She was married to another man for crissakes."

"You really should eat your soup, Bradley, before it goes cold."

He was not distracted. Emasculated, humiliated, embarrassed, annoyed and disgusted with his performance so far but not deterred from pursuing his point. "She had a husband. Maybe she regretted the affair. Maybe she was the one who ended it and wanted to save her marriage."

"Max knew the baby wasn't his so that's a moot point, Counselor."

He was floundering. "Maybe he wasn't in a position to assume responsibility for a family."

"Who? Max or the baby's father?"

"The father. I don't know." He rubbed his forehead. "Maybe neither one of them was ready for a family."

"Max and Phoebe were already married. So I assume they were looking forward to a family. In fact, I know that Max was eager to have children."

"His own, dammit! Farrah's not his child." He sank back, reddened up to his ears. He tugged at his necktie and reached for the Scotch. "Don't ask me to come up with all the answers, Philippa. I just wanted to make the point that maybe this guy wasn't given much of a choice."

"You mean maybe he was shut out from his daughter's life against his will?" Her eyes were downcast, and her voice was not the least reproachful. "Is that what you're trying to tell me?"

"Maybe something like that. I've been involved in cases before where that occurred. Maybe he didn't have a choice. That's all I'm saying. And maybe now he's entitled to his privacy."

"Quite honestly, Bradley, I don't know why he made the decision to abandon Bibi and her baby. My sister never talked about that, but I can tell you that I tried for years to get her to reveal something about the father. She never gave me the slightest hint. All I ever knew was that he was a marine, and I suspected he was an officer. Nothing else. It wasn't like Bibi to keep anything from me."

"It seems she could have asked him to assume some sort of role in her daughter's life if she had felt it was necessary."

"Maybe she tried."

"She remarried. Perhaps she wanted Farrah to have a more normal life and bond with her stepfather."

Philippa rested an elbow on the table and massaged her temple. For the first time, he saw the red-gold hair mussed, and it struck him as incredibly, inexplicably sexy.

"I suppose I should tell you, Bradley, that when Max came back from the war, he intended to divorce Bibi."

"How do you know that?"

"I know she told Max about the baby not being his, and they quarreled, naturally."

"That's perfectly understandable. But people do work these things out."

"Not Max. He consulted with a lawyer before he returned overseas. I know who it was, in fact. A lawyer right here in town."

"Who?"

"Someone practicing in a low rent district on the South Side. I found his card and some letters in Phoebe's things when I helped her move to Dayton with Dennis. I have it at home somewhere, I think. Can't think why I saved it really." She looked over his shoulder to stare at the wall.

"You've always had it in the back of your mind to pursue this, haven't you?"

She half-shrugged and redirected her gaze to Bradley's face. "I can't say really. I think Phoebe's death, dying so young and seeing what she went through with Dennis, the way her life turned out. It made me determined to see this through now."

"So long as you satisfy your morbid curiosity, it doesn't matter who gets hurt?"

"I wish you wouldn't put it like that."

"How should I put it?"

"You're not being fair. I don't think you've considered my feelings."

"This isn't your problem, Philippa. No matter how much you loved your sister, this was her choice, her call not yours. Leave it be for heaven's sake. If you cared for Bibi at all, then just leave it be."

"I have thought about all this. I do understand your concerns. Really."

He let up the minute he recognized her mood shift. "There's just so much to consider when you meddle in something like this. It was so long ago. How can we possibly know what was in the minds of these people?"

"I know that. But don't think I haven't tried."

He ventured a step farther. "What is the best thing for your niece? Our main concern should be her welfare. What will this do to her peace of mind?"

"She has a right to know who her father is."

"Yes, Philippa. I grant you that. Of course. But who is her real father? Is it her stepfather Dennis? Was it her legal father Max? Will her biological father turn out to be some disc jockey in Duluth with four kids who doesn't want to give her the time of day? Who? If you take away what little she has, what can you give her to replace that?"

Tears glistened in her eyes. She wadded her napkin and brushed crumbs away from her plate with a furious energy. "Farrah doesn't have to know about this. If I find out he's not a desirable person, someone who might cause her pain, then she need never find out about any of this."

He placed his hand on her arm. "Philippa, you know that once you jump in the water, you can't help but get wet. There'll be no way to turn off what you've started."

She dabbed at her eyes with the napkin. "Believe me, I would never want to do anything to injure Farrah. I love her. She's all I have in this world now that Bibi's gone."

He squelched an urge to offer her some tonic to ease her suffering, but he was drawn into her sadness. They had both lost someone. Philippa an only sibling, the little sister she had cared for when their parents were lost, the last, thin shred of family binding her to a kindred soul. Bradley Hammaker had lost someone, too. The one person who had promised him a future apart from his preordained, structured, stilted life with the law firm, the Tudor mansion in Hubbard Woods, Angela and in-laws who always expected more than he could deliver. It might have been different for all of them. He might have known this woman sitting across from him. In another world, it might have come true: Bradley, Bibi, Aunt Philippa and Farrah Lynn in a postwar, detached tract house in Mill Valley, California. A happy family.

He couldn't take the fantasy any farther than that. "Have you spoken to your niece about her feelings?"

She shook her head without answering.

"If she seems to be well adjusted, then why bring this up?"

"I think she may have an ache in her. I've already mentioned this. I feel it. Children sense when there is an emptiness. Farrah must know somehow."

"Has she ever said anything to make you think she suspects Max isn't her father?"

"Of course, not. But she did tell me she was having disturbing dreams since her mother died. About Max. I think that's very unusual, don't you? After all these years?"

He touched her arm again and was pleased to see she did not retreat from his physical overture. "It's only natural, Philippa. She's just lost her mother. It's normal for her to think about all these things, about Bibi, about Max, about when she was small."

She stared at him with moist, electric eyes. "I don't think I've heard anyone else call her that."

"Pardon?"

"You call my sister Bibi. She's always been known as Phoebe outside the family circle. I noticed you call her Bibi, too, as if you were an intimate in some way."

He backtracked awkwardly. "I didn't mean to assume any familiarity."

Philippa leaned across the table, pressed her hand over his and smiled. "I appreciate your kindness, Bradley. It's evident you care deeply about protecting your clients including my sister and my niece. I respect that. It means a great deal to me."

"I just want to help you through a difficult adjustment. I think you may be flirting with a very dangerous situation here."

"I know." She picked up her fork. "Bradley, I apologize for any unjust aspersions I may have made against your profession."

"Forget it. Lawyers have hides like alligators."

"You must be an excellent advocate. You've convinced me to act prudently. I'm going to give this some more thought. At least until I hear from my niece again. Then I'd like to meet with you before I make a final decision."

He finally dipped his spoon in the bowl. He didn't even like beef barley soup. "I'd like that." A two-ton weight lifted from his shoulders. "I'd like that very much."

22

Bradley switched off the headlights and sat for a moment looking across the expanse of manicured lawn and shrubbery lining his walkway. Angela would be asleep by now. These days she was getting up at five-thirty to jog around the neighborhood with a string of empty-nesters like herself. Bradley's wife was having a second wind at middle-age. With both boys grown and gone, she was casting her nets far afield to fill her days with meaningful activities.

He got out of the Mercedes and shut the door as quietly as possible. Inside the house, he put on the alarm, dropped his keys by the porcelain corgi and carried his jacket and briefcase up the spiraled staircase. At the second floor landing, he paused, turned around and felt for the switch to his right. Just before turning off the lights, he surveyed his domain—quiet, deserted and eerily artificial at this late hour. He and Angela had raised two sons in this house, climbed the stairs as newlyweds and burped crying babies in these hallways. When he stood still and closed his eyes, he could hear the echoes of all those years reverberating in his mind.

The house was a stone and brick Tudor fourteen-room mansion in Hubbard Woods, an old money enclave of Chicagoans who commuted to their banks and brokerages by train every morning and liked to think they left all the City's vulgarity behind when they boarded the five-oh-four in the evening. It was a planned community of plush plutocrats and artful dodgers who built their own Eden far removed from the grimy factories, tenements and steaming streets whose eastern European immigrants had never laid eyes on idyllic Hubbard Woods.

On Bradley's street there was a circular lane of capitalist ostentation. Each Republican baron vied with his neighbor to claim the grandest castle. The

Hammaker Tudor was the third house on the cul-de-sac. It was acceptable by Hubbard Woods' standards but decidedly modest set among the baroque monoliths crowding his hedges on Astor Circle.

The house had been built by Scottish industrialist Liam Keith who turned investment broker. He began by making wooden thread spools, graduated to transatlantic cable spindles and finally ended his career by sinking fellow investors' money in long distance telephone switching equipment. He made a fortune for himself and a decent return for his partners. There was a drinking fountain erected in his honor in the town square. The man had left an estate of twelve million dollars in 1929, conveniently cashing in just before the big Crash. Albion Perjamon bought the Keith mansion for his bride Mary at a real bargain price in 1933. Their only daughter Angela came with the house when Bradley married her in 1952.

Everything about Bradley Hammaker's present had to do with his wife's past. He lived in her house in her neighborhood and hobnobbed with her family's friends. Bradley's father-in-law bought him a place at the law firm when he left the service and returned home to Chicago after the war. His mother-in-law Mary decorated his office and even picked out the furniture for the nursery when the children came along. Every Sunday for as long as he had been married to Angela Perjamon Hammaker, Bradley had spent the evening dining with his in-laws at their Georgian residence on Greeley Lane a half mile from his own house. There was no escape. Their influence suffocated him at times. That was the rationalization he used most often when he visited on the South Side occasionally for some non-judgmental feminine company.

But without Angela's family influence and power, he wouldn't be standing there in a Hubbard Woods mansion, in his tailored three-piece suit with an Italian leather briefcase, a Rolex watch his father-in-law had given him for Christmas after making partner, a Mercedes 450SL in the driveway and a brand new Cadillac Seville in the garage. He had made a bargain. All this for keeping a small secret. It seemed like such a piddly price to pay for success at the time. The decision didn't occupy more than a fleeting instant of his time when he came to consider it.

Bradley turned off the lights and went into the dressing room. He sat down and took off his clothes. Angela was sound asleep in the master bedroom. He dropped his shoes on the carpet and tugged at his socks.

Bradley hadn't done much after receiving the first phone call from Bibi back in September of 1951. She had said she was pregnant, and there was an accusative edge to her voice. It had been his fault, his negligence. He should have taken precautions. He had. But he only had one condom, and the afternoon became more involved, and they had rushed into another round of lovemaking without a thought as to what lot Fate was waiting to cast upon their carelessness. When he heard Bibi's voice claiming he was at fault for her predicament, he felt nothing but anger. Not at Bibi. At himself. For the stupid assumption he could get away with anything. Even a one time random ejaculation out of all the thousands spent in aimless diversion and recreation. Bradley Hammaker had never been able to get away with anything in his entire life.

"*I'm pregnant, Brad,*" she had whispered over the long distance phone line. "*I saw the doctor. There's no doubt. It's about eight weeks along, he thinks. That fits, doesn't it? Doesn't it, Brad?*"

He was nodding over the phone but didn't bother to answer. He didn't need convincing. In a flash, he had seen the pharmacist's face barely note his disgust as he tired of waiting and left the Rexall drugstore without being waited on. One fateful condom short.

But Bibi had a husband. A husband she had fallen in love with when she was just a kid, when she didn't know what the hell love was all about. She found out the hard way. When she and Max married, she had expected a tender protector and companion to spur her self-confidence and create some space away from her dominating sister Philippa. She had counted on Max to give her the love and confidence she desperately needed. Instead Maxwell Swidnik was looking for a mother himself. He berated her for her less than perfect housekeeping, poor cooking skills and made fun of her winsome timidity he found noisome rather than appealing once they were man and wife.

After a year, Bibi was miserably unhappy and more unsure of herself than ever before. If she couldn't please this man, she must truly be a failure. No one in her whole life, she complained to Bradley, had ever been able to love her for herself. Her sister was so strong, so smart, so talented, so successful, so attractive, so independent. Bibi felt like a failure at everything.

Bradley assumed at first that Bibi could hoodwink her husband into accepting paternity for the baby. But then he realized that Bibi was thinking of telling Max the truth. It was important to her not to base a marriage relationship on deceit. And besides, she explained tearfully to him over the buzzing phone line to Honolulu, she didn't think she could stay Max's wife knowing she had borne another man's child.

They didn't speak for awhile after that. When she did contact Bradley again before the baby was born, he did not return her call. He hadn't meant to disappoint her, but she had decided to go back to Chicago to stay with her sister when he shipped overseas. Bradley assumed Max would come home, and Bibi would forget about their affair and get on with her life. His stake in Bibi's child seemed lost in the equation.

But when the letter arrived informing him that he had a daughter named Farrah Lynn, he was sick inside. He hadn't expected to feel an intimate connection with this person who carried his genes. He was engaged to marry Angela by then, charting a successful course through the smooth seas of old money to take her family's shortcut to a promising law career. That hadn't been the time to deal with his stupid mistake in California.

The first thing he had done after learning about Farrah was to call on his mentor Fran Lohman. The judge knew instantly what to do.

"*Bradley, don't worry about this. Give me her name and address. I'll take care of this for you. If there's a paternity suit, we can fight it.*"

"*No, no. She doesn't want that. She's married. She just wanted me to know about the birth, that's all. I'm not even sure her husband knows it's not his, but she hasn't said anything about involving me. I don't think she will, Fran.*"

"*What's on your mind, Hampster?*"

"*I'm not quite sure.*"

"*Is the kid yours?*"

"*Yes.*"

"*Positive?*"

"*Yes, dammit. I said it was.*"

"*Can you meet the burden of proof here, Hampster? She's married, isn't she?*"

"*Her husband was overseas. I got careless. I'm sure, Fran. It's mine. I don't want to argue that.*"

"*Okay. So do you want me to get in touch with her and see what she wants?*"

"*No. I'd rather make some sort of permanent arrangements on my own. I think I have a responsibility to help the kid in some way even if nothing comes of our affair. I mean, I don't imagine her mother will ever have much. She's an orphan, and her husband's a private.*"

Lohman had puffed furiously on a cigar as he made notes on a legal pad. "*Bradley, realize that you don't have to get involved in this. If the woman's married, you can walk away from this since she apparently won't want to press you for support or acknowledgment of paternity. I know how the emotional engines start racing at a time like this, but keep a level head on your shoulders here. You got a lot at stake.*"

"*I know.*" He was going to marry Angela. His future was set. If Bibi had wanted to hurt him, she could have forced him to his knees without a fight. He felt sorry for her, admired her honesty in an offhand way and wanted to make certain his daughter was raised with more opportunities than her mother had had. He could do that much. That much and no more.

"*You thought this over? Are you sure you want to stay involved?*"

"*Ever since I got her letter, I've been thinking about this, Fran. I want you to arrange some kind of trust for the child.*"

"*This is gonna cost you, Bradley.*"

"*I know. But it's what I want to do. I want to give her what I can so if she needs anything growing up, it'll be there for her even if I'm not.*"

"*Very noble of you, Hampster.*"

"*And in exchange I'm sure Bibi will agree to keep my name out of this.*"

"*The payments to the trust will be contingent on her confidentiality. There has to be a quid pro quo.*"

"*I understand that. I don't think Bibi will be a problem. Just get in touch with her and set this thing up, will you?*"

"*Will do. How much you got, Hampster? You got any spare cash at all?*"

"*I drained my bank account to pay for the ring and put a down payment on the car. I can't offer her a thin dime right now.*"

"*I'll advance you a personal loan, Hampster. This is just between us chickens—it'll never show up on the books.*"

"*Thanks, Fran.*"

"*You sure this is what you want to do?*"

"*Yes. I'm sure.*"

"*Well, okay, if that's how you want it, I'll do what I can.*"

"*Thanks, Fran. I owe you.*"

"*You're damned right. And I want interest, Hampster. Just to keep this thing honest between us.*"

"*Of course. I really appreciate this. I don't know what I'd do about this if you weren't around.*"

"*Say, is it a boy or girl?*"

He remembered he had closed his eyes at that moment and tried to visualize a cuddly infant nuzzling Bibi's pink breast. "*A girl. She named her Farrah Lynn.*"

"*Farrah, huh? Well, congratulations, Daddy. Have a cigar. Just picked these little Havana gems up at the Flamingo. Here, by god. Ain't every day you make Papa—take the whole damn box. I got plenty more where these came from.*" He waited while Bradley put the cold corona in his mouth and tried his best to muster a smile.

Bradley still had the box of cigars locked in his office credenza. After he had signed the papers Fran drew up for the trust fund, he didn't hear anymore about Phoebe or the baby until after the wedding. In fact, Angela was pregnant herself, expecting their first son Marcus when Fran showed up at his office.

"*He's been killed,*" he had said after sitting down across from Bradley's desk.

"*Who?*"

"*Maxwell Swidnik. Phoebe's husband. She's a widow with a baby now. I think I should have a talk with her and reinforce the terms of the trust agreement. Just in case she might decide to make herself a problem, Bradley.*" He had snipped off the end of a cigar and licked the tip with his tongue. "*Timing couldn't be worse for you.*"

"*I don't think she'll be like that. Tell her I'm sorry about her husband.*"

"*Well, just in case, I wanted you to know the developments. The life insurance money is going into the kid's trust. That's what Phoebe wants.*"

He had sat down behind his desk and held his hands against his head. "*That's a pretty damned decent thing to do.*"

"*She's a good mother so far as I can see. She won't be single long.*"

"*Let me know if she needs anything, will you?*"

"*She's fine. I would downplay the personal communications, Bradley. Just let me handle this. It's better if you keep the hell away from any of this. No trail to follow, no letters, no phone calls, nothing. Just let me handle everything.*"

"*I trust you, Fran.*"

"*Say, how's Angie feelin'?*"

"*Sick. Throws up every morning.*"

"*That won't last long. They always do it worst with their first. Thelma almost upchucked Corinne. Others didn't even make her belch.*"

"*Thanks, Fran. I appreciate all you've done for me.*"

"*By the way, your loan payment is overdue. You can buy me lunch.*"

There was a rustle of covers, and a lamp came on in the bedroom to break apart Bradley's painful reflections. Angela was awake, and he was thrust back into real time.

"Brad?"

"Don't bother to get up, Hon. I'm coming to bed." Bradley slid in beside his wife and pulled the sheet up to his chin.

She took a quick look, switched off the light and curled her backside against him. "Busy day?" she yawned.

"Yeah. Trial's gonna be a ball buster, Angie."

"You'll make out okay—you always do."

He stared up at the ceiling. He could see Fran's florid face puffing behind a veil of tobacco smoke as they left the office together that day in 1953. In fact, Lohman had kept his word. Bradley never heard a thing about Phoebe or his daughter. No personal tidbits of intimacy he could cherish as a father. Nothing. Fran handled everything. Over the years, he gradually increased the trust payments. And whenever the old judge told him there was an expediency which required an increase, Bradley always obeyed without questioning him. But there were never any Christmas greetings exchanged, no annual school photographs, no details of family life at all. As far as Bradley Hammaker was concerned his monthly trust deposits were like any other business transaction: sterile expenses, devoid of any personal baggage. Like paying the electric bill.

Five years later, Fran mentioned Bibi had remarried and moved to Dayton, Ohio. Over the years, especially after his own sons occupied so much of his attention, he thought less and less about the flesh and blood daughter growing up in Ohio totally unaware of his existence.

Now he had no idea where this strange pain was coming from inside him. After so many years, why should he be haunted by the image of this young woman out in the boondocks of Oregon? What had changed?

"You asleep, Ange?" He nudged her to make certain she was not.

"Mmmm…What is it?"

"You ever feel cheated only having sons?"

"What?" she mumbled groggily.

"You ever regret not having a daughter?"

"What?"

"I wonder what it would have been like to have a daughter, that's all. Just thinking. Go back to sleep."

"What are you talking about, Brad?"

"Nothing. Just talking. Go to sleep, Hon."

"Brad, are you thinking about having more children? At my age?"

"God, no. Go to sleep, Ange." He thumped his pillow several times and sank his face into the hollow.

"We have two wonderful sons. You'd think that would be enough. Most men want sons not daughters. You know, Bradley, you never said anything about wanting a daughter. I always thought you were satisfied having the boys."

"Forget I said anything. Goodnight, Angie."

"Are you having regrets at this stage of your life? If you really wanted a girl so badly, we could have adopted. I told you after Brad junior was born, I wasn't going to go through that again."

"Ange, please. I'm beat."

"But we could have adopted. Lots of couples do. I thought you were pleased with things the way they were."

"Look, just forget it. I'm sorry I brought it up—I didn't mean to wake you."

"You're sorry? You wake me up in the middle of the night to tell me you're suddenly dissatisfied with our children? Is it my fault we didn't have a girl?"

"Goddam it, Ange. I'm exhausted. Go to sleep, will you?"

"Have the boys been such a disappointment to you?" she whined in a practiced tone he had come to dread.

"I'm very happy with the boys. And you. I was just thinking aloud, that's all."

"If you're not happy with the decision I made to have my tubes tied, just tell me. I thought we talked this over, and now you decide you wanted another child?"

"No, I am not saying I wanted more children. I don't. Two is enough. I'm very happy with you and the boys. Just go to sleep, Ange."

"Then what is it?"

He bolted out of bed and pulled down the window shade with a violent jerk. The blind flew up and rattled around the roller bar. "Godammit!"

"What's the matter with you, Bradley?"

He reached for a cigarette. "Nothing. I'm just tired."

She got out of bed. When she put an arm around his waist in a tentative gesture of support, he flinched, and she drew back. "What's wrong, Brad? What is it?"

For the first time in his married life, he made an attempt to be completely honest with her. "I made a mistake, Angela."

"Is it something serious?"

"Yes."

"Well, can you fix it?"

"I wish I knew how."

23

It was so easy really. Josie didn't have to go any farther than the pay telephone at the trailer park. She just slipped her coins in the slot, asked for information in Chicago, Illinois, and requested a number for Charles P. Plack, the name at the bottom of Phoebe's affidavit. Josie figured Plack got copies of the affidavit because he was the lawyer representing Max Swidnik. And if she could find Plack, he might be able to tell her what she wanted to know.

When she dialed the number information gave her for Plack, it was a law office, and Charles Plack even took the call. As Josie fed change into the telephone at the operator's prompting every three minutes, Mr. Plack fielded her questions.

"Miss Wallgood, are you a beneficiary of Mrs. Poole's estate?" he asked in a smoker's baritone.

"No. I'm a human relations consultant, and Phoebe Poole's daughter Farrah Swidnik is my client. I'm calling you on her behalf." She agreed that Cain's suggestion to call herself a consultant on the credit application was timely. It was all a matter of respect. People never raised their eyebrows at the mention of a consultant. Psychic reader, on the other hand, was a real conversation stopper.

"Uh huh. You know, Miss, uh, Wellgood—"

"—Wallgood."

"Wallgood. You wanna know about a matter…uh, when was this again?"

"The estate has just been settled. But the information I'm after has to do with her father Max Swidnik twenty-five years ago."

"1952? Swidnik?"

"You were his lawyer. His wife signed an agreement not to ask him for child support for Farrah Swidnik."

"Why don't you write me a letter? I got a pretty full schedule right now."

"Can't you pull out the file and take a look at it for me?"

"You gotta lotta problems here, Miss Wallgood. First, I don't have files hangin' around here from twenty-five years ago. Lemme think…1952, huh?"

"It was August of 1952."

"Yeah, yeah. Well, in 1952, I was just outta law school. I took a lotta small cases like you're talkin' about. This was a property settlement agreement?"

"No. It was about paternity."

"Uh huh. Was there a complaint filed?"

"A lawsuit, you mean?"

"Yeah."

"I'm not sure."

"Well, if you have the dates and names of the litigants, you can write to the Cook County Court Clerk and request a copy of the documents you need."

"But I already have the document, Mr. Plack."

He burped back a guttural sigh, worn down by her persistence. "Then what is it you want from me exactly?"

"I want to ask you some questions about it."

He crushed his cigarette and started taking notes for the first time in their conversation. "And you're some kinda social services consultant?"

"Human relations."

"Are you a psychologist or a shrink?"

The question threw her off balance for a moment. Did it matter exactly what she called herself anyway? So long as she didn't come up with anything too outrageous this guy could probably care less. And if he thought she was a peer, he might even be more accommodating. "I'm a private consultant," she quibbled. "I've been helping Miss Swidnik deal with her father's death. He was killed in the Korean War—"

"—Uh huh—"

"—and his remains were never recovered."

"Uh huh. And what is it exactly you think I can do about it, Miss Willgood?"

"*Wallgood.*"

"Right."

"Well, you were his attorney in 1952, right?"

He leaned back until his chair squealed. "Could be. Maybe, maybe not. You think I remember all my nickel and dime clients for the last twenty-five years?"

"So you weren't his lawyer?"

"Look, I'd hafta check the records. What is it you want?"

"Just information you may have concerning his relatives, background, anything about his personal situation that may aid my client in reconstructing a history of her father. Since her mother was an orphan, and now she's passed away, he's the only family link she has."

"Uh huh. Well, like I said, I don't have those files here. I got all that junk stored away in a records warehouse. They got mice, rats, winos and who knows what kinda crap in that old loft. It'd take me awhile to have my staff dig up the file." His staff was one peroxided, pigeon-toed drop-out from the Acme Stenographic School in Joliet.

"How long would that take?"

"Who knows? Maybe a few weeks. Maybe a couple months. We're pretty busy right now, Miss Wallford."

"It's Wallgood."

"Yeah, right. Look, I'm busy with some big cases comin' up for trial."

"But you could find it, right?"

"If I represented this Max Swidnik in 1952 and handled a civil case for him, then I should have a file somewhere, yeah."

"Then could you find it for me?"

"There'd be a charge."

"How much?"

"A minimum fifty bucks. If we gotta make copies, that'd be extra."

"Okay. Do it then."

"You'll have to have your client write me, Miss Waldgood. Send the fifty bucks, and I'll get back to you when we locate the file."

"So you'll get started on it right away then?"

"If your client sends me a letter and the money. But I wanna make it clear that I can't release any information from a client file without authorization from the court, a sub poena *duces tecum* or a power of attorney specifically allowing your client—uh, this Miss Swidnik person—access to my files."

"Oh." Her lead balloon suddenly dropped.

He hung up before she had a chance to think of another excuse to keep him on the line. She put the receiver back. This looked like a dead-end. She had no idea anyone would want to conceal something in a file twenty-five years old. What were these lawyers afraid of anyway? Sneaky bastards. She'd end run this smart sonuvabitch.

She dialed Illinois information for Chicago one more time and asked for another name: R.B. Pester—the witness on Phoebe's affidavit. There were four

Pesters with the first initial R, seven Pesters in all. She sighed and took out a stack of quarters and dimes and fed her money into the machine.

There was no answer at the first number. The second listing had been disconnected and was no longer in service. The third turned out to be an old woman hard of hearing. Josie shouted for awhile, then gave up and went on to the fourth Pester.

"Hello?" a harried voice answered.

"Is this the Pester residence?"

"Yeah. Who is this?" The woman sounded tired and not the least bit friendly.

Maybe Josie's brilliant idea wasn't so brainy after all. She sighed and hunched her shoulders in resignation. Another blank, no doubt. "I was trying to locate R.B. Pester."

"Yeah? What do you want?"

"Is this R.B. Pester?"

"She's my mother-in-law."

"What's her name?"

"Who the hell is this anyway? Whatever you're selling, she doesn't want any."

"No, I'm not selling anything."

"Who is this?"

"I'm trying to locate the witness on a legal document from 1952. I'm not after anything from your mother-in-law. I just wanted to see if she could remember anything about the time she signed as a witness."

"Are you a lawyer?"

"No. I'm just trying to help a friend find out something about her father who died in the Korean War."

The voice still failed to yield a smidgen of civility. "What does this have to do with Rita?"

"She signed a document as a witness. She worked for an attorney, I think." She looked at her notes again. His name was right there: attorney for affiant. "I think she worked for a Mr. Lohman."

"He's retired now and so's Rita."

"Well, I was hoping I could speak to her."

"Hang on." She dropped the phone and shouted in the background.

In a moment, someone else picked up the phone and a pleasant, if timid, voice answered. "Hello? This is Rita Pester."

"Hello, Mrs. Pester. I'm calling for a friend—Farrah Swidnik in Oregon."

"Where?"

"Oregon. You see, I think you used to work as a secretary for an attorney named Lohman, is that right?" She aimed her pencil over her pad.

"Yes. I was his confidential secretary. Judge Lohman's retired now."

"I know, but I'm calling about something you did way back in 1952."

"Who are you again?"

"I'm a friend of Farrah Swidnik's—her mother Phoebe Swidnik was a client of Mr. Lohman, and he made up an affidavit, and you signed as a witness. Do you remember that at all, Mrs. Pester?"

"1952? That's so long ago. I always signed as a witness for Judge Lohman. There would have been hundreds of documents with my signature. I couldn't possibly remember each one."

"Do you remember anybody by the name of Swidnik?"

"No."

"Phoebe Swidnik's husband maybe? He was killed in Korea."

"I couldn't possibly remember that long ago. Judge Lohman had so many clients."

"Are you sure you can't think of anything that might help me?"

"No. I'm afraid not. Why do you want to know about Max after all these years?"

Josie's ears tingled. There were definitely strong vibes coming across the phone lines. She was certain she hadn't mentioned Max's name. "You know, his remains were never recovered after the war."

"Oh?"

"They sent back his dog tags with a coffin, but then they said there was a mistake, and the remains weren't Max's at all. So now Farrah, his daughter, is trying to learn more about him. Her mother Phoebe just passed away."

"You're a friend of Max Swidnik's daughter?"

"Yes."

"And Phoebe Swidnik is gone now?"

"She died of cancer. And Farrah wants to find out what he was like. Did you know her dad at all?"

"No." The denial shot back like a ricochet. Something stank, and it wasn't the cat pee in the phone booth.

"You know, Mrs. Pester, Farrah doesn't know that Max wasn't her real dad." Josie could hear the sound of pots and pans banging in the background. "She doesn't want anything—no money or anything like that. Her Mom left her a trust fund. She just wants to find out something about Max after all these years. I don't want to cause any trouble or anything, but if you could help me out…"

"Farrah wants to know more about her real father, you say?"

"Yeah, but he isn't Maxwell Swidnik."

"How do you know that?"

"Because of the affidavit you signed that this lawyer Lohman drew up. I have it, and it says that Max is not Farrah's real dad."

"How did you get that document?"

"Farrah's mother left it to her—some lawyer sent it after Phoebe died."

"Then why doesn't Farrah know the truth about her father?"

"Because she's afraid to read it. You see, if she finds out Max isn't her father, then it's like she has nobody. Her mother is dead. She didn't have any grandparents—Phoebe was an orphan. And Farrah's stepfather is a real shit. So can you help me out, Rita?"

"What do you want?"

"Well, did you know Max?"

"I don't think he was a client of the Judge."

"Do you know whose idea it was to make up the affidavit?"

"No. And that would be none of your business."

"Well, did Phoebe know Lohman for a long time?"

"I can't say."

"Did you know her?"

"Not really. We may have talked on the telephone occasionally."

"Can't you tell me anything at all about Maxwell Swidnik?"

"No. I'm sorry. I can't."

"Whose picture's attached to the affidavit?" Zaps of psychic energy were burning up the telephone lines. She was definitely onto something here. "It's Farrah's real father, right?"

"I don't know anything about a picture."

"Don't snow me, Rita. I got the picture, and it's Farrah's dad, isn't it?"

"I can't say."

"Were you and Max lovers?" she blurted in a bolt of brilliance that dazzled her. Sometimes her pyrotechnical genius just flowed out of her brain like electric current when she was really humming. Must be some sort of magical shit at work.

"Of course, not. That's absurd."

"But you knew him, didn't you?"

With a heavy sigh, Rita relented, relieved to be giving up. "I did know a Maxwell Swidnik from school. That's all. We lived in the same neighborhood. We knew each other slightly before he went in the service and met Phoebe."

"Was he your boyfriend?"

"Certainly not. That's ridiculous."

"Were you like dating?"

"We saw each other socially, if that's what you mean."

Josie banged her elbows on the sides of the phone booth in her unrestrained glee. She had hit the jackpot, plugged into the psychic mainstream. Goddam, she was good. "I bet it was a lot more serious than that, Rita. Weren't you like planning on marrying him or something?"

"It wasn't like that at all. While Max was in California, we both made other plans. I married someone else, but I was already widowed by the time I saw Max again."

"Was your husband in the war, too?"

"He was killed just a few weeks before Max was sent overseas with the First Division."

"So did you and Max hang out after your husband died?"

"Max wrote to me. We were just friends."

"And then he told you about Farrah, right? He found out he wasn't her father, didn't he?"

"Yes. He knew. But I don't know who the child's real father was," she volunteered hastily. "And even if I did, I would never divulge that information. That was a confidential matter between Phoebe and Max. Perhaps you would be better off just leaving things the way they are. I can't help you."

"Did Mr. Lohman know that you and Max were making it?"

There was a long hesitation on the line. Children could be heard bickering in the background; a door slammed then Rita Pester's voice lowered to nearly a whisper. "Are you calling on behalf of Farrah?"

"She's hired me as a consultant."

"What is your name again?"

"Josephine Wallgood."

"Look, I don't want to cause any trouble for anyone, Miss Wallgood."

"Neither do I. But shouldn't you have told your boss that you were involved with Max Swidnik? I mean, Lohman was Phoebe's lawyer, right? Isn't that like some kind of a conflict?"

"That's for lawyers. I was just a secretary."

"Well, it doesn't sound right to me."

Her voice squeaked as her throat tightened. "Please! Listen to me—it didn't matter. It had nothing to do with me and Max. This was just a simple matter between Phoebe and Max so he could get on with his life after the war. That's all."

Josie's brain was blazing like a Boy Scouts' campfire by now. "So you don't think Lohman will even care if I mention this to him about you and Max?"

"How did you find out about this? How did you know about Max and me?"

Josie grinned. It was in the stars. Plain as day. "Can't say, but I think it's something Mr. Lohman is gonna find pretty interesting, don't you, Rita?"

"Oh, no..." Rita whimpered. Criminy—Josie must have hit the mother lode. "Please, don't call him. He doesn't need to know. What difference does it make after all these years? Is Farrah going to try and cause trouble after all this time?"

"She doesn't want that."

"Then why can't you just go away and leave me alone?"

"Because she wants to know who her real father is."

"I can't help you."

"Who can?"

"How should I know? I can't help you."

"Then I'll call Mr. Lohman and see if he can tell me what I want to know."

"No! Just leave him alone! Judge Lohman would never reveal confidential information to you or anybody else. Just leave it be."

"Well, we'll see what he has to say about it."

"The Judge would never discuss a client's file with anyone, Young Lady."

Time to fire her silver bullet, her hole card. Josie's earlier labors were yielding dividends. She had called the information desk at the Silverton library and acting on a sudden hunch asked about the document's date. Josie was a real pro—she did her homework when necessary to make a score. Too bad there was nobody around to see how it was all paying off. This was phenom stuff.

"Look, Rita, I hate to bring this up, but I checked at the library, and you know what I found? This affidavit was signed on August 24th, and that was a Sunday. What were you doing in the office making up legal documents on a Sunday?"

"I haven't any idea what you're talking about."

"I guess I'll just have to call this Judge Lohman guy and ask him what he thinks about his secretary going down to the office on a Sunday and making up a bunch of legal documents for her boyfriend." Josie pulled the receiver away from her ear but stopped when she heard a frantic shout.

"Stop! Don't hang up!"

She pressed the phone against her cheek and grinned. Now she was really getting somewhere. This performance was star quality, good enough for TV. Too bad Josie lacked an audience. "So what can you tell me, Rita?"

"I swear, I don't know anything."

"A name?"

"No."

"Well, what?"

"You have to promise me—swear—that you won't tell anyone I told you."

"I can swear if you can."

"And you won't mention any of this to Judge Lohman. Nothing about me or Max or anything about the affidavit."

"He doesn't have to know if I can find out what I need from you."

"Just don't get him involved in this."

"Okay. So what can you tell me?"

"You swear?"

"Yeah. I swear. So do you know who it is?"

"I can't give you his name."

"But you know who it is?"

"Yes."

Josie's freckles stood out as her face flushed with excitement. She pressed the receiver closer to drown out the racket of a car engine roaring to life at a nearby trailer pad. "Was it somebody Max knew?"

"No."

Jesus, Josie was thinking as her cheeks swelled. This was getting good. Cain was going to love this. "Like somebody in the service?"

"Yes. They were stationed together at the same base."

"He was a marine like Max, right?"

"Yes."

"What else?'

"I can't give you a name." She sighed heavily. "I just can't."

"How about a good hint?"

"I can't. I've told you enough already."

"I need more than this, Rita."

"Look, if Phoebe had wanted her daughter to know about this man, why didn't she leave her something to identify him?"

"I think that was part of the bargain she made, right? Never to say anything?"

"Oh, please…I've said enough."

"The picture is him, right?"

"The snapshot. Yes."

"Who took it?"

"It was a picture Judge Lohman had."

"Jeez, you mean you like stole it or something and sent it to Max's lawyer?"

"It wasn't stealing. I just didn't think he would mind if I borrowed it. I meant to put it back. Max had no idea who it was. He didn't know the man—he just wanted to see what he looked like, that's all."

"All he had was this guy's picture?"

"Yes."

"I need more, Rita, or I'm gonna have to call and talk to Lohman."

"I've helped you all I can. I have to hang up now."

"You know what I think? I think he was somebody rich who wanted to make sure nobody found out about Farrah. And I'll bet that if he found out it was you who told, he'd be pissed enough to sue you or something."

"Why can't you just leave me alone?"

"Because Farrah needs to know who her father is."

"Well, I've told you everything I know."

"I don't think so."

"It's been so long ago. You don't know what will happen if you tell Judge Lohman about this affidavit, Miss Wallgood."

"If you don't want me to tell him, then you better help me out, Rita. This call is costing me a fortune already. I'm about to run out of quarters."

"If I help you, will you swear never to call me again?"

"If you swear to never tell anybody about my calling *you*."

"Alright. Then I have your word you won't contact Judge Lohman about this?"

"Sure. So what can you tell me besides he was in the marines with Max?"

"He was an officer."

"Yeah, so? I can tell that from the picture. He's got bars on his collar. What was his name?"

"I can't give you that—please, believe me. He was a lieutenant."

"What was his name for crissakes, Rita?"

Outside the phone booth, two little girls started jumping rope and giggling. Josie looked away. She shut her eyes and held her breath. This was like waiting for the dentist's drill to hit a nerve.

Rita sighed again. "He's a lawyer."

"So he's still around, right?"

"Yes."

"You aren't gong to tell me his name, but you know it, right?"

"I can't. I just can't."

"Okay. I already know his initial—it's B, right?"

"Yes."

"So give me his first name anyway. Is it Bob?"

"No."

"Bill?"

"No."

"Ben?"

"No."

"Bruce?"

"No."

"Brian?"

"No."

"Jesus, Rita. I don't have enough money to go through the entire alphabet here. Tell me his first name anyway. You know I'm gonna find him."

"You swear you won't ever call me again? And you won't call Judge Lohman?"

"What's his first name for crissakes?"

"Bradley."

She wrote the name quickly on her pad. "And he's a lawyer in Chicago, right?"

"Yes."

"It's gonna be easy for me to find him. Why don't you just tell me his last name? I know the initial is H, right? This is stupid, Rita."

"You swear—"

"—I swear. But if you don't give me the name, Rita, I'm gonna have to go through the whole list and tell each one all about why I'm calling. And I have a real strong suspicion that if I hit Lohman here with this copy of the affidavit, he's gonna shit little pearly pink bricks and totally freak out, right?"

"Please, don't do that!"

"Did you just make this up all by yourself and give it to Max to make him feel better, to screw Phoebe or what?"

"I did it because Max asked me to. Try to understand. Max was Catholic. So am I. We were hoping to be married when he came back from overseas. But there was no hope of our ever getting married in the Church unless Max could get an annulment. The affidavit was in support of his petition for annulment. It didn't hurt Phoebe. She didn't even know about it. I didn't think it would harm anyone since it was true anyway. Everything in that affidavit is true. I can swear to that myself. I felt that Phoebe would admit everything in the affidavit anyway sooner or later."

"So you made it up, and Lohman didn't ever find out?"

"No. Never. I sent it to Max when he was overseas so he could start the annulment petition with the Church. When he died, I just forgot all about it. It didn't matter anymore."

"What about Plack?"

"Who?"

"Charles Plack. You had him copied on the affidavit. I called and found out he's another lawyer in Chicago."

"Oh. Yes. Charlie. He was Maxwell's attorney. Max wanted me to send a copy to him, and I did."

"Why did Max even have an attorney?"

"Charlie Plack was going to handle the divorce."

"So Max was getting a divorce and an annulment?"

"He was going to divorce Phoebe, but he hoped to get an annulment so we could be married in the Church eventually."

"And did this Bradley guy ever have anything to do with Phoebe after Max died?"

"I don't know."

"Did Max ever talk to this guy?"

"No. I'm sure he didn't. Phoebe told him the baby wasn't his, but she never told Max who the father was."

"So you knew—"

"—Yes."

"Because Lohman knew, right?"

"Yes.

"But you didn't tell Max the name?"

"I couldn't. I couldn't have revealed confidential information like that to Max. They would have realized who told him. Nobody but the Judge knew who it was."

"How'd you find out?"

"I was Judge Lohman's private secretary. He used only an account number for the man who made the payments to Phoebe. But I overheard him talking on the phone once, and when I heard the word Farrah, I listened in."

"Did you know him?"

"I hadn't been working that long for the Judge at the time. This man is someone very close to Fran."

"Who's Fran?"

"Judge Lohman. Francis Lohman."

Josie drew a blank line on her paper. "So what's this Bradley's last name?"

A breathy pause preceded her barely audible admission. "Hammaker."

"Bradley Hammaker. Is that it?"

"You swore you won't ever divulge the source of your information."

"Not unless you tell somebody I talked to you."

"Please, don't call me again."

"I won't—as long as you keep our agreement."

"May I please hang up now?"

"Isn't it like a major crime to forge legal documents, Rita?"

Pester banged the phone down without another word.

24

Charlie Plack got up to shut his office door. He sat down and swiveled around to stare out his window at the alley. He had a second-floor view of a row of metal garbage cans, a brown dumpster filled with cardboard boxes, a brick wall with a slime trickle and an Olds Cutlass with no wheels and no plates. His professional situation had stagnated. He was up on the tenth floor once, across town in a high-rise on the Loop just off State Street. He'd shared space with four other attorneys and had a decent bank balance. Their secretary had all her own teeth, no tattoos, no runners in her hose or homicidal boyfriends out on parole.

But then there was a crisis: Bernie Shiggins lost a fourteen-day civil trial. It was a cinch, a slam dunker—a little old lady fell off the city bus and broke her hip. Then the driver went off and left her sprawled on the curb. But Bernie lost. Their investigator somehow had failed to discover their client was an ex-roustabout with the Ringling Brothers Circus, a professional slip and fall artist who masqueraded all over the country as a sweet little granny taking prat falls whenever she was in the vicinity of a hefty insurance policy.

The case bankrupted the firm. Partly because they were already overextended from another partner's gambling debts at the track, and partly because Plack had been dipping into the client trust account to cover his alimony arrearage. Now he was back in the low rent district handling dog bites, filing restraining orders and chasing down nickel and dime personal injury cases no reputable lawyer would consider. Plack's standards were considerably lower these days—he took on anybody with a discernible pulse who could mark an X on the contingency fee contract.

Plack picked up the phone and punched in a number. "Hey, guess who just called me?"

"I give up—the finance company."

"Farrah Swidnik's friend."

"Who?"

Plack grinned and lit a cigar, one of a dozen straight from Smoky Joe's Discount Smoke Shop. He planted his feet on the dirty windowsill. "She got the affidavit, and she's nosin' around already. I knew she would."

"That's Max's kid?"

"Caught in his trap."

"Oh, yeah, yeah. So you said."

"The kid doesn't know a thing yet. She will." He puffed a few times to make the stogie's tip glow. His gray shirt and knit tie were already peppered with ash.

"What'd you tell her?"

"It was some girlfriend of hers tryin' to get me to open up Max's old divorce file. Said she was a shrink or some shit, but it sounds like one of her hippie friends out there."

"You're gonna be sorry you poked your fat ass into this, Charlie."

"Bullshit. The kid has a right to know who her old man is."

"Why is that so fuckin important?"

"I told you why, dammit!"

"Yeah, yeah. Because of some old grudge that started twenty-five years ago. Who gives a fuck anymore, Charlie? Huh? Who?"

"Me, that's who. I care. I still give a shit. I don't forget about Sammy. I don't give a fuck if it was two-hundred years ago. I don't forget, Bernie."

"He's gone, Charlie. Christ, give it a rest, willya for crissakes?"

"What about my little Janice? You think I'm gonna forgive the bastard for that?"

"She's got nothin' to do with him, Charlie. Water under the fuckin bridge."

"Blow it out your ass, Bernie. What the fuck do you know about it, huh? How in hell do you know how I feel about that bastard?"

"He's gone. They're all gone for crissakes. Let it be, Charlie. Just let it be."

"You tell me that after they bring your brother home in a garbage sack. You gimme advice when you see your kid laid out like a slab of baloney at the morgue and your mother's heart breaks apart. Then you can tell me what the fuck to do, Bernie Shiggins."

"Charlie, look. It's over and done with, okay? What did Max Swidnik ever have to do with any of that shit, huh? He didn't have anything to do with your kid."

"He was a smart-assed sonuvabitch who always got away with it. Well, he ain't gettin' away with this any longer. The kid has a right to know what a shit-head she's been wastin' her time pinin' for, lookin' up to all these years."

"Give it up, Charlie. You don't know anything about this kid."

"She's the same age as my Janice. I know that."

Bernie didn't answer. Nobody could talk to Charlie Plack about his daughter Janice. It was like mentioning the Holocaust to the old Polacks in his neighborhood—nobody ever brought it up.

"I just think you should be careful. Watch your backside, Charlie. It ain't worth getting' disbarred for."

"I got my ass covered. You just make damned sure you keep your mouth shut."

"Jesus, Charlie, how long we been friends? How many years I know you? Who you callin' a fink here, Asshole? What the hell's got into you, you crazy sonuvabitch!"

Plack slammed the phone down and leaned back until his chair screamed.

Goddam assholes, he mumbled, knocking more ash on his trousers. Bernie Shiggins didn't give a flying fuck. Screw him. Charlie Plack's former partner was a two-bit hustler filing small claim judgments against deadbeat debtors for the Beneficial Finance Company in New Jersey now. Like he had some room to criticize. At least Charlie Plack still had a legitimate practice.

He reached inside his jacket pocket, took out a key and unlocked the bottom drawer of his desk. Inside was a metal strongbox. Charlie unlocked it and retrieved an affidavit embossed with Rita Pester's notary seal. He studied the original for a moment, then carefully folded it, replaced it in the box and relocked the drawer.

He was satisfied he had done the right thing. After all these years, while Farrah Swidnik was growing up with all the luxuries and bennies Charlie Plack's kids only dreamed about, he had this affidavit locked in his file. Max Swidnik had all the love and glory a kid could give a father who had died a hero. Farrah must have idolized the guy from the time she was old enough to hear about what a fantastic fellow he was. Charlie Plack knew better. A lot better. He had no love for his former client and Friday night beer buddy from Portelli's Produce Warehouse. That went back to when Charlie and Max were both working the day shift and going to school nights. But while Charlie was struggling to feed a wife and a kid with another one on the way, Max was just looking out for himself. Selfish bastard.

The trouble with Maxwell Swidnik was that he wanted it all. He wanted to come out of the service a decorated hero, stand for public office and end up in City Hall, maybe even the state capitol in Springfield. He had it all planned. He was engaged to a nice, respectable Catholic girl from the old neighborhood. He was planning on getting his law degree after the war, but then he met some cunt in California and got married. Dumped Rita like she had the clap, told her he needed a better future for himself than the old neighborhood could provide. California was wide open with opportunities, he spewed on the phone to Charlie just before he went overseas. Told Charlie he was crazy to stay in Chicago when he could come out to Oakland and make a fortune for himself.

"*This place is full of suckers, Charlie,*" Max had bragged.

When things had started to go sour for Max, who did he run to but his old friends for help? He had called from California just before he shipped out with Uncle Sam. "*I got the bitch where I want her now, Charlie. I want you to file for a divorce as soon as I get back from Korea. I'm gonna get an annulment, too. What do you think my chances are with that?*" He had referred to the document lying pristine on Charlie's desk blotter.

Plack had taken a quick look and puffed his cheeks out. "*About the divorce? No problem there. Is she amenable to a quick, no contest divorce?*"

"*Yes.*"

"*Then you're in like Flynn.*"

"*I mean about the annulment. I don't want this fiasco to queer any chances I have to get started when I come back. An annulment is the only way to do it clean so it doesn't leave any stink on my shoes, Charlie, right?*"

"*I can't give you advice about what the Church and His Holiness might do, Max.*"

"*Well, alright. But it makes my chances pretty good, don't you think?*"

"*No guarantees.*"

"*I'm gonna just erase this whole fucking mess from my life, Charlie—forget it ever happened. Forget about Bibi and get on with my life. I got big plans, Charlie. You know, I got a letter from Alderman Hennessey last week. It looks like I can get that job at City Hall when I get back. Hey, we're talking first step here, but it's a big leap up from our old neighborhood, huh?*"

Charlie's expression had frozen in a grimace. Bastard. He felt as if the slick sonuvabitch had ground his brogan into Plack's face. The old neighborhood, the street gang of rowdy steelworkers' sons, grocers' brats and factory flotsam was never good enough for Max.

Plack sucked hard on his cigar and held the smoke in his lungs. He siphoned the exhaust out slowly and watched it curl its way toward the window. Max didn't get the fancy-shmancy job working for the alderman. He didn't get to schmooze with the upper-crusties Plack loathed. He didn't even get a chance to jilt Rita a second time either. Charlie knew Max never had any intention of coming back to link up with that loser. Rita Pester was the only one who actually believed Maxwell would ever darken her doorway after he got what he wanted from her.

After all these years, it still made Charlie Plack wince when he thought about it. Not just his brother—that maybe was a heartbreak they had prepared themselves to accept: Sammy not coming home. Lots of boys went off to Korea and never came home. They could have stood that. But while they lowered Sammy into a plain grave with only four mourners looking on, Swidnik got a helluva send off for being a big, fucking hero. He was decorated posthumously with a Bronze Star and had a big write-up in the *Trib*, photos on the front page showing his ditzy mother hugging the flag they gave her at the cemetery. A couple of years later, a buddy from the First Division told Charlie straight out the guy was a fraud, a yellow rat who was the first grunt to jump out of the fox-hole and hightail it for the rear when the incoming mortar got him. In the confusion, with all the bodies shot to hell, the field CO got Max mixed up with another soldier who actually did stand up and kept firing at the advancing line until he was chopped in half by an NK shell. So Max Swidnik came out the hero and succeeded in fucking over decent guys like Sammy and the nameless schmuck in his platoon whose bravery was mistakenly overlooked.

What made it stick in Charlie's craw all these years was how every time he suffered a loss, got knifed in the heart, Max Swidnik came out smelling like a fucking rose.

Plack put his fist over his lips and squeezed out a tear that slid down his bulbous nose like an Olympic ski jumper. Plack's only son, his shining star from a marriage that never did work worth a damn, had hanged himself in jail awaiting arraignment. He'd been gang-raped by four bastards who held the seventeen-year old down and stifled his screams by shoving his underpants in his mouth. Charlie Plack was never going to forget that outrage, that final slap in the face. It seemed neither God nor any other living asshole on the planet would give Charlie Plack a chance to succeed at anything.

He wiped his face with a stubby finger and sniffed. Plack had two kids. After he lost his brother Sammy in Korea, he supported his widowed mother and doted on his son and baby girl. His son was demonstrating against the Vietnam war—burned his draft card right on the steps of City Hall. Got tossed in the can with a lot of degenerates who beat the shit out of him, raped him and then left him hanging there for two hours until the jailers found him. The shock and grief killed his grandmother—she passed away a month after they laid him to rest beside his Uncle Sammy. Then Charlie focused all his love and attention on his daughter Janice. She was the light of his life, a good girl who worshipped her daddy. Until a certain summer day in 1971 when she happened to be in the wrong neighborhood at the wrong time.

"Oh, Jesus," Charlie wept into his sleeve as he huddled in his ratty chair with the cigar dangling from his mouth. The painful memory of that day burned like battery acid in his heart. Janice had walked right up without a knock, no fucking warning at all. How could Charlie have ever guessed that his angel, his darling would surprise him in the middle of the afternoon, sitting in his own fucking automobile? When Janice pulled open the car door and saw the black hooker drooling with Charlie's jism, her phony orange wig askew, a half-dead Jack Daniels bottle open on the dash and Charlie's business end still throbbing like a Polish sausage in her fingers, she had let out a little cry like a wounded deer and run off before Charlie could even summon the courage to speak.

That was six years ago, and Janice still had not forgiven him. Never would. Plack still saw the look of shame and disgust in her face every time he closed his eyes, and it made him think of Max Swidnik—the lying, conniving bastard who had denied his own daughter, turned his back on her, and the kid still idolized the phony sonuvabitch.

Plack was going to change all that. It still mattered to him. Now that Phoebe was gone, he had nobody to answer to for his dirty work. Phoebe's kid had nobody left but Max's memory. And Charlie Plack was going to make sure she knew what a scumbag Max Swidnik really was, what a fucking shithead she had for a father. How he screwed over everybody he knew, used people up like they were toilet paper.

Finally Charlie Plack was going to destroy what was left of Maxwell Swidnik's bogus legacy to a daughter he never even wanted to know. It was enough to numb Charlie Plack's grief at losing his own little girl. After all the years of hurting, he was finally going to get even.

25

Philippa Mooney set her drink down and closed her purse. "I don't appreciate your choosing this place."

Charlie Plack shielded his face behind a tumbler full of whiskey and tap water. "I wanted to talk out of the office, that's all. No harm done."

"I don't like it. You can meet me at the University next time."

"You know, you're startin' to act like an old maid, Professor. You need to lighten up a little." Charlie Plack laid a finger on her arm and laughed as she recoiled. "What're you scared of? Afraid I'll bite, Teach?"

"It's Professor Mooney. Let's keep this strictly business, alright?"

"Okay, Miss Professor. Whatever you say." He offered her a silent toast and sipped his liquor. "But you're not a bad lookin' lady. I could make myself interested."

"Don't do me any favors."

"Suit yourself, Sis."

She pushed her martini away. "I wanted to see you because of Max Swidnik."

"So you said. And I'm all ears. What's on your mind?"

"You were his lawyer when he was married to Phoebe."

"Maybe. It's hard to remember that far back." He took another drink. Charlie Plack was enjoying playing with this uptight, smart-assed woman who rated her skinny butt so much purer than his. Goddam bitch. They were all the same. He hated her guts without even knowing her. Her sister, no doubt another spoiled princess, had taken Rita Pester's fiancé away then spread her legs for the whole damned fleet probably. These high-class bitches were all the same underneath, weren't they? Some tired old broad like Rita Pester had more integrity in her little finger than this snobbish dame had in her entire body.

"Look, Mr. Plack—"

"—Call me Charlie." His lop-sided leer forced her to look away.

"Can you please keep this conversation on a professional level?"

"Whatever makes you happy, Professor."

"I think you were going to help Max get a divorce from my sister. She told me Max had seen a lawyer, and when I was going through some of her things after she left Chicago and moved to Dayton with her second husband, I came across some letters you wrote to Phoebe on Max's behalf back in 1952. Since her death, I've gone through some of my sister's things, and I found your card. I don't forget names, Mr. Plack."

"Congratulations. I gotta lousy memory myself."

"Over the phone, you said you could help me. Was that just a line to get me here?" She looked around at the dimly lit, smoky lounge and saw no one who seemed to have bathed recently, including her scuzzy companion Plack.

Charlie sat up and straightened his necktie. Bitch thought she was too good for this, huh? This was a working folks' tavern. A place where real men and women threw back and had a few laughs after a ball-busting day answering to uptown pricks and bitches like this dame. "Look, I can do better than you any day of the week, Sis. Don't give yourself too many points, okay? I'm here on account of you asked me, okay? Let's get that straight—you asked *me*."

"The point is you said you could help me."

"You said you wanted to know about Max's divorce. But that ain't the only reason we're havin' this little chat, right?"

"I'm going to be straightforward with you, Mr. Plack."

"I'm really flattered," he smirked.

"I want to find out who fathered my sister's child. Max Swidnik knew it wasn't his. Wasn't that the basis for the divorce he planned to file?"

"Could be. People split up for lotsa reasons."

"Don't play games with me. You told me over the phone you remembered Max very well. So tell me—was her child's paternity the basis for the divorce?"

"What're you gonna do with this information? You out to blackmail somebody?"

"I won't even dignify that remark with an answer. My niece is entitled to find out who her natural father is."

"So how come your niece ain't here askin' questions about her old man in person?"

"I'm acting on her behalf."

"Very touching."

"My niece is going to be kept out of this completely. Do you understand?"

"Suit yourself. No skin off my nose."

"Tell me what you know about Max and Phoebe's intended divorce proceeding. You remember the details, correct?"

"Some."

"I want to know if the birth of my niece and her paternity were the bases for the divorce petition."

"Coulda been."

"Look here, Mr. Plack. Am I wasting my time? I thought you were going to share some information with me."

"What do you wanna know exactly about old Max?" He signaled the bartender for a refill. Philippa had hardly touched her martini.

"Do you remember Maxwell Swidnik or not?"

"Yeah. I remember Max. Him and me grew up together, lived within a block of each other in Chicago Heights."

"You knew him as a personal friend then not just as a client?"

"Him and me grew up on the same block. My old man got canned by Max's uncle—that's real neighborly, dontcha think, Professor?"

"I never knew much about his background. Phoebe didn't say much about Max's family."

"Never thought your hoity-toity flesh and blood could mix with the likes of Chicago Heights, huh? That it, Professor?"

"That's not what I meant at all. Were you close friends?"

"Since we were in grammar school. Only Max was smarter'n me." He smacked his lips. "Max figured he was better than everybody in them days."

"What do you mean by that?"

"Just what I said. Max had plans, and they didn't necessarily include your little sister, Honey."

"You didn't like Max?"

"Truth is, I hated the prick's guts." He grinned as he held his whiskey up so she viewed his contorted face through the rippled glass.

"Is there something else you know about Max you aren't telling me? Was there something he kept from my sister?"

"That ain't the half of it." He ran a thumb around the rim of his glass while he studied her. She might as well have been handling dead rats from the look on her mug. He slid off his stool and threw some bills on the bar. "Look, Honey, I gotta get back to the office. What's on your mind exactly?"

"I want to find out who fathered my sister's daughter Farrah."

"What's your angle?"

"I want to know the name of the bastard who got my sister pregnant and then walked away, Mr. Plack. If you know that, we can do business."

"You got nobody else to help you with this muckraking?"

"I just want the truth, that's all."

"What does truth matter to you, Professor? Can't you let sleepin' dogs lie?"

She stiffened and clutched her purse in both hands. "It matters a lot. You're a lawyer, and you're asking me if truth matters?" she challenged him sanctimoniously.

"Truth has absolutely nothin' to do with the law, Professor. Where'd you get that crazy idea?"

"How much do you want?"

Her frankness startled him. Not that Charlie Plack resembled a man who couldn't be bought, but her assumption rankled what little he had left of his professional pride.

"You're askin' the wrong guy. I'm a lawyer not a peepin' tom for crissakes."

He started to walk off, and she grabbed his sleeve with a grip like a stevedore. "Wait! I need your help, Mr. Plack. It's worth a lot to me to find out what you know."

"Why you wanna stir up trouble after all these years?" He was genuinely curious after all. She had appeared out of the woodwork all of a sudden. First Farrah's friend calling about the affidavit he had sent out to Oregon, and now Phoebe's sister getting on his case. The wheels were finally starting to roll under the old wagon. He enjoyed letting the bastards twist in the wind a little the way he'd done for years. Now it was his turn to tighten the noose.

"Please, sit down and talk to me, Mr. Plack. I'll buy the drinks." She opened her purse and took out a ten-dollar bill.

He sat back down and held his empty glass eye-high to catch the bartender's attention. "So what's the deal?"

"I know Max knew he wasn't my niece's father. Phoebe told me that. For some reason, my sister felt she could never identify the real father. All I know is that he was a marine in California. I think he was an officer. That's all I know."

In fact, that was as much as Charlie knew himself. Rita Pester knew, but Charlie and Max could never get her to spill her guts and nail the bastard. "So what gives you the right to pry into your sister's affairs?"

"Phoebe was my baby sister. My only sibling. She's all the family I have except for Farrah. We were orphaned as kids, raised in foster homes for the most part, and naturally my sister and I became extremely close. She was living with me in California when she met and married Max. I feel a responsibility for what happened with Farrah. Now that Bibi's gone, I want to know the truth, that's all. And I'm willing to pay for it. I think the lawyers forced my sister into an agreement to keep silent in order to receive money from the real father over the years. They bought her silence, Mr. Plack. I'm sure of it."

"Who's they?"

"Farrah's father and the lawyer he hired to handle the trust fund. I've talked to the attorney who handled Phoebe's estate, too. He won't tell me anything. In fact, he's trying to talk me out of going ahead with this. He says I should let it alone."

"So if you find this schmuck, what's in it for you?" He couldn't figure her out. Why should she be on the same crusade with no ax to grind?

"I just want to look the sonuvabitch in the eye and see him squirm. He walked out on my sister. He never even cared enough to see his own daughter. His own child. He just bought Phoebe off. I want to see the bastard suffer like he made my sister do all these years."

The words were sweet music to his ears. "What about the kid? Farrah is it? What's she gonna think if she finds out Max wasn't her old man?"

Philippa speared her olive with a plastic pick. "She doesn't know anything about it. I don't see a reason to tell her unless I have to. The last thing I want is to hurt my niece. This doesn't concern her at this point."

"The hell it don't," he snorted into his glass. "She thinks her daddy is some kinda fuckin war hero, right? He's her knight in shinin' armor."

"Please, watch your language, Mr. Plack."

"Ex*cuuuse* me, Your Ladyship."

"Farrah has only the memory of Max that my sister left her. She always tried to hold Max up as a good man, a loving husband and proud father. He was a decorated veteran of the Korean War, you know. Farrah has that much, at least."

"So she loves her dear, dead daddy, huh?"

"Of course, she does. Why wouldn't she?"

So the little protected princess adored old Max. "Idolizes the sonuvabitch," he growled into his glass. Charlie's Janice had thought the sun rose and set on her father's head once, too. He was glad he had sent the affidavit to Oregon, shaken up her britches a little. Max would hate it. Charlie loved it.

"Well, Mr. Plack. Will you help me or not?"

Charlie leaned so close she inhaled his alcoholic stench. "How much is it worth if I decide to tell you somethin' worthwhile, Professor?"

"It depends on how much it helps me. What can you tell me?"

"How much?"

"A hundred dollars for the name of the attorney in the Palmolive Building who was the go between. I know it's someone in the Hazeltine firm."

"Make it two hundred, and you got a deal, Honey."

"Do you know who it is?"

"You got the dough?"

"Yes. Of course, I do." She dug in her purse, unfolded the bills and curled her fingers around the money just as Plack reached out. "First give me the name."

"Is that the full two hundred?"

"Good lord. Count it if you like."

She passed him the cash, and he fanned the bills quickly. Then he tucked the wad in his pocket. "His name is Fran Lohman. He's retired now. Ex judge. Lives out in Brookfield."

"Does he know the identity of Farrah's father?"

Plack laughed. "Like shit knows stink, Missy. I got more for you. Lohman's secretary was a friend of mine from Chicago Heights. In fact, she and Max had a thing going before your sister ever heard of him. They got engaged before Max shipped out to California."

"Max was engaged to someone else when he married Phoebe?"

"That's right. You want more, Professor, I got more. You got any more cash?"

"I can write you a check."

"No dice. I deal only in cash. Strictly cash and carry."

She searched her purse again and came up with twenty dollars. "That's all the cash I have left."

"Well, it ain't enough. You come up with another hundred, and I may have somethin' else you can work on." He wiped his chin and headed for the door.

"Wait! When can I see you again?"

"When you got the dough, call me." He sank both hands in his droopy trousers and pushed through the swinging doors into the afternoon sunshine.

"Where's a phone I can use?" Philippa asked the bartender.

He jerked his head toward the restrooms. She handed him a dirty dollar bill, and he gave her some coins. While she fumbled with the phone book, the barkeep shook his head in disbelief. She didn't look like the type of dame Charlie was hustling these days. Maybe Charlie Plack was on a winning streak for a change.

26

Bradley interrupted the conversation to answer his intercom.

"Mr. Hammaker, there's a Professor Mooney on the line, and she says it's urgent. Shall I have her hold or ask her to call back?"

He glanced up at his colleague. "Go ahead and tell her I'll be right with her. Thanks. We're just finishing here." He gathered up his notes. "Well, I think we're ready to wrap up this afternoon. Any questions before I get back to work?"

"Well, Brad, sounds good to me if the litigants can quit the name calling long enough to read the new contract. I think we've covered all the bases." The junior partner shrugged and headed for the doorway. "You know how it is—these things bring out the beast in everybody. Maybe the judge can get these guys to see reason."

"Let's hope so. Thanks, Don."

He nodded at the flashing phone on Bradley's desk. "Well, I'll let you get back at it, Brad."

Once the attorney left, Bradley picked up the phone, pressed the flashing button and turned to face the window with the lake view. "Bradley Hammaker."

"Bradley, it's Philippa Mooney."

"How are you, Professor? Have you been thinking things over?" He tried to derail her petition. He could tell by the sound of her voice that it was coming.

"I wonder if I could see you. We need to talk."

"You couldn't have made a decision so soon after the other evening."

"I was disappointed in your not being able to help me, Bradley. What you said made a lot of sense, but I need to explain something."

Butterflies swarmed in his belly. "What exactly?"

"You remember I told you about the correspondence from the attorney I found in my sister's things—the one I thought was helping Max plan a divorce when he got back?"

"Yes."

"Well, this lawyer was Max's friend as well. He knew a lot about what happened out in California with Phoebe and Max."

"How can you be sure of that, Philippa?"

"Well, quite frankly, I wasn't. But I called him, and he agreed to meet with me."

"What?" He pinched his eyes closed. His intestines felt as though they were filling with lead shot. "Who is this guy?"

"Charles Plack. He told me that he was, in fact, going to file a divorce for Max as soon as he got back from overseas."

"Good god, Philippa, do you know what you're getting into?"

"He and Max were friends, Bradley. They grew up together in Chicago Heights. And he told me the name of the attorney who was the go between." She paused to take a breath at the same time Bradley Hammaker held his own. "Lohman. Francis Lohman."

"Do you know who Judge Lohman is? He was a State Supreme Court justice. A very respected jurist. He's an old man now. Why would you want to drag him into this?"

"Look, I didn't ask for any of these people to do what they did to my sister. If he's involved in this nasty deal to keep Bibi quiet and cover-up for a coward, then he has to answer for it. It's that simple. I don't care if he's a hundred-years old, Bradley. It doesn't matter. As long as he isn't so senile he doesn't remember anything."

"I thought you were going to wait before you did anything more about this, and then we could sit down and discuss it?"

"I thought very carefully about this, Bradley. I know this is the right thing to do."

"Jesus, Philippa, I don't know what to say. Except that I'm very disappointed that you've gone ahead on your own without speaking to me first."

"I understand that you want to protect my sister. She's your client after all."

"It's not just that."

"Well, what is it then?"

"It's complicated."

"You want to protect Judge Lohman? Is that it? Is he a friend of yours? A crony? Are you afraid if Lohman is embarrassed it will somehow affect you?"

"It's not just that…but yes. Frankly, I am appalled at the prospect of your invading the privacy of a respected jurist with some soap opera scandal."

"I didn't realize that's how you felt." Her voice cut through him like a surgeon's scalpel. "I'm sorry I bothered you."

"No, I only meant…" He heard a click and then the sound of the dial tone ringing in his head. Goddammit!

His head was pounding—he couldn't seem to think in a straight line. He punched another number into the phone.

"Yes?"

"Hi, Fran. It's me."

The deep, bearish voice was immeasurably comforting. "Hampster?"

"She's found you," he said with a deadened voice sated with guilt, fatigue and remorse at not being able to shield his old friend from this.

"Who for crissakes?"

"Philippa Mooney. Some attorney gave her your name."

"Who?"

"Plack I think she said it was. He was handling the divorce for Max."

"I didn't know he'd ever filed for a divorce."

"I guess he was going to. Anyway, Fran, she has your name, and she's hot to trot on this thing. I couldn't talk her out of it."

"Hampster, don't worry about it. Let her call me. She a looker?"

He was in no mood to be swayed by Fran's infectious good humor. "She's serious, Fran. Don't underestimate this woman."

"I can take care of myself against an old maid Latin teacher any goddam day of the week, Hampster. I ain't that old yet." The old barrister puffed on a cigar with the sound of hammering in the background.

"I'm sorry I have to put you through this, Fran."

"Nothin' to it. I'll put it to bed. If she wants to play games with me, she's gonna have to put her gloves on. I only play one way—to win. Quit worrying for crissakes."

"I expect her to call you."

"I'm ready. Now is that all? I'm in the middle of a high stakes gin rummy game with Napoleon Three." His Irish setter. Third edition.

"I'll let you go then."

"And quit your worrying—it'll make an old man outta ya, Hampster. Look what happened to me for god's sake. It ain't a pretty sight." He banged the phone down.

Bradley stared out the window. Lake Michigan shimmered like lime Jell-O. New spring greenery decorated the shoreline and beckoned pedestrians from the high-rises. He was thinking of a sunny summer day many years ago when he and Fran had gone sailing. Lohman was a senior partner at Hazeltine, Brown and was lobbying Bradley to apply for law school after graduation from Northwestern. The sunshine had sparkled like fireflies on the water as Fran chewed on a cigar while Bradley watched the wind-bellied gib strain in the stiff breeze.

"*Christ, Hampster,*" the old man had joked amiably with his cap set at a rakish angle over his oiled hair. "*Only way to steal legally in this country is to get your ticket to the Illinois bar and make thievery a respected profession.*"

Happy days. Fran always managed to infect him with enthusiasm. Not today. He didn't feel good about any of this. Maybe after all these years, it was time for him to ante up. His trust payments, conscience money in fact, hadn't expunged the debt. It didn't seem fair. What had he received for his charity besides peace of mind? Now there seemed to be a missing part to his life. A piece he couldn't fit back into the picture.

His phone buzzed. "Yes?"

"Mr. Hammaker, Mr. Brennerman is on line two. And there's a long distance call holding from a Josephine Wallgood."

"Who?"

"A Miss Wallgood from Oregon."

"Never heard of her."

"She says she's calling on behalf of a Farrah Swidnik. She said you would know Miss Swidnik."

His fist slammed into the desk. "Dammit!"

"Pardon?"

"Take a message."

He crossed his arms on the desk, put his head down and squeezed his eyes shut. Trickles of cold sweat slid down his sides as he sensed the walls closing in.

27

Josie hung up the receiver, closed the accordion door and trudged back to the trailer. The clouds were pressing down on the gunmetal-gray sky promising rain or at least a shower. She buttoned her sweater and scraped her boots on the porch step before going inside. For once, it made a difference if she tracked her dirty trail across the floor.

"You get him?" Cain asked, looking up from the sink where he was unwrapping two sirloin steaks.

"I left a message. The secretary said he was in conference. I don't know if she's bullshitting or if he didn't want to take my call. I'm gonna call him back."

"Well, you wanna know about the dog tags?"

She flopped in a chair and pulled her hair back. "Did you put em in the boat okay last night?"

"I got a knack for this stuff, you know? It's sorta like pickin' off the runner at second."

"Yeah, yeah. So did anybody see you or anything?"

"No way. I was in and out—slick as snot."

Cain dried his hands and leaned a hip against the counter. Motion seemed sculpted in his muscular legs and ass. Even when he was standing still, he radiated a primal earthiness which fanned Jodie's sexual fires. Cain Reeves was the kind of man any female of the species would pick out from a crowd just by looking at him. The way his eyes smoldered like smoky topaz, the curly hair, the Marlboro mustache and slow, infectious drawl as he slid his generous mouth into a smile just about drove women mad. Josie was no exception. Even if she knew her attraction was predictable, she was helpless to restrain it.

Josie accepted the cold bottle of Coke he set on the table. "Thanks."

"Nothin' to it, Babe. Easy as pie." He pecked her cheek. "So you're gonna have Max's voice sorta come outta the blue when you do the exorcism thing, huh?"

She took a foamy swig and paused a moment to catch her breath as the caustic cola scorched her throat. "Right." She wiped her mouth. "He's gonna leave a sign for us. That should add some authenticity. And I don't mean knocking on wood, blinking lights or some damned chicken shit thing like that."

"Pretty tough to have blinkin' lights with no juice, right, Babe?" he needled.

She ignored him. "This is gonna be good. Max Swidnik live and in person."

"So this ghost is gonna talk to us, right?"

"Yeah. You sound real good on the tape, Cain."

"Spooky?"

"Scary."

"Sexy?" he whispered, tickling her nipple through her blouse.

"Ghosts don't have to be sexy. Just believable."

"But it helps, right?"

"Doesn't hurt, I guess."

He snitched the Coke and finished it off. "This is fuckin freaky, Babe. Real spooky. The spirit world speaks. Then old Max is gonna mysteriously drop his dog tags in the boat, and Hobart and his old lady won't ever tumble to the real gig, right? How about if they get to thinkin' and figure out you coulda put em in the boat yourself when you go down there with Hobart?"

"Because I'm not that stupid. I'm not going near that boat. Hobart is gonna be the one who finds the dog tags in the boat not me." She ducked into the bedroom, poked under the bed and came back with a shopping bag—her case file. She took out the red jewelry box. "I'll have this with me, and when we find the tags in the boat, I'll ask Farrah to open the box and examine the tags."

"What tags? I just put the tags in the boat."

"I know that." She flipped the box open quickly to flash the contents. "These are dog tags I just got at the Army-Navy Surplus store. When they pick Max's tag out of the boat, then I'll like totally blow my mind and whip the jewelry box out and look for the tags Farrah gave me. And they're gonna still be here. Get it? Max has brought the tags down to the boat, and I still have the tags Farrah gave me. Hey, it's black magic. The unsolved mystery of the ages in person."

"But how'd you get two sets of Max's tags?"

"I didn't for crissakes. These are some throwaways I got from the surplus store, but nobody's gonna check the name too closely, because I'll freak out, go ballistic and toss em in the pond before they have a chance. It's for effect—the drama. When suckers believe, they see what they wanna see. I got this covered."

"But the name's gonna be different if they check it out."

"You don't get it. Look, the trick is to let people see what they want to see, believe what they want to believe. They're not expecting to see anybody else's dog tags but Max's—so why would they even look that closely? They're gonna be peein' their pants when they hear Max's voice and find the real tags in the boat. Then I freak out and toss these phonies in the water before they even have a chance to take a second look. Trust me. I definitely know what I'm doing."

"You really have this baby planned, dontcha, Josie Girl?"

"Of course, I do. Do I look like some kind of amateur to you?" She crossed her arms defiantly. "I told you I know what I'm doing. We're talking big pay-off, Cain. Everything has to go just right."

"I'm impressed. You're good, Josie."

"Thank you," she said with no hint of modesty.

He cuddled up beside her on the settee after she flipped on the Motorola.

"Hey, Baby," he purred, licking her neck. "You wanna fool around?"

She shook her head without even considering his proposal. "I have to think."

"I gotta hand it to you, Josie. You're a real professional. Business first, right?"

"Exactly."

"Nothin' rattles your cage, Josie Darlin'." He wrapped both arms around her. "I used to get to a guy named Manny Realto. He was a clean-up hitter for the Beavs when I was catching for Tacoma. See, Manny had this girlfriend—a real firecracker named Linda. And Linda had this tattoo on her butt of a little horse. I found out from my buddy Frankie about the tattoo, see, cuz he and Manny used to room together, and one time we're tied up three all in the top of the eighth, and Manny is up. Harley Stoup is on the mound, and he's lost all his best stuff. His arm is like Jell-O, see."

Josie was lost in her own thoughts, but Cain mistook her silence for rapt attention and continued with enthusiasm.

"And all we got is old Earl warmin' up. Hell, he's a lefty on his way down, and Manny is hittin' .340 for the season, leadin' the league." He fanned his fingers in front of her face. "Manny steps up to the plate, takes a quick spit back in my direction, and I hit him with the tattoo on Linda's butt. 'Hey, Manny,' I crack as he steps up, 'I hear Rubio's got saddlesores from ridin' that damn nag of Linda's all fuckin night while you was outta town.'

Goddam Spic practically swallows his chew. Then Harley winds up and flops one right over the fuckin plate—dead center, right across the belly button—but Manny is so shook he steps outta the batter's box and throws down his stick, then he runs all the way out to center field and breaks Rubio's jaw in three places with one punch and gets sent to the showers. The whole fuckin team pours outta the dugout, and we gotta slug fest goin' out there. Everybody's all shook up. Next two batters pop out to right field, and we win it four to three in the ninth with a stolen base." He slumped, spent from the spirited play by play and squeezed Josie's middle. "Some guys forget baseball is a head game, Babe. You know what I'm saying?"

"Yeah. Exactly." She could understand that logic, even in sports terms.

"You, on the other hand, Josie Babe, know how to keep your eye on the ball."

"Damn right, I do."

"Tell me what's on the roster. Who's up first, Girl?"

"I'm gonna call Hammaker back."

"That's Farrah's real dad, the lawyer in Chicago?"

"Yeah. Bastard wouldn't take my call, but he will."

"You gonna hit him up for some money?"

"He sounds like some fat cat who's probably got a lot more than Farrah does."

"So when do we tell Farrah about the letter Hobart gave you?"

"Max is gonna tell em with a message from the afterworld that'll knock their socks off."

"Yes, Ma'am." He saluted, put his feet up on the table and nudged the crystal ball aside slightly with the toe of his boot.

"Hey! Watch it!" She slapped his leg away.

"Cool it. It's just a prop, right?"

"That's not the point. It's like my professional credentials. Be careful." She rubbed a spot off the globe and settled back again. "I have to think."

He changed channels on the TV until settling on a wrestling match.

Josie crinkled her nose. "I hate that shit."

"You think. I'll watch."

"Can't we watch *Days of Our Lives*?"

"Nope." He ignored her and turned up the volume.

"I want you to take me over there after supper, Cain. We're gonna do this tonight."

"I'm ready."

"We can't waste any time. Somebody else must know about this affidavit. I gotta be sure I'm the first one with this information if it's gonna be worth anything."

Cain watched her out of the corner of his eye. "Say, Babe, where we goin' after you get the cash?"

"What do you mean?"

"Well, we ain't stayin' here, that's for damned sure. Legal or not, I ain't plannin' on hangin' around here after they hand over the dough, Josie Girl. If you wanna stick close to home, that's your business, I guess. But me—hell, I'm splittin'."

Josie hugged a tasseled pillow and looked passively on while one muscle-bound hulk tossed another swarthy combatant over his head and smacked his butt on the mat as if it were a hunk of bread dough. "I hadn't thought of that."

"You better give it some thought, Girl. I'm thinkin' of goin' someplace warm and dry. How about Vegas? You ever been there?"

"I hate the desert."

"How about Reno? It's got mountains."

"I hate mountains."

"You making a special effort to be bitchy or does it just come natural?"

"When are those steaks gonna be ready? I'm starved."

"I told you they gotta be tenderized first. Don't bug me."

"I'm hungry."

"Baby, you get the money from those suckers, and we can go to Hawaii. How'd you like that? Lay in the sun and bake like a couple chocolate chip cookies, drink mai tais all day and thump the mattress all night. Sound okay to you?"

"I hate the sun."

"Jesus, Josie, gimme a break. You're a real downer today. What's eatin' you?"

"I'm just hungry. You're supposed to be the cook so where's supper?"

He caught hold of her in one swoop. "You can get to be a real pain in the ass, Woman." He carried her into the bedroom, dumped her on the bed, ripped off her panties with one violent jerk and pinned her like a bug.

"Stop it!" she shrieked, slapping and kicking at him. "Get off me!"

"You gonna be nice to me?" He forced himself inside her and watched as Josie's anger melted into surrender. "That's better." He sealed his victory with a deep-throated kiss that smothered her moan. "Don't be such a bitch, Josie. I don't like it."

Then he rammed hard enough to wiggle the Nashua's wheels and made her bite her lip while she hung on. There was no tenderness in his ministrations—just masculine lust driven by his powerful loins working like locomotive pistons. When he was done and got up to fasten his jeans, the first word that came to her mind was "rape". It would have been if he hadn't just cleaned her kitchen, folded her laundry and helped her toward earning the biggest score of her psychic career.

But Cain Reeves was mistaken to think he could conquer Josephine Wallgood. Better men had tried and failed—like her father, for instance. Both her brother and sister were terrified of Manfred James Wallgood, Sr.. Even Josie's mother acquiesced to his tyrannical tantrums without protest. But not his youngest child. Josie fought any inference of arbitrary authority. And although Mr. Wallgood had reddened her backside a number of times, locked her in her room, restricted her to cold cereal and canned soup for a week, she never gave in, gave up, cried uncle. Not Josie. Never happened. No way.

If Cain thought he could best her with his physical strength, he was going to be disappointed. As she lay on the bed with her mouth bruised, a scarlet flush coloring her throat and aching from his assault, Josie was already planning to make him pay. She was going to ask Hobart and Farrah for more money. So far as Cain's weak brain had it figured, Farrah was going to be hit up for ten grand. So he'd settle for five with a smile, and Josie would score four times that much if she was lucky. She'd demand twenty-five grand and pocket twenty-thousand dollars for herself. Men were so easy to con—much less apt to see through a ruse than women who were always on the outlook for someone trying to take advantage of them. Trouble with men, especially good looking ones like Cain, was that they just hadn't been hustled enough to know when to shuffle the cards.

When he returned to the settee to watch wrestling, Josie dragged herself out of bed and cranked on the tub water. She needed a long, hot soak.

"Hey, Babe, get me a beer, willya?"

She looked at herself in the mirror, took note of the bruises on her arms, neck and thighs and promised herself she would deduct a hefty premium for his offensive behavior. Cain Reeves may have thought he had the upper hand, but Josie knew better. After all, she was the true professional. Cain was just a rank amateur.

28

She balanced a grocery sack on her hip and hung her purse from one arm. A meaty hand suddenly appeared and took hold of the bag of oranges she was about to dump on the pavement.

"Lemme give you a hand there, Rita." He reached for the other sack. "How you doin', Rita? Long time, no see, huh?"

She made a tentative move to reclaim her purchases, but he was one step ahead of her already, swaggering from beneath the Kroger's awning into the sunshine. "Charlie? Charlie Plack?" She pursued him into the parking lot.

"How you been, Rita?" He headed straight for his rusted Chrysler sedan.

"What do you think you're doing?"

"Thought I'd give you a lift home. You livin' with your son now, huh?"

"How'd you know where I live?"

He popped the trunk of his car, loaded her groceries then opened the passenger door. "You ain't that hard to find, Rita. Glad to see me?"

She frowned menacingly. "What do you want, Charlie?"

He feigned a hurt pout she knew better than to believe. "Hey, I gotta have a reason to look up an old friend? Stayin' in touch with the old gang some kinda crime?"

"It's been a long time, Charlie."

He slid behind the wheel and started the motor. Rita Pester hesitated a moment, considered the long hike to the bus stop multiplied by the bulk of her purchases, hugged her handbag and got in.

"Take me home then," she ordered as he cleared the lot.

"Lucky for me I was just drivin' by the old neighborhood and saw you go out shoppin'. Thought I'd tag along and give you a lift home."

She inspected her chauffeur suspiciously. He had less hair, more flab and even less tact than before. But it was Charlie Plack—the class jerk in high school who had tried to get her to suck on a whiskey bottle at the homecoming dance. Charlie always was a rounder, a con man and a thief. Everybody in Mr. Harper's home room knew damn well that it was Charlie who stole the senior class trip funds. It figured he'd go to law school and learn to filch other peoples' savings legally.

"What do you want, Charlie?"

"I gotta want somethin' just to be friendly?"

"Knowing you, Charlie—yes."

He grinned as he stopped for a light and rolled his window down. He lit a cigar and tossed the match out as he jerked the car through the intersection a step ahead of a cloud of noxious exhaust from the Chrysler's clattering tailpipe. "Know the trouble with you, Rita? You got a suspicious mind. Not suspicious enough, however."

"What do you mean by that? What are you up to, Charlie?"

"You got any ideas?"

"Absolutely not. If it's money you want, I haven't got any."

"Hey, you hurt me, Rita. That stings. You think I would be out scroungin' dough from my old pals? I'm doin' okay. I got my own practice."

"You still owe me four dollars you borrowed for gas."

"You're kiddin'. Four bucks?"

"We went to the Tip Top Drive-in for Cokes—you and Harry, Carole, Max and me. You ran out of gas in your old jalopy, and I sprang for the whole tab. You were going to pay me back the next Friday, but then you started dating Claudette Franks and didn't run with our crowd anymore."

He reminisced with a drooly smirk. "Oh, Jeez—Claudette. What a doll, huh?"

"You never paid me back, Charlie."

"You're all hot and bothered over four bucks?" He fished some crumpled bills from his trouser pocket and handed them over as he drove clumsily with one hand. "Now we're square."

"What do you think the compound interest would be after thirty-four years?"

"You were always such a hard-ass."

"This is about Max, isn't it?" she surmised as they turned a corner. "Why don't you just come out with it?"

"Well, you did work for Lohman all those years, right? I figure you got some information I need, Rita."

Her lips clamped shut like watertight doors on a submarine. She pulled her skirt down over her knobby knees and pressed her ankles together. "I figured it was you who sent that affidavit out to Oregon. You're just like a buzzard circling over a dying man, Charlie. You have no heart."

"How'd you know about the affidavit?"

"I already got a call from Oregon, Charlie. I knew it was you—who else had a copy? Who else knew about that affidavit? I figured you were up to no good. You sent the snapshot, too, didn't you?"

"So you do remember, huh? You still think about Max? Wonder what it woulda been like if he'd come back from Korea?"

"Not much anymore. That was a long time ago, Charlie. It's all in the past."

"Well, not anymore."

"Why'd you want to go and stir things up? You can get me in a lot of trouble, you know that?"

"Hey, I'm just tryin' to help out a friend. Gimme a break."

"I talked to that woman from Oregon—Farrah's friend. I'm not going to talk to you. Forget about it, Charlie."

He thumped his fist on the steering wheel and set off the horn. "What'd you tell that little bitch, huh?"

"Using foul language won't help."

"Sorry, Rita, but Jesus, I'm tryin' to get some information here. How'd she find you?"

"She got my name off the affidavit, I presume. I'm in the phone book. She wanted to know just what I'm sure you want to know. Forget about it, Charlie." She tapped on the window. "Turn at the next block."

"You mean to tell me you talked to her, but you won't talk to me—Charlie Plack, your lifelong friend? We go back a long ways, Rita. You and me—we're like family."

"No, we're not, Charlie. You and Max may have been friends, but I wasn't ever a friend of yours."

"Sorry you feel that way. I thought we could help each other out."

"Forget it. I have absolutely nothing to talk to you about. As far as I'm concerned, you breached a very serious ethical code when you sent that affidavit out to Oregon. You should never have done that."

"Hey, she's got a right to know the truth, goddammit!"

"You don't care anything about her. You don't care anything about anybody, Charlie." She put a hand on the door, but before she could open it, he stepped on the gas and sped down the street. "Let me out, damn you, Charlie! Stop the car!"

He drove to the end of the street and blew the stop sign. "Keep your panties on for crissakes. Lemme put you straight, Rita. Max was a grade A phony. You thought he was gonna come home and put the ring on your little pinkie, huh? Told you he was gonna get an annulment so you could be married in the Church with a fuckin white weddin' gown?"

"Charlie, take me back to the house. I want to get out."

"Well, I got news for you, Sister. He was using you. Max used everybody. Once he got what he wanted, you'da seen nothin' but his backside. You hear me?"

"I don't believe you."

"He told me," he lied. "He used to laugh at you, Rita. Called you a push-over—a real patsy. Round-heeled Rita. Max screwed you just like he screwed everybody."

"You're jealous. You want to hurt Max because you could never measure up, Charlie." She looked away so he couldn't see the tears glisten in her eyes. "You're so jealous it's pathetic."

"I ain't jealous of that asshole. But I don't think it's right for that little girl out there in Oregon to spend her life worshipin' his holy ass neither. The bastard didn't even give a rat's ass about her. Now she's gonna find out what a dickhead he was, Rita."

"Why would you want to do such an evil thing? What's wrong with you? I ought to report you to the state bar ethics committee."

He reached over and pinched her arm. "You listen to me, dammit. You know who Lohman was covering for. I want that name."

"You and Max were such buddies. You mean he never told you?"

"I figure Max never knew anymore than I did. But I'd lay odds you know damn well who it was, Rita."

"I don't."

"You're a goddam liar."

"What makes you think I'd ever tell you anyway? What I know about Judge Lohman's clients is confidential."

"Bullshit. You blabbed about every juicy goddam divorce petition that came outta that law firm, Rita. Don't give me that confidential crap."

"Take me home, Charlie. I'm warning you."

"What'd that dipshit from Oregon say?"

"Why don't you call her yourself if you're so curious?"

"She already called me. I didn't tell her a damn thing."

Rita was puzzled for a moment. Her eyebrows asked him "why not?"

"I figure nobody needs to know what I know just yet. Look, Rita, I can make a lotta money with this. There's somebody who wants the guy's name, and she's well off. Why just give this away, huh? You don't think Max owes you a little somethin' for screwin' up your life? I can split it with you, Rita. How about it?"

"Why would you want to profit from Max's misfortune?"

"Why not? The randy old judge's been covering up for this asshole for twenty-five years. It's time everybody came outta the closet, Rita. And if it ain't me or you, it's gonna be somebody else. Why shouldn't we make a little somethin' for our trouble?"

"You're insane. You ought to be put in jail."

His face swelled with outrage; the neck veins bulged in his frog-eyed face. "I oughtta be in jail? My kid was in jail—remember how the goddam pigs killed my boy?"

She had read the newspaper articles about that. It was a mistake. Charlie's son was arrested for protesting outside the Cook County draft board. Then he was assaulted in prison and died. It was a sad story, but no excuse for Charlie to try and destroy other peoples' lives. "That was unfortunate, Charlie."

"Unfortunate? That's what you call it? Fuckin *unfortunate*?" The car swerved over to the curb as he stomped on the brake.

"I'm sorry about your son."

"You're sorry. Well, that adds up to a big, freakin' zero, Rita. I had two kids, and I lost both of em while that asshole Max never gave a rat's ass about his kid, and she worships his ass."

"It's not fair for you to destroy her like that, Charlie. It's not fair. Max was a war hero. He would have made something of his life if he'd come back. Why would you want to tarnish his memory with filthy lies?"

"God, Rita, you don't see it. Can't you figure it out? Look—me and you got nothin'. Nobody gives a rat's ass about us. Your son probly can't wait to plant your butt in some old folks' dump. I had a beautiful family once. I lost the whole ball of wax after workin' my ass off for twenty years. Max? The bastard slides through, Rita. He cheats his friggin' way through school, screws every skirt who ever gave me a second look—"

"—That's a lie, and you know it."

"He was a bum, Rita. He never gave a rat's ass for anybody but himself. He pissed on you—he was gonna piss on Phoebe. He pissed on her kid. And you know what happened to the asshole? Huh? He got a fuckin medal. Got a goddam hero's funeral, big write up in the *Trib*—fuckin phony. Lemme tell you somethin', Rita. Max Swidnik loused up everything in my life I ever cared about. And now I've lost my Janice, and the sonuvabitch is gonna pay for it. His kid ain't gonna spend the rest of her life thinkin' he was such an almighty hero when my little girl can't stand the sight of me," he choked.

"What does Max have to do with Janice?"

He shifted the Chrysler into drive and pulled away from the curb. "He just ruined my life, that's all. He skated all his life, and he ends up adored by his kid, and she ain't even his. He never gave a holy shit. And I would give both my nuts for Janice—I'm so crazy about that kid." His voice cracked. "And she can't stand the sight of me, Rita." He pulled out a crumpled handkerchief and blew his nose. "I wanna see the look on the sonuvabitch's daughter's face when she finds out about her old man. I owe Max that, dontcha think, Rita? Huh? We both do."

"You're sick. You know that? You're going to cause a lot of trouble for a lot of innocent people, Charlie, and it'll get you nowhere."

"We'll see. You give me a call when you wanna talk."

"I'm not talking to you, Charlie. I have nothing to say."

He stopped in front of the weathered American Foursquare and unloaded the groceries. Then she carried her bags up the walk without looking back.

"Goddam loser," he muttered as soon as she shut the front door.

He climbed back in the Chrysler and headed for his office. When he got there, he returned a phone call from Professor Mooney.

"Well, Professor, you ready to do business?"

"Can I meet you somewhere?"

"Sure. How about the same place?"

"I hate that dive."

"Well, it's a sure bet you ain't gonna run into any of your college cronies then. See you at six."

"Don't play any of your stupid games with me, Mr. Plack. You know what I'm after. The only thing I'm willing to pay for is the name of Farrah's father. Do you understand that?"

"See you at six, Professor." He hung up.

He picked up the phone again and dialed another number. An elderly woman answered. "Hello."

"Is Judge Lohman in?"

"May I say who's calling?" Thelma asked politely.

"Charles Plack. Esquire," he added pompously.

She knew the Judge was napping upstairs in Bobby's room. He would probably welcome an interested caller. Being needed made his days pass more quickly. She was hoping it was a lawyer asking for advice. It pleased Fran to be useful to aspiring practitioners pursuing arcane tidbits to impress their prestigious clients. "Hold on, Mr. Plack. I'll see if the Judge is available." She put the phone down and walked to the foot of the stairs. "Fran? Fran, phone!" No answer. Sometimes her husband napped with the radio on, listening to a ballgame. She'd have to make the trip up the stairs. She returned to the phone and picked up the receiver. "Mr. Plack, I'm afraid the Judge is engaged at the moment. Can you wait while I go up and tell him you're on the line? I'm sure he'd like to speak with you."

"Fine. Thanks. I'll wait." Charlie relit his well-chewed cigar and rested his feet on the narrow window sill. The seamy tableau below was unchanged today except for a feral cat climbing out of the dumpster.

Thelma went up the stairs slowly, rested a moment at the first floor landing and ascended another eight stairs to the third floor. She paused to catch her breath before opening the door to Bobby's room.

The Judge was sitting in an old wing-backed chair with a newspaper folded on his lap. His head lolled to one side; the sunken eyes were closed, the bloodless lips agape. She saw a trace of spittle glisten on his chin. His right hand dangled over the chair arm. As she approached, she noticed a dark stain on his crotch. It would be humiliating for the Judge if he had wet himself in his sleep. Old age was treating him with more disdain than any of his clients or opposing counsel had dared to do over his long career.

"Fran?" she called, gently shaking his shoulder. "Fran? It's the phone, Dear."

She bent down and smelled the unmistakable odor of urine. His eyeballs were sunken deeply in the crinkled folds of sallow skin as she stroked his cheek. It was cool.

"Fran!" She shook him. "Fran!"

Then in a flash of bitter realization, she knew he was gone. She folded his right arm over his lap as the tears filled her eyes in a sudden flood.

29

Bradley looked over his shoulder as Penny entered the conference room.

"Mr. Hammaker, there's a call for you. It's Mrs. Lohman. She asked that I interrupt you."

He nodded and rose from the table. "Gentlemen, if this is a convenient time for a break, I have to take a call."

The two other attorneys glanced at the wall clock and nodded. "Sure, Brad. No problem. I could use some fresh coffee. Let's make it back here at the half hour."

Bradley closed his file. "Fine. See you then."

He strode out of the conference room and returned to his office. With the door closed, he sat down and punched the flashing light on his phone. "Hello, Thelma?"

"Bradley, I'm sorry to interrupt you."

"Not at all, Thelma. What is it?"

"I'm afraid I have sad news. The Judge suffered a very serious stroke this afternoon."

"Oh, God, no. When? Where is he?"

"He was upstairs reading the paper, doing the crossword actually, and apparently just went to sleep. I went up to call him down to the telephone and found him. I thought he was dead, but when the ambulance came, they were able to get a heartbeat, but the doctors say there isn't much hope of his ever coming out of the coma." She started to lose her composure but caught herself and cleared her throat. "I called you right away, Bradley, because the Judge asked me to be certain I notified you immediately if he was ever incapacitated in any way."

"I appreciate that, Thelma. If there's anything I can do…"

"There isn't. It's just a matter of waiting for his heart to stop, I'm afraid. We have to face the situation head on."

"Oh, Thelma. I'm so sorry." He closed his eyes to staunch the flood of tears. "You know how much I…I can't…Oh, God…"

"I know. He loved you like a son, Bradley. I want you to know that."

"I loved him like my own father, Thelma. I'll…I'll be so lost without him." As the reality of her news sank in, his knees buckled as if he had been hit in the belly with a baseball bat. For a moment, it was impossible to breathe. "I can't believe it… I mean, we just… Are you sure? Are the doctors certain there's nothing they can do?"

"Yes, Dear. We have to face facts, I'm afraid."

"What can I do? I'll come to the hospital. Is someone with you?"

"Don't worry about me, Dear. I'm holding up pretty well for now. Fran left me instructions. I want to carry them out while things are still slightly sane around here. He has a file in his safe, and it has your name on it. I'm to make certain you receive the file, or if that's not possible, I was instructed to burn it. Of course, I have no idea what's inside, Bradley, and I don't particularly want to know. I'm sending it over to your office by special messenger. I want to make sure I carry out all Fran's wishes while I'm still clearheaded."

"What can I do for you, Thelma? I feel so helpless—"

"—There's nothing, Dear. The girls are coming home. Mildred and Sam are with me—they've been our closest friends for forty years, and I'll be taken care of. We'll be fine."

"I'll call Angie."

"I'd like that. You don't know how much your friendship meant to Fran. You know, the last few years so few people came to see him anymore. He looked forward to your visits so much."

"Thelma, I…I'll miss him so much… I don't know how I'm going to go on from here without Fran around to…to help me…" His throat closed and strangled the words he wanted to ease the pain and calm the fear of abandonment enfolding like a shroud around him.

"I know, Dear. We all feel the same. He wouldn't want you to suffer, Bradley."

"Are you *sure* the doctors can't do something? Maybe if I called in a specialist—a top neurologist—"

"—It was a rather massive stroke. His heart just didn't know when it was supposed to stop, I guess. He's getting the best of care. He's in no pain."

"I'd like to see him."

"I think Fran would prefer to have you remember him the way he was the last time you visited. He would hate to have you see him lying in the hospital at the mercy of machines. But thanks for your prayers."

"You have them, Thelma."

"I have to run. God bless, Bradley."

He went to the washroom and splashed his face with cold water. It didn't help. He felt as if the underpinnings had been knocked out from beneath him. When his own father died, Bradley hadn't felt the pangs of bereavement he expected because he still had Fran Lohman in his corner. Now all his resources seemed to be shrinking. He wasn't ready to face the burden of middle-age and death alone. He still needed the old Judge. It wasn't fair that he should give up just when Bradley needed him most.

He stumbled through the rest of the deposition, and when he got back to his desk, there was a package from the messenger service. He asked his secretary to hold his calls. Then he sat down and opened the manila envelope.

Inside were photos of a little girl with a frilly pinafore, thick ringlets and a Shirley Temple smile—Farrah at two and a half. There was a picture of a grade-schooler on roller skates with braids flying out behind her—Farrah at seven. He studied each picture in the pile: Farrah with braces; Farrah blowing out the candles on her twelfth-birthday cake; her first formal dance; high school grad-uation with her mortarboard about to fall off.

Bradley was fascinated with the likenesses of his flesh and blood. This girl resembled him more than either Marcus or Bradley, Junior. She was tall, big-boned and sturdy like Bradley's mother. He looked longingly at the snapshots and felt the tingle of recognition in the dark eyes and thick, wavy hair. This was a part of him—his own marrow and tissue. His blood. She was his child, and as he studied her features captured by the camera lens, he understood the power of genetic inheritance. This was clearly his seed, his flesh reflected in the per-son he and Bibi made.

He took out a small packet of papers and began sorting them on his desk. There was Farrah's Brownie award; her 4-H Chapter Blue Ribbon for quilting; her report cards; a homemade Valentine card done in red crayon and pink felt; a fifth grade essay on "Why I Love America". He'd seen all the same childhood mementos in Angela's scrapbooks she kept for each of the boys. But this was something different. This was a dangerous discovery, an awakening of paternal instinct. He stared hard, fingered the yellowed papers lovingly and fought another onslaught of tears for what might have been, what different paths taken.

He was surprised to find that Fran had kept all these mementos. Bradley had passed the years away never realizing how involved the Judge was with Bibi, how much she must have come to rely on him just as Bradley had done for so long.

He took out a bundle of letters tied with purple ribbon. The letters were all addressed to Fran, and the postmarks were from both Chicago and Dayton. The last letter was postmarked 1958 from Dayton, Ohio. Bradley opened it and took out the neatly folded sheets of stationery. He read:

October 4, 1958
Dearest Fran,
You don't know how much it pains me to write this. I am sitting here at the window watching Farrah feed the birds in the backyard. Dennis is still at work and so I have the house to myself—to think and to miss you. I don't know if this was the right decision, but I felt I owed it to my daughter to give her the happiness I was denied in my life. I know what it is to grow up without a father, feeling a part of yourself missing. I have been searching for that lost love my whole life. I suppose those insecurities were partly responsible for Bradley and I being together. It's not an excuse, Fran, it's a reason I'm trying to sort out.

Don't be angry with me. Please. I need you now as much as ever. If things could have worked out differently for us, I like to think about what might have been. If Thelma and your children were somehow living in another world, and you were free, I would consider myself to be the happiest, luckiest woman in the world. But it can't be that way. I have only faced facts, Fran. You should be proud of me for that. For the first time in my life, I am being totally practical in looking out for the welfare of myself and my child.

Remember always that I love you, cherish you and miss you terribly. I have wonderful memories and someday maybe we can be together in a future when we won't have to worry about what our love would do to those we treasure most.

God Bless you, my dearest Fran. I do love you so.
Yours forever, Bibi

Bradley dropped the letter and sucked in a sharp breath. A knifelike pain stabbed at his eyes and hammered his temples. His hands were shaking as he folded the stationery, tucked it carefully back in the envelope and opened another. The more he read, the more he ached and weakened, but he was compelled to keep on like a moth circling the flame. He couldn't help himself.

April 13, 1954
Darling Fran,
I feel so guilty about the weekend, but yet I treasure our time together more than anything. I've never known such gentleness, such tender regard for my feelings, and I'm so in love my heart is ready to burst. I need to hear your voice—please, call. I will arrange some time for us to be together again soon, I promise.
Think of me, will you? My thoughts are full of your smell, the delicious taste of your body in mine, your loving arms tight around me. Oh, I love you so much, Fran. I can't live without you in my life—I'm counting the days, the hours and minutes until we can be together again.
Loving and wanting you always,
Your Bibi

He stared at the wall as he visualized the silver-haired judge holding tight to Bibi's slender, alabaster limbs, petting her silky hair and whispering promises in her ear as she cuddled in his bear-like arms. What a damn fool he'd been! What a stupid sonuvabitch! Where the hell had he been for the last twenty-five years? How could he have been betrayed by a man he admired and trusted? How could Fran have done this?

He stuffed the letters back in the envelope, redid the seal and shoved it in his top desk drawer. It lay there like a poisonous viper waiting in ambush.

He had to try and calm down. He was in no position to face Thelma and Angie feeling as if he'd been sideswiped by a Mack truck. He had to give himself a chance to put this whole thing in perspective. He reminded himself that Fran had lovers over the years. Thelma pretended ignorance over his little peccadilloes during the course of their marriage. She knew they were only transient dalliances, temporary flirtations which sparked, flared and simmered for a few months and then fizzled.

Bibi was a needy, attractive, vulnerable young woman when she met Fran. She was recently widowed, alone with a baby, and Fran was so goddam strong, secure and amenable. It made sense that he had seduced her, taken advantage of her natural inclination for infatuation. An older man coming to her rescue—the father she was always searching for. It made perfect sense.

Bradley stared out the window. The waters were serene, a pool of liquid mercury steeping in a slothful stew with only a lone sail cutting through the wake of a speedboat. His eyes couldn't focus. He felt dizzy and nauseous.

He knew he was trying to rationalize his sense of outrage. This was more than one of Judge Lohman's notorious escapades with a pretty lady in his debt. This was much more. This was a long standing, romantic affair that spanned years and sounded as if it may have threatened Fran's marriage. No wonder Bibi had married Dennis Poole and moved to Dayton, Ohio. She had to get away from Fran. She made another sacrifice to save somebody else's ass.

He pressed his temples with his forefingers. "Jesus, Bibi," he moaned, drowning in his own self pity. "Why, Bibi? Why?"

It wasn't fair. She could have fought for Bradley. They could have stood up to everybody if they had had the guts for it. Bradley didn't. And Bibi was never as brave as he was. Then she had given up Fran in the same way, laid herself across the altar again.

One letter had slipped from the envelope and lay like a white scab on his desk. He picked it up and bled as he opened it and read:

July 20, 1958

My Darling Fran,

You ask me if I have made my decision, and the answer must be—Yes—. The answer was ordained when I looked down at the innocent face of my young daughter and thought how selfish I have been. I want Farrah to have all the love and security I never knew, Fran. She is entitled to the same chances in life your children have. I don't let myself think about what might have been—it's too painful.

You also asked me if I love Dennis. The answer is no. But I feel that he will be a good father for Farrah and provide a good home for the three of us. What more can I ask? What more am I entitled to? He's suffered the same hurts in life as I and maybe together we can heal one another.

Fran, I have never lied to you. You looked deep into my eyes on Friday night and asked me if I still loved Bradley, and I must be honest with you. I was attracted to him for all the wrong reasons in California. I thought he could save me from feeling the painful rejection of Max's love. I was lonely, desperately insecure, and Bradley gave me the attention and love I needed at the time. But he abandoned me just as my father did, and I feel the same sense of loss from him. It was both our faults for falling in love so quickly and making Farrah before we had a chance to know our own hearts.

But you must know the truth—I do not regret the time I spent with Bradley. I am not sorry for a minute of the time I spent loving him. If I had it to do again, with all the heartbreak and pain I would have caused, I would choose to be with him and to have fought for the chance to make a real home for our daughter. I'm sorry if this answer disappoints you, but you asked for the truth, and I have offered it as best I can.

I hope we can see each other again before the wedding. You know I love you desperately…now just as much as before.

Your devoted and loving Bibi

Bradley's hands balled into fists. His nails dug into the flesh of his palms as he crushed the paper.

It had taken him a quarter century to come to this junction. He was at the crossroads, and he could read the signposts for the first time. This was what he had left behind for the security and opportunities marriage to Angela Perjamon offered. Bradley Hammaker had bartered away a chance for love in exchange for financial and professional rewards he considered more valuable than a clinging, immature woman who didn't seem able to make the tough choice. And now how ironic it was, he mused bitterly, to discover after all these years of self assurance and smugness from his high-rise pinnacle of success that Bibi was the one with the real guts. And he was the coward.

He locked his desk drawer, blew his nose, combed his hair and tugged at his silk tie. Then he took a deep breath and straightened the portraits of Angela and his two young sons which adorned the credenza. He looked into the handsome face of the woman he had been partnered with for so many years. Had she ever known? Had she ever guessed that she owned his body but not his soul? Was there ever a suspicion brewing in those lavender eyes that Bradley Hammaker had loved someone so deeply, so passionately that he could never trust himself to love again? Did she understand the reason for his tactful indiscretions over the years? She must know. If she cared anything at all about him, she must know what their union lacked—champagne without the bubbles, the waltz without the orchestra. Angela had to know all along. Fran knew. Bibi knew. Only Bradley had been able to dupe himself all these years into believing he had everything. In fact, he had nothing. Nothing at all.

He grabbed the phone and called his house. Their housekeeper Betty answered.

"Let me speak to Mrs. Hammaker, please."

In a moment, Angela was on the line, sounding slightly annoyed. "What is it, Brad? I was just on my way out to get my hair done."

"Angie, Fran's had a stroke. It doesn't look like he's going to make it."

"Oh, no. What a shame. Have you talked to Thelma?"

"She called me this afternoon. I guess they're just waiting for his heart to stop. The doctors told her there's no hope of a recovery." For the first time, his composure broke completely, peeling from his impeccable veneer to expose the raw agony of his remorse. Unabashedly he allowed the tears to stream down his cheeks.

"Oh, Brad. I'm so sorry. Are you alright?"

"Angela…"

"I'll send some flowers. Should I call Thelma? I suppose her daughters will be staying with her until after the funeral."

"We have to talk about this."

"I'll try to get home by six. Can you take an early train or should I come into town to get you?"

"Angie, we need to sit down and talk. It's important."

"Is it about Fran's will? Are you a legatee?"

His temper flared. "Goddamit! Listen to me."

"Bradley, is this the time to get into an argument? I'm on my way out the door. Can't this wait? I realize how upset you must be, but–"

"—Be quiet, dammit!" All of a sudden Bradley Hammaker felt a brave heart beating behind his Marshall-Field's tailored shirt. "Angela, listen to me."

"I'm trying to, Brad. Don't swear at me."

"I apologize."

"Can't we talk later? I'm late for my appointment, and I'm sure this can wait until you get home. But I will send flowers this afternoon. What hospital is he in? Maybe we should visit this evening. Did the doctors say he could have visitors? Is he in intensive care?"

"Listen to me."

"I said I was listening."

"Judge Lohman had a long love affair with a woman named Phoebe Swidnik."

"Well, so long as Thelma doesn't know. Is he possibly going to try and leave her something in the will, do you think?"

The truth tumbled out in a rush. "Phoebe Swidnik was Fran's client—he handled a trust fund for her that we set up. She's the mother of my daughter,

Angela. Her name is Farrah Lynn. She lives in Oregon and is twenty-five years old. She was conceived when I was stationed in California."

Angela crumpled into a chair, and the receiver flopped down on her lap. She sensed her insides freezing up. Stunned like a boxer taking a gut punch, she groped for the phone when she came to. "My God, what are you saying? You had a child out of wedlock?"

"Phoebe—Bibi was the love of my life. The time we spent together in California were the happiest days I've ever known, but she was married, and when she got pregnant, our affair ended. But I've been supporting my daughter all these years, and I've never really gotten over my feelings for her mother."

"Bradley, why are you telling me this?"

"Because it's the truth."

"It's a lie!"

"It's the truth, Angela."

"Oh, God! You sonuvabitch! You dirty bastard! How dare you tell me about this! How dare you do this to me!"

"I want to see my daughter. I ignored her for twenty-five years, and now I want her to know who her father is."

"Why? Why? For God's sake *why*?"

"Because I love her. I think I've always loved her."

"You must be crazy! Oh, dear God! What's happening to me?"

"I want to be a part of my daughter's life. I walked out on her before she was born because I thought so many other things were more important. I wanted you to know, Angela, that I made a mistake. I turned my back on Bibi and our baby because it was easier, hell...*safer* to marry you and get on with my life without complications. But there was always something missing from our marriage. I know you've always felt it just as much as I have."

"How can you say that? How can you have the nerve to say that to me, you sonuvabitch!"

"I'm sorry I never told you the truth, Angela. I should have a long time ago."

"Do you know what you're saying? Do you have any idea what you're doing to me?"

"I wanted you and everything your family could give us—the partnership and all the social shortcuts—more than I wanted Bibi and Farrah. It's as simple and as shitty as that."

"You goddamned bastard! You can go straight to hell!" She slammed the phone down as hard as she could, hoping it would break apart, fracture her arm, shatter both of her husband's eardrums and bring the plaster down from the ceiling.

Angela sat there shaking and hyperventilating—and waiting. Nothing happened. No plaster fell. Her heart kept on beating. The housekeeper peeked around the corner at her with wide, frightened eyes. The grandfather clock chimed the hour. The refrigerator hummed to life in the kitchen at the same time Chauncey, their Angora cat, crept from behind the sofa and flew up the stairs at sonic speed.

"Mrs. Hammaker?" Betty tiptoed from the kitchen. "Is everything alright?"

"The bastard! The dirty, filthy, lying, cheating, sinful bastard!" Angela screamed as loudly as she could until her throat burned and panic overcame her outrage.

"Can I do anything for you, Mrs. Hammaker?" Betty asked warily, ready to take flight if necessary for the back door. At this moment, her employer had the look of a homicidal maniac.

Angela got up without acknowledging her housekeeper, walked through the foyer, opened the front door and stumbled outside like a sleepwalker. She circled the driveway and then headed down the sidewalk without her purse or coat, her eyes awash with tears that burned her cheeks like acid as hatred blazed in her bleeding breast.

30

Cain slowed down at the end of Cully Marsh road and stopped the car so Josie could get out.

She opened her door, gave him a sly wink and clutched her bag. "Well, here goes," she said, sliding out.

Cain reached across the seat and patted her derrière. "Break a leg, Josie Girl."

She watched him drive off before she shouldered her bag and started down the road. Ruts sliced through the brambles like strips of raw bacon leading to Hobart and Farrah's trailer. At least now the mud had dried, and the trek was passable without waders and a paddle.

Hobart was feeding the dogs when Josie walked into view. "Hi, Jo. Sure glad you're here. Farrah is about to jump out of her skin. You walk all the way?"

"Hitched a ride."

"You read the letter yet?" He tossed a sack of dry food in the woodshed as the hounds dug into the chow with their jowls dripping and smacking.

"I gotta talk to Farrah about that. She inside?"

"She's out back doing some laundry."

Josie followed Hobart down the slope behind the trailer. Farrah was standing over a metal tub, both arms sunk in the froth. Beside her was a basket of wet clothes. Hobart had strung a clothesline from the top of the trailer to the woodshed eaves. Farrah had already started hanging up socks. Every one had a large darning scar on the toe.

"Hi, Josie. I'm so glad to see you."

"Hey, Farrah. I wanted to come as soon as I could."

Farrah dried her hands. "You want to come inside and have a lemonade?"

Josie had fortified herself with two Cokes before she left her place. She wanted no more natural, organic fruit sludge from Earth Mother Farrah. "No, thanks. I'm fine. Let's talk about the letter."

Hobart was leaning against the trailer with one knee bent. He tipped the brim of his hat and listened intently.

Josie waited until her audience was settled. This was theater, live and spontaneous. Psychic improv. A fitting test of her true talents.

"What is it, Josie?" Farrah asked with a jittery laugh. "Was it just a recipe for fudge or something?"

Josie frowned. "No way."

"Something about Max?" She turned to look at Hobart then answered her own question. "God, I knew it was. I knew it."

Josie put her hands on Farrah's shoulders, like grabbing a gunny sack full of antlers, and squeezed. "I have to tell you, Farrah. I didn't even open it. I was getting such strong vibes—I didn't even want to risk it."

"Risk what?" Hobart butted in. "What are you talking about? What sort of risk?"

"It just wasn't worth it, Farrah." She kept her eyes fastened on her primary victim. "There's something in this letter that will change your life, and I want to be sure you really want me to open it."

"What is it? Something about me you mean?"

"I want your permission before I tell you what's in here, Farrah, because I got such a strong reading from just touching the letter..." She took a deep breath. "I couldn't go ahead without your consent. It's so full of astral vibes, it's about to burst into flames. I think what's in this letter has to do with who you are, Farrah."

Farrah sat on the stump which served as Hobart's chopping block. She put her head in her hands. "Oh, Josie, I was afraid of this. I mean, it's just been so unreal ever since Mom died. First off I started having all these weird, freaky dreams about my dad, and then there's the footprints and seeing his ghost or spirit or whatever. I don't know what I should do."

"Open it for crissakes," Hobart suggested. "Get it over with—whatever it is."

Josie petted Farrah's curly mane. "Hey, it's cool. Don't worry. I think you can handle it. You know, maybe it's the spirits urging you to search for the truth."

She looked up with tears in her eyes. "I've thought of that, Josie."

She took the envelope from her bag. "I have to get in touch with my spiritual guides before I can go through with this. Do you have the money?"

Farrah blinked behind her pop bottle lenses and then looked at Hobart. "Uh, sure, Josie. You want a thousand dollars, right? I can write you a check. I got an account for the money."

"Two thousand—the letter is a thousand extra."

Hobart shrugged. "We can make out a check, Jo. That's no sweat."

"Great." She planted a foot on the stump and bent over in a conspiratorial huddle. "I have to tell you this is really serious, Farrah. Even more serious than exorcising Max's spirit from your place."

"Oh no, Josie. What's wrong?"

"Max's spirit is here for a reason."

"His dog tags, right?"

"The spirits always have a reason for intruding on the secular world. There's a price to pay for their connecting to loved ones—it diminishes their celestial powers with their peers in the spirit world. Max came back for another reason, Farrah—one much more important than just getting his dog tags. Spirits aren't tied to material objects."

"You mean it isn't the dog tags after all?"

"That's just a way of communicating with you, establishing a link. Max's spirit is troubled and not at peace because of what's in this letter, Farrah. I know it. I can sense it as plainly as if it spoke to me. The energies are that strong."

"What should I do then?"

Josie had been waiting to get to this point. It was the crux of the whole matter. The fee. It was the crowning glory of any skilled practitioner's art: the submission of the bill, the accolade for services rendered, the gratuity, the invoice with payment due on receipt, the final fillip for a sterling performance. It was time for Josie Wallgood to assert her professional priorities in this little drama she had scripted.

First she handed the resealed envelope over to Farrah and pressed it into her hands. "Hold it against your heart, Farrah. Now let your mind relax. I want you to be receptive to the message the celestial guides will reveal."

Farrah crossed her hands over her breast and closed her eyes.

The sun was just sliding behind the ridge. A rosy light suffused the marsh and made the pond shimmer like a nacreous jewel nestled among the susurrus rushes. Josie's timing was perfect. If there was ever a time of day when people were moved to believe in the spirits and goblins of fairy tales, it was at twilight when the shadows and dancing light played tricks on the imagination. If there was a moment for Max to make his appearance, this was certainly a perfect setting.

"Farrah Lynn…" Josie's voice hoarsened. Her face flushed, and sweats beads popped out on her brow and lip. Her hands trembled. "I'm getting a sign that there are two names on this paper which mean something to you. The first is Phoebe."

"My mother," Farrah whispered reverently.

"The second is Maxwell. They are speaking about your birth, their marriage. I see records, dates. It is a memorialization of your arrival on this planet, the genesis of your persona on Mother Earth."

Hobart pulled his hat down to shield his eyes from the sunset's glow. "It's like her birth certificate, Jo?"

"No. It's more…much more. I feel such a pain. A pain like a knife wound. *Awwwwwwwwww!*" Josie slapped a hand over her heart, sank to her knees, threw her head back and rolled her eyes.

Even Hobart was alarmed. He moved toward her, but Farrah motioned him back.

"She's in some kind of trance, Hobart. Let her alone. I think it might be dangerous to disturb her now."

They stood back and watched as Josie's entire body quivered like a fresh-killed steer. Her teeth chattered; her backbone shook until her limbs seemed about to detach from her torso. She moaned, foam bubbled from her mouth, and when she finally was able to speak, it was not in a voice Hobart and Farrah recognized.

"*Farrah Lynn, your pain is like a knife cutting out my heart. My gift to you…your birthright. The truth will set you free, Farrah Lynn. Search for him. Find the truth, and you will find yourself…*" Josie shuddered, sagged into a heap on the ground and panted like a long distance runner until Hobart bent down and wrapped his arms around her.

"You okay, Jo? Jesus."

Josie opened her eyes and looked around to get her bearings. The moment her gaze came to rest on Farrah, she jumped to her feet and snatched the letter from her hands. "It's all in here, Farrah! The truth! Burn it!"

"What do you mean, Josie? Was that my mom speaking to me? Was it? Tell me! She said I should find out the truth. About what? Tell me."

"Jeez, Farrah, I tried to warn you what's in there. If you go ahead and open it, you'll never feel the same about yourself again. It will change everything. But it's up to you, I guess. I've done all I can."

"Tell me what I should do."

Josie walked uphill to the other side of the trailer and sat down on the front step. She was in complete control now, and she loved it. It was time to make a grab for the cash. Farrah was ready to consider any price to find out what she now believed her mother wanted her to know.

Farrah and Hobart followed with concerned expressions on their faces and stood patiently waiting for their spiritual guide to lead on.

"Farrah, if you open that letter, you will discover that Maxwell Swidnik was not your father. I saw it clearly in my mind a moment ago," Josie confessed breathlessly.

Farrah staggered backward into Hobart's arms. "What? What do you mean? I'm illegitimate? Is that what you're trying to tell me?"

"That's only part of it, Farrah. Your spiritual guide is pushing you toward the light."

"What does that mean?" Hobart asked.

"Truth. Light means truth, Hobart. There is more truth to find." She bolted upright suddenly and grasped Farrah's icy hands in hers. "Farrah Lynn, your mother has called out to you from the grave to ask that you redeem her honor."

"How? What can I do, Josie?"

"Find your real father. Ask him to acknowledge you as his daughter, and then Max's soul can rest, Farrah. Until then," she let go and slapped her thighs, "it's useless for me to try to exorcise Max's spirit. He needs to stay here and convince you that he should be your rightful father."

Farrah hugged Hobart and buried her head in his chest.

He seemed genuinely worried for the first time. "Jo, you mean there's something in that envelope that questions the fact that Max was Farrah's dad?"

"It separates Max's spiritual connection with Farrah forever, provided she believes it and accepts her real father in Max's place. I think that's what Max has come to contest."

"Who's her dad then?"

"I don't see a name yet. The spirits haven't revealed that to me just yet. But I do see a face. I see dark eyes, hair...a stare. I see a beach...sand. There is something in the background...a skeleton." She closed her eyes and rocked back on her heels.

"A dead person? You mean my real father's dead, too?" Farrah sniffled.

"A skeleton that stands across the horizon...a steel skeleton." She snapped her head up. "It's a bridge, Farrah. I can see a bridge, sand, a beach. A striped towel. And a man. He's your father. I can also see an initial."

"Ohhh, Josie! It's just like my dream." Her hands flew up to cover her eyes.

"I see a B. Cold...very cold...Br...Brrr..." She sagged forward. "I'm sorry. That's all that is revealed to me. I can't see anymore. Everything in its proper time, Farrah. Open it."

"I can't."

Josie took the envelope and deliberately tore off an end. "We might as well have a look now. It's a beginning, a place to start the search. I can't go forward until this is disclosed to you, Farrah." She thrust it at Hobart. "The cosmic forces are too strong. Read it, Hobart."

As they watched, he pulled out the affidavit, read it silently and then handed it over to Farrah who only briefly scanned it. "She's right, Farrah. Your mom says Max isn't your real dad."

"But who is then?" Farrah looked to Hobart and then to Josie. "Who is he?"

"Look at this." Hobart whistled, holding out the photograph. "It's a man at the beach, and there's the bridge. Look, Farrah. Just like Josie predicted." He handed it over.

"It's the Oakland Bay Bridge! I know that beach! Oh, my god, Josie! I've dreamed about that beach. It's just like you said. My God, you saw this, didn't you?"

"He looks like you, Farrah." Hobart had noted the dark brooding eyes. He also saw Farrah's inheritance in the strong jaw, the abundant dark hair and big-boned frame.

"Ohhh God, Josie. It's him, isn't it? My dad?" She started to cry.

Josie braced herself for the hugs and feel-good schmaltz she knew was necessary. "Farrah, you love Max, right?"

"Of course, I do," Farrah blubbered. "I thought he was my dad."

"Well, don't you see his spiritual dilemma?"

Farrah shook her head. Until this moment, Josie hadn't seen it herself clearly, but there was something ripping her head open, blinding her with flashes of such amazing insight she was feeling genuinely weak. God, she was good. Just wait until she went on national television. Damn, she was going to be something special. She'd blow them all away with her act. The Hollywood stars would be begging her for readings. She'd be in all the celebrity mags, tour the juiciest parties, score a spot on the Johnny Carson show. Wow! This was far, far out.

"You are his only child although you're his in name only. He died before he could have any kids. So all these years you've worshiped him as a heroic father killed in the war before he had a chance to know you, right?"

"*Awww*...I guess so," Farrah sobbed.

"So now you received this document in the mail, and it destroys everything for him. Now his spirit is awakened. He's come back to claim you, Farrah, as his own daughter. He wants you."

"He wants to take me?"

"In a spiritual sense. If you find out who your real father is and deny Max, his spirit will forever be without mortal ties, Earthly energy, no one left on Earth of his flesh to mourn him. So he's come back to fight for you—he wants you as his daughter, Farrah. And with this paper, you've just found out there's somebody else who can claim you as their own."

"He's after her soul, Jo?" Hobart was flabbergasted with his own conclusion.

"I can't deal with this anymore, Josie. I have to sit down for awhile."

Hobart steered her into the trailer. They all sat on the bed. Hobart got up to fix tea. They barely spoke as evening shadows fell over the marshland.

Josie was content to wait out the exercise in histrionics. She had made her point, and come to think of it, it was no less than brilliant. So out of the blue, after all these years, Max's paternity was threatened, and although he didn't want to acknowledge Farrah as his after she was born, he had not planned on dying before he had a chance to father a child of his own. Now Farrah was his only shot at love and adoration on the Earthly plane so he was back to fight for her. Josie liked that. It was a brilliant stroke of drama. Made sense in a cosmic-connective sort of way, too. At least, Farrah and Hobart seemed to think so. The money was as good as hers. And she hadn't even started the real show yet.

Hobart gave Josie a check for two-thousand dollars, and she surprised the hell out of them by refusing to accept it.

"I can't. This is only the beginning, remember? Don't you see the bigger picture here?"

They both shook their heads.

"What do you mean, Josie?" Farrah asked.

"First you have to find out who your real father is."

"How could I do that? That could take years, and meanwhile Max will be terrifying us all the time. All I have is this old picture?"

"Don't forget the one person who loves you more than anyone else and knows who your father is."

"My mom?"

"Right. And she will let me know. I can promise you that, Farrah."

"Oh, Josie, could you do that for me? Really? I need to know, don't I?"

"I can use your spiritual guide to find the truth. I can give you a name, Farrah. You don't have to act on it, but at least you will know the truth, and then Max will be compelled to challenge him for your spirit."

Imagining the ghastly consequences of a cosmic battle for her soul was scaring the daylights out of Farrah. "What am I supposed to do?"

Josie was ready. She had already scripted this pitch in her mind. "I can give you peace. I can give peace to your mother who is suffering now knowing that there is a struggle for your soul between Max and your real father. I can guaranty that Max's spirit will be put to rest if you can confront him and tell him that you are no longer his daughter. If you reject him and accept your real flesh and blood father into your life, Max will have no choice but to go back and rejoin his spiritual circle."

"You mean, the next time he shows up, I have to tell him that?"

"No. I mean, I can channel through to the spiritual world and make a connection for you. I can find out the identity of your real father and exorcise Max at the same time."

"You sure, Jo?" Hobart wasn't convinced. "You can do that?"

"All I need is to know from you that you are ready to face the truth." Josie hadn't seriously considered the chance that Farrah might chicken out. Maybe her pitch had been so good, she had scared off her prospects. Just in case they were having any second thoughts about going ahead, she'd add a little more fuel to the fire. "You know, Farrah, if you do not go ahead with this spiritual cleansing, then Max may be with you from now until eternity. Spirits have no conception of Earthly time."

"What do I have to do, Josie? If my mother isn't at peace, then I think I have to do what she would have wanted. She sent the letter to me, didn't she?"

"Her spiritual influence was responsible. She knew Max would come back to claim you after she passed over. There's a great battle of spiritual wills going on in the celestial realm over your soul. Your mother is fighting for you. Can't you feel it?"

Farrah bawled, and her glasses splotched with tears. "Ohhh, Josie, what'll I do? What am I supposed to do?"

"I can help you. Are you ready to find the truth?"

"Yes," she blubbered, blowing her nose with a snort. "I'll do it. Tell me what I have to do. I'm ready."

First things first. That was the rule of business. Psychic stardom was all about mixing plenty of pizzazz with a little bullshit and a dose of drama to create a positive cash flow. "You have to be ready to renounce Maxwell Swidnik as

Gehla S. Knight 245

your father and no longer give him the love and loyalty you have shown him all your life."

She looked up at Hobart for an answer. He looked at Josie instead.

"He's not my real dad then, is he?"

"That's what the paper says," Hobart told her. "Your mom swore to that, Farrah."

"Okay, Josie. I can do that. I owe it to my mom. I never even knew him."

Josie forged ahead without even an extra eye blink. "And you need to give me half the money she left you."

Both Hobart and Farrah were caught off guard. Hobart found his tongue first. "Half of the trust fund?"

"Half. This is a turning point in Farrah's life—the money came from Max. It's poisoned. It's blood money. The spirits want you to divide the money—half for your aunt, half of the remainder for you, and half of that is Max's inheritance you must surrender in order to find everlasting peace. Twenty-five thousand dollars."

Hobart spoke first. "It's okay, Farrah. I don't want all that money anyhow. I think it's the right thing to do. Josie's right—it's his money. Let's get rid of it."

"I don't care about the money," Farrah snuffled. "You know that, Hobart. I never did. And what Josie said—about it being from Max, blood money from when he was killed—I think the only way for me to deal with this whole scene is to let it go."

"Then let's do it. Let's get this over with. I always thought it was the money that started this whole damn thing in the first place. I'll write you a check, Jo."

Josie's heart was skipping beats faster than a stoned drummer. This was too easy to be called work.

31

Charlie Plack had already downed a whiskey and soda before she showed up.
When Philippa Mooney came in, she looked right and left like a traffic warden
before approaching the bar where Charlie was rooted.

"Hi there, Professor. Have a seat."

"Can't we sit where we can have a little privacy?"

"Whatever your Royal Highness prefers." He made a grandiose gesture and
followed her lead to a back booth.

The bartender brought two fresh drinks and collected Charlie's money.

"Well? Do you have the information I asked for?" She ignored her martini
and tried to dodge his smoky exhaust.

"You rush into everything like a mad bull, Professor? No hello? No 'How are
you, Charlie'? No 'Thanks for the drink, Charlie'?"

"Let's just get to business. Do you have the name or not? If you don't, then
I'm leaving."

"I got somethin' even better."

"What?"

"Here." He flipped a snapshot across the table. It was a copy he had made of
the Kodak print Rita Pester had sent him twenty-four years ago. Now the original was out in Oregon, and he delighted in thinking about how Farrah would
study it and see how her biological father was obviously much better looking,
taller, stronger, better bred than Max. It showed in the cocky stance, the self-
assured smile, the ramrod posture. This guy, whoever he was, was class. No
wonder Max didn't cut the mustard—Phoebe knew class when she saw it. For
once, some lucky putz had beat Max out of a score. Charlie Plack almost
swooned with glee when he thought about it.

Although when Max had first called to tell him about his divorce plans twenty-four years ago, Plack had demonstrated the appropriate regret for the breakup of a happy marriage. But he had secretly rejoiced in Max's failure. The fact that Max revealed he had been cuckolded by an officer was even better and made Charlie's cheeks glow. If he could have had his way, Charlie Plack would have pinned a medal on the anonymous bastard. Every time he'd looked at the snapshot over the years, it gladdened his heart to know this was the one individual on the planet who had successfully stuck it to Maxwell Swidnik, rubbed his face in it and walked away clean.

"Who is it?" Philippa tapped the photo with a fingernail.

"Who do you think?"

She looked at the picture and studied the face smiling enigmatically from the shadows of a fading afternoon sun. "You're saying this is the man? This is Farrah's father?"

"That's the man."

She checked the back of the photo. "Well, who is it? Don't you have a name?"

"That's gonna be expensive, Professor."

Philippa grabbed her purse and started to get up.

"Hey, hold on. Siddown. We still got business to do."

"Look, Mr. Plack, you said you would have the name for me. You don't. What you have is an old snapshot of someone—it could be anyone."

"It ain't. It's him. It came from Lohman's office. It's him."

"Judge Lohman sent you this photograph?"

He nodded smugly. "Judge Lohman himself."

"Then you do know who this is. You do have a name."

"For the right price."

"You are the scum of the earth, Mr. Plack. This is simple extortion. I could have you arrested."

He raised his eyebrows in mock outrage. "For what? Helping a client locate somebody? Hey, Professor, my fee is whatever traffic will bear, okay? I put in a lotta time and trouble with this shit. You wanna know the name, you pay the fee. A thousand bucks up front. That's it."

She got up. "This is ridiculous. You're just a common crook. I'm going to see Judge Lohman. He obviously has the information I need. I intend to tell him about your outrageous behavior, Mr. Plack."

"Be my guest. But hizzoner ain't takin' too many calls these days."

"He'll talk to me."

"He ain't talkin' to nobody—he's like a fuckin zombie."

"What do you mean?"

"He hadda stroke. The guy's in a coma, gonna croak any minute. You're too late, Professor."

She sat down again. "Is this true? When did it happen?"

"Just today. I was talkin' to him for crissakes. He just up and croaked."

Philippa rubbed her temples. "Oh, my God."

"So now it's just you and me, Professor. What you wanna know, I already know. Only it's gonna cost you."

"You filthy scum. I have nothing but utter contempt for people like you profiting from the misfortunes of other people."

"Sticks and stones, Professor."

"You sonuvabitch. I'll find out what I need to know from my own sources." She scooted clear of the booth, tossed down a bill and closed her jacket.

"Call me when you change your mind, Your Highness. You know my number."

She was a step away from the booth, when he caught her. "Hey, you forgot your pinup, Professor."

"That could be a photograph of anyone. Without a name, it's meaningless. Goodnight."

He shrugged his shoulders, sucked on his cigarette and watched until she disappeared through the swinging doors. Goddam, uppity bitch. She'd come around. Soon enough.

He slid out of the booth and fished in his trousers for some change. Then he fed the coins in the payphone and dialed Rita Pester's number.

She answered on the first ring. "Hello?"

"Rita, we gotta talk. You have a chance to think this thing through?"

"Charlie, I'm not interested in talking to you. If you come by the house, I'll have my son call the police. Leave me alone. I'm warning you."

"Well, I gotta little love message for you, too, Doll." He closed the door on the phone booth. "I want that name. You should think about being nice to me. You wouldn't want your son to find out about you and old Max now, would you?"

"There's nothing to find out. How dare you try to threaten me!"

"Look, Rita, I know, you know, and old Max knew your kid was a bastard. He told me all about pinnin' you in the back seat of his old Mercury out at the Midway. Who you kiddin', you old biddy? You put out for the whole crowd in them days, Honey. Don't try to lay any of this holier than thou shit on me, okay? I know Max got in your britches first, but he wasn't the last, right? Don't fuck with me, Rita."

Her hands were shaking so much she feared she might drop the telephone receiver. A blind panic seized her. She was suddenly dizzier than a flagpole sitter in a hurricane. How could Max have told this loathsome man these intimate details of her life? She only confessed about her affairs to Max in order to stun him, hurt him half as much as she had been hurt when he married Phoebe. How could this ogre be so evil as to try to destroy her one triumph—her son? She could kill Charlie Plack if she knew how to do it.

"Charlie, I hate you. You're going straight to hell for this. Do you hear me? Straight to hell to burn in the fires of Satan forever."

"Yeah, yeah. Save all that fire and brimstone for somebody else, okay? I want the name. You gonna give it to me or not?"

"I was still a virgin when Max left for California. You're making up a filthy, disgusting lie! A filthy lie."

"Well, lemme put it this way, Rita. I happen to know that the guy you claimed married you and then went off and got himself conveniently killed in Korea—"

"—That's all true! His name was Sydney Pester, and he was from Philadelphia, and we were married at the Mary Magdalena Church."

"Rita, forget it. I checked. This joker, this Pester, was listed as a casualty from the First Division in Korea."

"He was decorated for valor, too."

"But he didn't get married in no Mary Magdalena Catholic Church. There's nothin' on the registry."

"That's a filthy lie! You can check at the Courthouse."

"I did. You took out a license, but there was no marriage, Rita. You made it up. Invented the whole thing for your family or whatnot. Hey, I can understand. Max steals your cherry then dumps on you and splits for California. And instead of comin' home on leave to put a ring on your finger, he marries some tramp he picked up on the beach, right?"

"You're a liar, Charlie Plack! A filthy, despicable liar."

"So you pick out some poor, horny GI on leave, and presto you're knocked up and then an instant bride before your sweetheart ships out, never to return. Sad, ain't it? Least ways that's the story you tell everybody. Except the State of Illinois's got no record of the special event, Rita. Convenient how you're widowed when Max gets back, too. I gotta hand it to you, Doll—I couldn't'ta done better myself."

She struggled to keep from crying and giving Charlie Plack the satisfaction of knowing he'd wounded her. "You're lying. You're making this up to hurt me, that's all."

"Well, I didn't figure it out either until I did some checkin' after our little chat the other day. You made me do it, Rita. If you had just been a little nicer to me, well, we wouldn't be havin' this unpleasant conversation right now."

"It's not true."

"I know you're not receivin' any widow's pension from the government, Rita. Neither did your kid. You never put in a claim—I checked the record. You know why? Because it's all a lie, and your dear departed husband ain't even dead. He's married and livin' in Hoboken. Works as a steam fitter. You want his number? Maybe your son wants to call him up and talk to his old man."

"You foul, filthy beast!"

"He probly never even gave you a second thought, Rita. You were just a weekend quickie. But I gotta give you credit—you had that kid and raised him all by yourself, and he's turned out pretty decent."

"You miserable, evil, evil man, Charlie. Your soul will go straight to purgatory!"

"Well, you wouldn't want your son to find out the truth about his mom now, would you, huh? How about just savin' me the trouble of talkin' to him?"

"Leave me alone!"

"The name, Rita. I want the name."

"How could you be so evil!"

Just as Charlie was about to press her again, there was the sound of scuffling on the other end of the line. Then a bass voice boomed over the phone like an air raid siren. "What the fuck are you doin'? Who is this?"

"I was talking to Mrs. Pester about some business between us," he stammered, backing up against the glass partition even though he was connected only by the phone line to the menacing voice.

"My mother doesn't have any business with you, Scumbag. You bother my mom again, and I'm gonna break your face for you. Understand, Asshole?"

"Sure. I'll call back later."

"You do, and I'll jump down your throat and rip you a new asshole! You got that? Leave my mother the fuck alone!" He slammed the phone down.

Charlie returned to the booth and finished his drink. Maybe it wasn't worth trying to squeeze poor little Rita. He almost felt guilty about threatening to expose her dirty little secret. He wouldn't even be surprised if her son already suspected the truth anyhow. These were different times. Charlie hated to come down on the spinster, but she shouldn't have treated him like shit when she had a chance to show a little gratitude to an old friend from the neighborhood.

Rita was one of the pathetic leftovers from Chicago Heights who was a perennial victim. She grew up the sixth child of a steelworker with a bum back who drank up his disability checks before Rita's mom had a chance to buy groceries. Rita's brothers and sisters all dropped out of school to take factory jobs, leave home and get away from abusive parents and grinding poverty. Rita hung in there for the long haul, finished school, got a job as a secretary downtown and was able to swing her own apartment.

She turned down a few good guys who could have offered her a family and a little postwar bungalow in the burbs. But she had her sights set on Max, had a crush on the jerk ever since she laid eyes on him. As far as Maxwell Swidnik was concerned, Rita was nothing more than a pastime, a way to spend his evenings when nothing better showed up. He had stolen her cherry and broken her poor, shriveled heart. And she got even the only way she could think of—by dropping her holy drawers for some randy serviceman. And when she found out she was expecting a baby, it must have been a frightening thing for poor little Rita. She made up a romantic story to preserve her pride, became a sympathetic, phony widow and waited for Max to return and marry her. But Charlie was betting good money that Max never intended to come back to Chicago and make Rita a bride. He had better things on his menu once he got rid of Phoebe. Rita didn't fit into Max's postwar plans. Once he'd used Rita to get the affidavit for his annulment, he tossed her aside like last week's stinky mackerel.

The fact that she continued to believe in him even after all the crap he put her through said something about Rita. She had nothing else in her drab life to look forward to. She must have always believed Max would get the annulment, make her an honest woman at last, and they'd live happily ever after.

The world was so full of suckers, Charlie chided himself. And bastards like Max could seek them out of a crowd the way a shark honed in on a crippled seal.

32

Down at Cully Marsh, crickets chirped like Spanish castanets as soon as the sun slipped behind the trees. Farrah, Hobart and Josie were standing at the edge of the pond. Hobart held a lantern aloft attracting a horde of flying insects as Josie wrapped her sweater around her bony shoulders and shuddered. A chilly breeze exhaled across the valley, ruffling the water and raising a mist from the cattail shore.

"Is this the place?" Josie asked Hobart, looking around. The light had faded enough to make it difficult to discern their footprints. Behind her, Josie had unobtrusively dropped the tape recorder in the tall grass. It was running.

"Yeah. Right over there is where I saw the tracks. Then they went down to the boat there, circled around the pond and just disappeared into the water."

"Did you see anybody at all?"

"Didn't see a damned thing, Jo. I waded out into the pond and couldn't find a thing. Damned if I can figure it out." He stood so close she could taste his pungent aroma. "I gotta tell you, I had my doubts about this whole business. But you've got something, a gift or whatever. I trust you. If Max is trying to get Farrah back, then I think you're the only one who can make him let go. Be honest with me. Can you really do it?"

Josie gazed up into his big, blue eyes. Jeez, she would have liked to get it on just once with Hobart Ames, but this was second best. It would have to do. And who knows? Maybe someday Farrah would split, and anything was possible, wasn't it?

"Yes, I can, Hobart. I can feel the power from Farrah's mom leading me. She's my spiritual guide. She's helping me."

"Thanks, Jo." He hugged her in a full body press. It was the first time she and Hobart had meshed in such a warm, intimate embrace. It was a bonus. Pure gravy.

"It's okay. We're friends, right?"

"Forever, Jo. I swear." He released her and stepped back. "Tell me what you want us to do. No sense waiting around."

"Let's just stand here and join hands for a moment. When I connect with the spiritual sphere, you will feel a charge of electricity and know I am on the other side. Then you'll just have to observe very carefully. I know there will be a sign."

"What kind of a sign?" Farrah asked timidly.

"You mean a ghost or something? Max is gonna like appear?" Hobart was hoping it didn't get physical. His philosophy was non violent in general, but he was prepared to do what had to be done to protect Farrah and Josie. It was the least he could do under the circumstances.

"I can't say. Sometimes the spirits take on earthly forms—other times they leave a physical sign of some kind. We'll have to see. But I feel very strongly that his presence is very close in this place. I feel I can make contact with his lost spirit here."

"Goddam." Hobart put his arms around the two women. "This is so weird, it's freaking me out. Do your thing, Jo. I'm ready. Farrah?"

"I have to pee first." She pulled away, gathered her skirts around her and stepped off into the pussy willows.

Josie waited as Farrah hiked her skirt and squatted. "I hope you're not afraid."

"I am. I'm just so glad you and Hobart are with me. I want to get this over with. I'm so grateful to you, Josie."

"Don't forget to get the money."

"Hobart will write you a check."

"It has to be cash. You'll have to go to the bank in the morning and draw out the money. When you get it, you can bring it back here, and I can take the final step."

Farrah rearranged her skirt and snapped her panties in place. "You mean you'll tell me the name of the guy who's my real dad? My mom is going to tell you his name when I give you the money?"

"Yes. That's her wish, Farrah. You understand about the money being poisoned by Max? It was blood money."

"You mean like he paid for my soul, sort of?"

"Yeah."

"Poor Mom. I feel so sorry for her. So you think Aunt Philly knows who he is?"

Josie's face clouded. What she didn't need was more salt in the stew. She wanted to discourage any independent sleuthing. "Your mother would never reveal her secret to anyone but you, Farrah. She kept it locked up inside her all these years. Jeez, she even took the secret to the grave with her."

"Yeah. I guess you're right. I think maybe Aunt Philly would have said something when Mom died, right? It must have been so painful for Mom to keep this thing locked up inside of her for all those years. I feel so incredibly guilty, Josie." She brushed tears from her cheeks. "I guess I know now why she was always so sad, had to drink to knock out the pain."

"This is strictly between you and the spirit of your dead mother, Farrah. She's crossed the spiritual divide to come back and give you the gift of truth."

"And I'm so grateful. Well, I'm ready, I guess." She parted the tall reeds and rejoined Hobart.

Joining hands, they stood in a close circle around the kerosene lantern glowing at their feet. Hobart and Farrah watched as Josie checked her watch. Timing was everything in theater, and she had to be certain she coordinated her act with the tape Cain had recorded. Certain she was right on schedule, Josie began to sway and tremble; her lips quivered as she drooled and moaned.

An owl hooted ominously as Farrah suddenly gave a yelp and sank to her knees. "Oh! Jeez, Hobart. She shocked me." Farrah rubbed her palm. "It felt like a bee sting."

"Jo? You okay?"

She was beyond the pale already—her body was limp, writhing in a semi swoon on the muddy bank. Her hands flew up to her face as her head lolled back. When her glistening lips parted, Josie spoke in a sweet, thin voice as frail and delicate as a child's.

Hobart and Farrah gasped, transfixed at the spectacle in spite of the cold fear which rooted them to the spot they were certain was being visited by spirits from beyond.

"*Farrah Lynn...my beautiful baby. Farrahhhhh...*" Josie sang in a high-pitched wail.

Farrah buried her face in her hands. Despite all this craziness, the hooting of the owl and the crickets in the pond, she recognized the unmistakable sound of Phoebe's lilting voice rising up from Josie Wallgood's throat. "Oh, Mom!" she squealed as she fell down bleating. "It's my mother, Hobart!"

Josie spoke with her eyes closed and her lips barely moving. "*Don't let any pain remain in your heart, Farrah Lynn. Trust Mama. This won't hurt you. I want you to know the truth. Your father loved you as I did. But he was so afraid to face the truth. Now he's ready to accept you into his heart, Farrah Lynn. Open your arms and take him in. Be kind and forgiving. He loves you so much. He always has really.*"

"Mama! Mama!" She flung herself at Josie whose body was as stiff as an ironing board. "Mama, please, tell me what to do. I love you, Mama. I'm sorry I left you. I didn't know you were so sick. I didn't know, Mama." *Boo hoo, hoo, hoo.* Tears were running like tap water down Farrah's cheeks.

Suddenly Josie's hand reached up and rested firmly on Farrah's head. "*I love you, too, and I understand. Don't cry anymore. Be happy…in love…so precious, so short. Time is so cruel, Farrah Lynn.*"

"Oh, Mama, I'm so sorry," Farrah blubbered, clinging to Hobart who hovered close by. "I didn't mean to leave when you needed me to be there for you. I love you, Mama."

"*You must tell Max he has to let you go now. It was wrong to keep you from the light for so long, Bootsie…*"

"Bawwwwwwww!" Farrah mooed.

"Jesus," Hobart gulped in astonishment. He knew Bootsie was the special nickname Phoebe had used when Farrah was a baby. How would anybody know about that? Farrah had only confided it once in a moment of total, introspective intimacy she shared with no one else. He felt his intestines turn to mush. He wanted to run up to the trailer, stand under the light of the Coleman lantern and hide out from all this freaky sorcery.

Then as Farrah collapsed in a heap, begging forgiveness from her mother's spirit ensconced in Josie's skinny frame, a second voice boomed out on cue from the reeds behind them and almost gave Hobart a heart attack. He couldn't even swallow his own spit or blink his eyes he was so shaken by the eerie intrusion.

Farrah was hysterical when she heard Cain's recorded voice rise from the reeds directly behind her. She quivered with fear, too scared even to speak.

"*Farrrrahhhhh…I…can't give you up. I'll nev…er let you go…*"

"Eeeeeeeeek!" Farrah pulled her skirt up and ran through the marsh grass for the light of the trailer as if she were one jump ahead of a King cobra.

Hobart was frozen in place with his heart thumping its way toward his tonsils and his bladder about to burst. "Jeeeesus!"

Cain's muffled baritone voice rolled on from the shadows of the dying sunset. "*Look for my sign. I left a sign to warn you. I won't give you up. You are my daughter. I've come back for you, Farrahhhh…to claim you…*"

"Jesus Christ Almighty, Jo! Where the hell is he?"

Josie never flinched. Her eyes were glazed and fixed. Her nostrils flared as her face shone with sweat.

The tape recorder played on: "*Keep these as my only inheritance to you. They are a part of me…a part of you. You cannot give them away. They are my link to you, Farrah. I have come to claim you, Farrah Lynn…*"

"Jesus, Jo! Wake up!" Hobart shook her by the shoulders until her teeth rattled in her head. "Jo! Snap out of it!"

The tape ran to the end in silence. Cain's soliloquy was superbly received. Just as Josie had known it would be.

Hobart slapped Josie's cheek until her eyes fluttered open. It took a moment for her to focus.

"Ooooooooooo…" she groaned, feeling all her muscles cramp at once. She struggled to her feet and hung on Hobart's arm. Her head ached as if she'd been slugged with a frying pan. Her ears were ringing, and she was drenched with sweat despite the night breeze cooling the marsh. Jesus Christ, what a trip! What the hell was going on? She was better than she thought, way beyond better. She was definitely going to play herself someday in the 20th Century Fox blockbuster *The Life Story of Madame Josephina, a Gift from the Stars* filmed in wide-screen Vista Vision and stereo sound.

"What's going on, Hobart?"

"Jesus, Jo, you like really flipped out on us. You were talking, and then Farrah's mom came out. Don't you remember anything?" He pulled her hair back and wiped her mouth. "You okay?"

She was still groggy, sick to her stomach. She couldn't smell anything besides the strong odor of burning kerosene. "I don't feel so good. You have any Coke?"

"Farrah's mom came through you, Jo. Scared the holy shit out of us. Farrah ran back to the trailer you scared her so bad."

Josie looked up at the stars overhead. The moon was rising over the ridge. "What did I say?" Funny thing—she couldn't honestly remember. It had been a stunning performance—she was certain of that. How she knew, she couldn't say for sure. Freaky. Maybe she had an attack or something at the end—epilepsy. That could be it. She had slipped into some sort of cerebral vapor lock.

Might even be low blood sugar. Better yet, caffeine withdrawal—not enough Coca Cola to keep her brain on an even keel. This was totally fucking weird.

Hobart guided her back toward the trailer. "Her mom called her Bootsie."

"What?"

"Her mom called her that when she was just a little baby. I know. Farrah told me once. Nobody else would know that." He crushed her against him. "Even you wouldn't know that, Jo. Jeez, I'm sorry if I ever thought about doubting you, Jo. You're so incredible. It's scary. Are you sure you're okay?"

She nodded. It felt good to have Hobart holding her like a lover. "I think so. I feel a little weird."

"Jo, look at that." He pointed toward the pond.

Josie peeked over his shoulder and saw a ripple spreading across the water. As they watched, the rowboat slid away from its berth, nudged its prow against the glassy billows and glided out into the pond on its own.

"Oh, shit!" Hobart let go of Josie, jumped into the water and waded out to capture the craft before it got over deep water. He took hold of the oar lock, lifted his body over the side, flailed with his feet and then with a grunt landed himself inside. He rowed it back to shore, got out and hauled it into the reeds.

Josie stood there and couldn't think of a single word to say when he stood up in the bow and held a glittery prize in his hand. "Josie! Look at this! Jesus, it's just like he said. It's a sign."

She was just too tired, too depleted by her own outburst of energy to respond. Instead, Josie sagged down on the bank and laid her head across her folded arms. She felt an overwhelming desire to sleep. Her brain was doped. What was a high blood sugar attack like? Maybe she'd OD'ed on caffeine—too many Cokes. Could be she was coming down with something—summer flu probably. PMS? And what was it that article said about sleeping sickness? She'd only skimmed that story at the checkout counter, and now could be she was about to go under like Rip Van Winkle. Too bad she hadn't read up on it instead of flipping ahead to check out the picture of a two-headed squirrel driving a golf cart on the White House lawn.

She barely paid attention when Hobart shined his light on the dog tags and read the name: "USMC Swidnik, Maxwell. Goddam! Holy Christ, this is for real, Jo. He's here!"

She came to her senses finally and realized she nearly missed her cue. She needed to get out the red jewelry case and flash the phony dog tags in Hobart's face.

She fumbled with her bag, plunged her hand into the assortment of junk and came up with the box. When she popped open the lid, Hobart was hovering over her with the light. Damn him. He was going to spoil everything.

Before she could protest, Hobart snatched the jewelry box and shined the flashlight on it. Damn him. He was going to ruin her whole plan. What a fucking, nosy jerk. This wouldn't have happened if Farrah had just stuck around. Now everything was turning to shit. Josie had to think of something. She tried to grab the case. Too late.

Hobart squatted in the marsh grass and put his arm around her. "Jo, it's just like he said. He left us a sign. He's really come back for Farrah, hasn't he?"

Josie looked for herself. Two dog tags were nestled in the case. Even she could see that they were United States Marine Corps tags with Maxwell Swidnik's name stamped on the metal as plain as day. Jesus Holy fucking Christ! She took Hobart's light and reread the tags. It couldn't be. They were exactly the same. This was absolutely impossible. No way. What the hell was going on? Cain Reeves must have set her up or something. He must have taken the real tags out and put them in the boat and then had some new tags made up and then… She stopped. Even she knew this was ridiculous. No way, no fuckin way. So what the hell was happening anyway?

"How could that be? This just can't be happening."

"Max left these, didn't he, Jo? Christ, he was here. Right here just like he said."

"My dog tags, my dog tags…" She turned her bag upside down, spilling everything into the tall grass. They had to be there—the Army-Navy Surplus store bogus tags. There must be an explanation.

Hobart held the jewelry box in one hand and the tags from the boat in the other. He balanced them inches from her nose. "They're here, see? Both of em—the ones Farrah gave you and the ones Max put in the boat."

Josie stared so hard her eyes crossed. "Those aren't the ones Farrah gave me."

"Sure they are—see? It says Max Swidnik right on em. Even has his serial number. I've seen these before, Jo."

"No," she insisted, pushing him away. "They couldn't be. No way, Hobart. No way Max could have put those tags in the boat—no way."

A shadow of doubt clouded his eyes. "You sure about that?"

"Those aren't the ones, dammit." This was all wrong. She couldn't figure out where she had gone wrong. This wasn't turning out like she had planned it at all. Damn it. "They couldn't be…unless…"

"Unless Max was really here, right, Jo?"

She began collecting her things and restocking her bag.

"Jo! Look at this!" Hobart aimed the light at his hands. His fingers were stained with blood.

"Did you cut yourself?"

He was examining his fingers, one by one, then his wrists. "No. So where the hell is this coming from?"

He threw the dog tags down. Josie picked them up. When she held them up to her face, she could see the red dripping from her own fingers. The dog tags were bleeding.

"Criminy shit!" She threw the tags into the pond with a major league lob even Cain would have admired. There was a soft splash when they hit the water near the middle of the pond.

She and Hobart clung to one another as a sudden gust of wind extinguished the flame in the lantern and left them alone in the cast of an unearthly, neon moon floating over Cully's Marsh.

33

She sipped at her drink as she sat by the window looking down on Jackson Park. It was raining softly, muffling the sounds of traffic below and emptying the sidewalks. Philippa Mooney was disgusted with her meeting at the lounge. Plack was little better than a street-corner thief. She was sorry she had ever given him any money in the first place. This was turning out to be a journey of hardships. Maybe there was another way to salve her soul. Maybe she had taken too much on. Maybe Bradley Hammaker was right. It could be time to begin healing after all these years.

She got up and traced a pattern in the carpet as she walked back and forth. It was nearly ten o'clock, and she was in her robe and slippers already. Too tired even to look at the papers she had brought home. Too exhausted even to think about school, Bibi, Plack, Farrah or anything other than rest. Maybe in the morning she would be able to make a decision on whether to let this go or pursue it to the bitter end.

First she would get in touch with Farrah. She was certain her niece didn't suspect what Philippa was trying to do, but she had to be sure. She would contact the lawyer in Oregon who had helped Farrah with the trust disbursement—Farnam, his name was. He'd know how she could reach her niece. As far as she knew, Farrah was living like a Neanderthal up in the Oregon woods in a shack without electricity, a phone or plumbing.

She set her glass down, poured a dollop of gin in a tumbler half-full with Collins mix and cracked open the freezer for some ice. Her doorbell chimed before she could dislodge the tray.

She wiped her hands quickly and walked to the foyer. Loosening the dead bolt, she peered over the top of the security chain. In the corridor lit with the saffron glow from the art deco chandelier was a familiar face she had not expected to see again.

"Can I come in?" His clothes were splotched with rain.

She could see a suitcase behind him. "Yes, of course." She closed the door, undid the chain and let him in. "What is it?"

Bradley set the bag down and opened his hands in a gesture of helplessness. "I can't go home."

"What's happened?"

"My wife's thrown me out."

He stood there with the reflection of the amber light behind him, his head to one side, hands sunk in his pockets, piercing black eyes riveted to hers, his silver-gray hair darkened by the rain. She looked at him, and suddenly she knew. In a lightning flash of recognition she saw the shadow of the man standing on the Oakland beach in the grainy snapshot, and she knew who he was.

"It's you, isn't it? It was you all along. I should have known."

"Do you hate me so much, Philippa?"

"I don't know. Give me a moment."

"Angela does. I'm afraid she's going to leave me." He looked away for the first time. "If you want me to go, I will."

"Why'd you come here?"

"If you want to spit in my eye, now's a good time."

"You told your wife about Bibi?"

"I don't know why really. I just couldn't hold it in any longer. God, Philippa, can you understand that at all? I can't."

"You ruined everything for yourself, didn't you?"

"I did that a long time ago."

"What do you want from me?"

He hung his head. The thoughts and emotions were tumbling too fast for him to sort any of it out. "Refuge, I suppose."

"A coward's retreat."

"Not just that. I need someone to tell me I'm doing the right thing—that the truth really does set us free. I never believed that before."

She opened her arms, and he lunged at her. They hung on like battered boxers trying to make it to the bell, dancing to silent music as they swayed on the carpet.

"Fran's gone," he murmured with his mouth pressed into her shoulder. "I wasn't prepared to lose him. He was my conscience all these years. I wanted to tell you I'm sorry, but it doesn't mean anything now. It's too late."

"It's not too late. It's never too late for that."

"God, Philippa, I never knew what Bibi went through. Fran never told me."

"Did you love her?"

He drew back. "I think I always have. I guess I didn't give myself a chance to get over the hurt when she left me."

"She left *you*? I don't understand."

"She was so guilty about the affair. She couldn't handle the guilt over the whole thing especially with Max headed for action overseas. Bibi was a lousy liar."

Philippa bit her lip. Wetness welled in her eyes. "She never loved anyone but you, Bradley, and you destroyed her." When he walked away, slumped onto her sofa and put his head back, she followed and stood with her arms folded across her chest. "You've had to live with that—what you did to Bibi—all this time. That's some consolation for me, I suppose."

"You're wrong. We were both wrong as it turns out. It wasn't like that at all. Christ, I just didn't have a clue. I didn't know what the hell was going on." He reached inside his jacket pocket, took out Bibi's letter and handed it to her.

"What's this?" she asked without looking at it.

"See for yourself. It's from Bibi."

Philippa sat down beside him on the sofa, opened the letter and began to read.

"Fran is Judge Lohman," he explained. "He handled all the arrangements with Bibi, set up the trust for me—everything."

"Yes, I know." As she read, her hands trembled. When she finished, she folded the paper carefully and handed it back. "I never knew. How could I have known? Bibi must have kept so many secrets…"

"Fran was a good man."

"She never even hinted—I never suspected there was ever anyone else. I always thought you were the one who broke her heart. I never knew anything about this. Never. This is a complete surprise."

"Judge Lohman's wife never knew about it either. This was something Bibi and Fran kept just between the two of them for all those years. What's it matter after all this time who Bibi loved? She's gone now. They're both gone."

"And I've wasted so much anger and bitterness over someone I didn't even know."

"All I want now is to see my daughter, Philippa. I want Farrah to know that I love her. That's all that matters to me."

When she leaned back, her robe fell open to reveal the swells of her body, still supple and inviting. He could count the pale freckles scattered across her skin like nutmeg on white rice.

"Is this going to destroy your marriage, Bradley?"

"I don't know. Angela says she wants a divorce, but she's just in shock right now. Terribly hurt. But I won't fight it if she goes ahead."

"How can you let this tear your family apart, lose everything you care about?"

"I love my sons. I suppose I love Angela, too, in a way, but it's different. I want more than that. I feel cheated, Philippa. I've lost so much by living a lie for twenty-four years—we all have. I want to get back what I can if there's still time."

"What are you going to do?"

"Check into a hotel, I guess. And then I'm going to get in touch with my daughter."

She reached for his hand. "I'll help if you want me to."

"You don't owe me anything, Philippa. I've lied to you for so long."

"That's over now. All I ever wanted was for my niece to be happy. I'm glad you're Farrah's father. You can be so proud of her, Bradley."

They sat side by side without speaking. The mantle clock chimed. Sibilant traffic sounds drifted up from the wet streets below and muted their sighs.

"I know it doesn't matter now, but I want you to know I'm sorry for the hurt I've caused. What else can I say, Philippa?"

She leaned over and grazed his cheek with a kiss. He could feel her eyelashes' caress. It brought to mind a tenderness he realized he had forfeited for so long it seemed brand new.

"It would mean so much if I could just stay here awhile and talk. There isn't anybody now that Fran's gone."

"Did anyone else ever know about you and Bibi?"

"No. I don't think she ever told anybody, but I always wondered if Dennis knew."

"No, he didn't. They used to argue about that all the time when they were drinking. She never told him, Bradley."

He pinched the bridge of his nose. "I feel what I've done is right, but the consequences are just starting to sink in."

"Is it going to be worth it? What about your sons?"

"They're both grown, involved with their own lives and problems. What happened was so long ago—before they were born. I doubt if they'll give a damn really except for what I've done to hurt their mother. Both the boys are close to Angela."

"Have you spoken to them yet?"

"No. Angela called Marcus and asked him to come home." He stared into space. "It's going to be a shock to discover they have a half-sister after all these years."

"You could have kept quiet about this. I think I'd decided to give up. What made you come forward after so many years? Did I have anything at all to do with it?"

"In a way—a catalyst, I suppose. I guess I've had trouble with this ever since Bibi died—like I suddenly discovered that a part of me was missing. Hell, I don't know. Maybe it's just my own brand of middle-aged crisis."

"You know, I have a feeling, Bradley, that Farrah feels the same thing about a part of her that's missing."

"All I want is a chance to tell Farrah I'm sorry and make it up to her somehow only I know that's not possible. Maybe she'll hate me. God, I wish I knew. I'm scared to death if you want to know the truth."

"Bradley, I think all she really wants to hear from you is that you love her. That's what we're all hoping to hear from our fathers, isn't it? What it all comes down to in the end."

"I suppose so. My father could never say it—the words. He was scared to death of being vulnerable, I guess. Never said it. Never told me he gave a shit."

"He did. He must have."

"You know, the funny thing is, I never really thought about how I felt toward Farrah until I was threatened with having to own up to it—the affair, California, the whole thing. What kind of a miserable, selfish bastard does that make me?"

"Don't. It's no good trying to make yourself a villain, Bradley. What she doesn't need from you is guilt. Farrah needs a father. That's all that matters, isn't it?"

"There has to be something more—dues to be paid."

"You want forgiveness, go to confession. That's not your daughter's burden."

"Now Bibi's gone, I'll never have a chance to tell her how I really felt."

"Maybe it doesn't matter. I wish I could have met Judge Lohman. Just to see what kind of man made Bibi happy." She touched his thigh. "How many letters do you have? How'd you get these?"

"Fran's wife sent them over to me. They were in a sealed file addressed to me that he kept in his safe. They had a thing going for a long time, Philippa—years. They must have loved each other very much. You read the letter—she gave him up to do the right thing just like she did with me."

"It's so sad, isn't it? Bibi never learned how to fight for herself."

"I've really messed things up, haven't I?"

"What counts is now, Bradley. Today. We can never go back and change the past."

Her eyes locked on to his in a silent embrace. Then they came together in slow-motion. Philippa broke free first, stood up and switched off the lamp. He followed her into the bedroom without a word being spoken. As he stood trembling in the shadows behind her, she drew the draperies closed, turned the coverlet down and slipped the robe off her shoulders.

"Philippa, I'm scared to death she'll hate my guts." What he hoped for was her forgiveness, a sign that truth encouraged redemption. But at this moment, he had never felt so rejected, so adrift, so alone at the same time he felt reborn. It was a painful delivery, a new beginning with a painful past he was facing for the first time.

She put her arms around his neck and drew him close against her. "It's going to be alright, Bradley," she murmured. "Everything's finally going to be alright."

As she sat him down on the bed and began to unbutton his shirt, he lost himself in her forgiving eyes and tried hard to believe her.

34

They huddled together around the table. The trailer was dark except for the single candle Farrah had lit. Shadows tattooed their pinched faces. Hobart sat with his arm around Farrah whose hand was linked with Josie's. Outside, the hound dogs howled at the full moon as a barn owl hooted from the rafters of the woodshed. At this time of night, the marsh was alive with the sounds of nocturnal critters closing in for the raucous midnight shift.

"I guess I must have cut myself climbing into the boat." Hobart's observation was muffled by his sleeve. There was a long rip just below the elbow where his skin was sliced open like a fresh melon. Beads of blood were strung in a rosary chain along his forearm when he held his wound up for inspection. "I thought the dog tags were bleeding. That just about made me lose it."

"Yeah," Josie said. "It's weird how you slashed your arm climbing into the boat."

"But, Josie, it's just like you said it would be, isn't it?" Farrah gushed. "Max left a sign for me. You said he would, right?"

"Yeah." She had to admit the obvious. So why was she feeling so creepy about taking due credit for this fiasco? What was tugging at her innards anyhow? It was just a screwy mix-up—she had probably misread the dog tags in the jewelry box. The light wasn't so good, was it? And in his confusion, Hobart had been mislead, too. That's all there was to it. Nothing to worry about. And about this Bootsie business that freaked them out so much. Well, Josie must have noticed the name when she was looking at the photo album Farrah showed her on her first visit. Maybe Bootsie was written on a picture. It had to come from somewhere, didn't it?

"Hobart, tell me the truth. Are you sure, absolutely one-hundred percent sure that you read Max's name on those tags you took out of my bag?"

"Sure I'm sure, Jo. Hell, you saw em, too. They were just like the ones in the boat. Same serial number and everything. They were identical."

"Something's wrong."

"Like what?"

"I can't say exactly." Well, hell, if she knew the answer to that, she wouldn't be sitting here shivering in the murk with these ignorant jerks. She'd be making damn sure she got her money before getting on with the final exorcism.

"Jo, if we get you the money right now, will you go ahead and do whatever you have to do to get rid of Max for us?" Hobart asked.

"It's twenty-five thousand dollars. You and Farrah understand how much I'm asking for this? That's half of your money, right?"

"Right. But it's worth it, Josie."

"Hobart and I don't want the money really. All we need is enough to fix up the truck and make some improvements around here. If you need the rest to put Mom's spirit to rest and make Max go away, you can have it."

How could these people be so fucking stupid? It was like taking candy from a baby—a crippled, blind baby. And they didn't even know that something was fucked up. There was a glitch. Josie wished she could figure it out herself.

"That money from Farrah's trust fund's got Max's blood on it, Jo. You said so."

"My dad's insurance money went into that. Mom told me. When Max was killed, the government sent her ten-thousand dollars. Maybe that's why Mom doesn't want me to keep all of it," Farrah pondered, twirling a ringlet around a bony finger.

"Think about this for a minute—be sure this is what you want to do. No hard feelings later. You pay me twenty-five thousand dollars, and you don't get a receipt or anything. That's how it works—cash and carry."

"And you get rid of Max, right? He'll be gone forever, never come back and try to steal my soul?"

"Yeah, that's the deal, Farrah."

"When I heard his voice, I thought I was going to die or something. I've never been that scared in my entire life, Josie. I've never heard his voice before, but somehow I knew it was Max. It was like seeing somebody get up out of the grave, you know what I mean? It was that scary. Something I never, ever want to have to repeat in my life. If you can promise me that this will be the last time I'm going to have to confront his spirit or whatever it was down there at the pond, then I don't care if you take all the money. It's still worth it. Hobart and I will have enough left over to fix things around here."

"Can you get the money?" Josie was ready to deal.

"Not tonight. But first thing in the morning when the bank opens, we'll go into town and draw it out of Farrah's account."

"You're not leaving me here by myself, are you?" There was just something spooky about this dump—dogs howling like banshees, fucking swamp gas or whatever playing tricks on her in the moonlight. Josie wanted to go home.

"Don't worry, Jo. You're the spiritual expert here, right? Max can only get to Farrah through you now. It'll be okay, won't it?"

"I don't like it. I wanna get outta this place. It's getting too spooky even for me." She stood up and wrapped her sweater around her. Cain would probably fix her a steak with home fries for supper. And she knew for an absolute certainty the Norge was stocked with icy cold Coke, too. This was a real bummer having to hang out down here in Pogo Land.

"Well, you can't leave until Max is taken care of." He blocked her exit. "You gotta stay until you carry through your end of the bargain, Jo. I mean, he's all riled up now and everything—God only knows what he might do. I'm not letting you out of our sight so long as Max can get to us. You can sleep out here on the couch."

"Tonight? I have to go home, Hobart. I got things to do."

"You can't. You can't leave, Jo. You gotta stay and see this thing out. That's part of the deal—you protect Farrah from Max until you can get him to go back where he came from. Permanently."

This was like trying to move Mount Hood with a scoop shovel—Josie wouldn't waste any energy trying. If he wanted her to stay, then she was staying. Cain would just have to figure things out for himself. "You got a real pillow and some blankets?"

"I'll fix it for you, Josie," Farrah volunteered.

The three of them sipped a midnight cup of herbal tea with Josie cuddled under the blankets on the short sofa and her hosts sitting at the table. They talked about Max, about Farrah's real father and how she had had dreams about him.

"You know, I'm not really surprised," Farrah said. "Maybe this was something in the back of my mind for a long time. Especially after Mom died, I just felt things."

"Uh huh." It was all bullshit. All a matter of suggestion. People were such suckers, Josie thought to herself. Willing to believe that their unconscious mind had all the answers, knew the real meaning of life. What a load of crap.

"So do you think my real dad is looking for me, too, Josie?"

She blinked herself into attention. Her mind had been wandering free of Farrah's rambling about her search for inner enlightenment. "Sure. Must be. Must be why Max feels threatened, huh?" She just made that up. It sounded damn good when she said it. Actually, she was convinced the sonuvabitch would never take her calls, would duck paternity like he ducked out on Farrah's mom.

"I've been wondering about him, what he looks like, what he's doing, if I have half-brothers and sisters. That sort of thing. And what if he doesn't want me to be a part of his life now, Josie? What do I do if that happens?"

She yawned. "Well, I'd say he must want you in his life now, Farrah, or he wouldn't be looking for you, would he?" One bullshit explanation was as good as another.

"That's right. You said it was my real dad looking for me that made Max's spirit return to try and claim me for his own, right?"

"Exactly." Sounded about as stupid as Jesus turning rocks into bagels or whatever the hell he was supposed to have done. People were so goddam gullible.

"Do you think he can find me?"

"He doesn't need to find you. That's what you're paying me for, right? I'm gonna find him for you. Your mother is gonna lead me to him."

Farrah snuggled against Hobart's shoulder. "Should I even tell my real dad about Max? I mean, his ghost coming back and everything?"

Josie sat up. "No way! Don't ever say a word once this is over, Farrah." To save my ass, she wanted to add aloud. "That's important. You could screw up the whole deal if you ever tell anybody about it. It only works if you never talk about it."

"You mean Max might come back?"

"Yeah. Like in triplicate. You could really put me in a box, Farrah." Josie chopped her hand on her thigh—the guillotine's justice coming home to roost right on her vulnerable neck. "Once you make a deal with the spirit world, there's no blabbing to the whole frigging universe. Never."

"I understand, Josie. I'll do whatever you tell me to, it's just that what if my real dad asks about Max? Won't he wonder how I found him?"

"People find each other every day. You could have probably found him without me, but it might take years. Just tell him your mom helped you."

"Yeah. She did in a way, didn't she? I mean, her spirit is telling you, right?"

"Right."

"But shouldn't I tell my real dad about the ghost? Maybe he's seen Max himself."

"Look, Farrah, Max is here to get you, right? You're his daughter, and he wants to keep it that way. He got killed off before he had kids of his own, so you're it—for eternity. I mean, it's like his soul will be wandering forever in the spirit world without any earthly tether, got it?" Of course, she didn't. Josie was pleased that she had been sufficiently obtuse to cow her questioner. It was simpler if they just left Josie to interpret all the celestial road signs and butted out of her business altogether. "So if I sever his connection to you, cut off his spiritual link, then you've got to agree not to mention him again. Ever."

"You mean not even say his name or anything?"

"Not even once, or you could screw it all up. He would just be waiting for a chance to get back in your life again."

Hobart shook his head in disbelief, a little overpowered by all the psychic super-speak his friend Josie was preaching. "This is too fucking much, Jo. Sounds like there's some kind of curse put on Farrah. Are you sure you know what you're doing?"

"What do you mean by that?" She was offended and not afraid to show it.

"Well, I mean, should we call in another expert or something? You think we need a priest maybe?"

"You guys already got the only expert you need. Max gave me a sign, didn't he?"

Farrah tugged at Hobart's sleeve. "Mom spoke through Josie, Hobart. I heard her call me Bootsie. I don't want anybody but Josie in on this. I trust her."

"Okay." Hobart relented. "But I'm thinking about you, Jo. Sounds like you're the one taking all the risks. You gonna be okay with this?"

"Sure. Fine. Don't worry." She was going to be fine with the twenty-five grand, she was thinking. After she gave Cain his split, the five thousand he was expecting, the rest was all bullshit, and it would take care of itself. All except that business with the dog tags, and she would straighten that out when she got back home. Maybe it was something Cain was up to. There had to be an explanation. She wouldn't worry about it now.

"Would you like to come in and sleep with us, Josie?" Farrah asked before she blew out the candle.

Yeah, she'd love to snuggle up to Hobart, but her idea of a dream date with this cuddly lug did not include a trio. Especially not with a bushy-haired coat rack like Farrah. She'd have to pass. "No. I'm fine."

Hobart unsnapped his suspenders. "See you in the morning, Jo. We'll get up and go in to the bank first thing. You don't think anything will happen till then, do you?"

She thumped her wimpy pillow. "Not as long as I'm here, I guess."

"Goodnight, Josie," Farrah whispered as she carried the lamp to the bedroom.

"Yeah. Night," she grumbled, pulling the covers over her head.

This was the shits. She'd rather be home in her Nashua with Cain. But if she had to wait here, plant her ass on this midget-sized sofa until after the bank opened, it was worth it to have the cash in her hands. Then she could dazzle them with some abracadabra shit and make them believe old Max was put to rest at last.

For the final act she was going to tell Farrah about her real dad and spill the beans on old Bradley Hammaker. That would give them all some grist for the mill. Validate her special powers. Then she and Cain would pack up the old Nashua and split. In the back of her mind, she was thinking that as soon as her money hit Cain's palm, he would split faster than a Sumo wrestler's girdle. But she had some plans of her own.

Besides, she thought to herself just before falling sleep, her Pinto was running again, and she could buy some new clothes and go home for a visit just to impress the folks. They never gave her credit for anything, and now she was ready to take a stab at launching her television career: *Stay tuned as the amazing Madame Josephina and her Crystal Ball penetrate the mysteries of the spirit world and reveal your future.* She was going to be fantastic. Absolutely fucking fantastic.

35

Alan Farnam cleared a space on his desk to plant both elbows. He looked down and surveyed a sea of disarray and disaster. He was at least a week behind in his mail. He had clients coming in at one to sign a will he hadn't even started drafting yet. Myrtle Mudsunk, his legal staff sergeant, was super at times like this. He only had to jot some notes, and she could fill in the blanks for him.

But he had a bigger problem. He had spilled sugared coffee on his one clean shirt, and he was supposed to attend a county bar association meeting at four. Things were always like this in his practice—one step from the edge. Made life interesting.

He grabbed for the ringing phone and knocked off an obese file which flapped its manila wings and spewed a trail of documents across the floor. "Farnam," he growled, trying to snatch up a few papers before Myrtle came in and gave him "that look" again.

"Mr. Farnam, this is Professor Mooney calling from Chicago. I'm Farrah Swidnik's aunt."

"Yeah," he grunted, stuffing papers back in the manila folder. "We, uh, sent you some money from Farrah's trust fund."

"Yes."

"Your niece must think a lot of you, Professor."

"Farrah is an exceptional young woman. I love my niece like a daughter, and now that her mother has passed away, all we have is one another. The reason I'm calling is to ask you about getting in touch with her. I understand she doesn't have a phone."

Farnam shrugged helplessly as his secretary came in and glared at him. "Uh, they live out in the boondocks. No electricity, no plumbing. It's a little primitive, Professor. You can probably get something to Farrah by addressing it to Rural Route Three, Cully Marsh Road."

"Well, I was thinking of coming out there to see her, Mr. Farnam. What do you think of that?"

"What do you mean exactly?"

"Well, is she able to accommodate visitors?"

"I see what you mean. Well, I've only been out to their place once, and let me put it this way. I mistook the woodshed for the house and the old trailer they're living in for an abandoned junker. Does that sort of sum it up for you, Professor?"

"I see."

"But she'd love to see you, I'm sure. Farrah's a good kid, and her boyfriend seems like a straight shooter. Looks a little homespun, but he's okay. They're not druggies or anything like that. It's just sort of a back-to-nature kind of life-style. But if I were you, I'd rent a good motel in town and a car. When you comin'?"

"I thought I'd take a few days over the spring break. I plan to fly into Salem."

"Well, you can rent a car at the Salem airport and drive to Silverton. It's a short trip. Just come out of the airport, take a right on Mission toward the free-way and take Lancaster Drive north to Silverton Road and head east. Can't miss. You wanna stop by the office, I can give you directions out there."

"Is it very far from town?"

"A ways. You know, out here we don't think anything of a twenty-mile drive to the grocery store for a jug of milk."

"I see."

"Hey, we'd love to have you stop by. When are you comin'?"

Philippa paused, conversing with someone in the background. "I'll be leaving this afternoon actually. You can expect me sometime tomorrow."

"Fine."

"Do you know if Farrah will be home?"

"Won't be far off. They never go anywhere."

"Oh, good. I wouldn't want to miss her. This visit is very important."

"Well, we look forward to seeing you then." As he started to hang up, he looked at the telephone message Myrtle was waving like a semaphore flag under his nose. He read it on the fly before a lucky snag landed it on his desk. "Say, Professor, something just came up. Do you know of anything in particular that your niece would want to use that money for?"

"What do you mean?"

"Well, I know she and her boyfriend Hobart were talking about a new truck and some plumbing, that kind of thing. I think they were gonna do most of the work themselves, but my secretary just handed me a note saying the bank is on the other line."

"Concerning Farrah?"

"It seems she wants to draw out half the money—twenty-five thousand dollars. In cash. Seems pretty rash since she just deposited the check."

"I haven't any idea. But it's her money, I suppose, isn't it?"

The attorney scratched a pudgy cheek. "Yeah, right. But this isn't necessarily like her. She and Hobart are pretty tight with a dollar. Real Scrooge types. Save tin foil and string like my mother did in the Depression. This hardly seems kosher, Professor."

"You think something might be wrong?"

"Don't know, but I'm gonna talk to Farrah. If anything seems out of place, I'll call you back."

"Let me give you my number."

He jotted down Philippa's number and hung up. Then he punched the other line. "Hi, Mel?"

The bank manager lowered his voice. He could look over his desk at the couple standing in the foyer, chatting, holding hands and nibbling on shelled nuts. They were dressed like gypsies, but he knew one of them fairly well and was acquainted with the woman when she opened her account. He had no intention of letting loose of that much cash to these people without some reassurance from Farnam.

"Al, you know your client is asking to withdraw a substantial sum in cash from her account?"

"How much exactly, Mel? Myrtle said twenty-five grand?"

"Of course, there'd be no interest yet. The funds only just cleared."

"Yeah. So what's she need it for? You ask her?"

"She won't say. The man with her—it's Hobart Ames. You know him?"

"Sure. He's her boyfriend."

"Well, my teller says he comes in to cash checks occasionally. Doesn't have an account with us. Small amounts, usually no more than a couple hundred or so. Does carpentry work. He's employed on and off it seems."

"So what'd you ask her about the need to withdraw that much money?"

"Well, she wouldn't say. She just said she wanted it in cash."

"No small talk at all to give you a clue?"

"What do you mean?"

Farnam sighed. His error. Bankers never made small talk when it came to giving up money. "Look, Mel, how does she seem? Okay?"

"Looks like they slept in their clothes, Al."

"Yeah, yeah. That's SOP for kids these days. So how is she? Under any duress you can see? Anything like that?"

Mel turned around and studied the pair. They were still holding hands, munching almonds and chattering. Looked like a couple of young people standing in line at the movie theater. "No. I can't say there is."

"Well, tell you what, Mel. Let me talk to her."

"Hold on." He laid the phone down, walked up to the front, signaled for Farrah to follow him and led her back to his desk. "Mr. Farnam would like a word with you, Miss Swidnik."

"Mr. Farnam?" Farrah looked back at Hobart. "He wants to talk to me?"

He waggled the phone at her.

Hesitantly, she put the receiver to her ear. "Mr. Farnam?"

"Hi, Farrah. How's it goin'?"

"Are they calling you about the money?"

"What's the problem, Farrah? An emergency or something just come up?"

"No. Not exactly."

"That's a lot of money to be walkin' around with in your pocket."

"I know."

"Have you thought about this?"

"About taking the money out you mean?"

"What's it for?"

"Do I have to tell you, Mr. Farnam? I mean, legally or something. Do I need a special reason like an emergency?"

"Not exactly."

"I thought maybe there was a penalty or something for taking my money out so soon."

"No. You got the money in a savings account, right?"

"I got half in a checking account and half in the savings account."

"And you want to close out one of the accounts?"

"The savings account."

He waited for an explanation to follow. It didn't. "Is everything okay between you and Hobart?"

"Yeah. Sure."

"Is the money for you or somebody else?"

"Look, Mr. Farnam, this is my money, right?"

"Sure is."

"And it doesn't matter what I do with it then, right? I mean, I already gave half of it to my aunt."

"Yes, you did. And that was very generous of you, Farrah."

"So I want half for myself now, that's all."

"Any special reason?"

"Do I have to tell you that?"

"Is there some reason you can't?"

"This is private. It's my money and nobody else's so don't they have to give me the money when I want it? Aren't there some kind of banking laws or something to make them give me the money?"

"You can have the money, Farrah. I just think people may be concerned over such a large withdrawal so soon. This inheritance created quite a responsibility. I'm just concerned that you don't make any rash decisions with that money."

"Uh huh."

"Is there anybody else asking you for the money?"

"I can't say. I just want to get my money and go on home. You don't have to worry about me or anything. I'm fine."

He rubbed his chin. Maybe he should try a different tactic. "Farrah, I heard from your aunt in Chicago. She just called me."

"Aunt Philly?"

"She's coming out to see you."

"For real? When?"

"Maybe by tomorrow."

"Great. Hey, that's super."

Farnam stopped to rethink. She seemed delighted to hear about her aunt's visit. "You think you could hold off on withdrawing the money until she comes out? Maybe this is something you would want to discuss with her."

"Not this."

"Farrah, you know I'm trying to look out for you. Can you tell me anything to make me feel better about this?"

"Like what?"

"Like assure me you are not being harassed by anybody wanting to use that money for some wild-assed scheme. That you're not under any pressure by anybody to withdraw that money."

"Nothing like that."

"But you'd rather not tell me the specifics?"

"That's my business, Mr. Farnam."

"Okay. Let me talk to Mel again."

"Mel?"

"The manager there."

"Okay. Bye."

Mel took the phone and looked at Farrah. "Al?"

"Mel, I can't get her to tell me anything. But I don't think it's gonna be a problem. Maybe these kids just wanna take the dough home and sock it under the pillow or something. If I were you, I wouldn't worry about it."

"Can you give me any sort of directive here, Al?"

"Well, you're the banker not me. It's her money. She wants it. So I guess you give it to her."

"That will close out her savings account with the bank, Al."

"Well, that's your business not mine. Look, if it makes you feel any easier about this, her aunt from Chicago is coming out here tomorrow. She'll make sure everything is kosher. You may have the cash back in a couple days."

"Alright. If you say so."

"Well, I'm just giving you my opinion. She's an adult. It's her money so give it to her."

"I'll see what I can do. That's a lot of cash."

Farnam laughed. "Hey, I thought that's what you guys specialized in—cash." He hung up and looked straight into the dead-eye glare of Myrtle standing with her short arms akimbo, each foot planted on legal litter.

"She wants to take out all her money so soon?" she snipped. "No kidding?"

"Half. Probly gonna bury it under the trailer. These young people don't trust banks, Myrtle." He winked. "They're part of the industrial, financial establishment screwing America."

"I think her mother should have appointed a trustee."

"Well, that ain't my concern."

Her eyes narrowed. "Have you started on that Jones will yet?"

"It's next on my short list. Don't worry. I got at least fifteen minutes before they show up." He checked his watch. "Make it ten anyhow."

"Alan, where is the Wendover file? Don't try to play dumb with me again. I know you had it last. You can't wiggle out of this. I need it. Now."

He frowned, scrunched his face into a pensive frown and pointed at the library table. There were at least thirty files piled there along with extra underwear, a broken coffee machine and back issues of *The Fly Fisherman*. "In the bottom drawer—right here. I was waiting on a call from Teddy." He pulled out the drawer. No file, but he did lift up a striped necktie with a clip still attached. "Hey, I was lookin' for this," he whooped with a triumphant grin.

"Look again. For the file not your dirty laundry. I already found a pair of socks behind the umbrella stand."

"The gray ones with the little purple checks?"

She shook her head and shot him a hopeless look. "They need mending."

"They're brand new. Almost."

"The big toe's got a hole in it."

"No kidding?" He was genuinely amazed. Seemed like only a few weeks ago he had picked those socks up at Meier and Franks when he was in Salem for a deposition. Wonder how long they'd been behind the umbrella stand? "Maybe the mice ate the toe out," he suggested seriously. "We got any mouse traps around here?"

"*Al-an*. Think. Where were you when you had that file last?"

"By the copy machine?"

"Wrong. I looked there first."

"Lemme think a minute." He knew he could finger that file and get this stalking witch out of his office if he just concentrated. Then it came to him. "The fridge."

He jumped out of his chair, went into the storeroom and opened the door of the broken-down Kelvinator that was now a warehouse for extra light bulbs, typewriter ribbons, coffee, sugar cubes and soda pop. He pushed a pizza carton aside and came up with a legal brief. "Aha! Right where I left it." He handed it over with a gallant flourish.

"Alan, there's tomato paste on the signature lines," she scolded.

"Such is life, Myrtle."

36

Josie had been gone all night. At one o'clock in the morning, after he had fed Goldie and done the dishes, Cain Reeves had driven down to Cully Marsh and parked the car. Then he had walked through the brambles to get a peek at the trailer. The lights were out. Hobart's battered truck was parked by the door. Josie must be spending the night—what a séance this must be. Josie had told him to come back and get the tape recorder. It should be in the weeds down by the boat dock.

He had come prepared with his vest pockets stuffed with hamburger balls. He took out a couple to grease his fingers, tiptoed down the muddy ruts and tossed some meat in the direction of the woodshed. The hound dogs came out wagging their tails and sniffing the ground for seconds. Cain dropped some more meat, threw a handful of bait into the stacks of alder wood piled by the woodshed door and slipped behind the blackberry bushes.

When he got to the marsh, he dropped on all fours, took out the flashlight and swept it right and left as he crept along. It took him only minutes to locate the cassette recorder Josie had dropped into the tall grass. He put it in his pocket, backed his way out, scattered the last of his hamburger in the hounds' path then stood up and hightailed it back to the road.

If the tape was out there lying in the boonies where Josie had set it, then he was certain that things had gone according to their plan. All he had to do now was wait for the money. She had said she wouldn't come home without the cash. That meant she was sitting tight on their tail until the banks opened. So by midday he ought to see Hobart delivering Josie Wallgood to the Nashua with ten grand in her bag.

Cain climbed back in his car, started it up and made a U turn. He headed for the Jewel Grove Trailer Park, fixed a fresh pot of coffee and lit a cigarette. Things were turning out better than expected. This was easy work. By tomorrow, he would be headed east with five-thousand bucks in his jeans. He was already thinking about Chicago. He had a buddy there: Frankie Alveras—used to play shortstop for Tacoma, had a drug problem and didn't last more than two seasons in Triple A. Shame because the guy had an arm like a rocket, but his head was all fucked up.

Cain put his feet up on a chair and took a long drag on the Camel. Frankie had been seeing a girl back home, and he got pretty serious about her. Seems he'd straightened himself out now since he got hooked up with this Janice—even got a good job working at the newspaper. Oiled the press machines or some damn thing for the *Chicago Tribune*. Made pretty decent money, was a union man and all that bullshit. So maybe Cain would just drive out to Chi Town and look old Frankie up. Could be Frankie could get him started somewhere. Hell, with this score of Josie's, he could afford to get himself some nice place to crash, a stereo, even go out and boogie a little on Saturday nights. They had lots of good booze, disco music and beautiful babes in Chicago. Frankie had told him about that.

Yeah, he decided, nodding in the darkness, watching the glowing end of his cigarette flare like a comet as he sucked. He just might take the money and blow this hickville town, go to Chicago and look up Frankie and his old lady Jan. Cain had a crumpled envelope he'd saved because it had Frankie's address on it. They were staying in a fourth floor two-bedroom apartment in the Varsity Building across from Jackson Park. Not far from the University of Chicago, Frankie had written him. Sounded like a pretty nice place. The couple was even expecting a baby real soon. Lucky Frankie. He didn't miss baseball. For Cain, he couldn't begin to think of attaching himself to any woman until he had anchored himself somewhere. Right now he had no idea where that was going to be. But one thing was certain: it wasn't going to be in this tin can Nashua with Josie the Psychic Phenom in Nowheresville, Oregon. Not hardly. Get real.

He grinned and blew smoke circles up toward the ceiling. No fucking way was he parking his ass in this drippy dump. He was going to be heading for the sunrise by tomorrow with cash in his pockets. But because Josie had been decent with him, taken him in and given him a stake, he felt he owed her a little something before he took off—his way of letting her know he was appreciative at least for this rest-stop romance.

Cain looked around searching for inspiration. Then an idea struck him. He could fix her something really special before he split. Maybe a big pot roast dinner with all the trimmings. Yeah. That was it. He'd fix her a fucking pot roast, buy a bottle of wine, and they'd have a helluva celebration before he took off. Might even pick up a Betty Crocker cake mix for desert. Seemed fair. More than fair actually because he knew damned well he'd have to do the dishes all by himself.

37

When Cain woke up, he scrambled three eggs, fried six strips of bacon, buttered four slices of white bread and drained the orange juice pitcher. Then he washed up and dressed, cleaned out the money from Josie's cookie jar to buy the groceries for his celebration dinner and headed for town. He gassed up his car then parked in front of the Dairy Delight Cafe and went inside. He ordered a cup of coffee while he read the sports page from a discarded newspaper.

Two women came in. They were talking faster than they were walking. One was wearing a floral-pattern blouse ruffled to her chin, flashy sunflowers printed on her skirt and a handbag with crocheted pansies. She sat down in a booth behind Cain and chattered with her companion, a younger woman with Gloria Steinem glasses and a brown ponytail.

"So what did you think of the show?" the younger one asked her companion as Cain read his paper.

"It was okay, but do you really think he's so sexy?"

"Don't you?"

"No. He's too young for me anyway."

"What'll you have, Myrtle?" the waitress asked from behind the counter.

"Same as always, I guess. Give me the tuna salad and an iced tea, Wilma."

"Me, too," her friend echoed.

Cain looked over his shoulder to take in his company with a swift glance. Two plain-faced women, one dumpy and middle-aged and the other about as interesting as vanilla pudding. He returned to his paper, scanning the page for the National League scores while the two women chatted.

The older woman stirred sugar in her tea. "Some days you just wonder why you even bother, do you know what I mean?"

"Uh huh. Today I was trying to–"

"—He makes such a mess, I can hardly keep any order at all."

"Uh huh. So I wanted to say to–"

'—and this morning just as I was getting ready to finish that Wendover will—they were coming in at noon—guess who called Alan?"

"Wendover—is that the couple who lives over by the IGA?"

"Yes, but never mind them. Guess who called this morning?"

"How would I know, Myrtle?"

"You remember that fellow who did the cabinets for the photo shop?"

"You mean Hallender's new store?"

"The man who did all the shelving and display cases. The curly-haired one."

"Oh. Him." She unwrapped a Saltine. "Yeah. He was kinda cute. I liked him. He did a job for us over at the pharmacy."

"That's the one. Well, he's living out at Cully Marsh, you know."

"Uh huh. I see him and his dogs sometimes when we go berry picking out there."

"He's living with Farrah Swidnik. You know her?"

"Uh uh." Her ponytail swung left and right as Cain turned around quickly and stared at her mention of Farrah's name.

"Well, she's from Haight Ashbury, I think. Alan represented Farrah for distribution of a trust fund her mother set up for her daughter."

"So Farrah and Hobart are living together out there?"

"Oh, yes. Haven't you ever seen them come in to town in that old truck of his?"

"Well, since the baby, I've been pretty house-bound. It's funny how we–"

"—That's who called Alan this morning. From the bank."

"Who?"

"Farrah Swidnik and her boyfriend. She was there to draw out the money, close out her account at the bank, and she just got the check a few days back."

"Yeah. Money goes right through your fingers. I wish I had some to slip through mine," she laughed.

Myrtle Mudsunk leaned over her coffee cup and spoke in a hushed tone that Cain could barely hear. "We thought she got taken in by somebody selling her something probably. She took out twenty-five thousand dollars in cash."

"She got that much, huh?"

"That was only half of what she had. Her mother left her a little over a hundred thousand, and she sent half of that to an aunt back east."

"Really? Half?"

Myrtle looked around quickly. "And she just took out half of the fifty-thousand she had left this morning. That's twenty-five *thousand* dollars—in cash." She rapped her knuckles on the table top. "Imagine that."

"That's a lotta money—more'n Kyle makes in a year. We'd like to—"

"—and that's not all. Alan tried to get her to say why, but she didn't tell him a thing. Just took the money and walked right out."

The waitress came over and slapped two specials down on the table. On her way back, she refilled Cain's cup.

"So God only knows what's happened to that money by now. These people have no sense of responsibility like we had when I was her age." Myrtle firmed her lips and stuck a fork into the tuna fish salad. "Imagine getting that kind of money and then going through twenty-five thousand dollars in just a few days."

"Uh huh. Must be neat."

"Too bad they don't have some kind of holding law, a time limit on when a depositor could draw out their money from a new account."

"You mean keep you from getting your money on demand? Hey, the banks get away with plenty now, Myrtle. I don't wanna give those suckers any more excuses to hang on to my money."

"Well, Lord only knows what she'll do with that much money. Something foolish no doubt."

"Hey, could be she's gonna remodel their house," she posited with her mouth full of tomato. "I've been trying to get Kyle to put some new vinyl in my kitchen for years."

Myrtle harumphed and nibbled on a celery stick. "Have you ever seen where they live out there? I board my dog in a better kennel than what they call a house."

"It's out there at the end of Cully Marsh Road, right? I've seen an old abandoned trailer out there in the blackberry bushes. That's on their property, isn't it?"

"It's not abandoned—they're living in it. You ought to see the junk they have around there." She dared anyone to find even a speck of dirt in her orderly bungalow. The last time her husband had tracked mud into the house, she had scolded him for a week. "That man looks like a lumberjack—always with a torn work shirt and muddy boots."

"Uh huh. But he's cute, isn't he? Hobart Ames, I mean. Real cute."

"If you like the type. But who would? Does he even own a clean white shirt or a decent tie?" She indicted Hobart like a fourth-grade slacker.

"Who cares, Myrtle? He's cute—a real hunk. I'd like to—"

" —Don't be silly." Myrtle puckered her lips in a scornful smile. "A porcupine's cute too, I suppose, but I wouldn't want to cuddle up to one."

Cain stood up, dropped some change on the counter and walked out. His blood was about as hot as a boiling radiator on the Mojave. His jaw was set, and the cords bulged in his thick neck. Twenty-five thousand dollars! And she had told him it was only going to be ten? Bitch! The conniving, lying, deceitful little witch.

He gunned the engine and squealed all four tires leaving Main Street.

Bitch! Two-timing, scheming cunt, he ranted as he sped out of town. The lying, sneaking bitches were always playing some fucking head game. Who in hell did she think she was, trying to cheat him like that? He wouldn't have been the least bit sore if she had demanded a sixty-forty split since she was doing the hard part. But trying to screw him out of seventy-five hundred bucks? The lying cunt. She was going to be sorry for this and regret the day she thought she could pull a fast one on Cain Reeves.

He screeched the car around a turn, bounced over the ruts and slid into the Jewel Grove Trailer Park. Goddam smart ass. She was going to learn an important lesson in human relations alright. One she wouldn't forget.

Cain jerked the Pontiac to a stop beside the Nashua, slammed the car door and tromped up the porch. Once inside, he flung open the cupboard doors and found a bottle of whiskey. He took a hefty slug and then began throwing everything onto the floor. When the last cupboard and drawer were emptied, he got around to the old Norge and with both hands jettisoned its contents. Eggs flew across the table and smacked against the knotty pine. A jar of Mayo crashed onto the stove top and oozed over the burners.

When he had trashed the tiny kitchen, he went to the front, smashed Josie's myrtlewood lamp and knocked over the settee. Then struck by an impulse of pure orneriness, he picked up the crystal ball and side-armed it through the window. The sound of tinkling glass and crumpling aluminum was music to his ears.

"Bitch!" he hollered as he wound up for a second pitch and hurled the new Motorola in the same direction. A sinker, right across the plate. *Crash!*

Satisfied with his work, he choked the bottle of bourbon and headed for the bedroom.

38

Charlie Plack kicked his overflowing wastebasket aside as he dropped himself into his scruffy chair. He stared at the brick wall and brooded. Damned rain. Miserable, wet fucking day. Dishwater sky, wet wind. No fucking clients worth a shit. Fuck all of them and their penny ante problems anyway.

He was going to get out of this shithole early today and spend the afternoon over at Tilly's. He and a few of his old beer-drinking buddies could shoot a few games of pool and then maybe find some moderately priced companions to fill a dull evening. He wanted to spit out the alum taste that bitchy Professor left in his mouth. Miss Holier Than Thou, Miss Christ Almighty herself. Piss on her.

His phone rang. Three times and no pick up. His secretary must be in the can down the hall reading bodice rippers as usual.

He answered. "Law office."

"Daddy?"

"Uhhh...Janice?"

"Hi, Daddy."

He fought off a lump the size of a Polish dumpling rising in his throat. "Is it really you, Honey Bun?" He choked back an outburst of unrestrained mush on hearing his baby girl's voice. She hadn't called her father for almost six years. A whole lifetime during which Charlie felt as if his balls were being nibbled by rats. She had drained his blood away drop by drop.

"Daddy, I wanted to call you."

"Oh, Baby. I'm...Jesus! I...I'm so glad to hear from you, Baby," he blubbered, mopping his brow with a soiled handkerchief.

"Daddy—"

"—It's been so long, Baby. I been dying, you know that? Dyin' a slow death without my little girl. How are you, Honey Bun? Are you okay?"

She laughed and made Charlie's heart flutter like a sparrow. "I'm fine, Daddy."

"You sure? You healthy and everything?"

"I'm fine. I just got a checkup last week as a matter of fact, and I'm fine."

"You're takin' good care of yourself, Baby?"

"Yes, Daddy. I'm fine. Really."

"Where you livin'? I been callin' Wendy and Cherie—all your friends, and they won't tell me a thing. You know the family won't tell me a goddam thing. Uncle Pauli said he couldn't even gimme your new address, Baby. I been goin' outta my mind with worry, Janice—you got no idea what it's been like."

"Daddy, I'm sorry, but I just didn't want to see you."

"Let's don't talk about that."

"I've been thinking things over lately, Daddy."

Sweat slid over his body in sheets and made the receiver slippery in his hand as he awaited his sentence. "Oh, Honey Bun, you know I'm sorry, Baby. I'm so friggin' sorry."

"I have something to tell you. You remember Frankie—the boy I was going with since tenth grade?"

"The baseball player?"

"Well, we're married now, Daddy."

He didn't care if she told him she had married King Kong, Malcolm X's brother or an unemployed Spic—just so long as he had his little girl's love again. "That's wonderful news, Sweetheart. He treatin' my little princess okay? Did you get married in the Church, Baby?"

"Yes, Daddy."

At least she had saved her soul even if he had not been there to share her happiness. He could forget about all that. It was in the past. Now she had called him. His baby princess Janice was on the phone to make amends. Jesus, this was wonderful news. This was a holy fucking miracle.

"Daddy, I've talked this over with Frankie."

"What's his last name, Baby?"

"Alveras. Frankie Alveras. He's a good Catholic, and he treats me like a queen, Daddy. Everything's going good for us. And the thing is, Frankie and me we've talked it all over, and he thinks you should know about this no matter how I feel about that other thing. Well, you know."

"Something's wrong? You need money?"

"It's nothing to worry about. I'm going to have a baby that's all. You're going to be a granddaddy in May."

He swiped at a snot dribble hanging from the tip of his nose. "My little Janice a mama? No kiddin'?"

"May tenth the doctor says. I wanted you to know, Daddy."

"Oh, Baby, that's wonderful."

"I was thinking that the baby deserves to know where he comes from, you know? He needs to get to know his granddad. If it's a boy, Frankie wants to name him Francis Charles. Francis is Frankie's Christian name, and we thought you wouldn't mind our naming him Charles after you. Of course, it might be a girl."

Charlie was snorting and blubbering into his handkerchief, giddy with happiness. "Sure—a little angel just like her mama."

"Are you glad to find out you're gonna be a grandfather, Daddy?"

"I'm so happy I'm about to bust wide open here. The angels musta heard my prayers. I been prayin' for the day I'd hear your voice again, Princess. The Virgin Mother answered my prayers today. I been lightin' a candle every Sunday so does this mean I can see you and the baby, Honey Bun?" He was shaking worse than the time he had double pneumonia as a kid.

There was a weighty pause while Charlie twisted in the wind. "Daddy, you know I still feel the same way about what I saw."

"Oh, Baby, you know I go to confession every Sunday since then. I ain't missed a single mass since, I swear. It was just a mistake, Honey. It wasn't anything really. You know your daddy wouldn't do anything bad to anybody, Janice."

"Like I said, Frankie and I talked this over, and he agreed that it's my decision. Someone told me the other day that he thinks I should just forgive and forget like Jesus did, that I only have one father, and my baby needs to know where he came from."

"He's right, Baby. We let this thing come between us, and it ain't right. A father and daughter should be together, you know?"

"So I just wanted you to know about me and Frankie and the baby."

"Can I come and see you?"

"Frankie would like to see us get back together and be a family for the baby's sake."

"What do you want, Janice? Do you wanna see your daddy?" He held his breath. His white knuckles gripped the receiver as if it were a live grenade.

"I've missed you, Daddy. Would you like to come over for supper on Sunday?"

He nearly fell out of his chair he was so excited. "Sunday?"

"Can you make it about six?"

"I'll be there if I gotta walk through hell fire. You sure he's takin' good care of my little angel?"

"Yes, Daddy. He even went out to the deli last night to get me some sauerkraut and Swiss cheese."

"He better treat my little girl good. She's a goddam angel walkin' on this earth. I'll bring over some pound cake. That was always your favorite, right, Sweetheart? Lemon pound cake? And maybe some strawberry ice cream, huh?"

"Get a pencil and write down the address. We're over by Jackson Park."

"This Frankie got you a nice place, Honey?"

"It's nice, Daddy. Frankie let me buy some new things for the baby already, too. He's got a good job at the *Trib*. He belongs to the union now."

"No more baseball, no more livin' on the road with a buncha bums in a broken down bus, chasin' women, boozin' and dopin'? That's no life for a married man with family responsibilities."

"Frankie's settled down now. He's home every night. He goes to church with me every Sunday. He's got a good job, and he's gonna get a raise the first of next month."

"Good, Baby. My little girl deserves the best."

"Frankie spoils me, Daddy. Anything I want, he gets it for me. You'll see. So come over for Sunday supper with us. You'll like Frankie. He wants to meet you."

She had been too ashamed to tell her husband the gritty details of her falling out with her father. Instead, she had told him Charlie was caught cheating with his secretary. It didn't sound so dirty, so sordid. Frankie couldn't believe she would turn her back on her dad for that. They often argued about it. It would take a great burden of guilt from her shoulders reconciling with her father.

As a matter of fact, the only person she had shared her awful secret with was the lawyer she had met in the stairwell recently when the elevator broke down. And it didn't seem so unforgivable a sin to that stranger either. Maybe the Holy Mother had sent this anonymous man to speak to her just at the right moment in her life. It was fate. She must be doing the right thing.

"This Frankie, he's the one with the pimples? The one who used to mow our grass up by the brewery?"

"That was his brother Ritchie. Frankie's just a year older than me, Daddy. He played shortstop."

"I remember him. He's not a bad-lookin' kid. He was kinda short."

"He's a man now, Daddy. He's taller than Uncle Pauli. Are you coming over on Sunday then?"

"You gotta ask?" He searched for a pencil. "What's the address?"

"And, Daddy...you know I still love you."

He nearly dropped the phone. Tears streamed down both his doughy cheeks and splatted on his wrinkled shirtfront. "God, I've missed you so much, Baby."

"Me, too, Daddy." There was an uncomfortable pause. "I'll see you on Sunday then. Let me give you the address."

He jotted down the numbers and hung up.

Charlie Plack swung around and looked out the streaked window at the alley which was his dismal backdrop. He blew his nose. "Thank you, Jesus. Bless you Sweet Mary, holy mother, for givin' me my little girl back."

As he wiped the snot from his upper lip, he saw a mangy cat creep from behind a vegetable crate and sniff at a rodent's carcass. Before it could haul away its prize, a raven swooped down like a red-eyed buzzard, snagged the booty and flew up to the roof while the flea-bitten tabby scurried under a garbage can.

39

Hobart laid the last hundred-dollar bill in Josie's palm. It felt better than the Pope's kiss as her fingers curled over the money. She had never seen such an accumulation of wealth let alone held it in both hands. This was capitalism at its very best. Absolutely.

"Thanks," she gushed still staring at the stack of bills in both hands.

"You better put that somewhere safe. You don't want to be carrying that around with you, Josie."

"Yeah, I'm gonna do that, Hobart. No sweat." She stuffed the money into her bag. It wouldn't all fit. She jettisoned a package of salted nuts, a rattail comb, a tube of lip balm, some Kleenex tissues, a mirror and a half-eaten O'Henry candy bar. The money ballooned out her bag nevertheless and gaped at the zippered closing. She took the last stack of fifties and divided them between her two skirt pockets. She was loaded up like a smuggler with brand new crisp bills smelling of rich all neatly bundled with red rubber bands.

When she finished stowing her loot, she looked up. Hobart and Farrah were standing by the door eyeing her like a couple of patients waiting for root canals.

"Jo," Hobart said warily, pushing his hat back on his head, "there's fresh tracks outside by the shed this morning. Fresh Camel butts, too. I think Max's been here while we were gone. You hear anything?"

"No. Nothing."

"Well, those look like the same tracks. He musta been here last night. Let's don't waste any more time. You got the money so get rid of Max."

Farrah slunk behind Hobart and wrapped her arms around his waist. "My Aunt Philly is coming out to see me, Josie. You have to do it right now, get rid of Max before she gets here."

Josie gulped back her surprise at the news. "Your aunt is coming out from Chicago?"

"Yeah."

"What for?"

"Mr. Farnham didn't say. To see me, I guess. Maybe thank me for the money." She glanced out the window. "You think maybe it could be another omen, a sign, Josie? Something to do with all of this? Has my mom's spirit called her, do you think?"

"Who knows? You can't read spirit's minds, you know."

"I didn't mean to imply anything. It's just that it's quite a coincidence, don't you think? Aunt Philly coming out here today with all of this going on? With my soul hanging in the balance?"

Hobart butted in. "Do you think she knows something about the exorcism, Jo?"

That was the last and worst thing Josie wanted to consider—some interloper horning in on her operation. She needed to perform the finale, drop the name, take her cash and head for the exit before anything else got screwed up. "Anything is possible in the realm of the paranormal. I think we should get a move on."

"Let's get this over with." Farrah sat down at the table and motioned for Hobart to join her. "I'm ready, I guess."

Josie took out the red jewelry box and set it down in front of her. Then she glanced around and frowned at the sunshine streaming in. It wasn't at all conducive to transcendental trances. "Close the curtains. Too much light scares em off."

Farrah jumped up and tugged at the flowery pillow slips drafted into service as draperies over the louvered glass and darkened the trailer instantly. She resumed her seat and grasped Hobart's hand in hers.

"What do we have to do?" Hobart asked.

Josie pulled her hair back from her face, licked her lips and closed her eyes. "Nothing. Just be quiet. Absolutely quiet. Under no circumstances should you utter a sound. If the spirits speak to you, do not answer. Got it?"

They both nodded obediently.

"Not a word." Josie kept her eyes tightly shut and flexed the muscles in her arms and neck for effect. She was going to get into this thing. And Max was going to fucking disappear. No doubt the tracks Hobart had spotted outside were Cain's. He had come back to retrieve the cassette just as they had planned. This was almost too easy. If there were such a thing, she would win the Psychic of the Year Award hands down. This was no dumb-ass con for twenty bucks a throw, phony tarot cards or palm reading. This was heavy. This was the Bigs, as Cain would call it. Josie had finally made it up to the major leagues of fortune-telling phenomena.

"When are you starting?" Farrah whispered.

Josie opened her eyes and shot a look of disapproval across the table top. "Shhhhhh! Don't say another word until I tell you to speak."

"Okay," she squeaked.

"And don't move. No matter what the spirits might say, don't obey. Got it?"

They both nodded with white-rimmed eyes.

"No telling who might be in possession of my corporeal and spiritual persona."

"What's that mean exactly?" Hobart winced at the thought of Josie being pulled apart like raw hamburger by pasty-faced ghouls.

"My body—my mortal self. It's not safe to communicate with the spirits at a time like this. It gives them a straight shot right into your soul."

Farrah gasped and held her hand over her mouth.

"You mean like a radar lock on? Like that, Jo?"

"Yeah. Exactly, Hobart. Only it's permanent. So keep your eyes closed and your mouths shut. Understand? No matter what you hear. This is serious shit. One wrong move, and you could be—"

"—Stop!" Farrah clamped her hands over her ears. "I don't even want to hear, Josie. Just hurry up and do it. I can't stand it. Just get this whole thing over with."

Josie suppressed a smirk at their dumb complacence. Too bad she couldn't order the spirits to call out for pizza and Cokes while these two potato-heads waited for the spooks to show.

Curtain up—she clasped her hands and rocked slightly forward in the chair. "Oh, Spirit Queen, Mother of the Universe, guide me to the celestial home of our departed soul Max Swidnik. His daughter Farrah Lynn is calling…" Josie chanted in a dramatic monotone. She was so good at this, she should definitely think about a movie career if the television show was a hit. Why not a sequel? *Madame Josephina Finds Love and Romance in the Cosmos!* Yeah, sounded good.

Farrah and Hobart went into a full body clinch.

Josie's chair rocked side to side then back and forth. Faster and faster. Then Josie's eyes flew open and rolled up in her head like a dead man's. Her body jerked in a spasmodic dance that climaxed with her stiffening like a corpse in full rigor mortis.

"Oh!" Farrah hid her face in Hobart's shoulder, too afraid to peek.

"Jesus!" He froze, wide-eyed and white-faced at the metamorphosis unfolding in front of him.

"*You lying, cheating cunt!*" Josie's masculine baritone thundered as she tipped straight back in her chair and crashed like a hat rack onto the floor. Foam bubbled from her mouth. "*You can't take away my only kid, you bitch! She's mine! I want her!*"

Farrah shrieked as Josie's legs stiffened like fireplace pokers and hammered a beat on the floor. Josie's eyes rolled around in their sockets, and spittle frothed on her lips. She stared blindly into a freaky void unseen by her stunned audience.

Hobart bit his lip. "Christ Almighty, she's having a fit."

"It's Max!" Farrah wailed, covering her face. "Don't look, Hobart! Don't look!"

Outside the dogs started barking like bloodhounds on the spoor of a skunk. Hobart and Farrah clung to one another and covered their eyes.

The trailer door suddenly flew wide open. A dark figure appeared on the threshold. The sun was at his back, and his silhouette floated in an oriel of orange light as he blocked the doorway. "*You lying, cheating bitch!*" The voice sounded as if it had bubbled up from the bowels of hell.

Hobart kept his eyes tightly shut against the ghostly intruder. He knew who it was. He knew that demented voice. He had heard its ghostly echo down at the marsh. It was Max Swidnik coming for Farrah. Hobart knew it could not be anything other than an apparition summoned by Josie's spiritual guide damning them all. She had told them not to heed any such outbursts, and he was determined to avoid temptation. No demonic thief was going to steal his soul.

Farrah took one peek at the wild-eyed manifestation and buried her face in Hobart's neck. "Awwwww!" She knew who it was, too. Max had come for her soul, and she wasn't letting him lock on to her with a careless glance in his direction. She squeezed her eyes shut, shaking so hard her teeth chattered.

With one jump, Cain Reeves was inside the trailer. He stepped over Josie's quivering body on the floor and grabbed her bag. Plunging his hand inside its bowels, he hauled out a stack of bills bundled with red rubber bands. "I don't know what kind of game you're playing, but you ain't gettin' away with this, Babe. You can't cheat me outta somethin' I earned fair and square. I'm here to get what's mine, you lying little witch." Cain stuffed the money back into Josie's bag and slung it across his chest like a Mexican bandoleer before staggering out the doorway. He turned for a final word. "Hey, it's only money, right? So long, Baby."

Then he slammed the metal door behind him, clomped through the bushes to his car and drove back up Cully Marsh Road with Josie's money and a half empty bottle of Jim Beam between his legs.

"Ohhh, please, don't hurt me," Farrah whimpered while the dogs barked. "Just go away. Go away. Please, just leave me alone!"

Hobart crushed her against his chest. His eyes were still clamped shut. "Remember what Jo said, Farrah. Don't answer him. Don't say a word. Just be quiet."

"I'm so scared."

"Me, too. But no matter what happens, just be quiet and don't move."

They trembled and hung on to one another. Josie seemed to be having a spasm of some kind. She jerked and kicked and turned as red as a Maine lobster. Her tongue protruded from her foaming mouth. Her arms flew out and knocked over a tenor banjo leaning against the wall. The instrument crashed to the floor and startled the couple anew.

"Oh, my god!" Farrah squeaked. "Max's ghost is killing Josie, Hobart. Do something!"

He cracked his eyes open and took a look for himself. Farrah may have been right. Josie looked like she was going to explode.

"How will I find out who my father is then?" Farrah whimpered.

Josie's mouth opened wide; her tongue rolled out, and her right hand raised. Then slowly her body relaxed and lay back as if she were simply asleep. The eyes fluttered closed. Her breathing deepened. Then she spoke in the sweet, fragile voice which made Farrah shiver. "*Bootsie, Darling, don't be afraid. It's Mama.*"

"Ohhhh...." Farrah moaned.

"*His name is Bradley Hammaker. And he loves you very much, Bootsie. He's coming to make amends. Forgive him and try to love him for my sake, Bootsie.*"

"Ohhhh, Mama." She bawled like a cow in labor as Hobart tried to comfort her.

Josie's expression softened. Her skin seemed to glow as she spoke in such a gentle, low-toned voice they had to strain to hear her clearly above Farrah's sobs. *"Don't be afraid. Max will never hurt you, Sweetheart. I promise. He's out of your life forever. Don't cry. The dark is lifted now, and a new day is beginning for you."*

Then with a long sigh, Josie started to snore. Her head turned to the side; she drew up her legs and scratched her nose with a forefinger.

Hobart peeked over the edge of the table. "I'll be damned." He got up, pulled the curtains back and let the light in. The dogs were finally quiet. "Hey, look." He pointed to the floor beside Josie. "Max took the money. I'll be god-dammed. It was just like Josie said—it was his money, and he took it. I guess Josie was trading your soul for the money, Farrah."

"Josie did that, Hobart?"

"Look. Her bag is gone. It's all gone. Max came and took the money."

"Is Josie alright?"

He knelt down and felt her forehead. It was cool now. "She's sleeping, I think."

"Poor Josie. She really risked a lot for me, didn't she, Hobart?"

"Incredible. Fucking incredible. I'd never believed any of this, Farrah, if I hadn't seen it with my own eyes."

"I thought she needed the money for herself. And it wasn't for her at all, was it?"

"This totally blows my mind. Freaks me out. She coulda like killed herself, I guess. Did you see her?"

Farrah half raised from the chair and peered down at Josie. "Is she okay?"

"I think so. Christ, she was foaming at the mouth like a zombie or something."

"Is Max gone now do you think?"

He felt for a pulse on Josie's clammy wrist and lifted a damp curl from her cheek. "I think so. You heard him. His voice was like right inside her, and then he was here in person. Josie said that might happen—the spirits sometimes take on earthly forms."

"I was so scared, Hobart, I almost peed my pants."

"You heard what he said?"

"He was pissed, right? At Mom do you think? Or Josie?"

"Both I guess. Jeez, Jo." He shook her tenderly. "Are you gonna be alright?"

Josie snored back at him.

"Did you get the name she said?" Farrah suddenly realized she hadn't had time to write it down. "It was Bradley something, wasn't it?"

"Hammaker, I think."

"Bradley Hammaker," Farrah sighed wistfully. "I wonder what he's like."

Josie's eyes flicked open. She tried to sit up, but Hobart restrained her gently.

"You okay, Jo?"

"What happened?" Josie coughed, trying to clear the cobwebs. Then she felt around on the floor, and the blood drained from her face. "Where's my bag?"

40

It was still raining. The sooty clouds had washed over the valley about noon, and by five o'clock, it was as dark as a train tunnel in the trailer park. Josie sat with her feet tucked under her on the horsehair settee. Goldie crawled up on her lap and purred. All around her, everywhere she looked, there was wreckage. He had even thrown her new color television set out the window, and now the rain was leaking in and beginning to stain the paneling.

She was brooding in the dark because he had broken her lamp, too. And the kitchen was like the aftermath of a spaghetti factory explosion. She didn't even have the heart to assess the carnage in there. The old Norge was as bare as a baby's ass—not even one cold Coke left. Cain had gone completely berserk.

Josie blew her nose on a tissue and pulled a blanket around her shoulders. Nothing to eat in the Nashua now. Unless she wanted to scrape peanut butter off the kitchen chairs or try scrambling the eggs dripping off the stove. No lights left except the feeble bulb over the sink. No dishes—he had broken everything. Even her favorite coffee cup with the astrological calendar on it.

But that wasn't the worst part. She could have forgiven him all that, written it all off as an aberrant rampage. But there was nothing she could do to assuage her pain at losing the crystal ball. The one icon of her ascendancy over the commonplace, and he had destroyed it. She could never forgive him for that. Never. In fact, she would plot her revenge. Somehow.

She had come home to find this mess, this sticky, splintery nightmare and no one to offer her an explanation. No one to share her outrage at the crime. Cain had stolen her money, taken it all, the selfish bastard, and run out on her. Probably laughing at her as he blew down the highway. It wasn't fair. Life was just shitty. The cocksucker had even cleaned out her cookie jar, smashed the glass in her Pinto and let the air out of all four tires. There was no more humanity in man. It was all her fault for expecting anything more. After all, men were just men, weren't they? No more—no less.

It had been such a fucking bad trip at Farrah and Hobart's. Something had gone wrong. One minute she was in the prime of her repertoire, and then the lights seemed to go out. She must have fallen back in the rickety chair and cracked her head on the floor. She might have killed herself, conked herself into eternal oblivion for all anybody cared. And while she was lying there like a landed fish in the boat, with a head wound, no doubt comatose and hallucinatory, that sonuvabitch had walked right in and grabbed her bag. And it was just as sad and simple as that.

She sneezed and sank her fingertips into Goldie's warm fur. "It's just so damned unfair, Goldie," she complained to a sympathetic listener who never argued back. "I can't believe that asshole is going to get away with my money, and I got nothing!" She sneezed again. "Nothing. Not even a lousy Coca Cola, Goldie. And now I don't even have a car that runs. Goddam it, Goldie. Goddam."

She dug into her pocket for a tissue, splayed her fingers and pulled out a fifty dollar bill. "Hey!" She bounced the cat off her lap, pulled out the bundles stashed in her skirt and counted out the money. There was twenty-five hundred dollars there. At least she wasn't broke.

She got up and paced back and forth. She had enough to start over—a down payment on another car and a new color TV. Maybe even a bigger-sized screen. And she'd get a new crystal ball like the one she'd seen at the Theater Crafts supply store in Portland. That ball had a black plastic base and a battery so it could glow a deep pink. Fantastic. She was going to go first class this time. Damn Cain Reeves to hell—he had robbed her, but she wasn't down and out yet.

Headlights flashed outside and temporarily lit up the inside of the trailer. Josie heard a car door slam and then footsteps pounding up her porch steps. It couldn't be Cain. He was long gone. Maybe it was a client, and now she didn't even have a crystal ball. She'd have to resort to a palm reading.

A big fist rapped on the door. Josie wiped her nose and stepped over the debris to answer the knock.

"Yes?" She saw the gold star pinned to his khaki shirt. My God, had somebody decided to arrest her for taking the money, and she didn't even get enough of it to fill her cookie jar? Things couldn't be turning out this bad. Who would have ratted on her anyway? Would Cain stoop that low?

"Are you Josephine Wellgood?" the lawman asked with a squint.

"Wallgood."

"Marion County Sheriff's Office, Ma'am. Deputy Hartack."

"What's the problem?"

He consulted a piece of paper crumpled in his beefy hand. "Ma'am, are you acquainted with a Cain Peter Reeves?"

Josie's heart raced as the rain pelted the sheriff's car and slapped against the trailer. Sounded like midgets tap-dancing.

"This space number twelve?" He flashed the beam of his light around her porch.

"I guess."

He moved just close enough to the open doorway to shield himself from the weather. "Ma'am, is he some relation to you?"

"No."

He lowered the brim of his hat. "You know this Mr. Reeves?"

This man just didn't send out any negative vibes despite his domineering appearance. "Yeah. I knew him, but he's not here. He split."

"Did he live here, Ma'am?"

"No. He was just fixing my car."

The sheriff took another look at the derelict Pinto being soaked in the steady downpour—busted out glass, flat tires, hood up and a dead battery sitting on one bruised fender. "Not much of a repair job, if you ask me."

"Yeah, well, I didn't pay him. But he cleaned me out anyway. He in any trouble or anything?"

"Ma'am, your name and address was in his wallet here." He reached behind him and took out Cain's weathered bifold. He handed her a crumpled slip with her name and address scrawled on it. "He didn't have no other current address. Can you tell us where we might be able to locate his next of kin at?"

Next of kin was about like asking to view the dearly departed. What the hell had happened anyway?

"They're from the Midwest I think he said. Somewhere in Ohio—Dayton. The place they make all the cash registers."

"He ever mention anybody in particular we might be able to get aholt of?"

"No. What happened to him? Was he in an accident or something?"

"Well, Ma'am, I think he was drinkin' pretty heavy. Ran his car into the ditch out on the Interstate and then looks like he tried to thumb down a ride, and with this rain comin' down like it is, the poor bastard didn't even see him until it was too late."

"What do you mean 'too late'?"

"He got hit, Ma'am. Runned over. A trucker got him. Couldn't help it. This Reeves fella just stepped out in the middle of the road, and there he was. You can't stop a forty-foot rig just like that, ya know."

She bit her knuckles. "Is he dead?"

"Wham!" He slapped his hands together and made Josie jump.

"Wham?"

"Kilt him dead as a doornail, Ma'am. Driver just had no time to stop. Pinned the poor sucker to the grille of that KW like a skeeter. Damn shame for the trucker to have to take somebody out thata way."

"Who hit him?" Something was buzzing in her brain—a psychic alarm clock going off.

"Trucker haulin' paper down to Sacramento. Jim Bob Pettiput outta Smoky Point, Alabama. Didn't even give him a citation, Ma'am. He done nothin' wrong, I can see. We had him file a report and let him go about his bizness."

Josie swallowed hard. "Jim Bob?"

"These crackers never figger one name's enough, ya know what I mean? Big black and yella KW."

She could see Jim Bob spitting tobacco juice out the window and calling her Sugar as he leaned over to close the door for her. "*Cain't never tell, Sugar, where our paths might get crosst—Wham!*"

"Well, if you can't give me no more information, Ma'am, I'll be on my way."

"He played baseball," she called out as he took a step off the porch.

He turned around and tipped his hat. "Say what?"

"Baseball. The guy that got killed—Cain Reeves. He played in the second string or something like that."

"Baseball? For the pros, ya mean?"

"Well, almost, I think. It was like the second or third string."

"The minors?"

"Yeah. Like that. He was a catcher for Tacoma, I think it was. But he hurt his knee and had to quit. He was selling TV's for Hall's Appliance in Salem."

The sheriff whipped out his pad and jotted down the information. "Thanks, Ma'am. That's a big help. Mr. Hall will likely have some background on him."

"Yeah. I guess."

He holstered the pad and started to turn away again. Josie could tell he had no intention of staying around to ask her any questions about herself. That meant there wasn't any money, right? Wouldn't he care enough to ask her about the money if they'd found it?

"Say there, you find any of my stuff with him? He took some of my things when he split."

"You wanna file a theft report, Ma'am?"

"Well, it wasn't much. Just some personal stuff. Did you find anything?"

"Weren't nothin' on him but this wallet with about fifteen bucks in it, Ma'am."

"What about his car?"

He shook his head and slid in behind the wheel. "Nothin' there, Ma'am. Just some spare underwear and junk like that. Nothin' worth a plug nickel."

"Sheriff, wait!" She jumped off the porch and got soaked by a gutter leak. "Did you find my bag? He took my bag with him. It had all my stuff."

"Sorry. Didn't find a thing except for his wallet on him and some old clothes, empty whiskey bottle, that sorta thing. Your name and address was on this slip of paper we found on him. That's all. Sorry. Why dontcha file a theft report?"

"You're sure you didn't find a purse or a bag or anything?"

"Nope. Didn't. Nothin' like that, Ma'am. You wanna file a report?"

"You looked through his car and everything, huh?"

"Ma'am, we went over that old car with a fine tooth comb. Didn't find nothin'. You wanna make out a report or not?"

She let go of the car door and stepped back. It was hopeless. "Forget it."

"Thanks for your help, Ma'am. 'Night now."

"Night."

Josie turned around and trudged back up the porch steps. Goldie hissed when she slammed the trailer door. Even the Fates were aligned against her. How could that be? How could her celestial vibes be so out of kilter?

She stumbled into the bedroom, threw herself down on the bed and snuggled under her purple India quilt. She caught her breath, closed her eyes and sneezed so hard her teeth rattled. "*Ahhhh-Chooo!*" She fumbled for a tissue, found a used one and blew her nose. Great—now she was coming down with a killer cold. How could all the stars be aligned against her? Where had she gone wrong? Everything seemed to be on target, headed for a three-point landing. This just wasn't fair.

Somewhere on the great ribbon of highway known as Interstate 5, southbound in his yellow KW cab, tapping his rattleskin boots to the tempo of Ferlin Husky on the eight track, Jim Bob was grinning like a cat-bird pussy—California bound with all Josie's money. His brain must have blown a fuse when he smacked into Cain, and all those brand new bills flew up into his radiator grille. Just tooling along, eating up the wet, black road, and he ran smack-dab into a frigging fortune. Exactly the way Josie had foretold. It just didn't seem possible that she could be punished for being so damned good. If she had known her corny, stupid-assed prediction at the T&R Truck Stop Cafe was going to come true, she would have kept her damned mouth shut.

"Shit, shit, shit…shit," she damned them all in one breath: Ginny Mae, Jim Bob Junior, Billy Boy, Pansy Ann, Zella Lu and Jim Bob. "Wham!" she cursed with a sinister curdle which made Goldie leap under the bed. "Wham, my ass."

41

Farrah grabbed Hobart's arm and pinched him. He looked up from the sink.

"It's her," she said, excited at the sight of the sedan pulling up beside the old GMC truck. She could spot her Aunt Philly's red hair in the weak light from the lantern hung outside their door.

The engine died; a car door opened, and Farrah flew outside and grabbed her aunt in a full body embrace as soon as she emerged from the driver's side.

"Darling, how are you?" Philippa was nearly overcome by her niece's exuberance.

"Oh, Aunt Philly! I'm so glad to see you!" Farrah kissed her cheeks and squeezed her aunt so hard she could barely breathe.

Philippa moved aside as the passenger door opened. "Farrah Darling, I'd like you to meet someone."

In the shadows, Farrah could see a man with thick, graying hair and dark eyes emerge from the car and take a step toward her. Those eyes were so familiar. She had seen their reflection look back from her mirror a thousand times before, and now she knew their source. She had no idea Josie's powers would work this fast. Life was a miracle. And now finally within her grasp was the answer to her prayers after so many years.

Farrah pushed her thick glasses up on her nose, extended a hand and found her voice again. "Hi. You must be Bradley. I'm your daughter Farrah Lynn."

Philippa and Bradley looked at each other—stunned into silence. Then the professor started to cry. The lawyer couldn't think of a single rebuttal for once. Life was just too incredible and wonderful to explain sometimes.

So Bradley just reached out for his daughter, folded her into his eager arms and said "Sorry I'm so late."

978-0-595-39940-6
0-595-39940-1

Coco's → Greg

818-419-6824
Notary 3924

Good Will → N. Hollywood
Vine / Lexington

Mona
818-730-1083

Lisa
618-531-2096

Printed in the United States
76967LV00005B/59